THE
PIANO
PLAYER

THE
PIANO
PLAYER

MAYBELLE
WALLIS

POOLBEG

Published 2022
by Poolbeg Press Ltd.
123 Grange Hill, Baldoyle,
Dublin 13, Ireland
Email: poolbeg@poolbeg.com

A catalogue record for this book is available from the British Library.

ISBN 978178199-474-0

www.poolbeg.com

ABOUT THE AUTHOR

A graduate of St Bartholomew's Hospital Medical College, Maybelle Wallis worked as a paediatrician in London and in England's West Midlands. She now lives and works in Wexford, Ireland. She loves the way her work always brings new patients and new challenges, as well as the comradeship of colleagues. At the same time, she is inspired by history and historical fiction and by the way society and medicine have developed over the last 300 years.

Her debut novel *Heart of Cruelty* was published by Poolbeg in 2020.

To the memory of my mother: Margaret Shea Thompson.

"When you are a doctor you can work anywhere in the world."

Chapter One

THE BANSHEE

London, 1849

Strangely, the City of London Steam Packet Company had named their ship after a fairy spirit whose keening is an omen of death.

'We'll miss the *Banshee*!' Edmond was halfway down the Alderman Stairs, head craned forward to show his pink neck and an inch of blond hair between collar and top hat. 'Do come on!' They were late because he had gone at the last minute to collect his winnings. Now he would not wait for her. *I was good enough to wait for you*, was what she might have said.

Jane gathered her skirts clear of the rain-slick granite steps that plunged between the mossy warehouse walls to the river. The porters were already dumping their baggage down where a strip of slimy cobbles stuck out into the Thames. The easterly wind of a January morning whistled in the rigging of the crowded vessels, a shrill counterpoint to the rumbling engines.

1

What if they did miss their passage to Dublin? She wished, in fact, that they would. Her letter to William, harder to compose than music, demanding much paper, ink and anguish, was only just in the post.

Edmond tipped the porters and hailed a waterman who rowed them amongst the river traffic to where the *Banshee* was getting up steam. Dense black smoke billowed from her funnel, scattering smuts.

'We'll be aboard in time.' Edmond patted his gloved hand over Jane's. He was smiling down at her. At least he was cheerful. He always was when he had won a good amount.

The boatman tied up alongside the pontoon and sprang up, holding out a hand to Jane. His hard grip propelled her toward the *Banshee's* gangway. As she clambered up after Edmond she wondered if her letter might reach William in Dublin before the bookings opened.

They were just in time, for the *Banshee's* whistle wailed, the anchor chains rattled up fore and aft, the mechanism grumbled into action, and they were under way, a flock of jeering seagulls wheeling above. The foredeck was crammed with soldiers, redcoats filling the benches, cursing one another, roaring with laughter, and sharing bottles of drink. Searching through rows of trunks were a respectable family: a bewhiskered gentleman in a black curricle coat and stovepipe hat, and his bustling wife with chestnut hair peeping from a jaunty green bonnet, who snapped at the deckhands and scolded her daughter for dreaming. Jane exchanged a brief smile with the younger woman, hoping she might prove an alternative to rehearsing Edmond's lines with him and hearing his talk of racing fixtures.

After their luggage was carried below, Jane stood at the stern to see the last of London beneath its grey pall. Edmond lit a cigar beside her. He was tall and fair, the star of Davenant's Players, with a nobility in his bearing that drew glances from women. Jane knew they made an elegant ensemble, their treble notes sparkling clear in a major key, even if their lower notes were mute.

Soon a steady wind came across the dull water, whipping up waves. Jane wrapped her shawl over her bonnet, tying it under her chin; Edmond, holding his top hat to his head, teased that she looked like an old peasant woman.

'I'm cold,' she shuddered, chilled by the journey ahead.

'Ah, now, Jane!' He opened his greatcoat to hug her against his canary silk waistcoat. He smelled of cigar smoke and bergamot hair oil. 'You've become too scrawny, my darling – I'm a bad husband for letting it happen. But I've a letter of credit for a hundred pounds, plus my gains today – perhaps in Dublin we'll find a sable wrap to warm you, and restaurants to feed you up?'

She quailed at the thought. They were used to touring the British provincial theatres, to waking late every morning with no idea of where to dine that night. But she had never expected that they would cross the sea to Dublin, or that she would have had to write about it to William:

My dear Dr Doughty,

I apologise for neglecting your letters. You were kind to have sent me your new address. I hope you have found success in your employment at the Meath Hospital. Unfortunately, despite your invitations, there was no opportunity for me to visit Dublin. She had only been able to continue the letter with the thought

3

that William might put it aside with a shrug. *But you may have seen in the newspapers that Davenant's Players are to open in Dublin at the Queen's Royal Theatre on the 14th of February, for a period of at least one month.*

After Dublin they would tour Belfast, Glasgow and Edinburgh, then perhaps Leeds, Manchester and Birmingham on the way back to London. Davenant had borrowed heavily, expecting takings to be high. Edmond had given up their lease, even selling her piano – a good one – back to the maker, saying they would find better on their return. If only the months away would also break some of his connections.

Escorted by pilot-boats, the *Banshee* made slow progress down the Thames, hampered by the rising tide, before tying up at Woolwich. A sergeant-major came on board and restored order amongst the military men.

'I'm getting queasy already,' Edmond complained.

Jane hoped that he was not becoming unwell. He was always ailing. 'The boat's barely moving.' It was rocking slightly as coal was winched on board.

'But it stinks here.' Edmond peered over the side. Below them, the brown water bore the effluvia of London out to sea, while moored in mid-river were the prison hulks, a pair of dismasted warships. The river lapped and slapped at their rotting hulls, as an ugly bunting of green algae flapped from their ropes. The old gunports were barred with rusting iron; men were confined on those gundecks and in the lightless holds below.

'Can you imagine how much worse it must be for those convicts?' Jane looked up at Edmond, who wrinkled his nose at her.

'I doubt it. This boat's no better. Is *Banshee* an Irish word for *floating shed*?' He shivered, despite his greatcoat. 'It's too cold. I'll have to go inside.' He led the way below decks. In the cabin they stumbled over their luggage, which occupied the floor. It would be too dark for Edmond to read the newspaper and he lay down on the lower bunk, pulling his coat around himself. 'This is a dismal rat-hole, isn't it?'

'It's only for three nights.' She stood looking through the dirty porthole at the hulk across the water. 'We'll be in Dublin by Tuesday evening.' William would have read her letter by then.

There is something that I could not bring myself to tell you before, but which I hope the passage of time enables you to accept. Edmond and I married seven years ago, in London. He only knows that I was your housemaid. So I ask you – I beg you – not to try to come to the theatre to see me. Any contact will only cause difficulties.

She could not meet William. She had never confessed to Edmond about him, even though Edmond's brief engagement to his leading lady, Maud Frith, was public knowledge. After Jane had left William and gone to London, she had tried to keep her distance from Edmond, reluctant to trust him. But he had continually sought her out. He had agonised over the several months that they had spent apart: if only he'd not left her in Birmingham, he should have married her then, should have kept her with him on the tour. If only he'd had money to send, and she'd not gone to the workhouse …

Brandy would calm Edmond to sleep but wake him to melancholy. He had begun to doubt his own worth, afraid he was ageing and that his public would desert him for a younger talent. He dried up in rehearsals, convinced that his voice could not project. Eventually Davenant had called him into his office for a quiet word, and after that had sent for Jane. He had reminded her that Edmond had made him take her on as a pianist, a role which, he assured her, she had fulfilled admirably. Her grasp of the repertoire was undeniable, her musical arrangements exquisite. But there was one thing wanting for the theatre company to truly succeed: Edmond must flourish into a great actor, which he could only do if she forgave him.

'You'll make a handsome couple,' he wheedled. 'You always did. A fine man like that. You must surely still care for him a little …'

She had reopened the old familiarity, tried to warm to Edmond, allowed him his kisses. Beside the breadth of his shoulders she appeared small, holding his arm as if he protected her. Only Davenant knew that she was not hanging on but propping him up; the fracture in their past was one that had healed just enough for them to limp along with an ache.

At least she had her music: her own income from playing in Davenant's orchestra, and her piano compositions that released her into an abstract world. Although William had longed for her to share his life in Dublin, had even transported his old piano from Birmingham, there had never been a future with him. She would have been playing that cottage piano at home, and nothing more.

She had tried to persuade herself, while writing her letter, that William would be indifferent to its contents. But if her mind was idle, or in the depths of the night, the truth would return to anguish her. If only she had not had to write it. How it would hurt him, to realise that he had waited in vain.

Chapter Two

THE MEREDITH–BROWNES

The tide turned, its outflow speeding the *Banshee* on between the water meadows. London was far behind, and they were about to leave England: a connection had been severed. At dusk the banks and mudflats of the Thames dissolved into the estuary where the lonely lightships rocked at anchor over the shoals. Gradually the *Banshee* turned south, following the Kent coast towards the English Channel. Jane and Edmond dined in the 'First Class Saloon', a drab compartment lit by a flickering oil lamp that swayed in its gimbals. The ship's cook, sporting a knitted hat and red neckerchief, doled out plates of bread and cold bacon; they ate little although Edmond drank a glass of porter.

The family that Jane had seen on the deck were across the table. They were Irish, by their accents. The mother raised her eyebrows at the cook's dirty apron and bare feet without pausing her conversation, which was of costumes, curtain material, and grand houses, and directed at her daughter, who smiled as she replied. The father, weary and grey, said little. The girl's white dress was smudged with soot but her face was luminous in the gloom, framed by glossy dark hair wound up with pink silk rosebuds. She pushed her plate aside and looked directly at Jane. Her eyes were lively, her expression open. The mother, chewing a tough mouthful, was at last quiet, and the girl smiled and craned forward a little.

They introduced themselves. The girl's name was Anna Meredith-Browne. The mother, Lucia, frowned as Jane explained their purpose in Dublin, but Anna exclaimed: 'How exciting! What's the production?' And without waiting for a reply continued: 'We'll come and watch you! Will we not get a box, Papa?'

'Possibly, Anna.' Her father patted her hand, which bore an inky black callus on the middle finger. 'If my work allows.'

The mother's disapproval softened as Edmond joined the conversation. Even though he was out of sorts, his voice, a melodious baritone, resonated.

'We're in repertory with five productions. The latest is *The Garden of Deceit*, where Prince Rinaldo woos Armida, daughter of the evil Caliph who compels her to place the prince under a poisonous spell. Yet Armida cannot resist Rinaldo's passion.'

Jane well knew the power of Edmond's gaze. Lucia Meredith-Browne took a gulp of water in silence, while Anna declared they would reserve tickets as soon as they were home in Dublin, the father nodding his acquiescence.

After the meal, Lucia, with her talk of fashions and furnishings exhausted, retired to her cabin with her daughter, while her husband read newspapers in the smoking room.

Overnight the *Banshee* passed the Straits of Dover and progressed steadily westwards along the English Channel. Edmond became more nauseous, refusing everything but brandy and water, yet insistent on smoking cigars in the cabin 'to clear his head'.

In the early morning Jane went on deck for air, leaving him below. The sky had cleared, and the easterly wind was behind the vessel; the cold air was refreshing. Anna was there at the starboard handrail, swathed in a pink shawl which held the dawn light. She started a conversation about the theatre company, seeming awestruck by Jane's ability to play the piano for an audience.

Jane named the actors: Madeleine Nisbett, who was to play Armida in *The Garden of Deceit*, her husband Tom Nesbitt, the Caliph, and others, but Anna did not know the names. She had not even heard of Edmond, who had become a celebrity in the last few years.

'We haven't been to the London theatres,' she said with a frown. 'When we're there, Mama spends her energies shopping, we have relatives to visit, and Papa's busy with work.' She said her father, a retired army colonel, worked in the administration at Dublin Castle and had quarterly meetings in London. He sometimes took a hotel suite in St James's for a week, so that she and her mother could accompany him.

'I suppose I enjoy it, but I'd rather be at my desk in my dressing gown.' Anna smiled across the water at chalk cliffs. 'Look – the Seven Sisters, forever in each other's company, never lonely, never concerned about fashion, or curtains.'

'What do you do at your desk?' Jane asked.

'I write,' she said, as though admitting an offence. Then more boldly: 'I write poetry.'

'You must let me read your work,' Jane offered, stifling a sigh. Young women's poems were often dull. Davenant had once made her set his daughter's verses to music for a production but even though she had done her best the lyrics had been too bland. They had not been a success.

Anna looked hard at her. 'I'm shy of showing my writing to others – I've a friend who writes far better. For all that she encourages me, I'm not ready.' She changed the subject, suggesting they should sit in the ladies' cabin, and led the way below. The small saloon was unheated but the banquettes were comfortable, and they were alone. They discussed books they both admired, Jane described favourite piano pieces, and Anna insisted they must meet in the future. She painted a picture of a glittering society.

'You'll adore Dublin. Such a beautiful city, and so many amusements: balls, races, musical events. There'll be a charity ball at the Rotunda soon – perhaps you'd subscribe for tickets?' She glowed as she spoke of her new dresses, of white damask, of yellow moiré, of taffeta the colour of apple blossom, of the V-waistline and how it flattered the form. And there were the cashmere shawls, the stockings, the bonnets, a wire hoop-petticoat four feet wide ...

Jane smiled without sharing Anna's enthusiasm. Her own tastes had darkened: greys, blacks and purples, paisleys, crimson. She was, in a way, still in mourning for a lost child, a lost love ...

Anna was asking her where she would be staying.

'Mr Davenant has found us rooms in Kildare Street,' Jane

replied. 'Do you know it?'

'That's so near to us, in Fitzwilliam Square – you must promise to visit. Now, say you will!'

As the voyage went on they found another reason to maintain contact with the Meredith-Brownes. Edmond discovered that Anna's father was happy to debate the detail of the Irish Racing Calendar, drawing on memories of years of race meetings. The Colonel even suggested over lunch that Edmond might enjoy a flutter at the Lucan Races, the next meeting being the 14th of February with a special train from Kingsbridge Station.

'That's the night of our opening performance,' Jane said.

'I expect the train will return in time.' Edmond had already made up his mind.

'I'll be busy at the Castle that day,' said the Colonel, 'but I'll get my son to place a few bets. There'll be hurdles, a flat race and a steeplechase, with a pony race to end.'

As he started to name horses and jockeys, Jane looked at the newspaper that lay on the table. An advertisement for **'Remedies for the Asiatic Cholera'** caught her eye … **'with which it is desirable families should be furnished, in case they be visited with that awful pestilence. Bewley & Evans, 3, Lower Sackville Street, Dublin'.** The awful pestilence she feared was Edmond's gambling.

Once they were alone in their cabin, she told Edmond she did not want to go to the Lucan Races.

'I only ever place half-crown bets.' His bright blue eyes met hers. 'You know that perfectly well, don't you? Watching me all the time, as you do.'

'What do you mean by that?' She had once been certain

11

that he had stopped betting. Now it was blatant; she did not have to spy on him to see it.

'I know you check my betting slips behind my back.'

She said she did not touch his pocketbook, but he would not have it.

'And why shouldn't I enjoy myself with my own earnings? The feeling of backing a winner – the excitement – that's second to none. This one thing can make me happy, Jane.'

'Only promise to be sensible.' It was hopeless – he would not be honest about it. 'You know how it affects you. Remember when you forgot your lines because your mind was on a triple bet?'

'You're always bringing that up – no one else noticed.' He laughed. 'Everything's under control.'

* * *

During that night and all the next day the *Banshee* followed the coastline until the sunset faded on the soaring cliffs and shattered rocks of Land's End. Then the sea grew rough: their half-empty dishes slid across the saloon tables while Edmond, greenish-pale, gulped down a brandy before going back to their cabin.

'He looks liverish,' commented Lucia Meredith-Browne, producing a silver case from her pocket, and passing Jane a card. 'My own physician, recommended to me by Lady Kildare. An eminent doctor.'

'Oliver Wright? A true gentleman of the turf,' added the Colonel. 'Excellent racing tips: as good a judge of the horse flesh as he is of the human.'

As Lucia began an exposition of her medical history, Jane pocketed the card with polite thanks.

'You seem somewhat pale yourself, Mrs Verity,' interrupted the Colonel. 'It's a hundred and fifty miles yet to Dublin. I should rest if I were you, it'll only get worse.'

She took his advice. That night her sleep was broken by the movement of the boat and the boom of waves against the bow.

In the early hours Edmond groaned, then started to stumble about. The cabin door opened and shut as he left her alone in the dark.

After some time he returned, evidently relieved of his nausea.

'A wild night!' he panted. 'You know, the mate's up there, keeping watch, wet through, and all he said was "*A roughish night, sir*". Roughish!'

He threw himself into his bunk.

'I've never felt sicker in my life.'

'You weren't well before we came away,' Jane said. She could not recall a night in the past few months when he had fallen asleep without brandy. He would rise in the early hours to light the dining-room lamp and pore over his racing notebook or pace the floor with a script. At dawn he would return to bed and sleep late only to wake with an aching, irritable head.

He said that he would see a doctor in Dublin.

'I'm sure you'll find someone.' She would not mention the Meredith-Brownes' recommendation and, of course, William was out of the question.

* * *

By dawn the storm had abated. Jane watched through the porthole as the *Banshee* passed the tower of Tuskar Light, white against a grey sky, then she went up on deck. A long low ridge loomed out of mist, followed by shoals and spits of land. Anna joined her and pointed out Wexford harbour, where a distant spire stuck up from a grey smudge. Further up the coast a fresh breeze blew the mist away, flattening the breakers on the beaches. Mountain peaks rose purple against a blue sky.

They spent the day chatting in the Ladies' Cabin, although Anna's compliments made Jane feel awkward.

'How I envy your success! The glamour, the glory, and the pair of you such an elegant couple.' Anna's face was alive with enthusiasm. 'If I could be free to live as you do …'

It was hard not to be cynical. 'I love music, I adore the piano, but the theatrical life – really – it's wearisome. It's Edmond who's the success – Davenant only hires me because he can pay me less than a man. In any case, Anna, you'll never need to work – you're bound to make a good marriage.' Jane looked down at her wedding ring. Those words had once been said to her.

'I'd only marry for love, mind,' said Anna, but when Jane asked if she had an interest in someone, she pointed out landmarks. 'Look! The Sugar Loaf Mountain! Soon you'll see the railway workings on the cliff at Bray, then it's Kingstown Harbour.'

'I do want to see Dublin Bay,' said Jane.

It proved to be as William had once described in his letters: the city lay like a jewel in a verdant setting ringed with mountains, overlooking a blue sea glittering in the sun.

Anna's mother came and told her to make sure of her trunk, so they all went below. As they parted Anna told Jane she must visit and gave her an address in Fitzwilliam Square.

When the time came to vacate the cabins, Jane returned to the deck with Edmond. The *Banshee* grumbled along the River Liffey between long granite walls. A dead horse drifted seaward in the brown water. Passing a crowded dockyard they continued upriver, nosing between other ships to moor just past the colonnades of the Custom House. Georgian terraces, black with soot, lined the quays on either side and there was a foul odour in the air.

After the ship's motion, standing on the quayside made them giddy. A porter carted their trunks, but they had to push on against a mass of people: men lugging bundles and bags, women with a baby on a hip or children at their skirts. There had been about eighty passengers on the *Banshee* but hundreds queued for the other ships.

Forced to halt, Jane turned to watch them massing on the decks.

'Are they potato famine emigrants?' she wondered aloud. 'Where will they end up?'

'Liverpool, Quebec, America?' Edmond shrugged.

'But I thought the government had sent thousands in famine relief every year?'

'Those handouts have achieved nothing,' said Edmond. 'The peasant farmers, the old cottiers, who know nought but potatoes, indeed will eat nothing else, must leave the land. It opens the way, I believe, for modern agriculture.'

A few of the emigrants looked prosperous, but most were gaunt and poorly dressed. Some faces were bright with hope, others drawn with grief. All were full of determination: they had set their faces forward, for they had no way back to the past.

'That can't be right. Anyone would grow new crops in preference to a voyage to the unknown.'

'To the bottom of the sea, if they're unfortunate. Imagine three weeks on a boat as bad as ours. Come now, we're moving.'

The porter went on. A line of jaunting-cars awaited the steamer passengers and a jarvey swung up their trunks and took the address of their lodgings. The elegance of the city belied the hardship displayed by the emigrants. Just as they turned on to a bridge to cross the river, Jane caught a glimpse of a broad shopping street where people promenaded alongside carriages, jaunting-cars, and equestrians. The Liffey itself ran gleaming in a long vista between bridges and stone walls, with spires and domes above. In the far distance the mountains were silhouetted against the sun. On the other side of the river an elegant street led to the grand facades of Trinity College and the Bank of Ireland.

* * *

They had rooms on the second floor of a well-appointed townhouse in Kildare Street, convenient to the fashionable centre but quieter. Their landlady greeted them warmly, their trunks were carried up, the skivvy brought hot water, and it was a relief to wash off the dirt of the journey and don fresh clothes.

Jane opened the window for air. Across the street was a

terrace of identical houses. How far was Harcourt Street, and was William seeing his patients?

'Everything's still turning around me.' Edmond lay down on the bed, his eyes dull with fatigue. She told him to ring for a glass of water, but he shook his head.

'I'd prefer a stiff brandy.' He closed his eyes. 'But it can wait. We'll eat at the chop house on the corner; the company are meeting there at eight.'

In her pocket was the card that Lucia Meredith-Browne had given her: *Dr Oliver Wright, MB BCh. Physician to the Gentry. Medical Attendant to the Turf Club. 92, Merrion Square.* She tore it into fragments and sprinkled them into the street.

Chapter Three

IN A FOREIGN COUNTRY

It had been in William's mind all day: whether to go or not? By late afternoon he still had patients to see when he was cornered by Dr Joseph Murphy. Now he might not get away at all.

'That cholera patient: it was inappropriate to give him chloroform,' pronounced Joseph, 'but I dared not question Dr Wright over it.'

At least a medical matter could be answered quickly. He'd known the young Irish doctor to rant about the British Parliament with his face as red as his hair, denouncing the famine relief effort as a sentence of death upon the population, demanding how many more must die before direct action was taken to replace the government? He was openly seditious: journalists had been imprisoned for less.

'Clearly the chloroform was intended to relieve suffering.' Professional etiquette forbade William to criticise a more senior colleague. It was not done, even if his diagnosis was wrong.

Joseph began to reassert his opinions, but somehow William persuaded him to see his waiting patients and, excusing himself, hurried with a thudding heart down the hospital steps.

He was going.

A wintry dusk filled Dublin's streets, obscuring ancient spires and decayed facades. A rat fled, its naked tail obscene, into a dirty courtyard. Gaslights flickered, the hiss of each one fading as he left its puddle of light to cross the slimy setts to the next. He sank his face into his scarf to keep contagion out of his lungs.

A gateway crowned with a wooden devil led to brothels, taverns, and lowly houses, where death did the rounds by night and the dawn discovered the remains. Here one contagion followed another. Cholera had recently arrived. It had spread through deadly miasma, via trade routes from India, through Hungary, across the Baltic and the North Sea. After a single family from Edinburgh had infected the Belfast workhouse, the epidemic had overtaken Ireland. The slum-dwellers who wasted away behind boarded-up windows, or lay crowded in filthy cellars, were its helpless victims.

But William went on past the cattle market and behind Dublin Castle, a stitch developing in his side and his calves smarting, building up a brisker pace along Dame Street. He was annoyed with his fool's errand, for which he barely had the time – he'd more patients to see at his rooms before supper.

He knew he ought to turn back. He should consider himself fortunate in his solitary life, in his comfortable home. His manservant Mr Nugent and his wife, who lived in the attic rooms, kept his house clean, his table replenished, his suits brushed and his shirts perfectly white. He had his work: his studies, the articles he wrote for journals, his own small laboratory in the hospital basement, his colleagues who'd made Dublin a centre of medical education that was the envy of Europe. His days were as set as those of an anatomy specimen sealed in a jar of arsenic and glycerine.

But the gas-lamps illuminated the notices for Davenant's Players outside the Queen's Theatre in Brunswick Street. *The Garden of Deceit* was opening on the 14th of February. He went into the red-carpeted foyer and asked for a ticket for the first night. He wanted to see the musicians, he explained to the booking clerk, he had an interest in music. 'I must see the piano. I'm especially interested in the piano. So that I can see the keyboard, you understand.'

'The piano's normally on the left in the orchestra pit.' The clerk frowned over the seating diagram. 'I suppose these boxes have the best view – and will seat four persons.'

William paid for a box, indifferent to the expense. He would see her face. He would watch her play. His eyes would be full of her once again: the flowing movements of her arms and shoulders as her fingers danced over the piano keys. *Jane*. It had been eight years and he still did not have the strength to keep away; there was no day in which he did not inhabit the past. He slipped the pasteboard ticket into his breast pocket, beside her letter of dismissal.

* * *

The following morning his breakfast was disturbed by one of the porters from the Meath. The hospital carriage waited outside. Dr Murphy had not yet arrived at work this morning, said the porter, and was not in his lodgings. 'Matron asked if you would be so good as to cover his rounds.'

William had his own patients to see in his rooms that day and would have to be quick. He said he would be there directly; the carriage waited while he grabbed his hat and coat, and his bag of instruments.

It was annoying, and typical of Joseph; the young man looked as though he kept bad company. It was not the first time he'd failed to arrive without notice, afterward offering a variety of excuses: sickness; helping Dr Wright at the races; the funeral of one of his many relatives. One absence last year had coincided with the failed uprising at Ballingarry, in County Tipperary. Joseph had made no secret of his support for that lost cause. But, as an Irish doctor, he could get away with what William could not.

William had worked at the Meath Hospital for eight years. Even though they were always short of doctors, he had not been received with the appreciation that he felt was his due. It seemed that experience outside of Dublin, even if gained in London, did not count.

On the face of it he was liked. He was greeted with great courtesy. 'How are you, Dr Doughty?' asked everyone – physicians, surgeons, housekeepers, porters, nurses, often several times in the same hour. Yet his instructions for his patients might not be followed, so that he would find the next day that another treatment had been given. When he quizzed the nurses about it they would recite a different plan.

Ireland was like, yet unlike England, he thought: a foreign country, uglier yet more beautiful, easier yet more

21

difficult. Harcourt Street was busy with traffic and as the hospital carriage dragged along he stared out of its window at the precise stonework of the footpath: the radiating lines of a granite fan forming a street corner, a double row of kerbstones making easy steps down to the road. In the fine details, Dublin often surpassed London; it was the same with medical education.

Then a disturbance of the passing throng caught his eye: a brief impact, three men suddenly running, a knot of people forming around a fallen man, screams …

'*Stop the carriage!*' William shouted, opening the door and jumping down. A huge mountain of a fellow carrying a book barged past, almost toppling him with the momentum of his flight. A second man shouted something in Irish. William saw all three vanish into an alley that led towards the slums. His arm felt bruised: perhaps the man's shoulder, or his book had caught it. He felt that he had seen those men before.

A handful of people stood around something on the pavement that might have been a bundle of clothing but for the stream of blood.

'Better get the police,' someone said half-heartedly.

The onlookers were already beginning to turn away.

'I'm a physician.' William knelt to turn the man face-up. The eyes were staring voids. Blood ran from a throat so badly severed that there was no chance of life.

'The big fella grabbed his arms from behind.' A woman stood hunched, her hands on her eyes, her fingers gripping her forehead. 'Holy Mother of God. I wished I'd never seen it. The other two drove the knife through his throat, one pushed, one pulled.' Her hands fell away, uncovering a face of horror.

'I saw that one of them had a book.' William stood up, rubbing his arm. 'Did it belong to this man?'

No-one replied.

The dead man did not look bookish: his greying beard was unkempt, his fingernails dirty, his coat threadbare.

The police were swift to arrive. After the uprising last year, small though it had been, Dublin had been reinforced with police and soldiers. As a pair of constables hurried along the street the crowd dispersed, so that by the time they reached the body William was the only one who remained. They looked at the blood, draining across the flagstones into the road. Then at the dead man's face, with its empty eyes and grey pallor of death.

'It's Jim Boylan.' One of the policemen retrieved the dead man's hat, which had rolled a few feet away, and placed it on the corpse's chest. 'Well, I suppose he had it coming.'

The other policeman, crouching, checked the coat pockets, pulling out only a few coins, a rusty key and a tobacco pouch. 'Nothing. I suppose it was all over too soon for you to see it, sir?'

'I saw it from the carriage. There were three of them, but no, I didn't see them properly. One was a huge fellow in a dark-red coat.'

All William could do was point out the alleyway into which the attackers had escaped.

'Ah, a big man, so.' The constable grimaced as he looked in that direction. 'Well, they'll be long gone. Three of them, eh? We'll not be able to find them if they're down there … well, you know yourself …'

William told them about the book.

'A loan book, I'd say,' the constable said. 'He'd have been out collecting.'

'We warned him, only the other day. No one does that round here by themselves. I'd say he strayed over the mark.'

'Is there nothing to be done?' William looked from one to the other. They were middle-aged and weary, neither willing to search for three dangerous men. 'A man has been killed in broad daylight.'

'We'll tell his wife to send for the body to be buried,' said the crouching man, replacing the key and the pouch.

'What about the Coroner?' William was shocked.

'He's a busy man.' The policeman got up from beside the corpse with an effort, pushing himself up with his hands. 'What can he say, but that the man was murdered?'

'Would you not want to catch the murderer?' It was indeed a foreign country, William thought.

'Well – they could be from one of the gangs. Or ...'

The lines deepened around his colleague's eyes. 'As long as they're not plotting against the Castle, we leave them to their loan-sharking and their cockfighting and their little rackets and feuds.'

'These be no harm to the likes of you, sir. They answer to their own masters and one gang keeps another in check – less for us to do.'

'What masters are those?' William asked.

'Best not to know, sir.'

Returning to the hospital carriage, William wondered if the policemen had masters of their own, who paid them to turn a blind eye.

24

* * *

That evening, after the day's work was done, he sat in his laboratory in the hospital basement with the forensic textbook written by Professor Edwin Charles, reading about strychnine poisoning.

He knew now where he had seen the three ruffians – on the ward with the patient of whose treatment Joseph had disapproved, a man called Tynan. They'd claimed to be Tynan's brothers and had caused a row when he died, not a complaint about his medical treatment, but a demand for a pocketbook that he had supposedly brought in with him. The three men had borne no family likeness to each other, nor to Tynan: a weaselly sneering man with a pointed nose, a second man with a fixed grin, the third a broad-shouldered giant with a bulbous nose and pockmarked face.

Patients' property was checked in and out by the hospital's apothecary. But in the face of vile abuse, Mr Carty had been adamant that he had not received the pocketbook, nor its contents. The arrival of a group of burly orderlies on the ward had ended the discussion. Nowadays a swift burial was vital to avoid the spread of pestilence, but even so it had been a shock to see, from the windows of the hospital stairwell, the weaselly man whipping up his horses so that the carriage bearing the coffin swerved out of the gateway into Long Lane, nearly colliding with a brewer's dray.

It was suspicious that Tynan had not had the diarrhoea or fever normally seen in cholera. Instead he had suffered cramps, violent enough to throw him out of bed, and in between them had gasped out that he had been '*pizened*'. Indeed, according to Professor Charles's book, these spasms were signs of strychnine poisoning.

William had once been a Coroner in England, years ago, when Dr Wright had been a mere workhouse doctor. His tenure as Coroner had been brief and unmerited, but long enough for him to realise that he should have reported Tynan's allegation to the police, retaining the body for a post-mortem until all the facts were known. Contradicting Dr Wright's diagnosis might not have gone well but, if Joseph had bled the patient, or washed out the stomach, some tests might have been possible. Even so, even if he had found proof, he could see now that the police might not have investigated.

William closed the textbook, then lifted the cover to see the title page again. Professor Charles worked at the Bellevue Hospital in New York. He would write to him and enquire whether any positions were available, whether he could train in forensic techniques. He would then not have to defer to Wright. He would make a new life in a new country.

He would go to the theatre. He would see Jane play the piano, but it would be merely a farewell.

Chapter Four

A LETTER FROM ANNA

29, Fitzwilliam Square

My dear Jane,

I enclose your tickets for the charity ball at the Rotunda, in aid of the Lying-In Hospital. Mrs Carmichael thanks you for your subscriptions. It promises to be a delightful evening. The Lord Lieutenant and Lady Clarendon are to be there, and it will be my first chance to wear my yellow moiré from London.

One of my friends, a writer, Jane Francesca Elgee, is eager to meet you, so if you like we might arrange to call on her. She lives with her widowed mother in Leeson Street.

Francesca maintains that poetry, with its fierce beauty, its intimacy of ideas and feelings, moves hearts and minds as prose cannot. Indeed, her poetry displays the tragedy of the Potato Famine in quite a different light. She inspires me to write, and to read aloud, is quite serious that I could be a writer, and has promised to help me all she can. Even so, when I compare my work

27

to hers, it seems trivial. She has already had her own poems and political articles published in newspapers, under a pseudonym – all without her mother's knowledge. I must admit to cherishing a secret ambition: to have my work published would make me happier than anything else.

I am so looking forward to the ball. It will be delightful to see you again.

With warmest wishes,

Anna

Chapter Five

A DINNER AND A BALL

With a week to go, Davenant fussed over rehearsals, resizing scenery and choreography to suit the shape of the stage, and trying voices and music in the auditorium, which echoed without its audience. He complained that the gas lamps were too dim, and that the stagehands were too slow. He even shouted at Edmond, who, still complaining of headaches, was hesitant with his lines.

'*Speak up, man!*' he bellowed.

Edmond scowled, but his voice increased in power as the rehearsal continued.

Only when he raised his baton to the orchestra did Davenant finally smile. A soft drumbeat began, followed by the high flutterings of the flute, the mellow notes of the oboe and the sighs of the violin and cello, until the piano with its vast ranges dominated the melody. The music, although of little artistic significance, still seemed to give him joy.

The cast worked until late that evening, whereupon

Davenant took everyone to dinner. A series of jaunting cars conveyed them through Dublin. Jane drew her new sable wrap around her, luxuriating in the soft fur. It was a dry evening, but achingly cold; the moon was a thin crescent and the stars faded in and out of the chimney smoke that streamed from the buildings on either side, dark hulks behind iron railings frosted white. Beneath a lamppost a young woman hugged herself in her satin frock, waiting for the client who would bring her into the warmth of the bawdy house. Near the Bank of Ireland, a line of the destitute lay huddled at the base of a long wall. Among them a woman and child were clasped together. So late, Jane thought, for a child to be awake, yet the small face, a thin white heart, stared, alert, at her.

Davenant had booked two long tables at the Royal Arcade Hotel, in a dining room with dark crimson draperies and painted panelling, overheated by two iron stoves. Tall candelabras with sagging candles dripped wax. Jane would have preferred bread, milk, and her bed, so the food when it arrived sank like lead to her stomach. The fish course was followed by slabs of roast meats with rich gravy and a burgundy heavy enough to appear black in the glass. Harry Barker, Edmond's understudy, sat beside her making conversation about Dublin's social circles but the wine dulled her, the day's music played itself in her ears, and she lacked the energy to raise her voice above the chatter. The table was heaped with wasted food: an entire braised duck with brandied cherries lay untouched.

Edmond guffawed to Tom Nisbett across the table while Madeleine giggled and gleamed, her golden hair bright beneath the candelabras and her eyes heavy with kohl. She wore her usual vivid colours: scarlet silk this evening, with strings of amber beads. One of the waiters, with an instinct for a leading lady, offered her side dishes, puddings, sweetmeats, which she declined, while, as was her way, wheedling out what there was of his life history: he was from Cavan with a wife and four children.

Madeleine flashed a smile at Jane. 'What an enviable woman, his wife, enjoying a simple life with a good man!'

Jane dropped her eyes to her plate, pretending to be occupied with her food. The man who had offered her such a life must be left in the past. She was grateful when Davenant started a speech, thanking everyone for their efforts, daring to hope that all would go well. Their first few nights were sold out, while a local journalist had promised a good review.

'*Bravo!*' Edmond applauded. 'Once the public realise our production is sublime they'll besiege the box office for tickets, and we shall all profit.'

'We'll drink to that!' Tom stood up, lifting a glass of the dark wine.

'*To fame and fortune!*' Edmond called out.

'Better: *to art and love!*' Tom clinked his glass to Madeleine's. 'They're the finer points of life.'

'*To music – the finest of all!*' Madeleine replied, to forestall any dispute. She smiled at Jane, who sipped her wine politely.

Later, as they were driven back to their lodgings, Jane looked for the child outside the bank, but no-one was there. A couple of constables, their muskets gleaming, patrolled further along towards the bridge. Perhaps all those people had been dispersed, denied rest on that freezing night. How could they survive such cold?

* * *

The cast had the Monday off but, even with all day to rest, Jane and Edmond arrived late for the charity ball at the Rotunda. The staff were clearing plates from the dining room yet a long row of buffet tables remained laden with food: cold meats in aspic, little sandwiches and pastries, pineapples and other hothouse fruit.

A chamber orchestra played in the ballroom as a grand and gaudy crowd chattered and drank champagne beneath chandeliers that were sparkling clouds of crystal. The gentlemen, if not in black evening coats, were in military uniform, bright with brass and medals. Their ladies, glittering with jewels, favoured the latest fashion – white silk and Valenciennes lace with coloured ribbons and sashes.

Jane, in the black silk and black garnets that she wore for performances, felt that her costume was too dark. It was a relief to recognise Anna, who, with another girl was chatting with two cavalry officers in dark-blue uniforms. One, tall and slender, was introduced as Anna's brother, Robert. His companion, more athletic, with a luxurious dark moustache, was Lieutenant Alex Royce, of the 17th Lancers.

Jane only had time to thank Anna for her letter before Alex resumed a conversation which had been about people whom Jane did not know. Clearly there would be no opportunity to discuss Anna's writing. Then the musicians started a waltz and the couples went to dance, Anna pairing with Alex. Jane tried to persuade Edmond to join the dance but heard a '*Halloo!*' above the din in the ballroom.

Lucia Meredith-Browne, in a white dress embroidered with red roses, rubies glowing in her chestnut hair, and lips carmined to match, bustled towards them, her hand on the sleeve of a stocky, bespectacled gentleman with his wife on his other arm.

'Charles is talking shop this evening,' she declared, inclining her head to where her husband stood with a group of military men, 'but allow me to introduce Dr and Mrs Oliver Wright.'

They exchanged courtesies, then took glasses of champagne from a waiter's silver tray. Dr Wright with the placid face and impeccable tailoring of a successful gentleman, gave them a rosy-cheeked grin. His wife Catriona was small and fair, with a soft Scottish voice which was too easily drowned out by others, and soon fell silent.

Lucia leaned forward to speak to Edmond. 'Mr Verity, you were ill during your sea journey, and I hope you're better, but if not I'm sure that Dr Wright will assist you. He's a senior physician at the Meath Hospital, and never refuses a call, even in the middle of the night, for a modest fee. He visits the sick poor for charity –'

'I'm a busy man, you know,' chimed in Dr Wright, his loud diction indicating an expensive English education. 'Very busy.'

'He provides medical cover for the Turf Club, so we often see him at the races.' Lucia fluttered her fan.

'The Colonel told me you knew a thing or two about the turf,' said Edmond. 'Tell me, what's your fancy for the Lucan Races?'

'The whole world's going to the Lucan Races!' Lucia laughed. 'If you bet on anything, you may bet he keeps his counsel!' She snapped her fan shut and tapped it on her nose, looking around at them all with an arch smile to which Mrs Wright did her best to respond.

'On the contrary, I oblige my friends, and am always delighted to encounter a fellow aficionado of the sport.' Dr Wright grinned, then leaning forward tapped the side of his nose, as if imparting a precious secret. 'Now, I've a horse running in the steeplechase – actually he belongs to Catriona – Kilfane. A four-year-old, son of Killarney and Royal Fanfare. Looking very good in training, and the favourite at five-to-two, isn't he, my love?'

'He's a magnificent creature.' Catriona Wright took back her husband's arm, her face brightening as she drew closer beside him. 'I love our horses.'

'In any case, I must make an appointment with you to discuss my health,' Edmond said to Dr Wright, not looking at Jane, as if he knew her eyebrows were raised.

'Excellent.' Wright took out his pocketbook and drew out a card. 'If fortune smiles, you may improve your wealth as well as your health!' He wrote on the card and handed it to Edmond. 'I trust that the afternoon of Monday the 12th will prove convenient.'

Jane would have drawn Edmond aside, but Lucia detained her with an account of the treatment of her 'female troubles' by Dr Wright.

'He's an expert!' She murmured the details into Jane's ear using coy euphemisms.

Hiding her impatience, Jane nodded and frowned,

hoping she could escape before being required to make confidences in return. Luckily a group of gentlemen gathered alongside Dr Wright to talk racing with him, and Lucia widened her eyes at one of them, raising a forefinger in greeting.

'You must meet Theodore Royce,' she told Jane. 'The richest man in Ireland, a widower, and a Member of Parliament!'

Theodore bowed deeply to both of them.

'I've just met Alex Royce,' said Jane. 'Are you related?'

Theodore had the same strong build and thick brown moustache. 'I must admit that young divil's my son,' he said with a grin.

'I expect you thought they were brothers!' teased Lucia.

As the orchestra struck up again, Theodore asked her to dance and they excused themselves to join the waltzing couples. She sparkled in his arms, her rubies on fire and his deep laugh seizing her until it bubbled from her throat.

What a vulgar woman, thought Jane; besides, the red pattern on that dress looked like blood.

The champagne had made her head throb. Pleading the heat, and a need for fresh air, she finally managed to detach Edmond from the group around Dr Wright. It was cold out on the terrace, but they found a bench in the shelter of a colonnade overlooking the gardens.

'An enjoyable evening,' Edmond took out his cigar case and clipped off the end of a cigar. 'I found Dr Wright very well informed.'

'About medicine?' Jane watched Edmond's profile as he struck a lucifer and puffed the cigar alight. He was so handsome, and so heedless. 'I hope you won't be foolish, Edmond.'

Edmond drew again on his cigar. He blew a smoke ring that floated slowly in the cold air, dissolving in the light from the ballroom. 'I know you don't like gambling. But what's the harm in a staking a few sovereigns here and there? I won't win if I don't play.'

She sighed. It had been half-crowns the other day.

'Well?' he asked.

'Just be cautious, Edmond, please.' They were not alone on the terrace, and she did not want to start a quarrel.

'Wright's a solid chap. You can see it in an instant. Everyone admires him.'

'You're too impulsive,' she said gently, and fell silent.

Mixed with the aroma of his cigar was the stink of the city, the miasma that misted over the Liffey and rose into the pall of smoke that gathered above the thousands of chimneys. Her mind reverted to a scene she had witnessed earlier: an odour that had made her cover her face. In a queue of vehicles, their jaunting car had stopped beside an entrance that was half-blocked by a pile of filth. She could still smell it.

'You worry too much.' He shifted closer to her on the bench, putting his arm around her waist so that she leaned into him. 'In fact, why are you so down in the mouth? You wanted to come to this ball, didn't you?'

'I've remembered something I saw today. It upset me.' The midden-heap had seemed to move, then she had realised that barefooted children were climbing it to jump into puddles of foul water. Their ragged bodies were black with dirt, their matted hair hung over faces disfigured with sores. While some had the vigour to fight, one sat listless, her stick-like limbs inanimate, and stared up at Jane.

Surely she had seen the same child with her mother near the bank?

'Suffering, squalor, far worse than anything I've ever seen, even during that time in Birmingham –'

'Oh, not that again – why must you always tax me with it? You know I can't bear it.'

'It reminds me …' She paused. 'It's a vision of hell. Once you've seen it …' She never spoke any more about her time in the workhouse, about Nathan, about how she still felt her dead baby in her arms. Edmond had complained that it haunted him, plunged him into melancholy.

'You overthink.' He squeezed her waist, briefly, twice, his signal to cheer up. 'Look around now, and tell me whether you're in hell or not.'

'I know – Dublin's a beautiful, elegant city – in places – this ball is magnificent.' She looked back through the tall windows at the prismatic brilliance of the chandeliers. Music and laughter echoed from inside. 'But everywhere I see abject squalor – it haunts me. How can we tolerate it?'

'What else can one do? Our entire earnings wouldn't feed the poor for half a day.' He coughed out a dense aroma of tobacco. 'It's no good moping – enjoy what you can.'

'No, Edmond, more should be done to save the people. I don't believe the famine's over. What's the government doing about it? It's criminal to allow such suffering.'

Grinding his cigar-butt beneath his heel Edmond glanced across the terrace. Another couple sat embraced at the other end of the colonnade.

'Mind what you say. The Colonel has his spies. You're in Dublin now, where *habeas corpus* is suspended.'

'What do you mean?'

'Come,' he said, 'you were a lawyer's daughter, you know these things.'

'Of course: imprisonment without charge or trial. But why?'

'The Colonel told me they had to crush an armed rebellion last year. They rounded up most of the Young Ireland leaders, but he thinks there's still a network of rebel clubs and secret societies trying to re-organise. Why do you think there are so many military men here?'

He was right: the ballroom was full of officers and she remembered the platoon on the boat.

'Davenant – you know what an old woman he is – has checked our scripts with a lawyer in case they lampoon the government.'

'So, I, a piano-player, must censor myself?' Her voice rose again. 'I only want the poor to find help – I'm not starting a revolution.'

Edmond hushed her. 'You and I, my dear, have been fortunate to succeed in the theatre, but remember that success is precarious.' His voice became low and persuasive. 'Beauty and talent are not enough. We need society's approval. So, speak with care, and not of the condition of Ireland. We may be bohemians, but best not express radical ideas, lest we attract bad reviews.'

'You think that reviews are more important than anything else?'

'You might have been your father's daughter, had he not cut you off. Then, as one of those dowdy women who visit prisons, or dole out blankets and soup to the poor, you might say what you want. But you're married to a celebrity. Remember, my love, to be elegant and beautiful, and to moderate your tone to match.'

'Edmond, you buy the newspapers. Don't just read the racing results and theatre reviews.' Perhaps, she thought, she should have been content to be dowdy. 'People are dying in their thousands from the famine.'

Edmund shrugged. 'We all die. All lives are a gamble. Mine and yours are gambled upon the stage – an actor's life, a musician's life – we have staked all we have, win or lose.'

His mind always came back to gambling. She would have challenged him further, but there was a gust of squally wind.

'The damned rain!' Edmond brushed his trousers as a spatter of drops blew in from the trees. 'It keeps raining. The ground's going to be too soft at the Lucan Races.' He rose, and gave her his arm, cutting off her protests. 'It's time we went in. You wanted to dance, didn't you?'

She went with him inside, to what now seemed a barbarous festivity, the costumes and chandeliers lending a mere gloss of civilisation. As they joined the quadrille, Jane glanced at the other dancers: Lord Wealthy, Lady Stupid, Lucia still flirting with Theodore Royce. What right had they to dictate society's winners or losers?

Edmond guided her. He was a graceful dancer, trained to move with precision. As she followed his lead with a swirl of silk skirts, they smiled sweetly at one another, aware that they drew admiring glances. Yet that public approval could be a poison that destroyed the soul.

She had never forgotten how William had once sacrificed his position in Birmingham for the sake of her testimony. He had reached a point where he had to act, when popularity was no longer important. Yet although she had loved him for it, she had forsaken him to pursue a life in music. But had it really been for this: for silks, for jewels, to dance with Edmond beneath chandeliers, dizzy with champagne? The calculation that had led her to take Edmond back, these ideas of success, did not add up. She could neither return to the past, nor feel eager for the future.

Chapter Six

JOSEPH MURPHY

Attendances at the Meath Hospital had doubled in the last month to two hundred a day, mostly the sick poor with cholera or typhus. The Meath was so full that they had to send patients to the fever sheds at Kilmainham, even though it was no better there. It was only the burial ground that made space for new admissions.

William prayed for spring: a change in the air might help.

'Cannae ye speak to Dr Murphy?' Dr Stephenson had come down from the fever wards to the Admissions Room with a handful of papers. 'He's prescribed mercury to a woman with a simple fever, and cold affusions to a man with chills, he writes one patient's record under another patient's name. I dinna think he knows one thing from another.' He dumped the papers on William's desk and stood glowering with his fists at his waist. 'Look at these. He cannae tell the different fevers apart.'

William grimaced. Did the man have nothing else to do?

Perhaps he could score his points when the admissions room was quieter. It didn't help that it was Mr Carty's day off; normally the apothecary dealt with the queue with brisk efficiency, sending home twenty patients an hour with Carty's Pills, Carty's Mixture, or Carty's Liniment, whichever was most in stock. 'I'll speak to him. But we're really busy.' It was lucky that Joseph was even back at work. 'Overwhelmed. I don't suppose you could help out for a short while?'

Dr Stephenson was taken aback: his mouth gaped for a moment. Then he replied that he was exhausted too, with two or three patients to a bed in the Fever Wards, and unable to admit any more patients. He had worked for twenty days in a row, ten or twelve hours a day, without a single day off. 'Cannae ye call on Dr Wright to help?'

'His wife's ill, so he's away from work. Look out there, if you will.'

Through the windows of the Admissions Room they could see the queue. The crowd of waiting patients filled the entrance driveway as far as the road; some lay on the ground in the teeming rain.

Dr Stephenson's conscience got the better of him. He sighed heavily but stalked across the Admissions Room and sat down at an empty desk. '*Next!*'

A nurse beckoned a patient forward who limped across the floor, supported by another man. As they sat down to speak to Dr Stephenson, William heard a groan and a splash and glanced across to where Joseph was attending a patient.

The pool on the floor was red. The patient, a young woman, was leaning over the side of the examination couch

42

vomiting blood; there must have been several pints of it. It stained the shoulder of her dress. Joseph was wiping it slowly from his coat as if he did not know what else to do. As William went over to help, Sister Aloysius arrived, to William's relief, and took charge. The patient, spectrally thin, sank back on the couch, her eyes rolled upwards under half-closed lids. William touched her hand: ice-cold.

'TB of the stomach, I think,' said Joseph. His eyes betrayed his helplessness. 'She gives a history of constant pain.'

'For heaven's sake, keep the poor girl warm.' Sister Aloysius called for a blanket and directed the housekeeper to clean up the blood. 'What's her name?'

'Rose Mahon.'

'Rose? Rose? Let's get you warm, now, look it.' She spread the blanket over the girl, tucking it up to her chin, covering the blood-sodden dress and the emaciated limbs. There was a whimper in response. 'May God have mercy on you.'

'There's no hope,' muttered William, and nodded silently when Joseph said he would prescribe morphia. Remembering what Dr Stephenson had said, he watched Joseph's trembling hand as he wrote. 'Let me see that … what's the matter with you? That's ten times the proper dose. Give me that.' William corrected what Joseph had written and signed it. 'What time did you start work?'

'Half past seven.' Joseph's reddened eyes betrayed utter weariness. His unkempt beard bore a stain of blood, his shirt collar was dirty and above it a long scratch, scabbed black, ran up towards his ear.

'It's past lunchtime. Have you eaten?'

Joseph shook his head, scowling down at his bloodstained

hands. 'They'll have stopped serving in the doctors' dining room.'

'Wash your hands and come back to me.'

When William had done what he could for the dying woman, he went to the desk where Dr Stephenson was already consulting with a second patient.

'I'll talk to Joseph over lunch.'

Dr Stephenson raised one eyebrow in acknowledgement.

Then, avoiding the eyes of the waiting patients, William led Joseph through the corridors to the hospital kitchen. The clash of crockery and the steamy smell of soup and boiled cabbage greeted them. Just inside the door was a table where food was collected by the orderlies.

'Let's sit here,' said William, and Joseph gratefully sank down on a stool beside him.

Maureen, greeting William like an old friend, served up bowls of her mutton soup with a plate of grey bread. Joseph thanked her effusively.

'You're not coping,' said William. 'Is it overwork?'

'It is not that. My duties are onerous but ...' He slurped soup.

'What's wrong? If you carry on like this you'll end up on the fever ward yourself.'

'Perhaps that would be better than where I am now.' Joseph dipped a large piece of bread in his soup and ate it in a single mouthful.

William watched him swallow, hoping he wouldn't choke.

They'd been unaware of their hunger beforehand, and now emptied their bowls in silence.

'*Cupán tae*, doctor.' Maureen had brought a tea tray.

William thanked her as she poured. It was the kindness in these places that kept people working when otherwise they'd have long given up.

'Is there something you need help with?' William asked after she left. He wished that Joseph would look him in the face.

'I lost something important.' Joseph stirred his tea. 'I have to replace it.'

'What was it?' William kept his voice low, conscious that if he probed too hard this young man might retreat.

'They attacked me in the street and took it.'

'Is that how you got that mark?'

'What mark? Oh ...' Joseph's fingertip went to the scabby line on his neck. 'Yes, I suppose it must have been.'

'Did you go to the police?'

Joseph shook his head. His face seemed to crumple, the eyes screwing up into slits and a deep furrow dividing his brow. As an orderly bumped through the doorway from the corridor with a trolley Joseph drank the tea, waiting for him to go. Then he put his cup down and leaned on his folded arms, muttering into his beard so that William had to strain to hear him.

'They took Tynan's betting slip – it was worth over a hundred pounds.'

'Did you say Tynan?' William felt uneasy. It was an enormous amount of money.

'The patient. The one who had chloroform.' Joseph spoke up more clearly. 'You were there when they came for the pocketbook.'

'Oh … yes … the three ruffians.' William remembered the big fellow growling that the pocketbook would be found even if he had to turn everyone over and shake them down. 'So, why did you have it?'

Joseph hesitated. 'He was after giving it me in the Admissions Room.'

'But Mr Carty's supposed to keep the patients' property.'

'Tynan told me to keep it safe.' Joseph shook his head slowly, still frowning into his teacup.

'Why you?'

'I don't know if I can say anything.' Joseph fixed him with a sideways glance. 'Sure I could be arrested.'

So, Joseph's ideas had got him into trouble, and now he couldn't go to the police. If only he could focus on his profession instead.

'It's to do with the Cause, isn't it?' William made a sympathetic grimace. 'Anyway, I'll not report you. Unburden yourself – you might be better able to cope with your work.'

'I meant to ask you for help,' Joseph muttered. 'Tynan was in the club with me, you see. He knew those three were looking for him, for the betting slip that belonged to the club. So, he slipped me the pocketbook when he was admitted.'

William sighed. He had heard rumours of the rebel 'clubs' that had been driven into hiding after last year's uprising. If Joseph were caught, he'd be transported. The whole hospital would be turned upside down.

'Tynan said he was poisoned.' William caught a doubtful look in Joseph's eye. 'Yet you treated him for cholera.'

'I didn't know what else to do. Anyway, it was the same three men that came after me. The ruffians, as you call them.

I was after taking the betting slip to Lydon's, on Grafton Street.'

'Lydon's? I thought that was an insurance office.'

'Well, it is and it isn't, if you understand me. Anyway, Lydon told me to bring it back the next day, as he hadn't enough cash to pay me. I was walking back to the hospital. Just by the old brewery they came out of the waste ground behind me. I spotted the big fellow straight away, and would have run. It was too late – they had a hold of me with the blade up at my throat.' Joseph's fingers travelled again to his wound. 'When they had got the betting slip, they knocked me down. I thought they were going to kick the life out of me, but then the little fella said that I could do nothing. They just left me like that. On the ground.'

'Suspicious, isn't it, that they'd attack you just as you were coming from Lydon's? Who are they?'

'I don't know.' He shook his head again. 'I really don't know. Not Tynan's brothers, at any rate. Anyway, I was going to ask you for a loan … I need a hundred pounds.'

'A hundred pounds!'

'Or fifty, at least.' Joseph stared down into his teacup again. 'I have to make up the money, somehow – there's my salary, the money I get from helping Dr Wright – I do his home visits, help him provide medical cover at the races – I'm working all hours. I've sold my books. The money has to go for the Cause.'

'Joseph, I'm planning to emigrate. I need my savings. I can't pay money into that kind of thing – it's illegal. What are they going to do with it anyway?'

'I can't tell you that.' Joseph hesitated, looking around

the kitchen; no-one was listening. 'All I can say is that there are places in the rural areas where the people have to help themselves, because the law won't. It's just a loan I need.'

William glanced at his watch: it was time to return to the Admissions Room to relieve Dr Stephenson. 'You're risking your life, Joseph, and it'll come to no good. You'll get no money from me.' He got up from the table. 'Look, I'll keep your secret but, please, have a care. Give up this madness.'

'I can't give it up.' Joseph rose to follow him. 'The club's forever. What I've sworn, I must honour.'

Chapter Seven

LUCAN RACES

The Valentine card that Edmond pulled from the bedside cabinet with a flourish was a pretty confection of ribbons, lace, and sentiment. But, as Jane opened it, a pair of train tickets to Lucan slid out.

'Why? Why must we attend the races today, when it's our opening night?' She scowled at his grinning face. 'I said I wouldn't go. We'll be exhausted. You know you haven't been well.'

Her arguments went nowhere. Edmond insisted that Dr Wright's pills were bucking him up, that their rehearsals were complete, and that a break would benefit them.

'What if we're delayed coming back?' She got up to wash and dress. A leisurely day had been spoilt.

'The special train will be back in time,' he said.

He had somehow been to the railway company offices in College Green for the timetable and tickets. Over breakfast he let slip that he had three guineas on one horse, ten on another, five on a third – as recommended, apparently, by Dr Wright.

'I must see the steeplechase first-hand,' he insisted.

'Eighteen guineas! When a working man might be lucky to earn a shilling a day!'

'It's a sum easily spared.' Edmond smiled at her, wide-eyed. 'Instead of wasting time on small bets I stand to win a small fortune. Don't be a spoil-sport.'

But it was with a sour face that she followed him out to the cab he had ordered.

They departed Kingsbridge Station at noon for Lucan. Jane had heard that rural Ireland was infertile bogland inhabited only by a miserable peasantry, yet the train soon ran through rich pastures and past the stone walls of elegant parks, clearly not the abode of famine. Here and there, between stately trees, she glimpsed the formal symmetry of mansions in the Palladian style. There were no starving masses at Lucan, instead a fashionable crowd, with women in bright bonnets, gentlemen in tweed, and army officers in uniform, surrounded the whitewashed station buildings, which were as charming as if magicked from the home counties of England. Another train arrived from the opposite direction, so that jaunting cars were much in demand, and Jane despaired of hiring one.

But a clear voice rose above the hubbub in the station yard.

'Jane! Jane!' Anna was in a black landau with its hoods folded back, driven by a liveried coachman, with her brother Robert at her side.

Soon Jane and Edmond were grateful to be seated in

comfort either side of a picnic hamper, as four black horses drew the impressive vehicle away from the station.

'Don't you adore this landau?' Peacock feathers trailing from Anna's sky-blue bonnet blew in the breeze, so that she had to keep brushing them away from her face. 'It belongs to Theodore Royce.'

Jane complimented her on her bright-blue velvet cape, lined with white fur. 'You've had a long journey today?'

'No – we're all staying at Royce Park, or at least Papa's hoping to join us if he can get away from Dublin. It's a house party, for the races. But Mama's unwell today, so it's just me and Robert in the landau – Theodore and Alex are riding over – lucky we had space, isn't it?'

'I do hope your mother recovers quickly.' Jane, suspecting more 'female troubles', was grateful not to hear the details.

At the racetrack the coachman brought the landau into a good position where they could see over the top hats of the men crowding along the course. He jumped down to see to the horses, while Robert went off to inspect the paddocks with Edmond.

Jane shifted into the seat beside Anna.

'I adore your wrap,' Anna touched a gloved fingertip to Jane's sables. 'How graceful!'

Jane, surprised, glanced at her and saw she was distracted by the jockeys as they paraded on their thoroughbreds. Some were clearly military men, sporting the blue uniforms of the cavalry.

Jane asked if she had written any more, after Francesca's encouragement.

'I've written something,' said Anna, 'but we'll see her for

tea on Friday if you're free? I'll read it out then.'

Jane accepted. Clearly there would be no talk of writing today. Instead, Anna pointed out various personages and racehorse owners in the other carriages – there were the Marquis of Drogheda and Lord St Lawrence with their wives – finally spotting in the distance Alex Royce, riding Lucius, his mount for the steeplechase.

'A handsome man,' Jane commented. Would Anna confess to more? A blush was the reply.

'He's a great friend of Robbie's.' Anna started to describe her brother's army career and the places where the Lancers had been posted.

Edmond clambered back up into the landau and, standing to get a better view, cheered aloud as the hurdle race was won in good style by Lord Lurgan's Fugitive, ridden by Mr Martin. He had staked money on the horse and Jane had not seen him so happy in a long time. But his mood reversed as the stewards were preparing for the steeplechase. Kilfane, Dr Wright's horse, which had started the day odds-on, had drifted down in the betting to 8–1, so he had backed the wrong horse to the tune of ten sovereigns, which would wipe out his winnings in the first race. Just as he had been buoyant over his win, he was pale with anxiety as he went down to watch the start.

The steeplechase was to be run over a course of three miles. After the crack of the starting pistol, they watched as the field galloped away to tackle the first fence.

Anna stood up and started waving.

'*Alex! Lucius!*' she yelled at the top of her voice, going on until she was flushed and breathless. 'Do you think he heard me?' She sat back down, billowing out flounces of sky-blue velvet.

'Undoubtedly.' Jane glanced sideways at her friend's profile. Anna's bright eyes were intent on the race, her lips parted in a smile.

Lucius, though not in the lead, at least cleared the first fence and looked to be going well, but after that disappeared from view. Then a shout went up: a horse had fallen and overlain its jockey. A large black carriage made its way to them as a group of stable lads hurried after it, carrying a hurdle to serve as a stretcher. Two men got out of the carriage. One, top-hatted and stocky, Anna identified as Dr Wright. His assistant, a leaner, younger man, was bare-headed, with ginger-red hair and beard bright in the sun as he crouched to examine the casualty. Shortly afterwards the little group eased the jockey onto the hurdle and carried him slowly towards the pavilion with the carriage following. Then the doctors were needed again, for another horse and rider were down, three fields away. A few minutes after the carriage departed a pistol shot rang out: the horse had been destroyed.

Anna was now afraid for Alex's safety and her hand crept into Jane's, seeking reassurance. But soon they saw the riders returning, whipping their mounts to the finish line, sweat making dark streaks on the horses' flanks.

'*He is nearly in the lead!*' Anna shrieked. '*Alex! Oh, Alex! Come on!*'

Alex was conspicuous in his Lancers' uniform. Beneath him, Lucius gained at every stride in a flat-out gallop, and finally stretched himself across the finish line by what looked like a length ahead. As Lucius slowed to a canter and then to a trot, Alex heard Anna's cheering, long after the crowd had quietened, and waved a jubilant greeting.

After Alex gave Lucius over to the care of his grooms and his father had warmly congratulated him, he strode over to the landau, muddy but glorious. He made Jane a polite bow before taking Anna's fingers to his lips. He then clambered up into the carriage to spend the remainder of the race meeting with them, dispensing sandwiches and champagne from the picnic hamper while delivering a merciless commentary upon the whole proceedings and gossip about the fashionables in the throng.

How fortunate Anna was, Jane thought – still with the freedom to choose her path. Whether Alex was the right path was another question, although at least he did not appear to gamble.

When Edmond rejoined them with Robert, he put on a show of calm.

'I might have done a little better in the steeplechase, I suppose.' He smiled ruefully. Kilfane had come fifth out of seven.

'The wretched beast looked half-asleep,' said Robert. 'A shame – a beautiful horse, well-muscled.'

'You shall look for my mount next time, to know where to put your money,' grinned Alex, displaying perfect white teeth.

Anna's eyes lingered on him.

'I hope you're not riding in the flat race,' said Edmond. 'Wright tipped me to back Enchantress.'

'Captain James Haworth's her jockey,' replied Alex. 'He's in my regiment, an excellent rider – your money's safe.'

And so it proved, as Edmond cheered Enchantress all the

way to the finish line. His complexion pinked up and a gleam of happiness lit up his eyes. His elated mood infected Jane and they were amused by the final race of the day, with five junior riders on ponies.

The stewards presented the prize purses to the victorious owners and their jockeys after which there was a kerfuffle in which small knots of people formed around men bearing notebooks who went here and there in the crowd. Dr Wright came over to Edmond.

'Your winnings, my friend,' he said, drawing a handful of sovereigns from his pocket and counting them into Edmond's hand. 'Mr Lydon's compliments – a fair day's play for a newcomer. Ten on the first race and twenty on the third, minus of course your stake on the second. I got you the best odds I could. A shame about Kilfane. But I've high hopes for him at the Curragh. He's a good runner, usually, and training hard.'

Edmond pocketed his money, shaking Dr Wright's hand warmly, clapping him on the back and pronouncing him a thoroughly good fellow.

Robert had not won in any race and moreover owed two sovereigns to Dr Wright, who had loaned him his stakes.

'How's the casualty?' Jane asked, as Robert felt in his pockets for the money.

'In no danger,' said Dr Wright. 'I was very busy, but I told Dr Murphy to put the broken leg in a splint and arrange for his conveyance home. He's my assistant at the Meath, and learning, fortunately – I'm very busy, you know. Here he comes now.' He looked as pleased with himself as if he had been the one who had treated the patient.

'Are you busy with the cholera cases, doctor?' Anna asked. 'I've read in the newspapers that –'

'Shocking, a terrible disease. Cases are crowding into the hospitals, people sick at home, even my poor wife has been terribly unwell.'

'I'm so sorry – to think that I saw her just a few days ago at the ball and she seemed in perfect health. I wish her a speedy recovery.'

Jane was merely making small talk, but Dr Wright turned as if to confront her, wide-eyed behind his spectacles.

'It happens in the best of households,' he said emphatically. 'One day a person is in perfect health – the next, struck down by the pestilence. Every single one of us knows of someone who has been infected or, indeed, of someone who has died. But I've engaged an excellent nurse. Catriona's receiving the best of care, and I fully expect her to recover.'

As Jane repeated her good wishes, Dr Murphy came up to tell Dr Wright that there was none of the morphia left, even though there had been a large bottle in the carriage earlier on.

'I'll come and check.' Wright quietened the red-haired doctor with a gesture and turned back to excuse himself. 'Forgive me, very busy, you know.'

'And shall we see you at the Curragh races, Dr Wright?' asked Edmond.

'Certainly.'

'I shall look forward to it,' Edmond said.

'I'll be in touch in the meantime.'

'Excellent.'

'It's time we left, Edmond,' Jane said. A queue of

carriages had formed at the exit from the field. 'We mustn't miss the train.'

Alex clambered up beside the coachman and took the reins, barging in at the head of the queue with an airy wave of thanks to the carriage behind.

They caught their train in style, and to Jane's relief arrived in Dublin at half past five.

Chapter Eight

THE FEAST OF ST VALENTINE

William received no post on the 14th of February, nor sent any. He had put his theatre ticket away in a drawer.

From early on the mournful tolling of bells – Christ Church, St Michan's, St Patrick's – had warned of the house calls that awaited in the slums of the Liberties – the Miseries as he called them privately. He was to have no tender Valentine's Day fancies. The chilly air was filled with keening over the victims of the night, the unearthly sound coming from the half-open doors which were the only source of light to those squalid lodgings. The slum dwellers were superstitious, and so many spoke of the *bean sí* – the fairy woman – that he was half afraid of seeing her himself, a wraith-woman sitting on a roof, running a silver comb through her ghastly hair as she wailed her lament, a harbinger of his own death.

Cholera fatalities multiplied in front of him: how could the authorities pretend to count the dead? One unfortunate had died without his relatives noticing, they having been so ill themselves. Beneath the befouled blanket the man's body was already cold.

At length, thinking he had finished and returning to the Meath Hospital to review his ward patients, William found that yet another list of home visits had been compiled. He missed lunch, the day grew dark, and the bells were striking four when, damp and dirty from the slums, he was able to go home. He'd cancelled some appointments – there'd be double to do the next day.

Mrs Nugent made his tea, and her husband brought a jug of warm water upstairs and laid out some clean clothes.

Thoughts he'd pushed away all the dreary day pushed their way back. Was he to have no sweetness in his life? For a long time, it was as if Jane had haunted him. He'd sought to glimpse her in the faces of other women, but it was hopeless: to him they were dull while she was luminous. They did not move as she moved, like a dancer with the bust held high and the limbs fluid; they did not have that delicate shape of the ear. They did not have her smell of cloves. Even the sweat in her underarm had that aroma. He could not clear it from his memory.

He'd tried to fill the ache of her absence with the faces and presences of others. He'd been charming to the nurses – those who were not nuns – in the vain hope that even one would prove to be educated. He'd paid his formal respects to stiff widows in Dublin drawing rooms. Worst of all, he'd even once paid a girl in the Monto who'd called him into the shadows with a beautiful, musical voice that had reminded him strongly of Jane's. But when in her dingy room she'd lit the lamp, he'd realised that she made him feel sick to the stomach. He put the money in her hand and left without even touching her.

Now he stripped off, shaved and washed, shivering as the water cooled on his skin. He dried himself. What might she think of him now? He applied cologne. His work had kept him active, his muscles were still firm, but his hair was shot through with grey. He dressed quickly. Mrs Verity, he reminded himself, was married to the young, handsome, and successful Mr Verity. She did not want to see him. But today was the feast of St Valentine. He would see her. Suddenly he felt afraid. He shouldn't have bought the ticket. He might still be enslaved.

A year ago on St Valentine's Day, he'd been coaxed to pray in the Carmelite chapel on Whitefriars Street nearby, before the reliquary of the patron saint of lovers, a decorative metal casket containing some bones of the martyr and a glass phial of his blood. The elderly priest was a former patient who, finding out that his physician was for some years a widower, urged him to beseech the saint to intercede.

William had tried at first to deflect the priest's attention. 'I had my fill of the Church and religion in England. I personally witnessed its corruption by cruelty and dishonesty.'

'It is certain that across the sea is a terrible place, full of liars and Anglicans.' Father Benedict's eyes gleamed between creased eyelids. His diction and manners had been polished in Rome. 'But how many times have you, with your physician's hand, palpated my chest, or my belly – there is no part of my anatomy that has been concealed from you. Do you think me cruel and dishonest?'

'But I was an Anglican.'

'The Blessed Mother and all the saints forgive all those who come in humility.'

In the end the priest had persuaded him, not with logic, or spirituality, but with superstition. What harm could it do, and it might be that it would bring good fortune? Even though William was a man of science, he still sought hope.

The cold had struck through his skin as he'd followed Father Benedict's flickering candle into the sanctuary. Seeing the casket lying in a niche in the wall he'd shuddered, as though a hand chilled his shoulder. Father Benedict rested his candle on an iron stand.

'Let us pray,' he said.

William's knees ached on the flagstones as the priest chanted in Latin, the prayer strong and resonant in that sacred space.

'May the spirit of Saint Valentine bless your hearth and home,' he concluded as the echoes faded. It sounded like *heart*, the way he said it.

'Amen.' Jane's face, the memory of her body, possessed William's mind, the sensation of her limbs touching his. Not in church, he thought, focusing instead on Father Benedict's withered hands.

'Pray every night. Say ten times in succession: the Ave Maria, the Gloria Patri and the Pater Noster. Here is the text of a novena to St Valentine. Know that the saintly spirit watches over you and by the love of God will draw unto you the companion of your heart.'

William had accepted the blessing and the slip of paper, praying silently that some of the martyr's power would enter his life. Then he'd walked out of the church into a world where Jane was in London, and not answering his letters.

Now a year had passed: it was St Valentine's Day again. He should have prayed every night that his memories of her would fade, so that he would be set free to love someone else. Yet he'd not said a single prayer and had lost the words of the novena. He took the theatre ticket from the drawer and held the pasteboard rectangle in his fingers, willing himself once again to discard it, so that he would never see her again. He was unable to do it.

He set out at half past six. A three-quarter moon shone down as he walked up past St Stephen's Green and along Grafton Street towards the twin hulks of the Bank of Ireland and Trinity College. As a drizzling wind blew down from the River Liffey, he saw a beggar girl crouching on the ground beside her mother with the railings of the bank at her back. From high in the wall the blind windows, like empty eye-sockets, stared down upon a long row of people, bundled in damp rags and sacking. The destitution in this city was of a scale no-one could comprehend, let alone try to relieve.

He gave the girl a farthing.

'Thank you, sir! Will I say a prayer for you?' Her voice was a tiny song, and her upturned face was heart-shaped, with a chin that came to a point. He stopped, then found a half-crown in his pocket for her. It was more than she'd get in a month of begging.

'Pray for me to Saint Valentine,' he said. 'For my heart's desire, that will never come true.'

'I will, sir! God bless you, sir!'

It was not far to the Queen's Royal Theatre. The foyer was crowded: if cholera could spread by miasma through the air, then he hoped that anyone sick had stayed away. Avoiding anyone who might know him, he took his place in the box. Of the four chairs he picked the one which placed the piano stool perfectly in his line of sight. His anxiety returned; his heart lurched in his chest.

As the audience packed into their seats, the musicians filed into the orchestra pit. Now Jane was within twenty feet of him. She did not look up and as she took her seat, arranging her skirt in a pretty curve, the musicians began tuning up. Beneath the domed ceiling huge gas chandeliers hissed in the void. He could see her brow and cheek, so shuffled his chair backwards out of the light, so that she would not glance up and spot him. With the theatre packed, the box he occupied alone might attract scrutiny.

'*Ladies and Gentlemen!*' As the conductor rapped his baton the audience hushed expectantly. 'It gives me unbounded joy to present to your esteemed attention our musical extravaganza: *The Garden of Deceit*. Pray silence! Let the magical mysteries of the Caliph and his daughter unfold before your eyes!'

As the overture began the chandeliers were turned down and William's heart began to calm. Now in relative darkness, he leaned forward again. A dim glow outlined her profile and the piano gleamed like glass. Her bare shoulders sloped softly down to her black silk dress and her hands caressed the keys. She seemed unchanged, but did he see her as she really was, or merely a vision of memory made flesh? A dark necklace was clasped at the nape of her neck and above it her hair was pinned in thick coils. He'd once unpinned that heavy rope of tresses, had once woken in the blissful mornings with her hair tangled across his throat ... A flash of red came from her necklace as she swayed sideways in a fluid movement to reach the highest notes. His answering pain was like a blade in the chest. He had never stopped reliving their parting: his useless pleading, the pouring rain, holding her, desperately kissing her before she hurried back to her train. He had watched it diminish along the railway tracks as it faded into smoke.

The curtain now rose on a garden with plaster statues. Unaware of his eyes burning her skin, Jane sat straight and still, her focus on the performance. The Caliph instructed his daughter Armida to beguile and poison her royal suitor, so that, intoxicated, he would surrender first his riches, then his life. They sang a duet then went off stage for Edmond's entrance as Prince Rinaldo, serenading with his hand now raised to the balcony, now placed over his heart.

William applauded Edmond with the rest of the audience, but as he did so his anguish deepened: the man – Jane's husband – was regal, evoking emotion merely through posture and movement, his voice powerfully resonant, his golden hair holding the light. William could not absorb the dialogue, but every scene led to a song in which every note of the piano was a pinprick of pain. A duet between Rinaldo and Armida ended the first act, then the orchestra played a grandiose fanfare.

But, rising out of what should have been silence, the piano accompaniment continued solo. Of course, he knew the delicate melody: it was a Nocturne of Chopin. The actors stood still, the applause from the audience faded, and the conductor paused his baton in mid-air. Jane played on, intent only on her own fingers. William could barely breathe. This was music they had once shared – music of which he'd once turned the sheets as he stood at the piano – now she had it by heart and played from the heart: a sequence that first surrendered to the pleasures of love, then grieved its passing. Had she somehow seen him? As Jane brought the piece to a close the audience roared applause, but she did not look up.

This had to be a tender farewell. Tears stung his eyes. It was the end. He was free. As the lights came up for the interval, he left the theatre and walked swiftly home. The bank was deserted now, the loiterers cleared by the police.

It was time to post the letter that lay ready on his desk, that listed his experience and qualifications and enquired about working for Professor Edwin Charles in the Department of Pathology of the Bellevue Hospital, New York. He would ask Dr Wright for a reference.

Chapter Nine

SPERANZA

'What in heaven's name happened at the end of Act One? You were in a trance.' Edmond sat at the dressing-room mirror in his shirtsleeves, cleaning greasepaint from his face with cold cream. 'What you played was not in the score. It was Chopin. Madeleine and I were stranded on the stage with our mouths agape. Davenant should have pushed you off the piano stool!'

Jane could not reply. Chopin. Evenings spent at the piano. William turning the music sheets even as his world turned to dust. Nights of impossible passion, of vine-like embrace, of poignant delight.

Edmond twisted round. 'How could you have been so careless?' His eyebrows were full of white cream and where he had wiped off paint his cheeks were greyish pale with kohl streaking away from his glaring eyes.

She stood in front of him, keeping her hands folded together, knowing that if she said nothing his inquisition would soon stop. How could she tell him what she had never told him about William? He would be incredulous that such a man – so old, so unfashionable – could rival a star like himself, perhaps would even mock her.

She had entered the orchestra pit and seen him. A single glimpse and no more, then bowed her head to hide her face, struggling to master the explosion in her heart. Keeping behind a tall violinist, she found her way to the piano stool, not daring to glance up. Even after eight years she recalled their last kiss, the closeness of his face. The look in his eyes as he crushed her against his coat soaked with rain. His skin and hair cold and wet, the warmth of his mouth, the scents of cologne and coal smoke, the iron pounding of the engine that was to draw her to London.

'You were lucky the audience liked it.' Edmond turned back to the mirror, wiping his face with a rag. 'But, Jane, what on earth were you thinking?'

'I have no idea. I suppose I was tired … after the races.' She wrenched her mind to the present. 'I told you it would be too long a day.' She made herself meet Edmond's eyes in the mirror, but he did not answer. 'But we enjoyed the outing,' she said, to distract him. 'And you did well with your winnings.'

'Yes. Yes, I did …' He leant close to the mirror to work the rag around his eyes. 'It was Dr Wright … he got me good odds …' His fingertip drew his eyelids closed.

'You're tired too, darling.' She went to rest a hand on his shoulder.

'I'm grand,' he said, disengaging with a shrug. 'That's what they say here in Ireland, isn't it? I'm grand!'

Indeed, all in the theatre company were jubilant about the success of the production. As they left the theatre to dine, Jane was the only one who was quiet. William's face in the shadows had been mournful, a wave of dark hair hanging over his forehead, those intense eyes deep beneath level eyebrows, his gaze like fingertips brushing her bare shoulder. She shivered with the half-hope, half-fear, that he might be there in the lamp glow, waiting outside the stage door. She ached a little with the relief when he was not.

She could only travel forward in life: that was the only possible direction. She hoped for William's sake that he would reach the same conclusion. It had been an affair. Now it was merely a memory; there was nothing to which they could return. That evening, as her colleagues recounted the best scenes and the ovations of the audience, she would do her utmost to enjoy her share of success.

* * *

At the end of the week Jane visited Francesca Elgee for tea, as arranged. Edmond, studying the newspaper, only glanced up when she told him where she was going.

'Enjoy yourself,' he said. 'I've an appointment with a tailor for a new coat this afternoon, then must go across to the bank.'

Behind the plain Georgian exterior of the Elgees' family home in Leeson Street was an old-fashioned interior in the Oriental style. Anna had already arrived, so Jane joined her on a blue velvet sofa, chatting while Francesca, reflected in gilt-framed mirrors, filled porcelain cups from a silver teapot.

'It will just be us three today. But you know, I intend to develop a little circle of writers – a salon, as it were – and you must join us.' Strikingly tall, Francesca had a presence which would dominate any salon: a husky voice, a languid red mouth and a full figure crammed into an antiquated damask dress beneath a profusion of baroque jewellery. She was perhaps in her mid-twenties, her faintly olive complexion retaining the freshness of youth.

She coaxed Anna to read out her work, gazing at her with rapt dark eyes, drooping her eyelids from time to time to dwell upon a poignant phrase. At the end, once she had exhausted her stock of compliments, she turned to Jane for agreement.

'I'm no judge of literature,' Jane protested, 'but I do a little musical composition and heard a rhythm that might lend itself to song …'

Francesca's attention switched to Jane's musical ability and, waving a jewelled hand at the piano across the room, she invited her to play. She was fond of a song of Schubert's, and coaxed Anna to sing the lyrics to Jane's accompaniment, applauding them both at the end.

'*Bravissimo!* You would do marvellous things with my poems if you set them to music.' She spoke with exceptional intensity and strength of conviction.

Opening a bureau, she extracted a folio of papers from a pile and handed them to Jane. They were her poems. On the first page, phrases such as *battle-cry* and *martyr's faith* suggested hymns. But further on, Jane read of the *crushed hearts of the famine-stricken*, and *patriots unafraid to die*. Avoiding Francesca's stare, Jane turned over the page without looking up. It was pure sedition: a ballad entitled

The Year of Revolutions glorified the uprisings of 1848 across Europe, urging the Irish likewise to rebel against the British. It seemed discordant, even eccentric, in that opulent drawing room.

Putting the folio on the music stand, Jane tried a popular tune to fit the lyrics, going on to improvise some variations on the piano as she sang in a soft voice, Francesca standing beside her and chiming in. It was embarrassing: her melodies were too trivial to match Francesca's lyrics of violent martyrdom. Yet Anna was enthusiastic, saying that she too had attempted a rebel ballad and would be delighted if Jane could look at it.

'Write the music down before you forget,' said Francesca. 'What a fine pianist you are, indeed, and what a lovely voice!'

'It might be safer if I did not,' said Jane. 'I've heard that –'

'I know all about the government,' interrupted Francesca. 'They mean to crush us. I have a friend, an innocent man, a newspaper editor, who has been in prison these many months. He appears in court for the fourth time next week. But the British cannot silence us. For anyone they imprison – for writing the truth – another one will spring up in his or her place.' She paced the room, tall and stately like a pirate queen, with jewels flashing in her hair. 'As I myself wrote last year in *The Nation*, under the name *Speranza* – meaning *'hope'* – *The Die Is Cast*. There is only one way: we must act. Silence is cowardice when thousands die of hunger and yet the produce of the land, the grain, the meat –'

'I'll write the song down if you have music paper,' Jane said in an attempt to divert her, but now Francesca's mind was running on politics. She opened a newspaper that lay on a side table and asked Jane her views on the state of Ireland.

'I'm not long arrived in Dublin.'

'Did you even read the review of your production in the *Freeman*?'

'Not yet.'

Francesca spread the newspaper out to read it. '"*The box circles contained their full quota of beauty and fashion and amongst the graceful groups of ladies flashed the scarlet and gold of the military.*" The military!' She stared at Jane. 'What civilised society requires the military to attend the opera? Are they to shoot you if they don't like it?' Before Jane could reply, she read on: '"*From the triumphs of theatrical genius our thoughts go to the misery in our city, to those dying of cold and hunger, whom we glimpse as mere shadows when we step from the theatre into our carriages and are whirled off to our luxurious homes.*" You must see, my dear, how the fortunes of the few contrast with the hardships of the many.' She smoothed a strand of black hair that had fallen from her hairstyle. It tangled amongst her rings, and she frowned as she freed it.

'The sentiments are noble,' Jane said, 'but, sadly, without the people in their carriages there would be no theatre. I'd have no salary.'

'Francesca, you must read the part about Mr Verity!' Anna interposed. 'That's the best.'

'"*The excellence of Mr Verity's acting … his exquisite delineations of the effect of poisoning on the mind of the prince … the convulsive clenching of the hands of the stricken victim and the moribund attitude in which he fell …*"' Francesca clawed at her own throat with an attempt at a death rattle.

'That's Jane's husband,' said Anna. 'Isn't she fortunate,

71

to both live for her music and be married to a brilliant actor?'

'How enviable!' Francesca put the newspaper aside, as if sensing a good story, and went to recline on a chaise longue. 'How did you meet him? Tell me about your lives.'

Jane had related this story before to others: she had known Edmond before he was famous, had first met him at the birthday party of a distant relative, he had heard her play the piano and found her a position with Davenant's Players.

'He must have been head over heels in love with you,' Francesca murmured, as if she sensed there was more, and wished to find it out. 'Do you not have children?'

'We have not been fortunate.' Jane never spoke of the dark period in her life. Even Francesca, with her lofty ideals, might recoil if she told her how Nathan had died, nine days old, starved and feverish, as a workhouse inmate bathed him in cold water. Now that she and Edmond had the means to support a child, no child had ever come.

Aware that Anna was looking away, Jane sighed inwardly. Women often sensed that she was hiding something. They did not pry, but soon withheld their friendship, pleasant to her face but dropping the connection afterwards. Perhaps one day she would confide in Anna, but not now, for she was too young, too sheltered …

Francesca now shot Jane a keen glance. 'And do you truly love him?'

'He can be a charming companion.' Jane gave her a bland smile. It was a question which she avoided asking of herself.

'So modest in your praise?' objected Anna. 'Such a personable gentleman, such fine eyes, his voice – I should worship him if I were his wife.'

'*Ha!*' said Francesca. 'You told me you were in love with Alex Royce! Your head has been so turned by him that you don't even want to know what the army's doing in this country.' As Anna protested, she spoke over her. 'No serious Irish poet could possibly love a soldier in the British Army. You should live for your art above all.'

'Oh, living for art is not as noble as it appears,' Jane protested.

'So, you have no more to say about your splendid husband and your life among the stars?' Francesca seemed to be skewering her under the guise of polite conversation.

'I'll tell you how he proposed.' Jane hoped the anecdote might satisfy them. 'It was quite theatrical really. We were at a banquet at a grand hotel in London. In front of two hundred people Edmond called for silence. He delivered a passionate speech about how he loved me, then went on one knee, imploring me to marry him, and holding out a ring. What else could I do but accept?'

'How romantic!' gasped Anna.

'Yet you seem unmoved by the memory.' Francesca, reclining on the chaise longue, supported her cheek on her hand, her dark eyes intent. 'Did you ever love anyone else?'

William. How deeply he had loved her, even though it had mired him in scandal. Yet she had returned to the theatre, to *live for art*.

'A long time ago.'

Suddenly Jane wanted badly to be alone, to be able to close her eyes before they started to prickle. She pretended to notice the ormolu clock on the mantelpiece. 'It's after four! I must go and get ready for this evening's performance.'

'Do call again,' Francesca said, still searching Jane's face, but not troubling to press her further. 'I'll ring for Theresa to show you out.'

As they waited for the maid, Anna remembered a piece of news. 'Oh – did you hear that Dr Wright's wife has just died?'

Francesca gasped. 'What happened?'

'Cholera,' said Anna. 'My mother is beside herself. Dr Wright had been telling everyone she was getting better. He must have had a dreadful shock.'

'We met her only the other day.' Jane remembered Mrs Wright at the Charity Ball, pale and softly spoken on her husband's arm. 'She seemed perfectly well. It's unbelievable that she could have died so quickly. I'm truly sorry to hear it.'

'How dreadfully unfortunate,' sighed Francesca, 'and how terrifying that a contagion like that can strike someone down without warning. It seems the epidemic is advancing rapidly – we shall all have to be more careful.'

'Poor Dr Wright has had a tragic life,' said Anna. 'They lost three children in infancy, with convulsions. Now he's alone, with no family to console him, and my father says he's deeply in debt.'

As Jane left, she had no doubt that every word of their conversation would be dissected. It seemed Francesca had an instinct for what was left unsaid; it would be best not to visit her again.

Chapter Ten

THE DEATH CERTIFICATE

Early on the Monday morning William went straight to Dr Wright's office at the Meath Hospital, hoping to catch him about his reference. Wright had rapidly accumulated wealth and prestige in Dublin. 'Dr Wright's widows' were a byword among the medical establishment for leaving him fat legacies after his assiduous care. He owned five carriages in addition to his country estate and a desirable townhouse on Merrion Square. He also had one of the best offices in the hospital, on the same corridor as Dr Graves and Mr Francis Rynd.

His brass nameplate was on an oaken door that muffled the response to William's knock.

William hesitated before pushing the door open and peering round. Wright was hunched at his desk with his head down. A large black book lay on the blotter. William recognised the silver crest of the death certificate book that usually was kept in the Head Porter's office; a black ribbon was tied around Wright's upper arm. Instead of stating his request, William began to apologise for his intrusion and tried to withdraw.

But Wright beckoned him in, gestured that he should pull a chair up to the desk.

'My wife has died.'

William muttered words of sympathy. 'I did not know that she was ill. What happened?'

Wright sank his forehead into his palm in a gesture of despair. 'Asiatic Cholera. She was taken ill the day before the Lucan Races.'

'I'm sorry to hear it.'

'I treated her myself,' continued Wright, 'with calomel and morphia. I engaged the best of nurses. But despite my best ... Oh God ... it was so fast.'

'You treated her yourself?' William grimaced. He stared down at the silver crest. Wright must know that he should have called in another physician – but it was hard to tax him with it in his grief.

'Who else could I have asked?' Wright seemed to sense his disapproval. 'There was no point in dragging another doctor away from their work – everyone's so very busy with this wretched epidemic.'

'Indeed. I suppose that you might have been obliged to consult a doctor who was junior to yourself.'

'And she who was in the prime of life, in the full flower of health, is now no more.' Wright sighed. 'I shall have a grand funeral for her and erect a monument in her memory. It will all be done properly, you understand?'

'Please accept my sincere sympathies.' William cleared his throat. He would not trouble Wright about the reference today – the man was too distracted. 'I should go across to the wards.'

'Of course, but was there something you wanted? No? Well, I won't detain you further, as I'm sure you have patients waiting.' Wright opened the black leather cover. 'But first, as you're here, I've completed the death certificate and I was going to ask you if you could sign …' He turned the book and pushed it towards William. 'I need it for the undertakers. She is to be buried at St. Werburgh's. My soul is beset with grief, yet I'm burdened with arranging the formalities. Once I have the certificate signed …'

'But I hadn't seen her,' William objected.

'You doubt me?' Wright's face darkened, although his melancholy expression did not change.

'I'm sorry, I'm unable to help you. I'm not in a position to sign.' William rose to leave. 'She wasn't under my care, nor have I seen her in the last fortnight. Perhaps if you spoke to the Coroner? I'm sure he'd understand your situation.'

'Doctors should help and support one another,' said Wright. 'Especially in this very busy time of a pandemic. We should all strive to be good colleagues. Surely there has been a time in your career when you have needed a colleague's support? No-one is superhuman.'

William wondered what Wright knew about his past. The medical establishment in Birmingham had been a small one, where secrets might be whispered. 'My point is that you're asking me to sign something which I cannot legally sign.'

'Do you quarrel with my diagnosis?' Wright's tone had grown cold.

'How can I confirm it? I've no knowledge of your wife's

case. In your position, as a highly eminent and respected clinician, you really shouldn't ask this of me. It's a breach in ethics. I find it unprofessional.'

Now Wright splayed his hands on the table, frowning, until he could no longer keep back his reply. 'Unprofessional! You call me unprofessional? It's you – you're unprofessional – you've never fitted in here, ever since you came from Birmingham. I'm not the only physician who sees you as difficult.' His grief had vanished, and a stinging anger took its place.

'I had no idea.' Startled by the sudden change in Wright's manner, William was wrong-footed.

'You had no idea that your practices were not in line with ours? Dr Stephenson told me of your inability to supervise Dr Murphy. Even the nurses, uneducated as they may be, distrust your judgment. They wait, then once you've left the wards, they ask me to review your patients.'

William was shocked. He might not have made as much money as Wright but had worked far harder. He studied the journals. He attended the Pathological Society every week. His methods were taken from the most up-to-date textbooks. This attack was so unexpected that he was unsure how to defend himself. He stared at Wright.

'I'd never considered myself badly regarded … I've always done my utmost for the patients … in any case I'm applying for a post in America. I'd come here to request a reference. But now I see that I'm asking the wrong man.'

There was an uncomfortable silence. Wright stared at him, his lips slowly parting. 'Forgive me.' Wright buried his head in his hands. 'I'm not feeling myself. The shock, you know. The shock. Please, forgive me. A misunderstanding.'

Now he wept, his shoulders heaving, and this abrupt reversal was harder to watch than the momentary display of spite. Bereavement could make people react in strange ways, William reflected: disbelief, anger, despair. This was the first time he had ever seen Wright lose control. He found he could after all pity him, with nothing to show for his years of marriage but dead infants and a dead wife.

'How can I face it all?' Wright mumbled into his palms. 'It is all too … oh God … I've lost all that was dear to me …'

William wondered if he should go around the desk to Wright's side. Was it appropriate to comfort him with a hand on the shoulder? He did not want to provoke another virulent outburst. There was one thing he could do for him. Surely Wright was capable of diagnosing and treating the cholera in his own family, when it was hard enough to find any physician with an hour to spare these days?

'Here, I'll sign it,' he said, lifting the pen from the inkstand and scratching his name on the death certificate.

'You're a good colleague, a good old chap,' mumbled Wright. 'I knew I could rely on you.

'I'm sorry for your loss.' William put the pen back and rocked the blotter over his signature. 'I shouldn't have refused you.'

'What I said, I didn't mean it, you know, heat of the moment.' Wright pulled out a handkerchief, blew his nose, then removed his glasses and gazed up at William, dabbing his eyes. 'So sorry.'

Nevertheless, thought William, someone must have complained of him to Wright, even if he had inflated their words. 'What you said about my colleagues has made me firmer in my resolve to move on.'

'You're of course highly respected among the medical staff … I hadn't intended … Look, I shall be delighted to write you an excellent reference, but there's no need for you to leave …'

'It would be an opportunity to work as a pathologist, applying scientific laboratory techniques to understand disease. I feel that in America science is the future and ability is more important than hierarchy.'

'I'm sure that you'd be better in the laboratory than on the ward – I mean, that it may prove to be the direction where your talents lie …' Now Wright was smiling blandly, his face resuming its usual placid expression.

Later when William relived the encounter, he felt a sickening qualm: Wright had contradicted himself time and again, dispensing his emotions as though from a tap. How much had been genuine and how much a show? Had he been manipulated into signing?

Chapter Eleven

PILLS AND BILLS

Edmond's new black frock coat had been delivered, just in time for them to go out to dinner.

'I hope it's hygienic.' Jane had seen a tailor's advertisement: orders were sewn in his workshop, not by out-workers in **'rooms where there is a deleterious vapour, with some member of the family lying in fever, or with the dreaded Asiatic Cholera, and at night the garment used for a covering, and by this means propagating disease'.** In the same newspaper she had read that six hundred people had died of cholera in Ireland in the last three weeks.

'It seems it.' He smelt the sleeve.

'Edmond! You could be infecting yourself.'

'I wouldn't patronise a cheap tailor in any case.' He shrugged the coat on.

That evening they were dining again at the Royal Arcade Hotel, with Tom and Madeleine, but there was no hope of a jarvey. Tom said that a notorious trial had just ended in the

81

Four Courts. A crowd streamed back from across the river, some exclaiming to each other about a sensation in the court, others arguing, or railing bitterly against the government. Perhaps it had been the trial of Francesca's newspaper friend.

'Let's walk,' said Tom. 'I'm hungry, and it isn't far.'

'Our dresses will get dirty.' Madeleine linked arms with Jane. She was in her usual bright silks.

'My dear ladies,' Edmond coaxed them, flourishing a gloved hand, 'the weather, in this most clement of cities, has been perfectly dry, the street has been swept to a state of perfect hygiene, and as for poor Tom …' As he sucked in his cheeks to parody emaciation, they laughed and gave in. It seemed to Jane that Dr Wright's stimulant pills were working.

Edmond and Tom strolled on ahead, threading their way through the crowd, and engaged in their own conversation, while Jane and Madeleine, arm in arm and minding their skirts, were slower.

As the courtroom crowds dispersed, the streets remained busy with ordinary home-goers: petty officials, clerks and shop girls. Jane had never seen so many beggars. The smart establishments employed uniformed doormen to clear their frontages. But wherever a shop was shuttered there would be a row of ragged people slumped against it, some with hands outstretched for pennies, others too far gone to beg. One unfortunate lay hopelessly sprawled half across the pavement, his arms flung up beside his head, so that they had to pick a way around him. Jane pitied them but was afraid of handing out alms: what if they surrounded her? What if they snatched her purse, or spread contagion?

Near the Carlisle Bridge a beggarwoman stopped their

path. The woman's audacity made Jane jump with fear, but all she said, in a quiet voice, was: 'Please, missus, if you could only spare something, for the sake of my child.' The woman's matted hair was loose to her waist and Jane's first instinct was to recoil from her and her feral smell, to find a way to walk on. But as the small girl beside her looked up with wide, shadowy eyes, Jane paused. She had seen the child before: her skin was tight over her cheekbones and her chin came to a point like the tip of a heart. Surely this was the child who had been sitting by the refuse heap, listless as the others played?

'Jane, come away,' called Edmond, over his shoulder, without altering his stride, but she hesitated as the mother pleaded.

'We walked from Mitchelstown, County Cork. The bailiffs from Mount Belvedere burned our roof, the whole family had only the road and beggary. Could you not spare me a little, for food?'

Jane felt that she must give something, if only to keep the child alive. She searched in her pocket for a coin.

Madeleine stayed her hand. 'Why do you not go to the model soup kitchen?' she asked the beggarwoman. A famous chef had set it up in Dublin Castle with much publicity about the cheap and nutritious soup. Tickets to see the apparatus were in high demand, and one could marvel at five hundred starving people being fed.

'Sure, the soup is only water boiled down to make it stronger! We're never any the better for it.'

'*Please*,' said the little girl, wilting against her mother's skirt.

83

Jane freed her arm from Madeleine and passed over a penny.

Madeleine interrupted the woman's thanks. 'Or you might go to the workhouse. At least you would have shelter there.'

'Madeleine!' Jane protested.

'It must be better than sleeping on the street.'

'Do you know what they do to the children? She'd be taken from me and given the black bottle. A few drops from that sends them asleep and they don't wake up.' The beggarwoman glared at Madeleine, resting her hand on her daughter's shoulder, drawing her close. 'Orla's the only one left. Everyone else passed away on the road from Cashel, including my mother and other daughter. I lost my husband outside the workhouse in Kildare.'

'Come away, Jane,' said Madeleine, taking her arm again.

Edmond and Tom had stopped ahead to wait.

'Whatever were you doing, talking to that creature?' asked Edmond as they caught up, but she did not reply.

* * *

After dinner, back in their lodgings, she told him what the woman had said.

'You're too naive.' He hung his new coat in the wardrobe. 'Most of those people aren't beggars at all – in fact the husband's working and the wife's spinning a tale on the street.' Edmond had picked at his dinner, yet the wine had given him hiccups.

'What do you know of poverty, Edmond?' Jane said, thinking of the gaunt face of the little girl. 'Of being hungry, and unable to feed your child?'

His face darkened: he had thought her comment barbed. She stood before him and put her hands on his shoulders. He was still tormented by the old demons.

'Edmond.' She reached up and smoothed his thick blond hair back from the side of his brow. It was moist with sweat. A hiccup shook his frame. His hands came around her waist and, as he rested his head onto her shoulder, still hiccupping, she surrounded him gently with her arms. His forehead was hot and heavy. 'You're unwell, my love,' she said, stepping back and raising his face with her hand. 'Do you have a fever?'

'Indigestion. Better in a minute.' He crossed the room and slumped into an armchair. His head drooped to his chest, bouncing as he hiccupped again.

'You thought that Dr Wright's pills had helped you?'

He glanced up. 'Wright? A capital fellow. Be better in a moment. Don't you worry.' But his eyelids closed again.

'Edmond?' She had to ask.

He let out a belch. 'Jane.'

'Is he encouraging you to gamble?'

His head jerked up. 'I did well. Came away with good winnings. You can't complain.'

'I just wanted to ask you –'

'It's up to me!'

His expression had hardened, but she continued. 'Be careful. You can't keep winning and with the Grand National –'

'I study the form. For every runner, I know the pedigree. I know the racing record of the horse. And its ancestors. It's not just hazard. It's a science.' He put his hand up to his forehead. 'I can't discuss it now. Pass me the pills. They're on the dresser.'

85

Jane sighed. 'The bottle's nearly empty,' she said, rattling it as she crossed the room.

Edmond felt no better after taking the pills and, complaining of nausea, put himself to bed.

She stayed up for another hour, forgetting her troubles in drafting musical compositions, missing her piano left behind in London, and waiting for him to fall asleep. He stirred a little as she joined him, but only snored when she whispered goodnight. She snuffed out the candle and lay awake, deciphering the shapes of the dark: the hanging gown that looked like a ghost, the looming mausoleum of the wardrobe, the faint light that crept around the edges of their door, as if from the next world.

The bed was too warm. Either Edmond had a fever, or her own physical tension was producing heat. She was losing Edmond again to gambling. She should never have given him a second chance, however much he had needed it. She slipped the coverlet away from her shoulder, allowing a cold draught to flow across her. Somewhere in this city, breathing this same cold air, was William, perhaps lying abed in the comfortable house he had described in his letters: the house with the old piano, with the garden where children might have played. She could not forget that sight of him at the theatre, how intensely he had gazed from the shadows of the box. She could not forget how they had long ago slept entangled, naked, her breast against his chest and her head on his neck, how he would rue a dead arm in the morning … Yet what life would she have had with him, once that brief passion had burned itself out? Dublin was a vassal of London, a backwater: there were not enough theatrical opportunities here.

Sighing, Jane turned over in the bed, cold again, pulling back at the blanket that Edmond had now snarled around his arm. She could not free it without waking him, and heaved a sigh, lying for warmth against the wall of his back, waiting for fatigue to dull her thoughts into sleep.

* * *

In the morning Edmond seemed refreshed and after breakfast went over to Dr Wright's rooms. He came back with more of the stimulant pills, as well as some new ones, pale purple this time, in a bottle labelled '*Anti-Cholera: One Pill Twice Daily*'.

'Just in case,' he said. 'Tom's taking them. Maybe you should as well?'

She frowned at the bottle in her hand.

'Do you think you have cholera?'

'No, of course not, these are just a preventive. You were even worried about my new coat, weren't you? By the way,' he kept his voice cheerful, 'I haven't any cash at present – could you lend me something to pay the tailor for it?'

'Really? I thought you went to the bank three days ago?' There had been a hundred pounds on his letter of credit, enough for two or three months, even without his salary.

'It's just for a day or so, until Davenant pays me.' He scowled at her hesitation.

'There must still be something left on your letter of credit, surely? How could you possibly have run out of money already?'

'Are you forgetting that I'm your husband?' He had

drawn himself up, as though affronted. 'I shouldn't have to justify my expenses, should I?'

'Edmond.' It was time to remind him of his obligations. 'We made a condition, before I agreed to marry you, that I would keep my own bank account, and you could not gamble with my earnings. It has worked well so far.'

'Other men gamble without being henpecked by their wives.' He stuck out his lower lip. 'You're being unreasonable.'

'So you're going back on your word as a gentleman? If you can't keep your word to me then why should we even be married?'

That should have paused him, but he redoubled his efforts. 'Jane, I only need twenty pounds.'

He knew that she had a circular letter from her bank in London for that amount, as yet uncashed.

'Twenty pounds! Do you know how long it takes me to earn that? And your coat was six, so what's the rest for?'

'In any case, I earn far more than that in a single performance. I'll give it back to you as soon as I'm paid. I'll write to my bankers in London to transfer more money.'

'Get it first, then spend it!' she snapped. 'Don't help yourself to my money.'

At that he started to wheedle, reminding her of all the things he had already paid for: the voyage to Ireland, lodging, dinners. The sable wrap. The day out at the Lucan Races …

'That was because you wanted to bet on the horses!' she protested.

But, he pleaded, hadn't he won? He fixed her with huge

eyes, and continued to plead, and sweet-talk her, and court her, until she gave in.

'Clearly then, your letter of credit must be used up?'

'Yes,' he said, with almost a shrug, as if it were obvious.

'I have one circular letter, that's all. I'll take it to the bank.' She turned her face away, setting her jaw, angry that he was forcing her to lie. She had another, also for twenty pounds, hidden away where he did not know about it.

* * *

Later that morning, when she had obtained the money, she refused to hand it over.

'It's my money!' She held out a sheaf of unpaid bills, her hand trembling with anger. 'I want to settle the tailor's bill myself – as well as these.'

'But you agreed.' His surprise was genuine. 'I'm your husband – you owe me your trust.'

She stared. It had to be said. '*I should never have given you a second chance.*' She said it with venom. It twisted together all her feelings of anguish, all the nights she had spent fretting over William, all her worries about their money. But what to her was a stinging slap went past him like the brush of a feather.

'At least you could give me the tailor's money,' was all he said. 'I'll go over to him this afternoon.'

It was hopeless. 'Do you promise?'

'Of course.'

She had enough to do settling their other bills, so doled out six sovereigns, which he pocketed, muttering thanks.

Despite the new pills Edmond grew more lethargic. He said he would go to the tailor's shop later in the week, settled in a chair with the newspaper and soon after that was asleep, groaning when Jane tried to wake him. She was tempted to take the money out of his pocket and pay the tailor herself, but instead spent the afternoon paying their other creditors. She paid their landlady a month's rent in advance, leaving two pounds and ten shillings, which would keep them in dinners until Davenant paid them at the end of the week.

Edmond awoke in the early evening. 'Time ish it?'

'Time to get ready,' said Jane. 'Are you feeling well, Edmond?'

'I all righ'…' He got up with a great effort from the chair, his eyes still dull.

'I'll get Mrs O'Reilly to make your tea. I hope you'll be better after that. You're on in less than two hours.'

Anxiety flooded her: she hoped to God he would be back to normal in time. Dr Wright's pills were definitely not helping, and his racing tips had lured Edmond back to gambling. She would have to persuade Edmond to consult someone else. Not knowing who else to ask, Jane decided she would find out if Mrs Meredith-Browne could recommend any other physician.

Chapter Twelve

SILENCE IN THE COURT!

'There must be someone else?' Jane sat on a frilled sofa in the Meredith-Browne's modishly chintzy drawing room. She had written to Anna about her concerns a few days prior.

'Truly, Jane, my mother says there's no better physician than Dr Wright.' Anna frowned earnestly. 'I really don't know what to advise you. She's gone to her dressmaker's, but I'll ask her again when she comes in.' Her smile was as winning as ever, but there was a new anxiety in her voice.

Jane had brought her the music for her ballad 'Liberty': she had made an arrangement of a couple of tunes from one of Mr Davenant's productions, first mourning in a minor key the nation's losses, then shifting to a freedom march in a major key.

Anna glanced at the stave sheets and said that she was delighted with it. 'But it looks too difficult for me to play.'

Jane's fingers ached to try out the music. She had been missing her piano, and across the room was Anna's. 'I could play, and you could sing –'

'Oh, but Papa might come home – I'll keep it for later.' Anna slipped the stave sheets between atlases in the bookcase then shut the glass doors. 'He's been in an awful temper with me all week.'

Jane was surprised. The weary, grey-looking gentleman she had seen on the boat had not seemed a domestic tyrant. 'Has something upset him?'

'It's his work.' Anna sighed. 'It's distressing him.'

'Does that mean that we can't play the piano?'

'Not to sing of freedom, at any rate. The British Parliament are cutting off the Famine Relief – Papa's beside himself. He says it will throw the whole country into chaos.' She stood in front of the bookcase, as if to conceal its contents. 'When you met us on the boat from London, he'd just been to plead with them. But now the MPs are ignoring his report.'

'But how can they do that? Everyone knows how disastrous the famine has been. You've only to go out in the street …' Jane remembered the hollow face of the little beggar girl. 'I spoke to a woman who'd been evicted from her farm and left with nothing: almost the entire family had died.'

'They said the relief money was squandered, so now the Irish landowners must pay. But Papa says that taxing landlords by the number of their tenants will just increase evictions.'

Jane heaved a sigh. 'I'm sorry your father's under pressure, but surely he doesn't mean us not to sing?'

'He found out about Francesca.' Anna raised helpless hands. 'I'm not allowed to see her now.'

'Why ever not?' Jane recalled Francesca's radical ideas, wondering if she had somehow irritated the Colonel.

'It was such a shock …'

'What happened?

'She made a scene at Mr Gavan Duffy's trial – the editor. He was charged with treason-felony.' She came across the room and sat beside Jane on the sofa. She lowered her voice. 'One of her *Speranza* pieces came out in *The Nation* last July, on the exact same day as the rebellion in Tipperary. It was a leading article. She called for a hundred thousand muskets, for barricades around Dublin Castle, and for revolution, just as in Paris and Vienna. *The Nation* was suppressed after that. The presses were broken up. Papa said at the time that famine was bad enough, but civil war would turn it into an apocalypse. He didn't know then that Francesca had written it.'

'But what happened at the trial?'

'She waited in the public gallery while the Solicitor General spoke for the prosecution. Then, as soon as he mentioned her article she stood up. She shouted out: "*I wrote that! I am* Speranza*! I edited* The Nation *that week – Gavan Duffy was in prison!*" It caused a sensation.'

'Unbelievable!' Jane imagined the striking figure of the young woman, her eccentric clothes and jewellery, and her husky contralto voice resonating through the court. 'Courageous – but so foolhardy – she must have been recognised. Was she charged with sedition?'

'No. She was quietened by shouts of "*Silence in the Court!*", then a policeman made her sit down.' Anna glanced wide-eyed at Jane. 'It was so fortunate that the Solicitor General's a friend of her family. He just said he was sorry that 'the young lady' – he didn't mention her name – should incur any risk by coming to the court, that she was respectably connected, and had been led into folly to write for such a publication. Then Mr Gavan Duffy spoke up to say that he was responsible for the article.'

'He was brave,' said Jane. 'If he hadn't said it, they would have locked her up on the spot.'

'But her mother's furious. And I'm supposed to have nothing more to do with her.'

'But have you seen her?'

'I had to see her – she's my friend. I crept out while Mama was at the dressmaker's.' Anna leant closer to Jane, her voice barely a murmur. 'She's in absolute anguish that it's made things worse for Mr Gavan Duffy – he's been in prison for months as it is. She says she'll never, ever, write sedition again, that the responsibility's more awful than she'd ever imagined.'

'She's certainly gone too far,' said Jane, 'but it's a shame. I can understand her anger about the situation here. Shouldn't a young woman be free to write of what occupies her mind?'

'Well, I certainly shan't be singing my ballad. My mother says that politics is an unsuitable interest for a young lady, as it causes wrinkles. Even worse, my pen was making an ugly blemish on my hand.' She stretched out her fingers. 'I think it's nearly gone now. I scrubbed it with lemon juice.'

'You ought not to give up your writing,' protested Jane.

'I'm to put my mind to the Patrick's Day Ball at Dublin Castle.' Anna took up the newspaper that Jane had bought for Edmond and found a report of a ball that listed the detail of every lady of rank, their jewels, and the fabric and colour of their dress. 'Mama insists that I have a new ball gown from Mrs Flannery's.' Rising, she put the newspaper aside and glided to the overmantel mirror as if on the arm of an imaginary partner. 'I had a lovely dress from London to wear, with pink lilies, but Mama said everyone wears green. So, I've ordered green watered silk overlaid with white tulle. She's lending me her emeralds.'

'You'll look wonderful.' Jane had divined the reason for Anna's sudden distraction. 'I'm sure you'll break all the young gentlemen's hearts, unless there's someone whom you've singled out?'

'What did you think of Alex Royce?' Anna's cheeks reflected in the mirror were the colour of a pink sugared almond.

Jane pretended not to remember him. 'Alex Royce?'

'You've met him twice,' Anna insisted, half turning round with a sidelong glance. 'The cavalry officer at the Lucan Races. My brother's friend. He came over and spoke to us after winning the steeplechase. Dreadfully handsome, dark, with soulful eyes. And he danced with me at the charity ball – you were there, at the Rotunda – so graceful, and he held me so firmly ...' Anna's arm crept around herself, her fingers exploring her shoulder. 'What kind of man do you think he is, Jane?'

'Well, you ought to know – he spent most of the race meeting with you.'

'But what do you think of him?'

'I didn't speak to him much. He's certainly handsome – athletic.'

'Isn't he, though? But he won't speak of serious subjects,' said Anna, with a smile. 'He's too light-hearted. If I mention what I'm reading he calls me clever and cultivated, but apart from the compliments doesn't seem to have an opinion.'

'Perhaps he's so infatuated with you that he can't think of anything else. But did you ask him about his life in the army?'

'Why, what should I ask?'

'Don't be naive, Anna! What did Francesca say? Why is the army here in such strength? With whom are they at war?'

'They're here to protect us, I suppose. Alex is in an Irish regiment, in any case.'

'Yet you've read Speranza's poems about foreign tyranny laying Ireland to waste and starving the people.' Jane lowered her voice in response to Anna's cautionary gesture. 'Your own ballad 'Liberty' is in the same genre. The army – British, Irish, whatever – is the instrument of that so-called foreign tyranny.'

Anna hesitated, blushing as her smile returned. 'But do you not think, that a husband should be someone who just by standing near makes your heart beat faster? The touch of whose hand is a shiver of delight? Love is more than agreeing over politics, is it not?'

Jane knew that shiver of delight: after Edmond had seduced her away from her parents their first months together had been a sparkling happiness. That crystal had been broken and glued back together, the fault line dulling its light. 'I suppose that a marriage should join minds as well as hearts. The former is rarer than the latter.' As she spoke, she thought of William: a union of the mind and the heart from which she had run away. 'There's also the money question: can he support you – or indeed, support himself, which tends to be the greater expense? Rarest of all, is he kind? If you find everything in one man, then you'll be lucky if he's faithful, or if there's not some other obstacle.'

'Alex's father is wealthy, although it's new money. As well as Royce Park, he owns Mount Belvedere in north County Cork. Alex told me his father made his money in property and insurance. I suppose one must admire him for it.'

'I met Theodore Royce at the Charity Ball. Your mother seems to like him.'

Anna laughed. 'She calls him an outrageous old flirt. But my parents had an odd conversation about him. My father said he had heard that Theodore Royce was a dangerous man to cross.'

'What did he mean by that?' The Colonel, working as he did in the administration, might know more than he would tell his wife and daughter.

Anna frowned. 'Papa said that property and insurance were not always respectable businesses. Someone whose wealth had risen so fast at a time of national crisis might be crooked. But Mama said it was all malicious rumour and that Mr Royce was a perfect gentleman.'

'Well,' Jane sighed, 'even if the father is a rogue, the son might still be a decent man. After all, you can't choose your parents.'

Anna brightened. 'Alex is funny. When I asked him about his father, he said that he was an appalling disgrace, and lots of other wild things that made me laugh.'

Jane smiled, remembering how Alex had entertained Anna at the races.

'Honestly, my stomach was hurting.' Anna chuckled, dimpling her downy cheeks. 'In the end I teased him, that he made everything a joke, and must be hiding his dark side.'

Jane watched the dimples flatten. 'You're still young, Anna, take your time. If you marry him you'll have fifty years together.'

'But I think I'd say yes,' said Anna, with a shiver. 'If he asked me.'

'Wait until you're sure,' Jane said, but her friend's eyes sparkled. Anna's decision was made: desire had triumphed over reason, and her writing ambitions had been put aside.

Chapter Thirteen

A MEDICAL REPORT

William had to hurry over to Grafton Street, having received a letter from a Mr Lydon which required an immediate response. Lydon's Insurances and Lettings Agency was above a dressmaker's shop, Mrs Flannery's. Behind plate glass windows a mannequin with enormous skirts of gaudy fabrics tempted ladies to look inside. Yet it was three men who emerged from the building and loitered outside in the sun, smoking pipes and deep in conversation, their faces shaded by their hats and collars.

From across the street William recognised the big ruffian's red velvet coat. He turned to look into a bookseller's shop, pretending to study the titles in the window as he watched the men's reflections until they parted and went away. As he crossed the road to Lydon's office, a lady in pink paused outside Mrs Flannery's, a graceful figure with tendrils of dark hair emerging beneath a bonnet trimmed with roses. She was, of course, not Jane, and returned his glance with a look of surprise.

Mr Vincent Lydon's name was on a brass plate: William entered the doorway between the shops and climbed a staircase where tobacco smoke lingered.

Letters and reports lay everywhere in Lydon's office, stacked in bundles on every surface. On the desk a steel spindle impaled the day's invoices.

'I'm glad ye came to talk to me.' Lydon, with his thinning hair and florid face, looked like a man who might spin you a tale in a bar. But his affable smile died as he spoke of his concern. 'It's consequent on the claim made by Dr Oliver Wright on the life of Mrs Catriona Wright. Regarding the circumstances of her death. Ye treated her for cholera, I believe?'

'Catriona Wright?' William's instinct was to stall for time. He had wanted to ask Dr Wright what to tell Mr Lydon, but Dr Wright was out of town until Thursday, at the Curragh Races.

'Yer signature's on her death certificate.' Lydon opened a folio and leafed through its contents. 'As passed over to me by Dr Wright's solicitor.'

'I can't remember the details – I've had so many patients –'

'But yer colleague's wife? She only died on the 16th.' Lydon held out a slip of paper. 'This might be yer signature?'

William glanced at his initials, overlarge on the bottom line, and waved it away. 'Yes. That's my signature. But I'd have to consult my records to provide anything further. I'm sorry.'

'Is it true that doctors don't look after an acquaintance, or one of their family? What ye call professional etiquette?'

'But all the physicians know Dr Wright – if that were the

case, she could hardly have been seen by anyone …' William continued on this theme, adding detail, until he realised that he was lying and Lydon was staring at him.

'He had insured her life for fifteen thousand pounds.' Lydon paused, sandy eyebrows bristling as he frowned. 'An enormous sum. His fine house on Merrion Square itself, and maybe his neighbour's as well, if not the whole row itself, could be bought outright for that amount. He was only just after finishing the first twelve months of the policy and was a few days into the period when he could claim. A young woman, too, only thirty-two years of age.'

'But in the present cholera epidemic –'

'There's more: Lydon's Insurances is after paying out a claim on Mrs Wright's mother just a few months before. I daren't even go to my underwriter with this one.'

'Certainly Dr Wright has been unfortunate.'

Lydon snorted. 'Mrs Wright was more unfortunate, in that her career as a racehorse owner was cut short. I found out that when the claim on the mother was paid, the grieving couple went to Liverpool to buy racehorses.'

'What's the relevance of that?'

'In my experience,' said Lydon, 'people who devote themselves to the turf tend to lose money by it, and sometimes it leads them to dishonesty.'

William stared at him. 'What are you saying?'

'All I'm asking is whether ye can confirm that ye treated Mrs Wright, and saw her after her death?'

'I believe she was a typical case of cholera, the fever, flux, and so forth …' His voice tailed away. 'I really would have to check my casebooks.'

'I'll need a full medical report before I approach the underwriter, mind.'

Then to William's unease, he spoke of sending his 'loss adjusters' to collect it.

'I'll reply to you myself by the end of the week.'

William took his leave and went back to the hospital. What if Lydon caused enquiry to be made at Dr Wright's house? The servants would deny ever having seen him. He knew he shouldn't have given in to Wright's grief, and was irritated that Wright had got him into this situation, but it would not do to show it. Wright was now the only person who could get him out of it.

* * *

On Monday morning, Wright was due to be at his consulting rooms in his home. William saw the first dozen or so patients in the Admissions Room, then told Joseph Murphy to take over.

Merrion Square was a short walk from the Meath, beyond St Stephen's Green, one of the best addresses in Dublin. The door knocker was still muffled in black crape and the blinds were drawn. An elderly housekeeper, her eyes milky with cataract, peered closely at him before she let him in. He had to explain twice that he was not a patient but another doctor.

Wright was not in his consulting room but in the dining room, staring down at the drinks tray on his sideboard as if watching something.

'I too had a letter from Mr Lydon.' He half-filled a

102

tumbler with whiskey and offered it to William, who declined.

'Have you replied?' William sat on a dining chair, studying Wright's frowning brow, the eyes partly hidden behind spectacles, the downturned mouth. 'I can't conceal the truth. You must tell him.'

A gold cufflink gleamed in a white cuff as Wright raised the glass to take a gulp of whiskey. His face crumpled as if he were about to weep.

William made quiet noises of sympathy and understanding. But a horrible anxiety gripped him: what if Wright persisted in the deception? What then? He'd already been forced to lie to Mr Lydon.

'I shall lose all that I have left of her. I shan't be able to bear it, you see ... to lose the horses as well ...' Wright took another mouthful of whiskey and sat down at the dining table. 'We were bereaved of our children, but we shared another passion – our racehorses. She spent her entire endowment on our stables and our horses' welfare. Now, her insurance payment is all that will save her beloved stables from being broken up.'

'So you haven't replied to Mr Lydon?'

'You'll have to help me, Dr Doughty, as a good colleague, as someone I trust.'

'But Mr Lydon's asking to see my casebooks.'

As Wright finished his whiskey, his cheeks regained their rosiness and his pain seemed to ease. 'Come into the consulting room.' He led the way across the corridor. There was a report ready on the desk. He handed it to William. 'I've written the dates and details of her final illness,' he continued as William glanced over it. 'I couldn't keep her alive, God help me. But we're in the midst of a deadly cholera epidemic, overwhelming the entire city, the country, what do they expect?'

'I know.' William heaved a sigh.

'That is what happened. All you have to do is transcribe it into your records. It will tally with my account if Lydon cross-checks.'

William hesitated. 'I still feel awkward that I never actually saw her. Nor was I entitled to be her physician, given that we're close colleagues.'

'But, Dr Doughty, do you not see that it was impossible to secure the services of any other physician, as all were – and are – so very busy with the epidemic. How was I supposed to proceed?'

'I'm sorry, but –'

'What's the alternative?' Wright came closer, staring at William through his spectacles, his pale eyes magnified and distorted. 'Will you claim that your own certificate was a forgery?'

'No ... I ...' William hesitated to answer. 'You know I signed it to help you out. But, perhaps, it would be better for both of us to admit the truth now rather than compound a falsehood which may lead us into deeper trouble. Could we perhaps say it was a terrible mistake? That I had confused her details with another patient?'

'Let me be frank.' Wright pulled out his desk chair and sat down, leaving William standing with the paper in his hand. 'You are applying for a position in New York. You asked me to provide you with a reference. How will it look, do you think, to your new employer, if you admit to making a false death certificate? You say you wish to avoid trouble later on. I propose to you that this is your only way. Take the information and do as I say.'

William read it: a textbook description of cholera symptoms developing over a couple of days.

'What's the matter?' Wright demanded, before he had finished. 'Do you not believe that was what happened?'

'Of course, of course ...' William folded the paper and looked down at his feet. There was nothing else that could be done.

Wright rang the bell and William heard the housekeeper trudging upstairs from the kitchen and her slow footsteps in the hall before she fumbled with the doorknob. The door creaked open.

'Bridget, this is Dr Doughty.' Wright spoke up, as if she were partly deaf. 'Dr Doughty has been a great source of help and advice to me, not least during my late wife's illness.'

The old woman curtseyed politely.

'Do you remember how often he visited her? He was always here to see her, wasn't he?'

'Yes, sir, he was, sir.' The housekeeper nodded, as if eager to show that she could still remember, and could still see through her clouded eyes.

'Even in her last days.' Wright raised his voice further. 'Her last days, Bridget.'

'Yes, in her last days, bless her.'

'You will show him out, now, please, Bridget,' said Wright.

Clearly Bridget's sight, and perhaps her mind, were failing, thought William. Either that, or she knew that if Wright dismissed her then there would be nowhere else for her but the poorhouse. Wright was twisting her so that Lydon, if he chose to question her, would discover nothing.

William felt that he had been twisted in the same way. He shoved the paper into his pocket and left. He had only to insert the notes, perhaps no more than a line at a time, into his daily casebook, for Lydon's inspection. He could forgive Wright that his wife had no other doctor at a time like this, when every physician was so hard-pressed. But – the thought was outrageous – suppose Wright *had* murdered his wife for the insurance money, and was making him an accessory to the crime?

The best way out was the post in New York. But William knew that, like Bridget, if he fell out of Wright's favour he would have nowhere to go.

Chapter Fourteen

INDISPOSED

A sinister arpeggio in A-minor accompanied the Caliph – Tom Nisbett – as he appeared among the plaster statuary of the *Garden of Deceit*.

'Have you not yet poisoned your prince?' he jeered at his daughter – Madeleine – to the groans of the audience, while weighing a golden flask in his hands. He rejected her excuses then exited to more foreboding chords.

Edmond came on as the prince, wandered dreamily in the garden, then knelt in front of Madeleine. 'Take this red rose, this rose of my heart.' It wavered as he offered it. 'Grasp it tight, let its thorns inject the same fever that burns my days and nights …'

'Though it may transfix my fingers it cannot infect me further, for I am already aflame …'

They continued, Edmond unusually hesitant, Madeleine in a higher register than normal. Jane sensed a tension that was not part of the scene: Edmond was not himself. As they linked arms with golden goblets in their hands, Jane accompanied their duet. Madeleine's voice soared into the gaps where Edmond's was too quiet. As the song went on he began to falter, at which, as the audience held their breath to listen, Davenant hissed prompts from the pit.

Between the verses the orchestra played on for the lovers to dance a few paces around the stage. The choreography was precise and well-rehearsed, yet Edmond lacked his usual grace. As the final verse began he leant on a plaster pedestal, which toppled with a bang, smashing its statue across the stage. A gasp went up from the audience as Edmond fell among the fragments.

The orchestra halted. Jane leapt up, the shock of it tingling in her arms. A few feet away Edmond lay motionless on the boards, an eerie whine issuing from his throat. Madeleine turned wide eyes on Davenant, waiting for directions. The audience were at first unsure if this was part of the show. But as the silence extended, they started to murmur. Davenant strode up on to the stage and a babble of voices broke out.

'*Is there a doctor?*' he shouted, then knelt at Edmond's side. Now that everyone knew his collapse was real, a babble of voices broke out.

'*Contagion!*' a lady shrieked, as people started to crowd towards the exits, murmuring about cholera.

Her heart pounding with anxiety, Jane rushed up the stage steps, glancing, despite herself, up at the boxes, just in case William might have been there to help, but of course he was not. Indeed, why should he have been?

'I think it's a seizure,' said Davenant.

Edmond's lips were purple, and his eyes rolled up beneath

their lids. His limbs had begun to clench and unclench; he was breathing noisily. A stagehand brought smelling salts which Jane, crouching, held to Edmond's nose so that they saw his eyelids flutter as he let out a moan. She put a hand on his forehead. It was clammy but there was no fever.

They turned up the gas in the chandeliers and repeated the call-out for a doctor, but no help came. Jane loosened Edmond's costume, releasing the tight ruff from around his neck, so that his breathing eased and to her relief his colour began to improve. He opened his eyes.

Davenant dashed to the front of the stage as the curtain came down. Panic had broken out at one of the exits and there was a scuffle.

'*Ladies and gentlemen, pray patience! Mr Edmond Verity is merely indisposed. No need for alarm. His part will be played by Mr Harry Barker, who will appear on stage shortly. Ladies … gentlemen …*' After a few moments he returned behind the curtain. 'We'll have to move him.'

The stagehands carried Edmond, who was now mumbling incoherently, into the wings.

'Get the costume off him, get him back to his lodgings and go for his doctor.'

Then Davenant went again to plead with the departing crowd to remain, for the play would shortly resume.

Harry Barker had donned the prince's cloak to stand in for Edmond, and with Madeleine took up position waiting for the curtain to rise. Jane prepared herself to return to the orchestra pit, trying to calm the shaking in her hands. She did not know how she would be able to continue playing, yet there was no one who could take her place.

As the commotion in the auditorium abated, Davenant came back through the curtains, shaking his head. 'Only ten people have stayed – I'll have to give them a refund.'

Although a relief, it was a disaster to cancel a show: earnings would fall. What would become of them?

Her anxieties mounting, Jane hurried back to the lodgings.

Their landlady, Mrs O'Reilly, had been watching out for her return. 'Is it the cholera? Jesus and Mary, I'll not have the cholera in my house.' She followed Jane upstairs. 'It'll kill everyone in the house stone dead, then the entire street …'

At the door of their rooms Jane turned, subduing her own anxiety. 'It can't possibly be – he's been taking the anti-cholera pills.'

'Well, he can't stay here.' Mrs O'Reilly was trembling with agitation, her face as crumpled as the apron that she twisted between red and swollen fingers. 'The doctor's in with him now. Ask for him to be taken to the Fever Hospital, in the name of God!'

'He has no fever. He's just not been right for a few days.'

Jane went in, shutting the landlady out.

She hurried through their empty sitting room to the bedroom beyond.

'It will be at least a week before you can resume work.' Dr Wright was sitting at Edmond's bedside. 'In the meantime …' He lowered his voice as Jane came in, speaking into Edmond's ear as if offering encouragement.

Edmond lay propped up while blood dripped from his arm into a metal dish in the doctor's hand. In the light of the oil lamp his pallor matched his pillows. His eyes were closed, but at least he was nodding and smiling at whatever Dr Wright had said.

'Mrs Verity.' Dr Wright glanced up in Jane's direction. 'I am, as you see, bleeding him, which has helped him to come round. I've brought him some stronger stimulant pills – on the dresser.' He had a black ribbon of mourning on his coat sleeve: perhaps she should offer him condolences on his wife's death. But he was steadying his lancet in Edmond's arm as he watched the level in the dish. She merely thanked him for attending so quickly, then waited as he finished his task. He released the band he had tied around Edmond's arm, applied a dressing, and wiped the lancet. 'Would you be good enough to clean the dish for me?'

Jane picked it up from the bedside table then followed him out to the sitting room. 'What's the matter with him?'

'He's suffering a little nervous debility, but I expect it to be helped by the stimulants. See that he takes one pill three times a day with a little water, in addition to his previous regime. I'll review him in a few days' time.'

She detained Dr Wright as he was about to leave. 'Edmond has been taking your pills since the 13th of February – it's been a fortnight.' She was sure of the date: Edmond had first been to Dr Wright's rooms the day before the Lucan Races. 'This evening ... I ... I thought I'd lost him.'

'You will see recovery soon.' Smiling, Wright made to side-step her towards the door. 'Already there are signs of it which I, as a medical practitioner, can discern.'

'But he's just collapsed on stage. He's barely eating. What's the matter with him?'

'My good woman,' he said, still smiling, 'I'm afraid

111

you're overwrought. I understand your anxieties, but please remain calm. Simply ensure that he adheres to the treatment as prescribed. It is merely a nervous affliction, which with rest and care and careful observation of the medical regime, will soon resolve. You will see.'

'But every day what I see is that he's *getting worse!*' Jane could not keep her voice from rising. 'Are you sure it is not something more serious?'

'Jane?' Edmond had heard them through the open door.

'Your wife is solicitous on your behalf, sir!' Wright called back to him, before raising his eyebrows at her. 'Now, my dear, I've agreed the course of treatment with your husband, so no need for you to worry your pretty head.'

'But when will he get better?' How dare he dismiss her like that? 'What do you mean by *soon* – when? I can't even stay here to look after him – I have to work, Mr Davenant has no-one to take my place.' She was too proud to mention their money worries, yet Dr Wright sighed, as if he thought he had divined her problem.

'I know an excellent nurse at the Meath Hospital. She may be able to offer a few extra hours in the evening to care for your husband, but you must adhere to the treatment regime. Do you promise?'

'A nurse would be a great help,' she conceded, feeling she had no other choice. 'But I don't know if we could afford to pay her.'

'It will just be a modest contribution to the Sisters of Charity. In any case, in a few days you will see an improvement in him.'

A rap at the door revealed Mrs O'Reilly, unable to wait

any longer. 'Is it the cholera, doctor?' She shifted from side to side, trying to see past Jane's shoulders.

'No. It is not the cholera. I think it no more than a nervous affliction. Rest, and the stimulant pills, should bring the patient round.'

'Oh, please God! I'll say my prayers for the poor gentleman until he's better, so I will.'

'Could you kindly clean this for the doctor, Mrs O'Reilly?' Jane thrust the dish of blood into her hand and shut the door in her disconcerted face before she could pry any further.

Once Dr Wright had gone downstairs Jane gave Edmond one of the new pills and sat beside the bed.

'I'm sure I'll improve,' he said weakly. 'Dr Wright says my nervous function has improved.'

'You must get better, Edmond.' She leant across and put her arm over him, resting her head against his chest. Without him there would be no theatre company and she would be alone in a strange city. 'I don't know what I'll do if anything happens to you.' His left arm was bandaged up but though he lifted the other it was too weak to return her embrace.

She sat up again. 'What did you arrange with Dr Wright? You were talking to him about something when I came in.'

All Edmond would say was that the doctor was coming to bleed him again. She recalled her glimpse of the two men with their heads close together: Edmond with that smile.

'I hope that you have not done anything foolish, my love,' she said carefully.

'He is the kindest of men,' said Edmond. 'He told me today about a poor patient of his. The man complained that

113

Dr Wright had given him a healthy stomach but nothing to put in it, so he gave him a shilling to buy food.' He ended with a sigh. Despite the stimulant tablet, his eyelids fluttered shut then he fell asleep.

Leaving a night-light burning, Jane crept downstairs to the dining room for a glass of water and a few biscuits; she had not eaten that evening. When she returned to their room Edmond was sprawled snoring across their bed, but she changed into her nightgown and curled up, exhausted, beside him.

* * *

It was after midnight when Edmond abruptly sat up, retching. He heaved himself out of bed and staggered to the window, pushing up the sash.

'What is it, Edmond?' Jane sat up, empty-headed, from a deep sleep.

He hung over the windowsill, unable to reply, gasping in lungfuls of the damp air.

She went to him and put her hand on his back, unsure what else to do. His muscles twitched beneath her hand.

Outside the rain fell heavily from a black sky, with snakes of water flowing down the empty street. A smell came in, of dank basements and sewage, of coal smoke and horses in harness. Edmond's body tensed and he vomited into the street below. Then he stumbled back to the bed and flung himself down with a groan.

Jane closed the window. If only they were back in London, in their house in Cheyne Walk, and she could have called in Dr Lewis. Here in Dublin they knew no-one. She returned to the bedside. Edmond was soaked in sweat, and she wiped his face with a handkerchief soaked with cologne. The scent of juniper and lavender took away the bitter odour of his vomit.

'I'm sorry, Jane,' he said. His hand wandered across the bedclothes and found hers, pulling her down to sit on the bed beside him. 'You're very good to me.'

'I'll fetch you a glass of water,' she offered, but he passed his hand gently over her thigh and cradled her hip to detain her.

'After last night I … my confidence … I hope I'm still of use. What did Davenant say?'

As he rested his head in her lap, she stroked his shoulder mechanically. 'Don't worry about Davenant,' she said. 'Just rest and get better.'

'Tell him Dr Wright says I shall be back to work next week.' His head weighed down upon her thigh, and she touched his cheek, feeling how sharply the bone stuck out. 'Don't worry about money,' he whispered. 'I've written to my bankers in London. And I'm guaranteed to win on the Grand National. You'll see –'

'Of course.' It was pointless challenging him. As shadows encroached on the feeble glow of the night-light, she had an overwhelming conviction that he had stood for the last time upon the stage. His next words betrayed that he sensed it too.

'I want you to know something. You've always been the only one, always been my true love.'

'What about Maud Frith?' she asked quietly. 'You got engaged to her, do you remember?'

His gaze dwelt upon the folds of her nightgown. She had once so admired his classical profile, the almond shape of his eyes, had adored the chilly, blank beauty of his face. Yet now she often avoided looking at him.

'It was a bet,' he muttered, without glancing up, and when she asked him to repeat himself said: 'I got engaged for a bet.'

She suppressed an angry reply. All those years ago, desperate for Edmond to return, reading of that engagement in the newspaper had broken her.

'Tom Nesbitt wagered fifty pounds that I couldn't get her to say yes. But when she found out and broke it off, I had to give him half the money back.'

'Did you ever think,' she said, her voice carefully controlled, 'that I might find out about it?'

'I needed the money. It tided me over to the next race day – I won something then.' It was as if he had thought it justified.

Jane stilled, feeling tension flow through her; her thigh muscle hot and angry under his head.

'I came back for you. I did what I said, mostly. But it was you, then – you were the one who wouldn't come with me.'

'We won't argue over it anymore,' she said, remembering how William's arms had become a consoling haven.

'That led to another wager,' murmured Edmond. That smile again. 'You were so cold, for so long, that Tom bet me a hundred pounds I couldn't get you back.'

She opened her mouth to protest.

'It paid the bills for the ring and the banquet,' he said.

'That's loathsome!' She remembered, with a sickening

feeling, his speech at that birthday party, the dramatic proposal that she had retold to her acquaintances. 'All you ever cared about was gambling!'

He looked up then. His smile faded. 'No, Jane, I always loved you. I know I haven't loved you properly, whatever that is, but I can't, I don't even know how to, and I hope you'll forgive me for it.'

She closed her eyes. It was the nearest she would ever get to an admission of guilt from him. 'Well, if it weren't for you, I'd never have become a professional pianist. It's almost impossible for a woman. But you got me in with Davenant, you encouraged me to keep practising, praising me, keeping me going, advising on my compositions ... you never failed me there.'

'Now, we're at peace with one another,' he said, and drew her down for a kiss. 'How wonderful you are. Lovely Jane. I wish I could still ...' His breath was bitter, but his mouth was gentle and his hand slipped a caress inside the neck of her nightgown.

She straightened up again, and stroked his hair back from his forehead, but did not reply. It was no use going over the past in the middle of the night. Here they were in Dublin, running out of money, and running out of time.

Chapter Fifteen

SISTER ALOYSIUS

The nurse from the Sisters of Charity came at five o'clock the following afternoon. Mrs O'Reilly brought her upstairs, left hot water and clean linen, then retreated hastily.

Sister Aloysius chuckled. 'Afraid of the cholera, yer wan.'

'It isn't cholera!' Jane protested.

'People still remember the thirties.' Sister Aloysius put a jug of hot water on the washstand. She was small and wiry with freckled cheeks and bright brown eyes. 'Well, if God put me on this earth to care for the sick people, I'd better get on with His work. Now, Mr Verity …'

It had been a wearisome day, with Edmond plagued with painful limbs and reluctant to move. Jane had an evening performance ahead of her, yet now Sister Aloysius filled the wash bowl and bustled around him, expecting her to help.

'Let's freshen you up, Mr Verity. Help him, now, bring his knee up, so …' She showed Jane where to place her hands to move Edmond for a wash. 'Ah, you're not willing for it even though he's your husband. You'll soon learn.'

Jane would rather not have learned, but did as asked.

Sister Aloysius continued, plying the sponge: 'I had to learn. The thirties – the last big epidemic – that was when I started as a nurse at the Cholera Hospital in Grangegorman. I was only seventeen, and terrified even to walk up to the place. There'd be people outside wanting me to read the dead list pinned to the door. It had been a prison once, and the bell tolled out from the tower whenever another poor soul had passed on. Here, wash him down there ...'

'I would not have had your courage.' Jane took the sponge and wiped Edmond, who flinched as she touched him, so that she tried to be gentler.

'Faith gives you courage.' Sister Aloysius, rubbing Edmond with a towel, met her glance with shrewd appraisal. 'You'd have found the courage, sure enough – we had to. We had over five hundred cholera patients. All over the place – on the stone benches in the cells, on the floors, in the corridors – with only straw for bedding. They'd cry like animals, in agony from the blue cramps, the poor souls.'

'What on earth could you do?'

'Oh, we found plenty to do. Time to change your sheets, Mr Verity.'

Edmond merely nodded. Neither of us, thought Jane, can resist this woman's energy.

Sister Aloysius showed Jane how to change the bedlinen without getting Edmond out of the bed. Her thin wrists belied her strength.

'We saw that the people needed help, and we helped them. We worked in fours, four hours at a time, day and night around the clock, we washed them and fed them, we prayed with the sick and the dying and we swept the slops and straw into the yard.' She lowered her voice as she gathered the bed linen up into a bundle. 'Every morning we sent the dead to be buried side by side in a long trench, may God have mercy. And the priest who prayed over them fell sick and himself was buried there.'

'You were lucky to survive.' Jane smoothed Edmond's sheets, imagining the hopeless cases in a decaying institution, recalling her dark memories of the workhouse. 'I couldn't have borne it.'

'Well, I was young and strong but, sure, if that didn't destroy me, I don't know what would!' Sister Aloysius chuckled again, her rosy cheeks outlined by the crisp white borders of her veil. 'We washed ourselves and our clothes in lime and water, and we prayed in the oratory – it worked, for only one of us got the sickness, and she recovered. At last, when we thought it would never be over, then it was, thank the Lord, and they closed the hospital. It was a prison before, now it's a prison again – for women and children awaiting transportation. Yet now the cholera's come back, heaven help us ...'

Sister Aloysius finished cleaning and tidying, then said it must be time for Edmond's tablets and gave him a pill from the green bottle, which he swallowed obediently.

'You're very kind.' He thanked her, then lay back on his plumped-up pillows, in crisp new sheets, his hair brushed and his limbs arranged so comfortably that he forgot his pain.

As the nun sat down on the chair beside the bed, continuing her chat, he turned his head to give her a wan smile. She proved to be effusive in her praise of Dr Wright.

'He's such a good, kind man,' she assured them. 'Everyone speaks well of him.' She repeated with enthusiasm what Jane had heard before, that Dr Wright was hard-working and did not charge the poor.

'He seems affluent, nonetheless,' Jane commented, thinking of the elegance of Merrion Square.

'Oh, he has a great many patients. He won't charge them much, sometimes not at all, but usually the wealthy will leave him a legacy, you know, that's how it works, sure.'

Jane caught a knowing glance from beneath the nurse's brows. Was she hinting that Edmond should remember Dr Wright in his will? She did not know, of course, that Edmond had no money to leave. Worse, was she taking it for granted that he would die?

'Do you often visit his patients like this?' Jane asked her.

'When requested – it's a little extra income for my Order.'

'It's burdensome, isn't it, at the end of a working day?'

'Ah, sure – it never goes on for very long.'

It was nearly six o'clock. As Jane put on her black silk and garnets and arranged her hair, she wondered what Sister Aloysius had meant: was her evening work shortened by the patients' recovery, or by their death?

'I wish I didn't have to go out.' The dense folds of her dress billowed away from a corseted waist. She smoothed it down and was ready. 'But it's time – they need me – there's no-one else to play for them.'

'You look marvellous, as always,' Edmond rested his hand on his heart, then stretched it out to her. 'Beautified for your one true love. Good luck with the performance.'

121

Sister Aloysius likewise urged her to go. 'Your husband will be perfectly comfortable.'

Jane kissed Edmond. His admiring glance, the pleasant weight of the silk, the feeling of freedom as she stepped out into the street to hail a passing jarvey: they all weighed on her heart. When would they kiss farewell for the last time?

* * *

She arrived at the Queen's Royal Theatre with enough time to catch up with George Davenant. He was deep in discussion with Mr McFadyen, the theatre's proprietor, but broke off to ask her about Edmond's progress.

She shook her head.

'Dr Wright says it will be at least a week before he can return.'

'And then?'

'I hope he'll be better.' Anxiety gnawed at her, the sense that Edmond was getting steadily worse, and the next week would see a continuing decline, rather than recovery.

Davenant's smooth face wrinkled for a moment but then revived. 'In the meantime …' he shuffled through the papers that lay on McFadyen's desk until he found a slim, paper-bound folio. 'Take him this: a new libretto he can learn while he lies in his bed. A musical tragedy by a brilliant new writer: John Percival. Do you know his work?'

'I don't think Edmond's well enough.' Jane glanced through the libretto: *The Emperor of Persia*. She could not imagine that Edmond would be able to focus on it. 'To me he seems worse, despite Dr Wright's treatment.'

Davenant raised his eyebrows. 'Then he should consult a different doctor.'

'Dr Wright was highly recommended, and Edmond likes him.' She did not mention that they shared an interest in racing. Davenant had already nurse-maided Edmond out of that addiction once before.

'Well, there must be others as good or better in Dublin,' said Davenant. 'Edmond's always had a strong constitution, never missed a performance – it can't be right, collapsing on stage like that.'

'I'll find out if there is anyone else,' she said. 'But Dr Wright was recommended by an acquaintance, and I don't really know who else to ask.'

Of course, that was a lie: she did know another doctor. Later as she sat at the piano with the audience hushed as she played, she thought back to the opening night, to the glimpse of William sitting alone in his box.

Back in Kildare Street that night she wrote and rewrote another letter until nearly two in the morning, removing any words that could possibly evoke their past attachment and replacing them with polite formality.

Dear Dr Doughty,

I thank you for your attention to my earlier letter. I now regret to confess that I desperately need your help with a medical problem, and hope that you will, as a physician, forgive this intrusion.

My husband developed headaches during our voyage from England last month and he has been seeing Dr Oliver Wright, who was highly recommended to us, and who continues to visit regularly and prescribe stimulants and anti-cholera pills for what he terms 'a nervous complaint'. Despite Dr Wright's optimism, Edmond recently collapsed during a performance and since then has been confined to bed.

I wonder if you would be so kind as to grant me the very great favour of a second opinion. We will be prompt in settling your invoices.

I am sorry if I embarrass you with this awkward request, but I know not on whom else I may call. I thank you in the hope that you might help me in my difficulty.

Sincerely,

Jane Verity

She slept fitfully, rising early to busy herself with Edmond's care. He was looking brighter and, when at ten o'clock she said she was popping out to Dawson Street to post a letter, he merely asked her to get him a newspaper on the way.

At the receiving house she paid for the postage automatically, yet as soon as she had stepped back out into the street, anxiety overwhelmed her so completely that she stood still and almost turned around to ask the clerk for the letter back. She should not have written to William. Then she reminded herself of how much Edmond needed help, and went on.

Chapter Sixteen

DEBTS

William looked at the address: a genteel lodging house in Kildare Street. She was so near. His instinct was to go to her. Then he halted, his finger and thumb pinching tight the paper that had come from her hands: a letter from a dutiful wife.

He reflected: a favour to an old friend – as she was – still risked a conflict of interest. What if, despite his best efforts, her husband died? It might be worse than the Catriona Wright case – he still had to complete his report about that for Mr Lydon.

In any case the cholera epidemic had become a monster that found the unfortunate in their tenements, piled them up in the hospital, then sent them to a mass grave. His workload was exhausting him; he had neither the stamina nor the skill to take on a complex case.

No: the thing to do was to raise Mr Verity's case with Dr Wright, to prompt him to undertake his own review. Unfortunately, when he went to his senior's office at the hospital it was locked up and there was no answer to his knock.

Two gentlemen were waiting in the corridor outside.

'Are you Dr Joseph Murphy?' they asked.

'No,' said William. 'Why?'

They were there on behalf of the Turf Club, they said, but would not give a reason. They would wait. As Dr Wright was absent a porter had gone to find Dr Murphy.

Joseph then appeared in haste.

'May I assist you, gentlemen?' Joseph explained that Dr Wright had gone to Bray to see patients on behalf of a colleague who was unwell.

Having confirmed that Joseph had assisted Dr Wright with his medical cover duties at the recent Curragh Races, the gentlemen asked to interview him in private. Feeling himself dismissed, William went back to the Admissions Room where he was to be in charge for the rest of the day.

Later Joseph confided in William that Wright had in truth gone to Liverpool for the Grand National, where he had a horse running. He had also to visit the gunmakers there, to replace a brace of pistols that had gone missing, so would be away until Saturday morning. Joseph had been left to carry out Wright's home visits for him.

'He's given me so many written instructions that I don't know where to begin.'

'What did the Turf Club ask?'

'If Dr Wright had ever medicated the horses.'

'Has he? I didn't know he had any veterinary experience.'

'On the racecourse, all we can give them is a bullet,' Joseph said. 'I told them I've had to do it myself if a horse has broken a leg. That's why Dr Wright keeps the pistols in the carriage – sometimes there's no farrier.'

'But why would they ask about medication?' Another strand of doubt had emerged, to tug at William's thoughts. 'Do you think they suspect race fixing?'

'They didn't say. I told them nothing was given.' Joseph frowned. 'Although, now I think of it … no …' He fell silent.

'What?' asked William, but Joseph would only shake his head.

They were in the physicians' common room – one of the housekeepers had brought them a plateful of egg and onion sandwiches and a pot of tea. Joseph was hunched in a battered armchair within reach of the plate, and ate rapidly. William probed a fragment of onion from a gap between his teeth, studying him. Joseph was getting thinner and his hours at the hospital were becoming even more erratic. He was always getting Dr Stephenson to stand in for him. Joseph was not lazy, and often worked early in the morning or late in the evening, but it was never certain when he'd be present. Dr Stephenson was often unsure why his colleague was absent: he was 'maybe sick'. Yet if asked about his health, Joseph would say, with a sardonic glance, that he was quite well, and had never felt better.

'I suppose you enjoy the Turf Club duties?' William asked him. 'Is a day at the races like a day off from the hospital?'

Joseph scowled. 'How could I enjoy it, now? In this country destroyed by famine, to see the rank, the fashion and beauty of Dublin, crowding on to the racecourses with their horses and carriages and picnic hampers?' Joseph was a handsome young man, but not when the hatred of the Anglo-Irish Ascendancy struck like knives through his face. 'In the fox-hunting season they're riding out past paupers crawling to the workhouse. The yelping of their dogs – that are fed every day upon meat – and their hunting horns, drown out the groans of the dying and the cries of their starving children.'

'Why do you even go to the races?' William took another sandwich, relishing the sharpness of the onion and the buttery fragments of the hardboiled egg.

'I need the money. I get more from Dr Wright for a few hours than I do in a fortnight here.'

'Still paying off your debt?' William studied Joseph: the long scar on his neck was nearly healed.

'You know I'm in debt – we're all in debt, for sure.'

'Are we?' William thought of his own comfortable lot – but then he'd nothing to waste his money on: no vices, no politics, no woman …

'We ought to go back to the Admissions Room,' said Joseph, draining his teacup. 'It's busy this time of the day, and Mr Carty is there by himself.'

'He'll send them all home with Carty's Mixture,' said William. 'Have another sandwich first.' He'd be off home soon to see his own patients in the relative comfort of his rooms, while Joseph would have just a few moments more rest before facing that pandemonium until midnight. Earlier the corridor outside the Admissions Room had been full of queuing patients, and the room itself busier than a Saturday market.

'Sure, but it feels – it's not right, you know – to be resting and eating, when the people down there are in such desperation.'

'They'll still be desperate when you've starved to death,' William warned him, and pushed the plate across the table.

* * *

On the Saturday morning William made his way over to Merrion Square, where black crape still swathed Dr Wright's doorknocker.

The housekeeper asked him to wait. From the opulent hallway he could overhear Dr Wright's secretary going through his list of house calls:

'Miss Danvers, on Leeson Street, has an ague –'

'Oh, Lord.'

'Mrs Mulligan a headache, the Dowager Lady Ellimore is complaining of her right knee and says it is urgent –'

'Oh – Lady Ellimore – does she not know how very busy I am? But I suppose …'

'She says she cannot walk, and to remember the codicil in her will.'

'Very well …'

'Then there's Mrs Prendergast: her daughter has developed a squint …'

William glanced at the newspaper from England that lay on the hall table: **Sporting Intelligence: Liverpool Grand National Steeplechase. Despite the coldness, the climate being almost Siberian, the attendance from all parts of the United Kingdom was immense, including many fashionables. The race meeting was particularly**

successful and, except for the untoward accidents to The Curate, and Equinox, who were killed in the steeplechase, would have passed off perfectly. The race was run at a great pace throughout – Peter Simple winning in a canter – the distance having been accomplished in a few seconds under eleven minutes. Value of the stakes £720.

William read on: the owner of Equinox was Dr Oliver Wright. It would take Wright weeks of house calls to those rich old women, of the most obsequious attendance, of prescribing a pharmacopoeia of medicines, of invoicing and repeat invoicing, to earn back the money he had invested in that horse. He might not manage it until he had benefited from the codicil in Lady Ellimore's will.

William considered his elegant surroundings – the immaculate plasterwork, the fine furniture, the gilding – 'Dr Wright's widows' expected their physician to have the trappings of rank, with rooms on the smartest square in town. But how much was owned and how much was loaned? Perhaps the whole lot: the town house, the country estate, the carriages, the racing stables, depended on debt? Wright had said himself years ago, that you couldn't succeed on the turf without a good stable of thoroughbreds, that to build that up required investment, and to attract the necessary credit required a good standing in society. As Joseph had said: *'We're all in debt, for sure.'*

Another caller arrived. The housekeeper admitted one of the porters from the hospital, who went straight in to see Dr Wright, as if familiar with the rooms. After acknowledging curtly that it was a good day and answering some enquiries about his health, Dr Wright interrupted the man and told him to get to the point.

'Sister Aloysius wants you to attend one of your outdoor patients, sir. Mr Edmond Verity, she says, is very ill.'

William's fingers closed over Jane's letter in his pocket.

'Why was I not told of this before?' Dr Wright demanded, as if he had not been the past few days at Aintree and, before receiving a reply snapped: 'I'm very busy this morning.'

'I'm very sorry, sir, but Sister Aloysius said to tell you that your treatment is not working and, though it may well be of the very best, the patient is not improving.'

William got to his feet and, as the porter continued to cajole Dr Wright, went in with Jane's letter, apologising for the intrusion. 'I was asked by Mrs Verity to provide a second opinion. I thought you should know.'

'How do you imagine that you could provide a superior opinion to my own?' Dr Wright beckoned him to hand over the letter. Grabbing it with a scornful glance, he read: '*Dear Dr Doughty.* Why would she have addressed herself to you? You're hardly pre-eminent among the doctors in the city.'

'I have no idea.' William felt himself blush as Wright darted him a keen glance. 'That is – I haven't seen her since … years ago …'

Wright turned to the porter. 'Tell Dr Murphy to see this patient and report back to me directly.' As he waited for his secretary to leave the room, he reread the letter in his hand. 'The elegant wife of an English actor – so was there some previous connection? Years ago?'

'She's merely an acquaintance.'

'*I am sorry if I embarrass you* … I suppose she means about

131

the second opinion, but even so ... something about this letter is a little unusual, if you will forgive me, Dr Doughty. *My earlier letter ... I now need your help with a medical problem* ... there's a history here.' Dr Wright lowered his spectacles to stare. 'Is this to do with your scandal in Birmingham, I wonder? There was a great deal of gossip at one time, wasn't there?'

'No. Of course it isn't –' The back of William's neck prickled under his collar. He had not realised the letter would give anything away. What did Dr Wright remember from Birmingham?

'You're a bad liar, sir.' Dr Wright replaced his spectacles. A smile developed at one corner of his mouth and spread into a grin. 'Is this her, I wonder? Your servant girl who turned up at your inquest in the workhouse to accuse your brother-in-law? Your wife died, you kept the girl on in your household, everyone knew what was going on. Astley-Scrope had to write the death certificate. You lost your position as Coroner for a pair of pretty eyes –'

'*Enough!*' William snatched the letter back. His pulses were pounding. Wright's words had reminded him how he had lain every night with his limbs wrapped around her. 'That's all in the past. She went to London to marry Mr Verity, as you can see. I've no interest any longer – if I had, why would I have brought you her letter? I haven't the time to see him: I'm so beleaguered by cholera cases that I haven't even completed the report for Mr Lydon.'

'Of course,' said Dr Wright, his smile fading. 'Of course, I understand. I understand completely. I won't mention it again.'

William took a deep breath. 'Are you going to see your patient or not?'

'It seems I'll have to. Although, I am very busy at the moment …'

'So you'll review Mr Verity's case yourself, I take it?'

Dr Wright clasped his hands over his waistcoat. His gold cufflinks chinked against his watch chain and his signet ring glinted as his hands embraced.

'You may be assured, sir, that his treatment will receive my closest attention. As soon as I have had time to consider Dr Murphy's report, I shall arrange to review him myself.'

Chapter Seventeen

THE BANSHEE ON THE ROOF

Jane heard nothing from William, and it was Dr Murphy who arrived to see Edmond that morning.

'Dr Wright is very busy and has asked me to report back to him.' He went in to see Edmond.

Their voices were a murmur in the bedroom, then Edmond grunted and coughed, perhaps moving himself in the bed.

Dr Murphy came back through into the sitting room.

'May I see his pills?' The young doctor looked gaunt and weary. Half-hidden by his beard a purple scar ran down his neck from his left ear to his shirt collar.

Jane indicated the tray. 'In the green glass bottle are the newest stimulant pills – the other pills were stopped – the pale purple anti-cholera pill he takes twice a day. The brown liquid is a chalybeate tonic.'

Dr Murphy rotated the bottles, reading their labels, which she knew were uninformative: *The Tablets, The Compound*.

'Continue as you are, then.'

'But he's been so low in spirits over the last few days, with constant headaches – he's been vomiting, will barely eat, sometimes he has ringing in the ears … painful limbs …'

Dr Murphy opened the brown tonic bottle and sniffed at it. 'I've seen Dr Wright prescribe these treatments many times before and his patients swear by them. Your husband ought to do well, Mrs Verity.'

'But do you think he's improving?'

'I'm sure he will. I wouldn't make any major changes. Dr Wright's diagnosis was nervous exhaustion, so best continue the stimulants. To speed recovery a little alkali mixture may be beneficial. I'll write a prescription – I don't dispense as Dr Wright does – take it to the pharmacy on South King Street – you will find the pharmacist very good.'

Jane asked him about his fee.

'It will be five shillings, but Dr Wright will invoice you in due course. I deputise for him and he pays me directly.' He made to leave, but frowned as he saw her face. 'Is there anything else?'

Cautiously Jane asked him if he knew of any other doctors she might approach for help. Edmond's improvement had been very slow, she explained, and she was thinking of getting a second opinion. Dr Wright had been very warmly recommended by her friends, but nonetheless …

'The English like to consult Dr Wright,' said Dr Murphy, 'because they trust their own countrymen.'

'But that can't matter. The countries are the same, aren't they?'

'Well.' Dr Murphy gave her a hard stare. 'That's a matter

135

of opinion, if I may say so. But you'll find there are some excellent Irish physicians in the city. I'd advise you, however, that it may confuse matters to have two separate physicians and two different courses of treatment going on at the same time. So, a doctor may decline a patient who's already under the care of a colleague.'

'But Edmond used to have such energy, such power in his voice. He's hollowed out. You're used to looking at invalids all day. I am not.' Jane hesitated. This young man worked for Dr Wright, and perhaps could say nothing against him. But her anxieties nagged: the unknown treatments, the unclear diagnosis, encouraging Edmond to gamble. 'What's your honest opinion of Dr Wright?'

'I have nothing to say against him,' said Dr Murphy. 'An eminent physician, popular with his patients.'

'And when you have deputised for him, have you found all his treatments to be appropriate?'

'He's my senior, with far more experience than myself, so I'm in no position to criticise.'

'And what of his racing tips? Do you think those appropriate?'

For a moment Dr Murphy was at a loss for an answer. 'I don't know about that – I think his patients do very well … a little amusement to keep the mind occupied is no bad thing, I suppose.'

'Edmond is not doing well.' Weariness dulled her mind; she was running out of argument and close to tears. 'Sometimes I'm afraid that he's going to die.'

Dr Murphy told her she could do no more than continue with what was prescribed, and that he must be going as he had other patients to see.

136

Jane followed him to the door. 'There must be someone else I can ask. A second opinion? Can you recommend anyone? Just to set my mind at rest?'

Dr Murphy shook his head.

'I've already advised against it. Remember that every physician in the city is fully occupied with the present epidemic, working night and day, seven days a week, some even going out into the provinces to assist single-handed colleagues. But I will make Dr Wright aware of your concerns and ask him to visit.'

* * *

Soon afterward the tailor called with the same invoice for the frock coat for which she had already given Edmond six sovereigns.

'The coat was delivered on the 19th of February, and it's the 12th of March today.'

'I'm so sorry – my husband was taken ill. He's still in bed, so I suppose he hasn't been able to go to pay you. I'll just fetch it.'

Jane left the tailor waiting on the landing and went to ask Edmond for the money.

'I don't have anything,' he said. 'You wouldn't give me it. You said you were settling the bills yourself.'

'That's untrue!'

But Edmond was obdurate. Furious, Jane searched his pockets and found nothing: not even betting slips. In his pocketbook a letter from his bankers in London informed him that he was overdrawn to the sum of eighty pounds, twelve shillings and sixpence.

With some effort, she persuaded the tailor that Edmond was indisposed but the invoice would be paid the following week. As he went away grumbling, she knew that she would have to encash her last twenty pounds. She asked Edmond again about the coat money when she took him in his pills, but he was vague.

Despite his protests she showed him his pocketbook. 'I need to know where our money is going, Edmond. What happened to the letter of credit? To the hundred pounds? Why are you so heavily overdrawn in London?'

'Don't worry about it, Jane. All will be well.'

'What do you mean?' Could he still be gambling when he was too ill to leave his bed?

Edmond merely tapped the side of his nose, a half-suppressed smile sharpening his mouth, and repeated that all was well.

'But even the six pounds, Edmond – I did give it you for your coat! Where has it gone?'

Edmond did not meet her eyes, so she sat down on the edge of the bed and got into his line of sight.

'Be honest with me – have you lost it on the horses?'

'Don't be tedious, darling,' said Edmond. 'Nothing has been lost. Wait and see, Jane, even though I'm not working you'll soon have earnings greater than you ever dreamt of. Nothing ventured, nothing gained, eh?'

As she opened her mouth to protest, he clenched his teeth and doubled up in the bed. Her first fear was that it was another seizure, and she felt a wave of anxiety; but he was still conscious – it was a spasm of pain. Panting, he said he would be better in a moment, it was passing, then sank back on the pillows with his eyes closed.

She could not question him any further in case it worsened his condition. Once she was sure that he had settled she went downstairs to the dining room hoping that Madeleine would still be at breakfast, but only Mrs O'Reilly was there. Jane felt compelled to join her, dealing with her enquiries about Edmond, until she heard the morning's post arrive and found that at last there was a letter.

Still standing in the hallway, she broke the seal at once, but as soon as she unfolded it she knew the answer just from the shape of William's handwriting. Years ago, it had seemed as if his mind had been so leaping with hopes and imaginings that he paid no attention to his untidy writing. But this letter was as good as a fair copy to be read out in court. Her heart that had pulsed with hope now contracted with regret.

He begged her forgiveness for not replying sooner, as he had been occupied with the cholera epidemic, which was raging in the slums around the Meath. He added that according to professional etiquette he could not treat a personal acquaintance, or a member of their family. Moreover, Dr Wright was his superior at the Meath Hospital, being a senior physician, whilst he himself was only a clinical assistant. He had however requested Dr Wright to review Edmond's progress in person.

She read his final sentence over and over: '*I also hope to take up a post in New York at the Bellevue Hospital, pursuing my earlier interest in pathology, and expect to be emigrating to America this September to make a fresh start in life, so find that this venture presently occupies my time.*'

She returned to the dining room and sat down again in her place.

'Bad news?' Mrs O'Reilly glanced at the folded letter.

Jane shook her head. 'Someone I know is planning to emigrate.'

'Well, I'm sorry to tell you this but a man down the road heard the cry of the banshee last evening. He said she was sitting on my roof.'

'The *Banshee*?' Jane was bemused. 'That was the boat that brought us from London.'

Mrs O'Reilly's eyes were suddenly intense in her wrinkled face. 'The banshee is an old woman with a witch's nose, and her cry is such as you never heard, at first you think it the scream of an animal, but it's unearthly, from the other side. She warns of death, and if she throws her silver comb and strikes you, then the death is your own.'

'What an odd thing to name a boat for.' Jane felt her skin prickle. 'I suppose ship owners don't believe in such.'

'If Patrick Kinsella saw the banshee on the roof, then he was likely out of his head from the drink. But a great number of us are still afraid of her.'

Making an excuse, Jane left her breakfast unfinished. She did not want to listen to the old woman's superstitious fancies. She went upstairs without Edmond's cup of tea – he was still asleep, in any case. As she looked at his inert shape, and the beads of sweat that gathered amongst his stubble, the myth of the banshee took shape in her mind. William's refusal, though reasonable and predictable, had filled her with despair. She heard a new keening from the seagulls overhead and looked through the window at the houses across the road, imagining a dark shape by the chimney stacks, running a silver comb through long grey hair.

* * *

Sister Aloysius arrived in the afternoon bringing the twin protections of sanctity and common sense. Jane said nothing to her about the banshee – it seemed foolish now – but repeated her concerns about Edmond, and anxiety to get an opinion from another doctor.

Sister Aloysius reassured her: where she worked at the Meath Hospital, Dr Wright was held in the highest of regard, and the Meath was one of the greatest centres of medical learning in Europe. Now if Jane would assist her …

They washed and shaved Edmond and helped him into an armchair where he sat reading the newspaper while they changed the bedlinen.

'You're getting handy enough in the sick-room,' the nun said.

'I'm gaining a little experience.'

'You have more than that. Do you never sense a calling?'

'I already have a vocation as a pianist, to which I find I am well suited.'

'But you might still make yourself useful at the hospital – we're always short-handed. If you ever want the work just report to the Matron's office between nine and ten of a morning.'

Jane was taken aback, but thanked her for her appreciation.

'You may find a mission,' said the nun, her eyes bright beneath her white veil, 'that has more meaning than playing the piano.'

'*Jane!*' Edmond called out. '*I've won!*' He read from the

newspaper, which trembled in his hands. '*Sporting Intelligence – Curragh Races. Lucius, the favourite at five to two, came fourth, and Kilfane was the winner at twenty-five to one!*'

He was more animated than she had seen him in the last fortnight, his face alight with glee.

'You can't have placed a bet,' Jane protested. 'Edmond, you've been ill.'

He ignored her, his face falling as he read on: 'We hear that Kilfane collapsed after the race and, though entered for the Naas races … may be … withdrawn.'

His eyes had grown blank and his speech indistinct. At the next moment he tensed as if he had been struck by lightning. His body straightened in a spasm and, as he jerked his head back, the top of his skull rammed the armchair into the wall.

'*Edmond!*' Jane gasped, trying to calm her rising panic.

His reply was a shrill, animal whine, as he bared his clenched teeth. His eyes were crescents of white between his quivering eyelids, while his breath seemed to have caught in his throat and his face turned purple, then black.

Was this the moment of death? Even Sister Aloysius seemed afraid, uncertain what to do, or how to help him. Was it too late? Then his stiff posture collapsed. He slithered from the chair to the floor as his limbs jerked and his eyes stared blindly. He gurgled and gasped. Bloodstained saliva ran down his chin.

Jane blundered out into the corridor and screamed for help. As she got back to him the limb jerks were slowing down. A smell rose up as if he had soiled himself, but his face, wiped clean by Sister Aloysius, was a better colour. She realised with relief that he was after all alive.

As Mrs O'Reilly rushed in, he seemed for a moment to relax and open his eyes, then fell into a snoring stupor which was interrupted from time to time by startles and jerks.

'Jesus, Mary and Joseph!' Their landlady stood horror-struck, her hands to her mouth as if to stop all her fears from tumbling out. 'He's dying! I knew this would happen. The cholera!'

Jane regretted calling out for help, but then Madeleine came in and although her eyes widened remained calm.

'I thought I'd lost him.' Jane burst into tears.

Madeleine hugged her, waiting for her sobs to subside. Then she told Mrs O'Reilly, who was crossing herself and murmuring about the banshee, that Edmond was not dying and to calm down and fetch fresh linen.

Indeed, Edmond opened his eyes, and as they helped him up and across to the bed was groggily able to say that he was all right.

'Shall I ask Tom to fetch Dr Wright?' Madeleine bent down to hear his reply.

Edmond said nothing but lifted and let fall his hand before closing his eyes again.

'Dr Murphy was going to ask him to visit in any case.' Jane doubted what Dr Wright could do. Weeks of treatments, of pills and tonics, and now this.

Edmond's limbs jerked and he let out a gasp.

Jane's skin prickled with anxiety. 'What if it happens again, what will I do?' she said, but neither Madeleine nor Sister Aloysius could give her an answer.

One person could.

William had refused her in writing but surely he would not refuse her face to face?

Chapter Eighteen

THE PATRICK'S DAY BALL

My dear Jane,

I'm so sorry to hear that your Edmond has been unwell but I'm sure that Dr Wright will soon have him better again. Mama is quite definite that there is no better physician in Dublin.

Yesterday I attended the St Patrick's Day Ball at Dublin Castle. The green dress with the tulle was a success and I danced with Alex Royce more than was proper – he really is a graceful dancer, and so handsome in his uniform. I understand your point about the army, but surely everyone must have a career nowadays – it is not the modern way to be one of the 'idle rich'. I don't find Alex to be political – he says that the cavalry suits him because of his horsemanship.

Do write soon, Jane, or call – I haven't heard from you for a while and it would be delightful to continue our friendship.

With my kindest regards,

Anna

Chapter Nineteen

BERNARD MORRISSEY

Late in the evening, well after surgery hours were over and William had seen his last patient, his manservant Mr Nugent entered the study and closed the door.

'A couple of fellows' – he did not say gentlemen – 'demand to see you, doctor.' He flicked his eyes over his shoulder, meaning that William must come and look. 'They would not say what it was about. A big fellow in a red coat, rough-looking, a weaselly companion.'

'What do they want?' William felt a current of fear pass through him.

'Would you like me to fetch the police?'

Quietly crossing the room, William opened the door a crack and peered out over Mr Nugent's shoulder. 'Best not.' Those men had been at Lydon's office. It might be better for the police not to know the reason for their visit. 'I'll see them, Mr Nugent,' he said, as he stepped out into the hall.

Only the big fellow in the red velvet coat remained

standing, while his companion, as if obeying a silent instruction, sat down to wait on the bench.

'Bernard Morrissey, loss adjuster.' He doffed his hat. 'Dr William Doughty?'

'You can come in.' William led the way, trying to master his rising tension as he felt his body grow hot and sweaty.

'How are yeh, sir?'

Even the banal greeting, to William's nervous ears, sounded like a threat.

Mr Morrissey merely held his hat in his hands, yet there was menace in the way he bore himself, in the bulk of his arms and shoulders, the way he strode into the room, his boots almost stamping on the floorboards, and the way that he scraped a chair into place without being asked, then made it groan under his weight. He dumped his hat on William's desk.

'Sit down, sir,' he commanded.

A strong smell of stale tobacco smoke rose from the hat, making William feel nauseous as he obeyed. He realised that his hands were trembling.

'Mr Lydon tells me that yeh promised him a report, about Mrs Catriona Wright. He is yet to see it.' Mr Morrissey, who wore no gloves, planted a meaty fist on either side of his hat. ''Tis a week overdue.'

'I'm sorry. I've been too busy.' William looked across the desk at the dark stains on the man's red velvet coat and a heavy signet ring on a hairy finger. 'The cholera epidemic, my patients ...' He was afraid to meet Mr Morrissey's eyes but noticed that two gold teeth glinted amongst his incisors.

'So, my job as a loss adjuster,' said Mr Morrissey, 'is to make certain that the claims on the underwriter are not going to be an excessive sum. All the more in a case where the details of the claim are in question. Have yeh begun yer report, sir?'

William hesitated. He had a draft full of corrections and crossings out that tried to strike a delicate balance between Dr Wright's notes and telling the truth. Looking again at Mr Morrissey's bare hands he decided that he would have to rebalance the report for his own protection.

'Mr Lydon also requires a sight of yer casebook.'

'No.' William had found there was no space to insert Dr Wright's sentences into his casebook, so that he would have to rewrite the entire ledger dating back at least three months. 'That is, I think it's at the hospital.'

'I've a carriage waiting.'

Outside, on the box of a carriage, silhouetted in the glow of the gas lamps across the street, sat the third man. He had evidently positioned himself to see in and, noticing William watching him, raised his cap mockingly.

William looked away at once, but now had to face Mr Morrissey. He shrank down a little in his chair.

'We can be at the hospital in five minutes,' said Mr Morrissey.

'It's not convenient.' William longed to bury his head in his hands, so that he could rub his eyelids as he would do when tired.

'Let's be honest,' said Mr Morrissey. 'Dr Wright poisoned Mrs Wright, did he not?'

William's breath stilled in his throat.

''Tis clear enough, don't yeh think? The debts – the first year paid on the policy – the means easily to hand – an epidemic of cholera to hide in ...'

'I don't believe you,' William protested, even though that same fear had been stabbing at him like a lancet for days. 'You can't prove it.'

'But we know it, don't we, Dr Doughty? Or – what's yer diagnosis?'

'She almost certainly died of cholera.' Yet he was tormented by the opposite certainty: that Mr Morrissey was right.

'We could dig her up, so, find the poison. Then yeh could be strung up alongside her husband, maybe?' Mr Morrissey yanked up an invisible noose, then dropped his head down and sideways as he stuck a big tongue out between his jaws.

William fought down his horror, and the urge to panic at the thought they might report him to the law. But – no – he was certain now who these three men were.

'You won't dig her up, though, will you?' he snapped. Even though he could feel himself shaking, he did not care any more if he came to harm. 'I've seen you before, Mr Morrissey. You're no better yourself. I saw you cut James Boylan's throat in the street. You attacked one of my colleagues, didn't you – a young doctor, Joseph Murphy? And was it you that gave strychnine to Mr Tynan, before you attempted to help yourself to his pocketbook? You're hardly in a position to go to the police.'

Mr Morrissey's reply was not the aggressive outburst that William feared, but a broad grin that displayed his patchwork dentition.

'Yeh've seen how we work, now – we dole out our own justice. In any case, Dr Doughty, yeh're no good to us in the hands of the law. Alive though, alive, alive-o, yeh might be a source of income. The underwriter's always looking to avail himself of income.'

'Who do you mean – the underwriter? Do you mean Mr Lydon?'

'Lydon?' Mr Morrissey laughed so contemptuously that his fists came off the table and he cradled his own belly. 'Best for you not to know. Otherwise …' He stopped laughing. His forefinger came up to his own left ear and slashed down across the stubble of his throat, harvesting the course of the left carotid artery, internal jugular vein, and continuing just below the larynx before stopping above the right clavicle. 'So, it'll be twenty guineas a month, Dr Doughty.'

'Twenty guineas! That's outrageous.' William stood upright, thrusting back his chair and leaning forward across his desk. Anger pulsed through him, tightening his jaw and forming an aching mass in his chest.

'A discount – just twenty sovereigns then, as a favour.' Mr Morrissey sniggered. 'Think of it as a fire-insurance premium.'

'That's outright extortion! I'm not paying it, whatever the consequences. *Get out!*' He pointed a trembling finger at the door.

'Yeh'll only have to see a few more private patients.' Mr Morrissey was clearly not budging.

William sat down again, desperately trying to imagine a way out.

'Get them to pay their bills on time. Inherit some legacies from old women, the way that other doctors do.'

William thought before replying: next month was April. By September he might be leaving for New York. Six months at the most – a hundred and twenty pounds.

'I think if yeh can find the payments, Dr Doughty, that the underwriter will no longer require your report. ' Mr Morrissey grinned. 'Very likely we can settle Dr Wright's claim without it.'

It was a large sum, but manageable. As the man had said, there were ways to earn it.

'Very well,' he sighed. It was, after all, only money. What was more troubling was that something that he had tried to prevent himself from even suspecting had been stated by Mr Morrissey as a bald fact.

Chapter Twenty

THE HAPPIEST GIRL IN DUBLIN

Friday 29th March

My dear Jane

It is decided! I must be the happiest girl in Dublin. We are to be married on the 28th of August in the Chapel Royal at Dublin Castle. Five months seems an age to wait but my father says a state visit to Ireland is planned by Queen Victoria and Prince Albert in early August, so it is best to wait until that is all over.

My mother is organising the wedding breakfast in Dublin, at the Shelburne Hotel, but Alex's father insists that afterwards we all travel down to his Mount Belvedere estate, at Ballyhamon near Mitchelstown, for a house party and a steeplechase meeting. Extra servants are to be taken on and the house is to be refurbished so that Alex and I will be able to live there in comfort. Alex intends to breed horses there. It's a long road journey, but one can travel by train to Kilmallock, and be met by the estate carriages.

I should be delighted if you and Edmond were able to join us for either or both events as guests.

I saw Francesca in secret and was able to present the ballad 'Liberty' with its music to her. She was delighted with it. She may claim to have given up nationalist writing, but I think her sympathies remain strong in that direction.

With sincere affection,

Anna

Chapter Twenty-one

DOCTOR'S ORDERS

Jane could not compose a reply to Anna, who had not troubled to ask about Edmond. When Sister Aloysius arrived in the late afternoon she went out, dressed for the evening's performance under her sable wrap, telling her she had some purchases to make before the theatre. The nurse's support for Dr Wright was so wholehearted that Jane would not tell her she was seeking a second opinion.

William lived in a handsome house on Harcourt Street, where, according to his brass plate, surgery hours were between four and six. Her heart misgave her as she climbed the steps from the street, knowing they would soon be face to face.

His manservant opened the door and, when Jane explained her business, asked her to wait on a bench in the hallway. Four patients were waiting and one of them, in between coughs, nodded a greeting, to which Jane felt too awkward to reply. She should not be here.

Across the passage from her was a door from behind which came voices and a hacking cough; William was evidently busy with a patient. After a while they emerged: a gouty gentleman who heaved himself along with his walking stick was followed by William. He stopped short as he saw her.

She stood up, but without greeting her he said that he was extremely busy. He indicated the other patients.

'I'll only take a moment – please let me speak to you in person.' She scanned his face for some feeling, for some kindness, but found none.

He sighed. 'Go in,' he said, muttering an apology to the four waiting as a fifth was being admitted by the servant.

She stood before his desk. He had changed. His mouth was set about with lines of unhappiness, the furrow between his brows was permanent, his wavy black hair fading to grey.

He held his hand out as if to shake hers but as she hesitated he turned it into a gesture, indicating the chair beside her. 'Do sit down.' Behind him the gilt-lettered spines of his library gleamed in mahogany bookcases.

The room was very warm; a fire spat in the grate. She loosened her sable wrap and sat, hiding her face below the brim of her bonnet, fussing with her black silk skirts. There was a leather couch in one corner, beside a table with instruments laid out. She studied the pattern on the Turkish rug and heard the floorboards creak as he strode to the window.

She glanced up. He stood with folded arms looking out at the street, profiled by the light. She cleared her throat and swallowed, thinking she should not have come here. 'How are you, William?'

'How the devil d'you think I am?' He leaned his shoulder

against the white shutter that was folded back in the window reveal, half turning towards her, crossing one ankle over the other. 'Changed. As, I suppose, are you.'

She always pictured him in coroner's black, but a brown coat hung over the back of his chair, and he sported a green silk waistcoat and tie. What if someone else had changed him? She could not keep back the very question that she had already determined she would not ask.

'Are you married?'

'No. There we have the difference. I tried, but ...' He stared at her, his jaw hard.

'I'm sorry,' she said. 'I –'

'Sorry for what? Your marriage?' He came back to the desk and sat down heavily, scraping his chair across the floorboards.

'No – yes – that is – I'm sorry for disturbing you.'

On the desk was the old pewter inkstand from the house in Newhall Street. His familiar things: the blotter, the letter-opener, rested on the worn leather inlay. Unwilling to look up, she saw them all in minute detail – the mirror image of the handwriting on the white blotting paper, the jacquard pattern on the waistcoat – while his shirt collar and his gloomy face above it were blurred. After all the years, all that distance, it was enough to make one weep for the past.

'You're going to America.'

'Yes. But in any case ... you're here ...' He was looking at his hands on the desk as he waited for her to recollect her errand.

His quietude made her calm herself. The past had to remain in the past.

'It's about Edmond. He has a nervous complaint. Last night he had convulsions. I thought he was dying.'

'You saw my reply to your letter?' He looked her over then looked away: as if he held her, then let her go. 'I can't involve myself in his case. And you can see how busy I am. Please don't –'

'Yes, but …'

She described the failure of all Dr Wright's treatments: the stimulant pills, the chalybeate tonic, and when William asked if Dr Wright had seen Edmond recently, she said not.

'I did ask him to review your husband's case when I received your letter.' William grimaced.

'He hasn't visited. Dr Murphy came on his behalf.'

'It's unethical to criticise another doctor. And he is, as I told you, my superior.'

'But?' She recognised his face of unease.

'You surely must remember him from Birmingham? He was the physician to the workhouse. You were in the infirmary whilst you were an inmate there.'

'I never saw Dr Wright,' she said. 'He never came to the infirmary.'

William cocked an eyebrow, pressing his lips together, indicating that she must draw her own conclusion.

But she continued: 'He seems so popular here – everyone speaks highly of him and how he gladly visits even the poorest patients. Yet …'

'He is indeed very successful.' He hesitated, as if considering what to say. 'Even I contrived to make a new start here. They call it the 'City of Doctors'. Best clinical teaching in Europe – our expertise and knowledge is unrivalled –'

'So, surely you could at least suggest another physician? For a second opinion? Even if you can't treat him yourself?'

'Well.' He vented a breath. Still considering her, he took his pen from the inkstand. 'I'll write a referral to Dr Samuel Grattan. I suppose it makes no difference to me now.'

He took a sheet of paper and focused on it, his hand moving rapidly across it, the veins and sinews more prominent than in the past. She knew a place at the base of his thumb where she had felt the warm pulse. What if she reached out to touch –

'Headache, collapse, biliousness? Weight loss? No flux … any cough?' He questioned her in detail: the time course of the illness, the sequence of symptoms and treatment, the seizure, so that she racked her brains to provide the answers.

She asked if it could be cholera, but he said not, and that he thought Dr Wright's diagnosis likely to be correct. At length he blotted the letter, sealed and addressed it before standing up and handing it to her.

'I am grateful to you,' she said. 'And … for all your letters.' As she reached out for the letter her sable wrap slipped, revealing a bare shoulder and the black garnet necklace. Remembering that she was dressed for her evening performance, she drew it close again.

The colour had darkened in his face. She knew that he was still in pain, and felt that pain in her own body, as if connected by a wire. But what if now, she went to him, to rest her hands on his chest, to caress and console him? No, it was too late. The time for that was years ago.

His patients were grumbling in the hall. He raised his eyebrows, as if to say: was there anything else?

'I ought to go, I'm sorry.' How could she bear to face what she had done? She put the letter in her pocket and stood to leave. William showed her out politely, without even offering a handshake. As they passed the waiting patients a memory intruded again: their parting on the station platform.

'Do call again.' The tone of his voice indicated that it would be unwelcome.

She told the jarvey to go via Dr Grattan's rooms. As he turned the jaunting car around Jane looked back at the house. She had half expected William to seek to resume their affair, as if, no matter how far she wandered, her paths would wind back to his constant point. But now the eyes that had hotly adored her, and the lips that had whispered that she was the most beautiful girl in the world, had turned to ice. He had grown old in bitterness; while as for her, grief, anxiety, and the constant weariness of her life were propelling her into middle age. Her girlhood was gone.

At Dr Grattan's the housekeeper displayed a face of distress. The gentleman himself had that very day fallen ill, of the fever, so could not help her. Jane asked if there was another physician she could call upon, but the housekeeper shook her head.

'There's no doctor available to assist with the patients,' she said. 'Dr Grattan has even been obliged to treat himself.'

It was hopeless. Jane went on to the theatre, feeling she was in a trap. One evening followed another at the same piano, playing the same music, over and over again, and for what? A gambler, a string of garnets and a sable wrap?

* * *

Early the next morning there was a rap at the door. Jane, having given up their bed to Edmond's painful, restless limbs, had slept on the sofa. She put Edmond's greatcoat aside and rose, pulling on her wrapper.

'*Jane!*' It was Madeleine Nisbett. '*Jane!*'

Madeleine was bleary-eyed, with tangled hair and her dress unevenly fastened. 'Tom's fallen ill.'

'Really? But he seemed perfectly well yesterday evening.' He had played the role of the Caliph with his usual energy and, afterwards, accompanying Jane and Madeleine back to the lodgings, had been in good form, hinting at a successful wager on the horses.

Madeleine said Tom had been stricken in the night with diarrhoea and vomiting, could keep nothing down, and was barely awake.

'Is it cholera?' Jane wondered if, with another of the company sick, perhaps Mrs O'Reilly was right. The epidemic had found them after all.

'It can't be,' said Madeleine. A muffled groan came from their room, and she glanced back in alarm. 'He started the anti-cholera pills a couple of days ago.'

'Go and help him. I'll dress and go for Dr Wright. He'll have to come – he's due to see Edmond as well.'

Jane hurried through the awakening streets. Housemaids queued with their jugs beside a green cart of milk churns, the horse standing still and quiet. The beggars were in their usual place – doubtless had been there all night – she looked for the girl with the heart-shaped face and saw her nestling under her mother's arm. Jane paused and stooping down, gave her a halfpenny.

'Thank the lady, Orla,' said the mother.

'Thank you, missis,' said Orla, her eyes huge in her wan face.

Jane hurried on, wondering if she and Nathan might have become like them, had their lives taken a different path.

In Merrion Square the house that bore Dr Wright's brass nameplate was the largest house in its terrace, double-fronted, and with a palatial entrance hall where his elderly housekeeper told her to wait. In the morning sun the crystal prisms of chandeliers exploded rainbows across the walls. Jane overheard the rising growl of voices, until three rough-looking men came out of the front room. The first one, a squat fellow in black, had his hands in his pockets. The middle one, towering above his companions in a huge frock coat of blood-red velvet, paused and glared at her fiercely.

'What d'ye be lookin' at, missis?' He held her widening eyes with his own: bright blue, cruel and cold.

'Come on, yerself,' said the first man, over his shoulder, and the big man dropped his stare and followed him out into the street.

The third man, with a peaked cap above his pointed nose, whistled as he went out. The front door banged to behind them, then there was silence.

Dr Wright must have been alone then, in his consulting room. Jane went straight in to him. Her apology met with no response. He sat motionless at his desk, staring through her as though she were transparent. She was there to ask him for help but found herself asking him instead if he was well.

He still did not reply but, removing his spectacles, took a handkerchief out and wiped his face. He replaced his spectacles, thought better of it, and wiped those as well.

'Dr Wright?'

'What?' He had not even recognised her.

She explained that she was Edmond Verity's wife and told him about Tom having been taken ill.

'Yes, yes, of course,' he said. 'I'll come along with you now. I'll review your husband as well.' He jumped up from his chair and took up his black leather bag.

Jane started to tell him about Edmond's seizure but he went at such a pace that she nearly had to run to keep up, all the way to their lodgings in Kildare Street.

As Jane led Dr Wright upstairs, Mrs O'Reilly emerged from her rooms to intercept him. 'Is it the cholera? I heard a whole family died of it, in the next street. The McGraths – a mother, a father, four children – God have mercy upon them.'

He fended her off. 'I could at least see the man first. Where is he?'

'He can't stay in the house if it's the cholera. For God's sake take him to the hospital and I'll lime-wash the room. I have nine lodgers here, with a servant, so if every one of us be sick, what will I do then?'

'Let me be about my business, madam, please. I'm a busy man.' He pushed past her and went along the landing as she shadowed him.

'I've kept the house well aired, so I have, and gave them no sour fruits nor uncooked vegetables. Yet these people – all these theatre folk – bring the disease in with them.'

Dr Wright went in to see Tom without replying.

Mrs O'Reilly lingered as the door was shut in her face. Had Jane not been there she would doubtless have pressed her ear to it.

'You actors, bringing in the contagion, the late hours you keep, the drunkenness. Rowdy. Your Mr Davenant assured me that you were respectable people. Well, I never saw the like.'

'But our performances are in the evenings. We don't finish until ten o'clock. So, we eat afterwards in a restaurant, or a public house. Indeed, at Mr O'Flaherty's by the theatre he keeps a stew hot for us. What's the harm in that?'

Mrs O'Reilly humphed with folded arms, clearly not budging until she heard the diagnosis.

When he emerged, Dr Wright was calm. 'It is not cholera,' he said. 'Mr Nisbett has a mild gastric attack. There is no fever, and no need for him to go to the Fever Hospital. Instead, I have given him some pills which will ease any pain and relieve tension, and he is to rest for two days and two nights.'

He said he would see Edmond by himself, yet Mrs O'Reilly followed him along the corridor as he rebuffed her anxieties with instructions about Tom's diet: he was to have beef-tea, or wine, but no solid food. Then he went in to see Edmond, firmly shutting her out.

Jane looked in on Tom and Madeleine. The stench in the room was overpowering even though the windows were wide open. Tom lay contorted in the bed and cried out.

'Oh, Tom!' Madeleine wiped his face with a cloth. 'I don't know how to help you.' He did not respond to her.

Jane feared Mrs O'Reilly might be right about the cholera. Was she also right about the Fever Hospital?

'I'll have to speak to Davenant.' Madeleine was trembling. 'Someone will have to play Tom's part.'

It was a Saturday, so they had a matinee and an evening performance. There was no understudy available as Harry Barker was playing Edmond's role.

'Perhaps Matthew Charlton can do it,' Jane suggested. 'They're never on together. He'll just have to get changed for Act Two.'

A spasm tightened Tom's limbs and he gave out a long groan, clenching his teeth together. Did he have the blue cramps of which Sister Aloysius had spoken? But then he relaxed: perhaps a drug was taking effect.

'What did Dr Wright give him?' Jane asked.

'I wouldn't know one medicine from another,' said Madeleine. 'The pills were costly enough so perhaps they may help him.'

'How could Tom become so unwell so quickly?'

'He was on top of the world last night. He'd won on the Curragh Races – he said the winnings were to be staked today at Naas, and he'd get a fortune for the sake of a few pounds.' Madeleine had tears in her eyes.

Jane's instinct was to embrace her, but she remembered that she might expose herself to contagion.

'I didn't know Tom gambled.'

'Not usually, but he said he'd had some cast-iron information.'

163

'Dr Wright and his racing tips?'

'He didn't say any more, just …' Madeleine tapped the side of her nose.

Jane thought back. It was the gesture that Wright had used at the ball, as if pointing out an important secret … that Edmond had used when trying to persuade her …

'Edmond said something about Naas, and a horse, Kilfane – Dr Wright's horse – but I can't remember – he's been so unwell.'

'Edmond had a problem with gambling, didn't he? There were rumours.' Madeleine had never known the full extent of it.

'He overcame it, but now – he's so secretive that I don't even know how he does it. I'd watch Tom if I were you.'

'He can't even get up, Jane, look at him.' Madeleine folded her arms tight around herself and her face crumpled with distress. Tom was comatose.

'I'm sorry, Madeleine, I have to get back to Edmond and see what Dr Wright said.' Jane hurried along the corridor to their rooms, but Dr Wright had already left. A new green glass bottle labelled *'Take one, three times a day,'* was on Edmond's bedside table and he seemed in good spirits.

She told him that Tom was ill.

'Two of us unable to work!' was his comment. 'Well, by the time we get better we'll both be rich at any rate.'

She waited until her urge to rebuke him had died down, then said: 'I thought there had been a problem with Kilfane running at Naas.'

He shot her a sly glance. 'How did you know about that?'

'You told me yourself – you read it out from the

newspaper – it was just before you had your seizure. Perhaps you've forgotten.'

'Seizure?' He looked genuinely puzzled.

'Don't worry, Edmond.' She saw in his face that his obsessions preoccupied him and waited to see what more he would say.

'Well, it's lucky the newspapers printed that Kilfane collapsed after the Curragh Races. I'm hoping for fifteen or twenty to one at Naas. I won three hundred and seventy-five on the Curragh, so depending on the odds it could net me thousands.' He chuckled. 'Without even moving from my bed!'

'But how will Kilfane even be able to race?'

Edmond pointed at the new bottle of pills. 'Doctor's orders.' He tapped the side of his nose, then lapsed into silence.

Jane sat with Edmond until Sister Aloysius freed her to go to the theatre. But she learnt nothing more. He read through *The Emperor of Persia* even though it seemed unlikely he would ever play the part.

* * *

At both of that day's performances the audience was much diminished. Rumours were mounting about cholera and at Davenant's announcement of the substitutions due to illness there was a murmur of unease. The understudies performed well, Matthew Charlton playing the Caliph and his wife taking Madeleine's place, yet some of the audience did not return after the interval.

At the piano, Jane was aware that every small ache in her body, every rumble in her stomach might be the onset of illness. What if she died? What was the sum of her life, and had she found her calling? Every note she played was intangible, briefly occupying the air, fading away … Was it truly worthwhile? After the finale came the applause – but after that came silence, then the turning away of attention as the theatre emptied.

At O'Flaherty's pub Mr Davenant bought them ale and she swallowed down her stew with it. She had to get back so that Sister Aloysius could leave.

'Bookings are right down at the moment,' Davenant said. 'Disappointing. People are afraid of contagion. I hope we can keep going until Tom and Edmond are well again.'

'I know.' Jane could say nothing to cheer him up. They lapsed into silence, each contemplating in their own way the loss of their livelihood.

They shared a jaunting car on the way back to the lodgings. The city was sinister in the freezing darkness, as though harbingers of death haunted the night.

Jane told Davenant how she had failed to find Edmond an alternative physician. 'They're overburdened with the epidemic.' She steadied herself as the jaunting car lurched around a collapse of rubble that half blocked the road. 'The physicians are themselves falling ill. I wish we'd never come here.'

'We've survived worse,' said Davenant, attempting a cheerful tone.

'But Edmond has started to gamble again,' she said.

He shook his head and fell silent.

They arrived back at Kildare Street to a scene of chaos.

Mrs O'Reilly was piling luggage in the street, the skivvy helping her, while Sister Aloysius tried to calm them both. Madeleine Nesbitt sat on a trunk, with her face raised to the sky, crying with an unearthly wail that darkened the soul.

Davenant swore. 'What in the world has happened now?' Leaving Jane to pay the driver, he jumped down to argue with their landlady.

Jane went to Madeleine and put a hand on her shoulder. It was stiff with grief.

'*Tom's dead!*' Madeleine wailed.

Jane crouched down and held her as she sobbed.

'I'm so sorry.' What else could she say? In the space of a day Tom had passed from a celebrated life into darkness. 'He was a brilliant actor, Madeleine. But to you … a husband … your love …'

As she hugged Madeleine, she could hear Mrs O'Reilly shouting: 'I'll not have actors bringing in contagion. Whatever Dr Wright said, it's the cholera. I'm certain of it.' Davenant was trying to reason with her as she blocked him from entering the house.

'What's become of Edmond, and our belongings?' Jane went over to them. 'I must go up and see my husband.'

'You'll go up to him all right, and then bring him out with you!' Mrs O'Reilly was trembling with agitation. 'I'm not giving my life away. I've a respectable lodging house – clean and healthy. I won't have diseased people traipsing in and out.'

In the end Davenant, producing a handful of sovereigns, persuaded Mrs O'Reilly to calm down. All their belongings were returned to their rooms, but she insisted that they would all have to leave in the morning: the only place for Edmond was a hospital. 'I'll not have contagion in my house.'

Jane finally went up to Edmond.

'What's all the racket?' He lay listless in the bed. 'Why did they move our bags?'

'We have to move out,' Jane said. 'Sister Aloysius told me to take you to the Meath Hospital.'

Edmond turned his head sideways on his pillow and shut his eyes with a groan.

Chapter Twenty-two

THE MEATH HOSPITAL

'Please, Edmond,' Jane said, 'you must walk.' She handed the jarvey a sixpence, double his fare, yet he was too afraid of contagion to get down to help them, sitting with his collar turned up and his scarf over his mouth. So she reached up to Edmond who stumbled down from the cab into her arms, almost toppling her over. As she held him upright her hands sank into his coat as if there was nothing left but bone. The driver slapped the reins along the horse's back and drove off.

Even on a Sunday morning the queue of sick people, coughing and groaning, stretched from the hospital doors back down the steps and for twenty yards or so back to the stone gateposts. Some stood, helped by friends or relatives, but most sat or lay on the ground. It was a dry, grey day and a biting March wind blew through the hospital courtyard.

They might be waiting for hours, amongst the indigent, the starved, and the filthy, but Edmond did not seem to notice. His eyelids drooped; she supported him to the end of the queue where he sank down on the ground. She stood for a while, then sat down beside him. He started to shiver so she tucked his greatcoat around him, found his gloves in the pockets and helped them over his hands.

'I don't know what will happen to us,' he said. 'Poor Madeleine, with Tom dead. And everyone turned out on the street.'

She squeezed his hand. 'Just think about getting better.'

'Something will come up. I won on the Curragh, and I'm sure I've won at Naas. If only I could find out the results.'

'I'm sure,' she said – he was too weak and helpless to argue with. Tears came to her eyes. Where would they live? She had some money left from her last circular letter, but even with her salary it would last no more than a couple of weeks in a hotel. There would be medical bills to pay. She would have to rent a cheap room and might yet have to pawn her garnets and her sable wrap which were still in the luggage that she had persuaded Mrs O'Reilly to store.

'I love you, Jane,' Edmond sighed. 'How fragrant, Vauxhall Gardens … the fireworks … your rose silk gown. The champagne. How beautiful we were … how exquisite …'

'It will be like that again,' she promised him. With his eyes shut he was mercifully oblivious to the misery around him. 'Rest now.'

She pillowed Edmond's head on her lap and leaned her back against the gatepost behind them. His fair hair was dull with sweat; he smiled as she stroked it away from his forehead and after a while he fell asleep. Her own head drooped but, hearing other people shifting, she jerked awake, watching out for their place in the queue.

When Edmond had to move up, he tried his best, but on the third time he cried out and crashed to the ground.

A cold fear gripped her. Another seizure: she was losing him. A murmur went up the queue, that a man was dying. People turned to look, and a couple of orderlies came down the hospital steps.

'Has he the cholera?' a woman asked, jiggling a fretful infant in her arms. She drew back, afraid of contagion.

Jane shook her head. 'He's been ill for weeks.'

Jane was afraid that the hospital staff would refuse Edmond admission, but instead they fetched a stretcher and carried him in. Jane followed them. They laid him down in a crowded hallway, among scores of sick patients. It was fearful to hear the groans of distress.

'Yeh can't stay wit him, missus.' Despite his blunt words, the orderly gave her a kindly smile.

'He's barely conscious. I must stay until I can speak to the doctor.'

He drew his finger from ear to ear. 'Them nurses'll trow yeh out. Or yeh'll get the sickness yerself.'

With a shrug the orderly went away and she waited beside Edmond, leaning after a while against the wall for support, wondering how long her own health would hold out amidst this chaos of contagion.

Sister Aloysius, thank heavens, at last appeared and felt Edmond's pulse. 'I'll get him up to the pay ward,' she said, hurrying away to summon help.

The orderlies took him to St Aidan's Ward, Sister Aloysius herself directing the nurses where to put him, so that at least Edmond had a bed to himself.

As Jane helped him to get comfortable, there was a cry.

'Nurse! Nurse!' An elderly patient, attempting to get out of bed, had fallen.

Jane went over to him. She looked up and down the long, gloomy aisle between the rows of beds but could not see a nurse.

'Help me.' He looked up at her, trembling, fear heightening his unwashed odour. His withered hand scrabbled weakly at the floorboards.

'Calm yourself. I'll get you up in a minute.' She stooped and put out a hand to steady him, waiting to see if his shaking would subside, while trying to suppress her own anxiety.

He whimpered.

'I have to go to Sackville Street,' he muttered. He straightened his wavering arm, lifting his head and shoulder.

'Can you sit up?' Jane knelt beside him and took his lower shoulder, raising him sideways. 'Well done.'

'Thank you.' His legs, protruding askew from his nightshirt, looked too thin and weak to bear the weight of his body. 'God bless you.'

'Don't thank me until you're up.' Jane thought of what she had learned from watching Sister Aloysius, of how she guided Edmond with deft movements when he was unsteady. 'Can you bend your knees up? Put your hand on the end of your bed.'

He obeyed as best as he could. The bed was merely a wooden platform with a thin paliasse of straw, but it would serve to support him.

Now she crouched behind him, moving her arms under his.

'After three, I'll say *up*. Push up as I lift you.' She counted slowly, as if conducting a grand overture. 'One, two, three … *up!*'

He was standing, shakily. She gave him a moment to steady himself then stepped him around like a bizarre dancer, slowly releasing him and propelling him to the point where he could sink back down on his bed.

Sister Aloysius was hurrying down the ward.

'Good woman, yourself! My nurses are all down in the Admissions Room. Now, sir …'

'He wanted to go to Sackville Street,' Jane said. 'He must be wandering in his mind.'

'This is Sackville Street, sir! You're here, now! Isn't it just grand?' Sister Aloysius smiled as the old man relaxed with his hands clasped behind his head. She turned to Jane. 'Could you possibly keep an eye on him? I have to go back to Admissions – twenty-two patients are waiting to be admitted and we have three nurses out sick.'

Jane nodded.

'You've a good pair of hands, Mrs Verity, and a kind heart.' Sister Aloysius eyed Jane approvingly. 'You might take a job here. You may find your true calling, as I said before.'

'I'm a pianist, not a nurse.' Jane smiled at the nun's eagerness, thinking as she did so that she would have to go over to the theatre to check what was happening.

'I could get you an interview with the Matron.'

'I've so much to do that I've no idea where to start, Sister. I must find new accommodation. And what am I to do for Edmond? Should I wait with him until the doctor comes? I have his pills here and I don't think he can properly speak for himself at the moment.'

'I'll take the pills and speak to the doctor,' said Sister Aloysius. 'You sort yourself out and come back to me when you're ready. Think on it, now.'

* * *

At the Queen's Royal Theatre 'CANCELLED' had been daubed in black over the notices. It was chained and padlocked but a light glimmered within. Mr Davenant was there, shabby in his old tweeds.

'Jane.' He looked destroyed, and stared anxiously at her miserable face. 'Come in. How's Edmond?'

At that she stopped. They were in the corridor that led to his dressing room. 'I had to leave him there,' she blurted out, and leant her forehead against the wall. The cold plasterwork met her brow. Hot tears welled up.

'Oh dear God, my dear …' Davenant sighed. He put a handkerchief into her hand. 'Come, a little brandy. Madeleine's here, and Mr McFadyen, the theatre manager. We'll see what we can do.'

He coaxed her into his dressing room, where he gave her the only vacant chair and perched on the lid of his trunk. His evening suit hung like a headless man on the back of the door. Madeleine was hunched in a chair in the corner, with a mourning veil that hid her face. Davenant held out a bottle.

'Best Napoleon, smuggled in from Armagnac.'

Jane accepted it and took a sip, coughing as the spirit burnt the back of her nose and throat, realising as it went down how empty her stomach was. Shaking her head, she passed the bottle back. 'What to do?'

'We can't reopen. One sick, I can manage. One dead ...' Davenant puffed out his cheeks, then exhaled between pursed lips. 'Today both Matthew and Susanna Charlton are feverish and Arnold Marchant's said he's going home as he doesn't want to get sick – so we've no cello either.'

'Is there any kind of show we can put on?' Madeleine's voice was faint with grief.

McFadyen said that the whole of Dublin had fallen silent in the grip of the epidemic. 'People aren't going out: afraid of contagion, sick themselves, or caring for family. Druggists are running out of medicines. The hearses are queuing for the graveyards.' He sat on Davenant's trunk, took the brandy bottle, swigged, and handed it back.

'Our audiences are gone.' Davenant sipped and swallowed as he looked from one face to the next. 'We'll have to refund the tickets. We'll have to get home somehow. I can't see how we can perform the rest of the tour with so many lost. Poor Tom. Tom was in his prime, had great things ahead of him ... great things ... but now – a funeral.'

With a whimper Madeleine drooped her veiled head into her black-gloved hands.

'Without doubt ye can earn a living back in England,' McFadyen replied. 'As for me, I'll be ruined. I can't see my way to reopening.'

'I can't pay salaries now,' said Davenant. 'I've borrowed heavily to bring the show here. I'll have to borrow even more to get home.'

As he shared the brandy bottle with McFadyen, the discussion went back and forth until the bottle was empty and the conclusion that faced them, dizzy though they were from alcohol, was that Davenant's Players must disband, each making their own way back to England. It was the end of the theatre company.

'Well, I have to close up now,' said McFadyen. 'Make sure to take yer things.' He rapped his knuckles on Davenant's trunk.

Jane's head throbbed. Now with no work and no salary, she would still have to find somewhere to live.

As they filed out towards the stage door, Madeleine put her hand on Jane's wrist to detain her. 'Be careful.' She put her black veil aside just enough to show a long red scab running down her neck from below her ear.

Jane's mouth fell open.

'What happened?' she whispered in horror.

'I was moving our luggage from Mrs O'Reilly's to a hotel on the quays. I went out to pay the driver, and by the time I went back upstairs to my room three men were there.' Her fingers probed the line of the wound . 'They held a knife to my neck.'

'You must have thought they were going to murder you!' Jane said, putting her hands to Madeleine's arms to comfort her. '

'They wanted Tom's money. They said he had thousands of pounds. But I knew nothing of it. I had about fifteen pounds in cash. That was all that I had, so I offered it them, but they refused it and threatened me. Then they emptied out our trunks all over my room, and made me go through all his things.'

'Did they find it?'

Madeleine shook her head. 'But they said they'd come back and if I didn't find the money – seven thousand pounds! – he'd won it gambling, they said – they'd do the same to my face.'

'What will you do, Madeleine? Have you told the police?'

'The hotel manager said he didn't understand how the men could have got into the room and he'd fetch the police himself. But no-one came.'

'You should go to the police station yourself – it's by Dublin Castle, I think.'

'I'd be afraid to do it. I'm moving to a different hotel and went straight away to book a first-class passage to Liverpool. It's in a week's time. Won't you travel with me, Jane? We could share a cabin.'

Jane shook her head. 'I can't leave Edmond. I'll find a cheap room somewhere.'

'Be careful of yourself, Jane. Whatever Tom was involved in, this betting thing, I think Edmond is in it as well.'

* * *

Francis Street was not far from Lydon's Insurances and Lettings Agency and the pretty shopfronts of Grafton Street. It had once been elegant; merchants had thrived in the spacious rooms. Yet it had decayed into poverty, the ground floors taken over by dealers in rags and bottles. Sooty brickwork crumbled amongst swirls of bituminous smoke and broomsticks stuck out from upper windows, supporting washing lines from which tattered clothing flew in the wind like the phantom flags of death. Ferns grew beneath over-spilling gutters, water splashing over them and down to the street.

Jane followed the landlord's agent into a house where a

mother stood on the front step as her children scrambled indoors. She wished Jane a good evening with a friendly smile before following them into the front room where she could be heard restoring calm.

Mr Lydon led the way upstairs, reciting the terms of Jane's tenancy through the mouldy air. A cold sweat of damp was disintegrating the structure of Number 85, blackening the broken ceilings and rotting the wood. In the stairwell, plasterwork that had once framed grand portraits had fallen off the walls. The banisters had gone and one of the treads was missing so that she had to steady herself against the wall. A gap where the dado rail had broken provided a handhold.

'Rules be set by the owner. Yeh follow them – or yeh're out. No men allowed in the room. He wouldn't often be letting to young women, but if yeh're sure yeh can manage the deposit …'

'I already told you – I'm married,' objected Jane. 'I'm a successful pianist. My husband is Edmond Verity, the famous actor. We had played the Queen's Royal Theatre but he's sick and in the Meath Hospital.'

'That's as may be, Mrs Verity.' Mr Lydon took off his stovepipe hat to enter the vacant room: second-floor front. 'But the rent must be paid every Friday, no subletting. Accommodation kept tidy, nothing broke. No burning of fixtures and fittings.' He unlocked the door and went in before her. 'And if I want yeh out of here, yeh're out, no other way about it.'

Mr Lydon grinned beneath his sandy moustache, blue eyes gleaming, grasping the crown of his hat between his hands as if they encircled her neck. The furniture consisted of a sideboard and an iron bedstead. There was a brownish mattress but no bedding; most people, Mr Lydon said, managed with a coat.

The wind blew in through the rag-stuffed holes in the window frame, stirring the tattered remnant of curtain and howling in the chimney. Yet the plaster flowers on the ceiling were exquisite while below a speckled mirror the fireplace, of grey marble with finely carved pilasters, retained grandeur. On the serpentine grate stood a cooking kettle, while a water bucket rested nearby on an upturned drawer. A waste pail in the corner of the room would have to be cleaned before she could think of using it. He told her the water pump was outside in the street, while the privy was in a shed in the back yard. Likely to be planks over a hole in the ground, she thought.

'Happy?' asked Mr Lydon.

A couple of flies emerged from holes in the ancient Chinoiserie wallpaper; perhaps there were maggots behind it.

'The stairs ought to be mended. They're dangerous.'

'Mr Royce will not have me waste good timber where people may thieve it for firewood.' Mr Lydon smiled again. 'Best stay quiet if yeh wish for a roof over your head.'

'Mr Royce?' She recognised the name. 'The MP?'

'Mr Theodore Royce,' confirmed Mr Lydon. He held up the key. 'Now, will you have the room or no?'

The landlord was Anna's future father-in-law. He had waltzed with Lucia in the Rotunda ballroom. It would do no good to mention the acquaintance, not now that she was

179

looking at the reverse side of his wealth. The room would have to do; she had no time or energy to look further. Edmond would not like it, but they might move on when he came out of hospital. She gave Mr Lydon ten shillings as key money and a half-crown for the coming week's rent. After he had handed over the key and gone downstairs, she stood at the window looking down into the street. She delayed lighting the candle; one never knew who might look up.

People had lit their fires against the cold of the evening and the smog thickened in the air, mingling with the malty smell of breweries and the reek of the river. Here and there, faint light glimmered behind shutters or partly boarded windows; across the street flickering shadows moved in the window dust.

She heard a piano in a room below, but it must have been the children tunelessly hammering the keys: *plink-plink-plink, plunk-plunk-plunk-plunk*, followed at last by a reproachful voice, perhaps that of the woman who had greeted her, then the racket hushed.

The sounds of the night became the songs of the balladeers, the grunts of brawling drunks, the soft words of prostitutes. Screaming ... if you heard the banshee there would be a death. It was only a baby. Yet a hearse trundled below. The clop of hooves and the grind of iron wheels on stone faded away. Even at this late hour it was going to the burial grounds, a box of death on wheels, the driver hunched in his seat, the pony's stunted body as concave and gaunt as its master's.

* * *

Jane took a cab back to Kildare Street for her luggage.

'Will you not come in for a minute?' Mrs O'Reilly, to Jane's surprise, hurried her inside. 'There's a letter for you, missis, just in the dining room there.'

'But I should be away. The cab's waiting.'

'The servant can bring your bags out. Just a quick moment.'

Mrs O'Reilly had lit the lamp on the dining table and the envelope beneath it bore Anna's handwriting. Jane took the letter but it seemed there was another reason for the landlady's concern. She closed the door and, after glancing out at the street, closed the curtain.

'There were three fellers here asking after your husband,' she said in a low voice. 'They said he owes them something.'

'But we have no debts.' Jane had paid all their bills. She would owe Dr Wright and the hospital, but doubted they would pursue her as yet. Could she have overlooked one of the tradesmen?

'They'd have had all your trunks and bags away had I not said that they belonged to someone else.'

'Did they say who they were? Maybe I should find them and try to settle the debt?'

'I was afeared to ask them. I told them that you were after leaving and I had said you were not to come back. Maybe you had gone back to England.'

'I wish we could. But Edmond's too ill.' Jane caught a wary look in Mrs O'Reilly's eyes. 'Why were you afraid?'

'They were a rough lot, you know that kind of way? I wouldn't have any dealings with them. Not that type of person.'

'Edmond never had any business with anyone like that.'

Jane shook her head in puzzlement. 'What exactly did they want?'

'They wanted him. Or yourself.'

'Were they tradesmen?' Jane had a compelling feeling that they were not. Were these the three men who had threatened Madeleine? Who were somehow connected to gambling? Mrs O'Reilly was shaking her head. If she knew anything else she was not telling.

'If they ask me again, I won't say to them that you came here. But mind yourself. Stay away from the bad areas.'

'I've taken a room in Francis Street.'

Mrs O'Reilly's face crumpled. 'Be very careful.'

Chapter Twenty-three

SHOPPING ON GRAFTON STREET

My dear Jane,

It is a while since I heard from you. I do hope that this letter finds you well and that Edmond is making a speedy recovery.

You must forgive my neglect of you, but I have been completely occupied in preparations for my wedding. The fruitcake alone took three appointments with the caterer: it is to weigh fifty pounds. The number, size and style of its presentation boxes occupied myself and my mother for some hours. Alex unfortunately won't pay attention to anything he considers 'domestic', so all the decisions are left to Mama and myself, while his father is footing the bill for everything.

I have been back to Mrs Flannery's on Grafton Street, this time to choose my wedding dress. She told me to take my pick of the most sumptuous fabrics and styles and that I would look like royalty. I first chose a heavy satin but the weight of all that fabric – twenty yards, imagine! – would have been too much to wear all day, so instead I settled on a thin silk taffeta and what she called

'Valentian' lace, with a simpler version of the same for the bridesmaids. At the same time, I am to have a 'costume de voyage' of blue 'moiré antique' with a matching bonnet. I won't bore you with the details of my mother's costumes.

Theodore is paying for the dresses and had also presented myself and Mama each with a diamond parure from one of the jewellers on Grafton Street. Evidently, he is the landlord for the shops and the apartments above, so, the shopkeepers being his tenants, he is able to purchase from them at a discount.

I must confess though, that I got the pieces confused. As the bride I had imagined the larger set was for me, but he said laughingly that the mother of the bride took precedence and insisted on fixing it on her himself. Even though mine was more modest it is the most dazzling set of jewellery I have ever possessed, and I was effusive in my thanks. My father — he is such an old bore sometimes! — said they were both excessive and ought to be returned, but gave in to me and Mama, else he would never have heard the last of it.

I only wish you could have been with me at the dressmakers — you have such taste and style, while my mother is inclined to be fussy.

I managed to see Francesca, who is in better spirits. Mr Gavan Duffy had another court hearing, after which he was released on bail. We hope he will be able to stay out of trouble in the future.

I do hope that we will be able to maintain our friendship, and that you will call over and see me when you can.

With sincere affection,

Anna

Chapter Twenty-four

A WORLD APART

My dear Anna,

I am sorry that I have been too busy to write to you. Edmond has become severely ill, Davenant's Players have been forced to disband and, as you can see, I have had to move to a less fashionable address. Edmond had to be admitted to the Meath Hospital when we were turned out of our lodgings.

It is impossible for me to come to visit you at present as I have found work at the hospital. My duties are menial. Mostly I help to wash the patients and to lay out anyone who has died during the night. At least I am able to keep an eye on Edmond, although unfortunately he does not improve.

You are fortunate to have made such an advantageous match and I do enjoy reading about your marriage preparations. However, it seems to me that you are entering a world that is very much apart from mine. I fear it will be impossible for us to attend your wedding ceremonies – and offer my sincere apologies – but would be glad to remain your friend. I hope that you retain your ambitions as a writer, and will be patient with me during this time of difficulty.

With affectionate wishes,

Jane

Chapter Twenty-five

GROWING UNEASE

William, followed by a medical student, went from one hopeless and emaciated patient to the next: from the tubercular to the syphilitic, from the agonised to the paralysed. Even on the pay ward he lacked time to teach the student, as the routine of examination and prescribing had to keep pace with the numbers arriving from the Admissions Room.

Above the usual coughs and groans, a high-pitched whine shrilled out at the other end of the ward, then there was a thud as a man slid from his bed to the floor.

'Dr Doughty!' A nurse called out for help. *'He's having a seizure!'*

By the time William reached him it had already stopped.

'Sister Aloysius says he's a famous actor. You wouldn't believe it, would you?'

It was Edmond Verity – Dr Wright's patient – pitiful and dishevelled. William had not known he was in the hospital. He was still breathing but the crystalline blue eyes stared blankly up and there was no response even when he tapped him on the forehead.

'Get the orderlies to lift him into bed. He'll sleep it off. Check him over for injuries when he wakes.'

He went back to his own work.

He knew no more of the case than what Jane had told him, that day when she had come to his rooms, when he had tried not to look at her, despite her beauty. His eyes had strayed only at that last moment when the black fur had slipped down over her bare shoulder. It had been merely desire that he had felt then, for less than a second – only a physical impulse, not love. Thank God she had not noticed. He felt nothing for her now, he told himself; his jealousies and longings had gone. Her husband was merely another patient, whom he would of course help if required.

'What do you think these contain?' Joseph Murphy, at the nurses' desk, held out a green glass bottle. 'Mr Verity's after bringing these in with him. *The Stimulant. Take one twice a day, complete the course.* There must be another fortnight or so of them left.'

William took the bottle and peered at the label, recognising Wright's precise copperplate script. There was no pharmacist's name; Wright must have formulated these himself, rolling the chalky pill dough into strings before slicing them into tablets.

'Why do you ask?'

'To my mind they seem to be after making the man worse. Every time he's given them he starts vomiting. This morning the nurses gave him a double dose because they'd forgotten it last night and – you saw what happened – he's still unconscious.'

'What's his diagnosis?'

'Nervous debilitation.'

William raised an eyebrow. That was what Jane had said, but what did it actually mean? Hypochondriasis? He had known such patients to present with collapse, headache and even vomiting. Hysteria, less common in males – although the gentleman was after all an actor – could also produce prolonged and dramatic seizures.

'Why not try stopping them?' He rattled the bottle in his hand.

'You know yourself I can't alter Dr Wright's treatments, especially for one of his private patients.'

William opened the bottle and tipped out a sugar-coated pill, which lay glistening on the desk. Taking out his pocket handkerchief, he put the pill into its folds.

'It's possible to discover the contents. It's an interest of mine. I'll be able to tell you in the next couple of days.' He closed the bottle and returned it to Joseph. A sugar crystal stuck to his finger and without thinking he licked it off. It did not taste sweet. It formed a tiny burning spot on his tongue, with a bitter hint at the back of his throat as he swallowed. He grimaced. 'In the meantime, if the treatment is not benefiting him, it probably should be stopped. Perhaps there's an alternative? You ought to discuss it with Dr Wright.'

For a moment he thought of his meeting with Mr Morrissey with a shudder of horrible anxiety: *Dr Wright poisoned Mrs Wright.* What if this was white arsenic? That would explain its ill effects. He thought he would be able to identify it. He had the apparatus downstairs in his laboratory, and had studied the methods of Marsh and Orfila in Christison's *Treatise on Poisons.*

He left Joseph to put the bottle away and pondered. White arsenic, given in small amounts, was still in the pharmacopoeia, used in fever drops and the like. Its mere presence in the pills would not prove deliberate poisoning. After analysing for the presence of arsenic and other substances, he'd try out a new method he'd read up, to estimate the quantity of arsenic present.

It was hard to believe, however, that Wright could possibly have any motive to poison his celebrated patient. Dead men did not pay invoices, and Wright could not be expecting a legacy after only a few weeks as Mr Verity's physician. Wright had spoken of Jane's elegance, of her pretty eyes – but surely he could not be aiming to supplant her husband? William pondered how to probe him, to discover what he would say about the pills.

There was another matter to be discussed in private – a letter from Mr Lydon that read: *'On foot of further discussions with our loss adjusters, I am informed that Dr Oliver Wright will no longer pursue the insurance claim on Mrs Catriona Wright. You may regard this matter as concluded.'*

Dr Wright, when he arrived on the ward, briefly conferred with the nurse then strode up to William, who was stooping to examine a patient's chest. 'What do you mean by stopping my treatment?'

Wright, arms akimbo and feet planted wide, could be heard up and down the ward. Was this man, with his ringing, educated voice, really a murderer?

'Do you mean Mr Verity's pills?' William straightened up under his patient's anxious gaze. 'I didn't. What I said was that they probably should be stopped. I told Dr Murphy to discuss it with you but he must have acted straight away.'

'You both acted with reckless ignorance,' Wright declared. 'You know nothing of this case. Those stimulant pills are keeping Mr Verity alive in his advanced state of illness.'

William moved closer to Wright so that they stood in the long aisle that ran between the rows of beds. 'I was told that the patient was unable to tolerate them.' He looked down at the stocky man: his face was crumpled in a scowl, the chin thrust out like an English bulldog. 'That he was vomiting them, and that after this morning's dose he had a seizure.'

'If you stop them it could kill him!' barked Wright, as the nurse turned to watch them. 'Is that what you want?'

'Of course not!'

'Perhaps you'd prefer him out of the way? Don't forget I know about your past, about your scandal, about your love –'

'I assure you,' William interrupted, raising his voice over Wright's, 'that he's just another patient as far as I'm concerned. I had no intention of interfering but was asked my opinion by another doctor.'

'You have no right to an opinion on matters of which you know nothing. If Mr Verity comes to harm, I'll hold you responsible.'

Wright was distorting the truth, and William felt it. For a moment he was tempted to mount a challenge: over what happened to Catriona, over what was in Verity's green glass bottle. But he knew that he had no firm evidence. Moreover, this was no place for a heated argument, in the middle of the ward with everyone watching. Instead, he quelled his anger.

'It's a simple matter to correct – the missing dose can be

given.' William went on to placate Wright as well as he could, the nurse coming over to help. 'No-one has any intention of going against your decisions or, heaven forbid, doing anything that might delay the patient's recovery.' It was not a good time to ask Wright what the pills contained.

When Wright had calmed down, William said there was another matter he wanted to ask about, in private.

Later on, when they met in Wright's office, he said: 'Mr Lydon wrote to me saying he had concluded the matter of your late wife.'

Wright waved a hand. 'Yes, naturally he accepted my account.'

'Perhaps I had delayed my report for too long – I'm sorry.'

'It's paid up, so there's no need for you to do anything further.'

William studied him with growing unease. Lydon's letter had been clear that Wright had dropped his claim. 'I wanted to tell you that I haven't made the – additions – to my records that you suggested. I'm unsure how the queries were settled?'

But Wright, now smiling, shook his head. 'No matter, all is resolved to the insurance broker's satisfaction. As to my list of dates, there's no need for you to keep that now. You may destroy it if you so wish. There will be no further enquiries.'

William turned to leave.

'Dr Doughty ...' Wright's voice became ingratiating. 'I wish to apologise for losing my temper. It's just that I've been so very busy after my return from leave, quite overburdened, in fact. I may have spoken over-sharply about my patient's treatment. I realise now that you were trying, in your own way, to help Mr Verity.'

Wright's belated apology would have been better if it had arrived in front of the other staff in the ward. But it was best accepted.

'You must understand that I no longer have any personal connection to his wife,' said William. 'Even if I had, I would not harm the man – what do you think I am?'

'Of course,' said Wright, 'of course I understand. I'll say nothing more about it.'

Exactly what he had said the last time it was discussed, William thought. The man was a liar.

Later, in his laboratory, William studied Professor Charles's textbook. He would have to decompose the pill with zinc and vitriol, and capture the resulting gas, which when ignited would deposit a black metallic film on a ceramic vessel. To gauge the quantity, he would have to put a known solution of arsenic through the same process for comparison. He needed that solution, so spoke to Mr Carty, the hospital's apothecary, describing the methods of the pathologist in New York.

'I'm hoping to go over there and work for him, but in the meantime I need practice in his chemical methods,' he told him. 'Could you recommend a supplier of reagents?'

'Sure, I have what you need in stock,' said Mr Carty. 'The housekeepers use it for rat poison. Come over to the apothecary's stores.' As they went along the hospital corridor Carty added that, even having worked fifteen years for the hospital, he was himself saving for a ticket to America, as it was hard for an honest man to prosper in Dublin.

In the storeroom Carty stooped to check through bottles at the back of a lower shelf. '*Liquor Arsenicalis*, one per cent,' he said, bringing a green ribbed flask to the work bench and decanting a small bottle. 'Be careful, 'tis a powerful poison. A tenth of a drachm could be lethal.'

* * *

In the end William was unsurprised to discover that the black stain of Wright's pill was almost as deep as that produced by *Liquor Arsenicalis*. According to the textbook, the next step was to analyse the patient's vomit, to prove the poison had been taken. He found and carefully cleaned a glass jar which would do for a sample.

He felt a sinking sensation of dread, knowing that he should, in all conscience, challenge Wright about the treatment again. There was still the possibility that Wright did not realise how strong the pills were. Perhaps if Mr Verity could be switched to a better regime he might yet improve. He determined to speak to Wright first thing the next morning.

Chapter Twenty-six

MUCH LEFT UNSAID

'I thought you'd left me.' Edmond reached for Jane's hand and held it.

'Why would you think that?' Her day of work was at an end, and the light fading outside. She had come from the roaring chaos of the Admissions room to the crowded men's ward. The elderly man she had helped was no longer there; she hoped he had been discharged home. The nurses here believed in the cleansing properties of fresh air, so a cold wind whistled through the open windows.

'Each time you leave, I think I might not see you again.'

'But I've started working here so that I can see you every day.' She let go his hand to pull the thin coverlet up around his shoulders. 'Has Dr Wright been to see you?'

Edmond nodded. 'Dr Murphy changed my treatment, but he soon changed it back. He brought me good news about the Naas Races, too.'

'You seem weaker, Edmond.' She did not want to hear

about the Naas Races. 'Are you in pain?'

'No, only a little tingling, numb if anything … you know, my feet, I can barely feel them. The numbness spreads upwards a little each day.' His voice was hoarse. 'Do you remember how I used to stride across the stage? I've given my last performance. Did you tell Davenant that I shan't be back?'

'Let's hope you improve.'

'I have regrets, Jane. Things I can't undo. The time we were apart – when I deserted you – I was foolish.'

'There's nothing more to be said.' She writhed inwardly. She had not yet told him her side of the truth.

'I was grateful to have you back.' His eyes opened fully and even though they were sunken in their sockets she was drawn by their familiar beauty, by the many shades of blue in the fibres of the iris, by his long dark eyelashes. 'But you'd changed. How cold you were to me … your awful experience … the workhouse … you were never the same. I'm sorry.'

He pushed back his hair with a weak movement. It was thinning, falling out, always sticking to his nightshirt and filling the hairbrush.

'There was something else that changed me … that you never knew …' She still hesitated. From somewhere came a cry. Perhaps from one of the patients. There it was again, rising so high in the register that she strained her hearing to detect it. It was unearthly. She shivered, as though she was washing in icy water on a winter morning. Edmond's time was coming to an end, she thought.

'When I learned that you had got engaged …' she said,

then checked herself. 'No. It was not your fault. I had someone else, a man who loved me.'

Again, his incredible eyes, but now wide with wonder. 'I thought you so much altered,' he said. 'Maybe … but no, I could not be certain, and surely the fault was mine, for if I had never …'

'Do you remember when you found me working as a maidservant? And you met my employer?'

He smiled ruefully. 'You were so angry that you rejected me.' Then his face fell. '*Him?* The coroner?'

She nodded.

'He looked so dull. Him?'

'Yes.'

'How?' Edmond displayed no jealousy. A half-smile curved his mouth as if he were eager to hear it. It was too late for it to divide them, for it was Death that waited to bring down that blade.

'I thought William harsh at first. The house was a dreary place, and his wife was an invalid.' How dark had been the secrets of Newhall Street, the inquests recorded in the coroner's black ledgers… 'I discovered that she was seduced by her own brother, a man of evil. But as I tried to convince William of it, he fixed his affections on me. Harriet took her own life and afterwards … William and I …'

'Consoled one another?' Edmond supplied.

'I thought I had lost you forever.' But she had to be honest: it had been her choice. The memories of pleasure were still physically palpable. 'No. In that moment I loved him, body and soul.'

Edmond lay back against his pillow and raised his eyes

to the ceiling, his lips forming a calm smile. 'I almost knew it, that something had happened. You're too pretty, too passionate … But not him – I never spotted him. So old. He didn't seem your type.'

'He was forty at the time.'

'Do you still care for him?' Edmond raised himself again on his elbow to study her face. 'You do. That change in you … it's still there, isn't it?'

'No.' She met his eyes. He had taken her news so calmly that she began to wonder if his own affections had, all this time, been elsewhere.

'Twenty years between you.' Edmond had been doing the sums. 'I'll suppose you'll soon be free to go back to him. But you'll have to watch him age while you're still in your prime.'

She shook her head. 'He's here in Dublin – he works here. I told him not to try to see me. He agreed.'

'Is he still single?'

She nodded. She would not reveal the humiliation of that recent encounter.

'He'll have you back, who wouldn't?' Edmond's eyes brightened. 'You needn't be alone when I'm gone, Jane. Mourn me, then live your life.'

She wanted to say *no* but couldn't and looked at the floor. Why was everything so impermanent? Her eyes prickled.

'Or perhaps you'll settle back down in London.' Edmond reached over and patted her hand. 'Your parents might yet forgive you for going off with an actor.'

'They'll never forgive me. You know they cut me off, when we first eloped.' Her father, sober and high-minded, had a disdain of theatrical folk and 'bohemians'. Jane pulled a handkerchief from her pocket, wiped her eyes, and blew her nose.

Edmond sighed. 'I always thought the distance between us was because of Nathan. Did you forgive me?'

'More than I forgave myself.' She tried to grasp the truth. 'You see, if I'd had money, Nathan wouldn't have been born in the workhouse. My milk might have come ... I couldn't feed him, you see, no-one could save him.' She blew her nose again. Her arms, as always, ached with the memory.

'I had not meant you harm.' He had said that so many times. 'It was just that – I had no money to send ... my gambling debts. I was careless, and foolish. I'm sorry, Jane.'

'Not everyone can be saved, Edmond, it can't be helped, and what we can't help we must forgive. But I wish you could have seen his face. He might have grown up in your image.'

Edmond heaved a sigh. 'At least I'll leave you better off than the last time – there's money ...'

'You've done a lot in your life.' She had not the heart to tell him they had nothing, or to ask him about the three men who sought him: what difference would it make? Her past might be discussed without rancour, but his gambling was another matter. He would never tell her the truth. Let him pass away content in his illusions. 'Do you remember when you played Hamlet? How you delighted the critics?'

He looked up and smiled. 'I captured the public. Better one year of fame than three score and ten in obscurity.'

'I'll miss you, Edmond.' No-one was looking. She kissed his lips with gentle affection. 'You altered the course of my life. I have my music, thanks to you.'

His head drooped sideways, his voice failing as he spoke. 'I would not … have become a great actor without you. I have understood love … the pain and tragedy and glory of love. When I stare into the abyss the audience looks over my shoulder.'

Soon afterwards he was racked by vomiting. Jane ran to fetch him a bowl. His stomach must have been empty for all he brought up was a little clear liquid, speckled with blood.

'That's to be kept,' said a nurse. 'For one of the doctors. Leave it on the floor by the bed.'

Edmond's vomiting eased off but now his speech made no sense, randomly naming racehorses and their odds as he faded in and out of consciousness. The thin cry continued, piercing Jane's mind.

* * *

Edmond had already gone from confusion to coma when Jane left the hospital late in the evening. At Francis Street she slept briefly, waking in the early hours. The dawn was arriving earlier as the spring progressed. The grey outlines of the room and the luggage that lay about on the floor appeared half an hour before it was time to get up. Restless yet weary, she lay waiting for the bells of Dublin to toll the hour of seven as the red light of a clear morning glowed on the walls. The shrilling that had threaded through her dreams had stopped.

As she walked back to the hospital, the early sunlight made the city beautiful, gilding the sooty brickwork of the tenements in memory of their former glory and illuminating the symmetry of the graceful Georgian terraces, the handsome oblongs of the windows and the fanlights above the doors. The cruel classes and the criminals were still abed and at that hour the people who made or sold things, served, or took care of others were going to work. There was a gentle mood in the streets, a scent of spring, and neighbours greeted one another in passing.

Jane was early to work and went straight up to St Aidan's Ward to see Edmond. The nurses were raising the blinds and opening the windows; sun and air flooded in where he lay. She knew it had happened yet disbelieved it at the same time. He was ashen white, his mouth open, his eyes unseeing and his hand, though placed elegantly across his chest as though he were about to deliver a speech, was hard and cold. No one knew the time of his death. Her tears gathering, Jane went into the sluice room to be alone. Whatever his faults, he had been her husband. She wept into her apron, for the handsome man whose velvet voice had once held her enthralled, and for the life and the hopes that they had shared, which were now at an end.

* * *

By mid-morning Edmond lay in the mortuary. Jane would never see him again; all that remained to her was a slip of paper signed by Dr Murphy, which gave 'nervous debilitation' as the cause of death.

The Head Porter told her that the burial could not be delayed as the mortuary was overflowing, which, as he was sure that she knew herself, was causing miasma and disease.

'The hospital can provide a winding sheet and a burial at Broadstone – there'll be a priest but we won't allow mourners for fear of contagion. I'm sorry, m'love.'

'I don't want him to have a pauper's burial.' Would her little family have no memorial? First Nathan lost in the cesspit beneath the Birmingham Workhouse, now Edmond to lie in an unmarked grave with the dead of Dublin, his limbs resting forever beside unknown strangers. 'Let me speak to the undertakers about funeral arrangements.'

The Head Porter frowned. 'They're all overwhelmed.'

'Please!'

'I'll give you until eleven o'clock. The burial cart leaves each day at twelve noon.'

She hurried away, grief stinging her eyes. After queuing for an hour in a register office crowded with the bereaved, she took the certificate to the nearest undertaker where she was told by a weary gentleman that coffins must be made to order in elm or oak, as the ready-made and the cheaper woods were in immense demand, and that she would find that every other undertaker in the city was in the same situation.

On reflection she realised that she did not have enough money – the last circular letter had long been cashed and the little that she had raised from the pawnbroker was running out. She would have to accept the pauper's burial offered by the hospital. On the way back to the Head Porter, with the church bells already tolling eleven, she felt with dread that she would be next to lie in an unmarked grave. Perhaps around the next corner she might hear that cry again, see a silver comb at her feet and feel the spirit of the banshee mark her.

Chapter Twenty-seven

THE ANALYSIS

William went to St Aidan's Ward to see if the sample of Mr Verity's stomach contents had been collected. The nurse handed him the jar, but the bed where the patient had lain was now occupied by another man.

'We had to send Mr Verity to the mortuary this morning.'

'He's dead?' William stared at her in shock. He was too late. If only he had stood his ground against Wright. Or if he had acted earlier. He had not expected it so soon.

'That's Mr Phelan, just up from the Admissions Room.' The nurse was one of those who avoided following his instructions, preferring Dr Wright's advice. 'Dr Murphy fears he may be a case of consumption. He asked would you look at him, please?'

William glanced over at Mr Phelan. He was perhaps in his thirties but shrunken like an old man. There was no fat on him at all: his facial bones were sharp beneath transparent, dark-veined skin. He was hungrily eating a bowl of stirabout. Many patients were simply victims of starvation, who, if their stomachs did not reject the offered food, gradually returned to strength.

'I'll be back in an hour.' Sometimes the dead were more important than the living. William hurried away, sweat dampening his palms. He knew he had to do the analysis. But what would he do if his fears were correct?

The basement corridor, dimly lit by thick glazed gratings, was almost deserted. An orderly pushed a trolley in the far distance, clattering away towards the laundry. William unlocked the little room; everything was as he had left it.

William went through the same process that he had used for Wright's pill. He poured the contents of the sample jar into a glass flask and carefully added powdered zinc and vitriol. The mixture began to fizz. He plugged it with a cork, running through which a fine glass tube took the gas through a filter and towards a white ceramic tile held vertical in a clamp stand.

William waited a few moments then lit the outlet. A tiny blue flame appeared, with a thread of smoke. He moved the tile closer and a black metallic stain spread across the white surface. When the flame had burned down William took the tile out of the clamp and marked it with a grease pencil: *VERITY – GASTRIC CONTENTS*.

He still had the series of tiles that he had exposed in the same way using different dilutions of the *Liquor Arsenicalis* that Carty had given him. The concentration of arsenic in the stomach contents was about a tenth of that in the standard solution. Without doubt a lethal dose had been administered.

William sat at his workbench, staring at the tiles, feeling

that malice was present in the room. There would be little time to investigate this death further before Verity was buried. As soon as he attempted it Wright would challenge him to confirm his findings: to prove that the results were accurate; that the stomach contents were genuinely those of Verity and had not been contaminated after collection. And what if Wright's treatment had been given with the best intent? If his practice could be scrutinised, then why not everyone else's?

William folded his arms on the edge of his workbench and hunched over the stains, thinking. It could not be doubted that Wright was a liar. Yet surely all doctors told lies? Most had no right to the respect that they thought was their due: they prescribed useless or toxic medications; they persuaded patients to undergo surgery in ignorance of the complications; they even told dying patients they were getting better. Yet any physician, even if incompetent and dishonest, would be disgusted at the idea of deliberately causing a patient harm. Was Wright a murderer?

Their conflict over Mr Verity's pills stood out in William's memory. Despite his arrogance, Wright was usually content to delegate his patients' care to his deputies, once they had been admitted to the Meath. So the vehemence of his insistence upon those pills was extraordinary. What if the poisoning had been intentional? But why poison a patient who had been a minor celebrity, and whose endorsement might have enhanced Wright's reputation? And Verity had only been Wright's patient for a matter of weeks, so, unlike 'Dr Wright's widows', no legacy could be expected. In fact, as he had been unable to work, Mr Verity's money had likely run out, driving him to enter the hospital instead of receiving treatment in his lodgings, and perhaps forcing Jane to find work in the hospital. William had glimpsed her passing in the distance, but had not had the chance to approach her.

What of Bernard Morrissey's bald statement: *Dr Wright killed Mrs Wright*? There had been all the fuss about the insurance reports. Lydon, the insurance broker, had stated that Wright had made a similar claim on his late mother-in-law, and had said that people like Wright, who devoted themselves to the turf, lost money by it and became dishonest. The Turf Club had been investigating Wright for doping.

William was inclined to believe Lydon's letter on that matter, rather than Wright's statement that the claim had been paid. But he could not rely upon anything that Bernard Morrissey said. The man led a gang of murderous criminals and no doubt had intimidated Wright into giving up the insurance claim.

William cupped his jaw in his left hand, rested his cheekbones on his thumb and forefinger, and blinked. When he had lost patience with Morrissey in his consulting room, he had been confronting a murderer. At times, when anger lanced through him, he became too outspoken. Now it was time to be outspoken again. He was taking a risk: he doubted that Wright would be in a position to harm him, but what if he sought to block his appointment in New York? He heaved a sigh. There was no other way. He locked his laboratory and went upstairs in search of Wright.

He would have preferred to have taken Wright quietly aside but found him berating Joseph in the corridor outside the Head Porter's room. 'You've completely disregarded my instructions. I told you the woman was to be bled –'

'Sure but I haven't had the time.' Joseph's voice was insultingly languid. 'It's always busy in the Admissions Room.'

'If you were punctual in your attendance and didn't disappear to the Lord knows where – the nurses tell me about you, don't imagine that they don't –'

'Dr Wright.' William raised his voice to be heard. 'I have a matter to discuss with you. It's about Mr Verity. You may as well join us, Joseph, as I promised you I would give you an answer regarding his pills. Should we go to your office, Dr Wright?'

A hum of voices and a reek of tobacco smoke issued from the open door of the Head Porters' room, but Wright merely backed away to the opposite side of the corridor.

'I'm sure we can deal with the matter quickly.'

'Very well.' William went up close to him, Joseph joining them. 'There was a huge quantity of arsenic in Mr Verity's stomach contents. What say you to that? What did you state as the cause of death?'

'Dr Murphy wrote out the certificate.'

William looked at Joseph.

'Nervous debilitation,' Joseph said, with a lift of one ginger eyebrow.

'And what exactly is that?' William hissed, his jutting chin close to Dr Wright's. 'Debilitation caused by what?'

'The patient had a degenerative nervous complaint.' Wright backed away, lifting his hands defensively. 'In all likelihood a tumour in the brain, or ...'

'What proof do you have? Why did you allow Dr Murphy to issue a death certificate?'

'For him to be buried, of course.'

'I was obliged to write it,' said Joseph. 'The bed was needed for the next patient.'

'Mr Verity's body ought to go to the Dublin Pathological Society on Saturday,' said William. 'If there's a tumour, we'll find it. Otherwise, I'd ascribe it to arsenic poisoning.'

'Indeed? And how would my patient have taken such a great quantity of arsenic?'

'Your so-called stimulant pills. That's why they made him sick.' William balled his fists at his sides. 'Headaches, vomiting, seizures: they're all symptoms.'

'Those pills were harmless. They only contained a very tiny quantity. You know it may be a beneficial medication in a low dose. If some person had given him arsenic, why should my stimulant pills be the only source?'

'I analysed one,' said William.

Dr Wright hesitated momentarily before resuming his bland expression. 'How could you have done that? You're no chemist.'

'On the contrary – I have the apparatus downstairs in my laboratory. I have proof that the pill contained a large quantity of arsenic.'

'I must come and inspect.' Dr Wright showed no surprise. 'Will I also find in your so-called laboratory the bottle that you got two days ago from Mr Carty, containing a powerful solution of the same substance?'

William frowned. 'Of course. It was a control solution. To compare the strengths.'

'Mr Carty told me about the strength of the liquid he gave you. The housekeepers use it against vermin. So, Dr Doughty, my pills were not the source of the arsenic, I think?'

Dr Wright's gaze shifted over William's shoulder and along the corridor. He raised his voice. 'You had already attempted to interfere with Mr Verity's treatment.'

'I merely advised – when asked. I'd no wish to interfere in your patient's care. Moreover, *your* treatment – which you insisted on restarting – did nothing to save him, quite the reverse!'

'Indeed, and what about this lady?'

William turned his head to see Jane behind him.

Wright pulled her forward by her wrist. Her hand twisted in his grip and William fought down an instinct to punch him. 'This – pardon me, madam – this ravishing widow? After so many years, you finally had the means to free her – didn't you?'

Jane stilled and her eyes met William's. They were wide in shock, as if she had received a blow to the head. Her eyes the same that had absorbed him years ago, eyes grey like rain. A visceral memory caught his breath beneath his ribs and gripped his belly.

As Wright released her, she dropped her gaze to the floor. His cruelty had compounded her distress. She looked exhausted, the poor thing, her face puffy with grief.

William drew himself up.

'I have absolutely no association with her! How dare you say that? I'm the one who seeks the truth, while you merely wish the patient to be buried.' He was in the right, yet he feared he had gone down in her esteem.

'In this situation the next-of-kin should give consent for a post-mortem.' Wright was smiling now, relishing his advantage. 'What say you, Mrs Verity? Should the doctors of the Dublin Pathological Society anatomise your late husband, for us to accuse one another over his death, or should he be buried intact?'

'I don't know.' Jane faltered. She darted another glance at William's face, then at Joseph, who was looking away, then back at Wright.

'The question is,' added William, 'that his diagnosis was not, to my mind, clear. A post-mortem examination might establish the cause.'

'What do you mean?' Her voice quivered as if with pain.

'I'm concerned that his death was due to his medication.' William might have said more, but her hands came up to her face and rested there. He pitied her. It was horrible to put her through this added ordeal.

'Your husband was a handsome fellow,' Dr Wright said softly. 'I am sorry for your loss. It would be a shame for us to saw his head open, would it not?'

'The door of the Head Porter's office is in front of you,' pleaded William. 'You have only to go in to amend the arrangements. We could find out the truth.'

As she lowered her hands and looked from one to another, her tears trickled down her face. She wiped them away with her apron. 'Let him be buried as he is,' she said. 'Edmond had been ill for a long time before I brought him into the hospital. Perhaps I'll never understand what it was.'

William plunged his hands in his pockets and now stood apart.

'My deepest condolences, Mrs Verity,' said Dr Wright, and after a pause added: 'I see that you have now joined the nursing establishment at our excellent hospital.'

210

Jane, blowing her nose, said, 'Yes.'

'Then we had all best return to our duties, had we not?'

* * *

William saw her later in the Admissions Room. They were too busy to talk. He did not acknowledge her, save to issue instructions. He had said that there was nothing between them and aimed to bear this out by his behaviour. In any case, anything they may have felt was soon forgotten in dealing with the surge of patients. Five poor wretches, brought in by their relatives in the last moments of their lives, lay there freshly dead. The orderlies, who they asked repeatedly to move the bodies to the mortuary, were too busy stretchering admitted patients to the wards. In a roaring ocean of disaster, Edmond Verity's death that day had been but the breaking of a single wave.

Chapter Twenty-eight

THREE DIVILS

Jane did not return to her room until late in the evening. She locked the door behind her, lit a candle and sat down on the bed, trembling. Overwhelmed by the miseries of the day, she had no energy to undress. Edmond's greatcoat was her blanket; for comfort she drew it around her shoulders just as she had on the *Banshee*. The bergamot scent of his pomade still clung to the folds, with a deeper reek of cigar smoke. She embraced it and slept.

It was not until the rain drumming on the window woke her in the first light of morning that she noticed that her belongings had been disturbed. The lid of her trunk had been shut on a triangle of fabric. Her black silk dress lay crumpled inside, as if its skirts had been hastily stuffed in. She straightened out the dress and refolded it. Likewise, she found that her bags had been emptied and repacked. Nothing was missing, yet it seemed that everything, even her most intimate belongings, had been pried into and rummaged.

A man must have done it: men did not know how to fold clothes properly. But how had he got in? With a key? Or by picking the lock? It gave her a chill of fear. What if he came in again, and found her? She should go to the police about it, but what would she say? They would not understand how her dresses were folded.

She washed quickly and went downstairs to empty the slop bucket into the privy and refill the jug at the pump. When she came back in from the rain her ground-floor neighbour Nellie was in the front hall, sweeping out her room and calling back through the doorway, settling an argument between her children.

'Give that back now, and mind ya finish yer tae – there now, best boy!' She looked up at Jane. 'How are ya, missis? A rainy day today?'

Jane bid her a good morning as though she had not properly heard the question. Nellie stopped sweeping and leant on the broom handle, her green eyes narrowed with concern as she read Jane's expression. 'That bad, is it?'

Adversity closes the heart, but kindness opens it, so that pain finds a way in. Jane paused and leant on the wall, afraid she might crumple into a ball of misery. 'My husband died,' she muttered. 'He was in the Meath Hospital.'

'Ah, ye poor love!' Nellie heaved a mournful sigh. 'Leave yer buckets, come in, have a cup of tae, won't ya? I've plenty left in the pot. Hisself has gone to work.'

It would save her lighting her own fire for breakfast – Jane did not need much more persuasion to follow her in.

Nellie's room was warm and crammed with furniture: a large bed for the whole family, a table where four children squeezed onto two chairs, an old piano. It smelt of musty clothing. There was nowhere for Jane to sit until the eldest boy stood up. He was off out, he said, and downed his tea with a grimace, shoving a crust of bread into his pocket as he left and pecking his mother on the cheek. He had outgrown his clothes and his bare feet were black with dirt. He sold the newspapers, Nellie explained as she poured from a large pewter teapot. There was no milk or sugar.

Nellie displaced a couple of children from the chair beside the piano. 'Don't be so bold! Leave that piano alone!' She rubbed their finger-marks off with her apron and sat down. 'I'm always afraid they'll wreck it. It was here when we moved in – I don' know who owned it or why they left it – but I'd be afraid they might come back for it someday. So! Tell me what's ailin' ya.'

Jane cradled the chipped teacup in her hands and sketched out her story as the bitter brew restored her.

'Yeh'll be goin' back to England, so?' asked Nellie.

'I can't. Not yet. I haven't the money for the journey, nor anything to go back to.' Her parents would not welcome their prodigal daughter. 'I'm needed at the hospital, anyway.'

She told Nellie about the Admissions Room.

'Yer workin' yerself to the bone, ya poor crayture.' Nellie's hands were reddened by work, like Jane's, contrasting as she raised her teacup with the pallor of her face. Her small daughter leant against her skirts, staring up at Jane.

'At least I can keep myself on my earnings. I suppose I should sell Edmond's clothes really – as long as no-one steals them. Someone was in my room.'

'When?' Nellie frowned.

'Yesterday, I think. I was late back, and so tired I didn't notice it until this morning. Someone had been through all my things. Did you see anyone go up?'

'I heard some bumping up there.' Nellie pointed at the ceiling: Jane's room was above. 'In the afternoon. I thought at first yeh were back from work, then I heard them – they were after coming down the stairs, talking out there in the hall. I went out to the children, the fellers went over the street and drove off in their carriage. I've seen them three divils many a time.'

'Do you know who they are?'

'Yer men work for Mr Lydon, and Mr Royce.' Nellie put a protective hand on her daughter's shoulder. 'If ya get behind wit yer rent they'll come and see ya – and God help ya.'

'But I'm all paid up,' said Jane. 'Why would they go through my things? They didn't even take anything.'

Nellie shook her head in defeat.

'Who knows? 'Tis not our place to ask. There's eight families live in this house, and none would so much as raise a whisper when them three come calling. It's as well ya weren't here.'

The cold fear returned.

'I can't live in a place where the landlord's men can walk in and out as they please. They must have had a key.'

'Ah sure, they'll probably leave ya alone now. Look it, if they took nothing then ya have nothing they want. Just pay the rent and keep quiet, and yeh'll be grand.'

'But I can't tolerate it – I'll have to find somewhere else.'

'Well, it's like this all over the town, wherever ya go there's a racket. Corporation Street they'll lend out money

215

and kill ya if ya don't pay back double, the Monto it's all about the girls, round here it's mainly the horses. And wherever ya go, if yer renting, ye'll be renting off Mr Royce. Sure, he owns the whole place, rackets and all.'

'I met him once. He's an MP, a very wealthy landowner, a respectable gentleman.'

'*Ha!* Very likely.' Nellie's eyes narrowed. 'We respect him here all right, but for different reasons, ya know?'

* * *

Jane had spent too long talking to Nellie and hurried on her way to the Meath with her apron and her nurse's cap bundled beneath her jacket to keep them dry in the rain. She was still weary from the day before, but work she must; it was all she had to live on, for now.

Before she had gone twenty yards, a resplendent black brougham came past, drawn by a pair of roans. The vehicle was far too grand for the dismal street and juddered on the setts as it went on slowly alongside her.

'*Hoo,*' said the driver, and reined the horses to a halt a little way ahead. Rainwater slid from the carriage roof and splashed on the road.

'Mrs Verity?' The carriage door opened and a gentleman with a narrow, sharp-nosed face leant his head out into the rain. 'I thought I had recognised you.'

She averted her gaze, hoping her face was hidden by the brim of her bonnet. He greeted her again.

'Mrs Jane Verity, the famous pianist?

She paused.

'Yes.' He obviously knew her; there was no point in denying it. 'And you are ...?'

'How extraordinary to stumble across you!' He tipped his hat with a smile. Brass buttons gleamed on his coat sleeve. 'How delightful! I much admired your performance, alongside your husband, at the Queen's Royal Theatre. His acting was utterly compelling. Such a pity that he became ill and, it seems, if you'll forgive me now, that you've fallen upon hard times.'

'My husband has passed away.' It was hard to say the words; she almost felt ashamed.

He gasped. 'Isn't that the most terrible tragedy?' Yet it seemed as if he had somehow known; he was ready with his sympathies. 'I am so very sorry to hear that. You must accept my sincere condolences on your loss. If there is anything at all I can do, I would very much like to be of assistance, out of the very deepest respect ...'

His eagerness to help was so convincing that she did not think to ask how he had noticed her in the street.

'It's very good of you, but I must be on my way to work. I don't play the piano any more, in fact. I'm to be at the Meath Hospital at half past eight.'

The rain became heavy, thudding on the carriage roof and enlarging the puddles in the street.

'Well now, you're nearly late, Mrs Verity.' He consulted a gold fob watch. 'My timepiece is showing twenty past the hour.'

She well knew it – she had heard the churches striking the quarter.

'Allow me to offer you a lift, madam?'

'It would most be improper for me to get into a stranger's carriage!'

He threw up his hands. 'How can I drive past and leave a talented lady like your good self walking in the rain, with the streets in such a filthy condition? It'll be only a few minutes to the hospital – a twenty-minute walk, I should think, for you?'

He would not desist and in the end she agreed, for her legs were aching and her feet were getting soaked as she stood trying to dissuade him. He reached down a gloved hand to help her step up into the carriage, and immediately rapped on the front glass with his cane, ordering the driver to the Meath Hospital. They set off at a good pace as she sat down facing him, her back to the driver.

She was at least under shelter and settled back on the black-leather, tobacco-smelling seat, brushing raindrops from her skirts and sleeves. When she glanced up again, she was startled to see that there was another man on the back seat, silent. She nodded politely at the fellow but he made no response. Between the shadow of his hat brim and his black scarf only a bulbous pock-marked nose could be seen. He sat with his legs spreading out the dark red velvet of his coat and his fists balled loosely on his thighs, his top hat brushing the carriage roof and his shadowed bulk occupying such a breadth of the carriage that the sharp-nosed man's narrow shoulders were squeezed against the upholstery beside the window.

Her route to the Meath was straightforward but after a few twists and turns they were bowling along Cork Street, away from the town, clattering past the canvas awnings of the shops as passers-by stared at the grand carriage. Now she would really be late.

'I said the Meath Hospital, not the Fever Hospital,' she said in alarm, but her companions took no notice.

She twisted around and knocked on the glass behind the driver. He briefly glanced back at her then merely shook the reins with a '*Ha!*' to urge the horses on.

'I must thank you for your help, but you're taking me out of my way,' she said as they approached the Fever Hospital, but the smaller man merely smirked.

'Unfortunately, Mrs Verity,' he said, 'there is a small question which someone wishes to discuss with you first. A kind of debt that wants to be settled.'

She had to get out. Outside the Fever Hospital there was a queue of traffic. As they slowed, she determined to jump down. She shifted on the seat, squeezing her bundle under her arm.

'I owe nothing to anyone.' She grabbed the arm-strap and made to stand up, but the big man planted his foot on her skirt and she sat back down with a bump. 'How dare you!' Her protest was cut short as the brougham jerked forward and she almost slid off her seat. They overtook the queue, causing an oncoming cart to swerve, and went on, picking up speed. She was being abducted.

'The Guvnor wants a word,' grinned the big man. Two gold teeth glinted in the shadow of his upper lip.

She could not think of getting out now, for the brougham was going too fast. With the horses at full gallop the vehicle lurched over a canal bridge and passed between open fields, swaying and bumping on the road. The rain had stopped but the carriage wheels splashed and dragged through deep puddles.

'I've settled my debts. How dare you take me away like this! I'm needed at the hospital – I'll be missed. The police will come after you. You have to let me go!'

But the men were silent, the sharp-nosed man wearing a malicious smile and his companion's heavy boot still weighing down her skirt. With the driver, that made three – were these the same men that had searched her room? The 'three divils' that Nellie had said worked for Lydon and Royce?

Before long the carriage passed between a pair of black stone gateposts topped with sculpted horseheads, disturbing a flock of crows. The driveway, planted either side with elms, wound between paddocks and pigsties, around a tall grey mansion with a stately portico set amongst lawns and cedars, and into a stable yard.

They left her locked up in the barn, alone, and her anger gave way to fear. For a while she stood still, in shock, as her eyes slowly adjusted to what little light crept beneath the eaves, then wondering if she might try to find a way out of this prison. Even if the chances of crossing the fields and making her way back to Dublin were small, she would rather not see 'the Guvnor' for 'a word'.

Chapter Twenty-nine

ROYCE PARK

She began to explore, feeling her way with a hand on the rough stone wall, but after a few yards tripped over a pile of pickaxes and shovels, landing on a wheelbarrow which seemed to be full of mildewed clothes. Something scuttled away. Grimacing, she stood up and dusted herself down. She was investigating the tools, wondering if she could dig her way out and wishing she could find a wood-axe, when the door was flung open with a bang.

'This way, Mrs Verity.'

The big man beckoned her out and she had no option but to follow. As she collected up her bundle her eye was drawn back along the line of light from the open door. In the far corner of the barn a rat ran over a dentist's chair. She shuddered. Straps dangled from heavy wooden arms.

He led her towards the big house, his heavy boots thumping the ground. She had seen him somewhere before, half recognised the stained frock coat of blood-red velvet and the harsh blue eyes. Perhaps at the hospital.

Entering through a back door, they went first along a service corridor and then through a spacious gilded hallway with Persian carpets and Chinese porcelain. All was silent apart from their footfalls. A fine white dust had stuck to her gloves and was difficult to dislodge.

She was brought into a room lined with gun racks, above which silver cups were displayed behind glass. A hunting rifle had been leant against a leather-topped table. A painting of a chestnut thoroughbred hung between the cabinets while elsewhere the walls bristled with stags' antlers. The big man remained impassive by the door as she studied the winners' names engraved on the silver trophies – racehorses and their owners. Each one bore the name of Mr T. Royce. The father of Alex Royce – Anna's future father-in-law. But what did he want with her?

Soon Theodore Royce himself strode into the room, attired as a country gentleman, his riding clothes perfectly tailored, boots gleaming with polish, his collar and cuffs starched and white.

'Bernard, of what were you thinking?' He laid a pistol on the table.

'Ya want me to search her, sir?'

'No! What were you doing, putting this exquisite young lady in the barn?' He shut the giant out. 'Good morning, Mrs Verity, and I trust that all is well with you today?'

Her anger resurged. 'How dare you treat me like this? Your men snatched me off the street, abducted me, unlawfully, against my will – I demand that you return me to Dublin immediately!'

Royce smiled, indifferently. 'I do apologise, Mrs Verity, for treating you in this unmannerly way, and assure you of your safe return to Dublin. But first, there is a small matter with which I require your kind help.' A mahogany armchair with claw feet creaked as he sank into it. He gestured that she too should sit down. Behind her was a stool with tripod legs of spiralling antelope horn and she perched awkwardly upon the nasty object.

'I don't see how I can possibly be of help to you.' She scowled at him.

His smile faded as he eyed her, stroking his glossy brown moustache with a manicured finger. 'You see, Mrs Verity, shortly before your husband unfortunately died – please accept my heartfelt condolences – he was one of two punters who won a huge sum on a horse called Kilfane, running in the Naas Races on the 14th of April – last Saturday. Kilfane had been at a hundred-to-one after a supposed injury, so when he came in first it was – unfortunate.'

'He came in first?' She stared at him. Was this the win of which Edmond had dreamed? No – it could not be – Edmond was ill in bed – he was in the Meath Hospital on the Sunday.

'My agent paid out twelve thousand pounds between the two gentlemen concerned: your husband and a Mr Tom Nesbitt.' Royce settled back in his chair, crossing one riding boot over the other, but his gaze was intense. 'I intend to recover it, Mrs Verity.'

'But Edmond never received anything. And Tom –' She stared at Royce, trying to remember: so much had happened. 'Tom was sick as well – he had cholera – the same day as your races. Tom was dead the next day. Edmond was in

223

hospital and died on the 19th of April. How could either of them have won money?'

'Perhaps they had placed their bets through an intermediary.'

'I don't believe my husband even had such a betting slip in his possession. I had been through his pocketbooks. I was worried about his gambling. Who collected the winnings? Your agent must know to whom the money was paid.'

'With almost a thousand punters a day,' Royce shrugged, 'I expect you know better than I, Mrs Verity.'

'In any case, if they did place bets, then they were entitled to their winnings.'

'Not if the race was fixed.' Royce bared his teeth and crinkled the corners of his eyes; it could hardly be called a smile. 'Both men had bet on a single horse, Kilfane: the money won from his race at the Curragh was evidently staked on his race at Naas. What were the chances of Kilfane winning both races, especially a horse as beset by problems as we were led to believe? He ran fifth at Lucan, collapsed after winning the Curragh and was rumoured to be unfit for Naas until the last moment.' Royce rose from his chair and went to inspect the oil painting of the chestnut horse. 'This was my horse, Lucius. Did you ever see anything as beautiful that was not in human form? Lucius was the favourite at Naas, had been very strong in training, yet ran erratically. He fell at the fourth fence, broke his leg, and had to be shot. He'd been named for a dear, dear friend, and we grieved at his passing.'

'I'm sorry for your horse. But I still don't think I can help you. I have nothing. Edmond was buried in a pauper's grave.'

Royce continued as if she had not spoken: 'As for Kilfane, I suspected the rumours of his injury had been exaggerated. I demanded a Turf Club investigation, which found nothing – those gentlemen have no real powers. So, I sent my men round to Dr Wright, Kilfane's owner. He maintained that he was not connected with the bets and had not bet on his horse himself, having been in two minds about entering him for Naas. And that, surely, brings me back to you.'

'But I know nothing at all of it.' A memory arose, however, of Edmond's green glass bottle of pills. *Doctor's orders,* he had said.

Perhaps Royce saw her hesitation. 'You're taking me for a fool.' A nasty edge entered his voice.

'You've no right to question me like this.' Jane knew that she was the one who had been wronged, and who had lost money. 'I knew nothing of my husband's bets. He kept it all secret, or I'd have stopped him. He gambled away all our savings with nothing to show for it. I've lost everything. Why do you think I'm renting your miserable room and working for a pittance at the hospital? I'd have gone back to London if I had the money.'

'Maybe you think it better to conceal your newfound riches to avoid attracting attention. Perhaps you already knew that a large amount of money was unfairly won – seven thousand in your husband's case.'

'Well, I can't help you.' But she wondered if Royce was partly in the right? What had Edmond said about the races and the stimulant pills, and when had he said it? In any case – 'I don't have any money.'

'You see, Mrs Verity, my son is about to marry. The

celebrations to be held on his country estate must mark him out as a man who will advance in life. If he is not to be a general, then at least he'll be a baronet. Money is required for his advancement and required at the present moment – this is not the time for me to be made into a fool. You must be hiding your husband's winnings – and I will have them back.' His expression hardened. 'If you're bamboozling me …'

So, it had come to this: he was directly threatening her. This supposed gentleman had no scruples about extorting money to buy his way through society. Her heart thumped with fear, but she would not waver.

'You're outrageous. You even had my room – in your rack-rent ruin – searched before you abducted me. So you must know that I don't have the money.'

'Then where is it?' Now Royce glanced at the pistol where it lay on the table. 'I must have answers. What are you hiding? You must have known something.'

'I can tell you precisely nothing.' What if he shot her? Cold fear sank from her heart into the pit of her stomach. She kept her tone calm. 'Rather than issuing threats, you should return me to the city before I'm missed. I have no winnings, and know nothing about your horse racing.'

'Return you.' Royce stood and walked over to the table. 'Indeed? Or make you into a warning to others?'

She flinched as he picked up the pistol and tapped the butt against his palm, as if he weighed what to do, and did not care if he shot her or not.

'*Bernard!*' he shouted.

Immediately the big man came in; he had been waiting.

Royce pointed at her. 'The stable yard,' he said.

As Bernard made to grab her arm, she fended him off.

'I can walk.' She was determined to stay dignified. She was not going to beg or plead.

Royce led the way. They returned through the service corridor. She walked behind Royce, keeping pace with the footfall of his polished boots, uncertain of everything except that every step took her nearer to her fate and that Bernard was behind her, ready to drag her forward if she failed.

'Go and stand by the barn. Don't turn round,' ordered Royce once they were outside. He trained the pistol on her as she passed in front of him.

She stood with her forehead to the wall; her nurse's apron, she realised, was still clenched under her arm. Would her absence be noticed at the hospital? Would anyone ask the police to search for her? Might they question Nellie? Or perhaps she would not be missed? She heard Royce's footsteps behind her, then all was silent. She wished him to hell. Then, in that moment, she knew that William would miss her. His aloofness was a front. If only she could see him once more, even just for one more kiss, one more farewell –

The pistol shot was at close range. The crack of it echoed in the yard. Crows flapped up and cawed.

Something clattered on the ground.

'Take her back to Dublin,' said Royce.

She turned around, her ears still ringing. The pistol's smoking muzzle was pointing up into the air.

'Come back to me with answers. Or you'll not leave Dublin alive.' Royce brought the pistol down by his side. Then he strode back into the house.

As Jane walked to the black brougham, she realised her

legs were shaking. Bernard, replacing his hat on his head, offered her a steadying arm.

'*Hup yeh go!*' He handed her up and slammed the door.

The carriage pulled swiftly away down the drive, between the black gateposts and back towards Dublin. Alone inside, Jane leant back trembling on the upholstery. If only Royce's threats were empty. But what about the dentist's chair? The old clothes in the barn? Where the white dust had clung to the hem of her skirts it had made tiny holes with burnt margins. Quicklime, she thought, for disposing of the dead.

What were her options: go to the police, get out of Dublin, or find a huge sum of money which she didn't have? And what to tell Anna? Dazzled by Theodore's wealth and seduced by Alex's masculine charm, she would soon be wedded to that family for good. What did Alex know of his father's murderous methods, and what was he capable of himself?

Chapter Thirty

THE NAMESAKE

Jane heard the bells striking twelve as the brougham arrived at the Meath Hospital. Easing its way past the waiting patients in the forecourt, the carriage came to a halt at the front steps.

'Jane!' Sister Aloysius bustled up to her as soon as she arrived in the Admissions Room. 'Are you all right?'

'Yes, thank you. I'm sorry I'm late – I overslept.' It was a relief to be within the hospital's solid walls and in the company of the nurses and orderlies.

'You don't look as if you've slept at all. Poor woman, you look exhausted.'

'I'll manage, Sister.' She was still trembling.

'It was only yesterday that your husband passed. Take what time you need. If you're not able for it, then go back home and rest.'

'But there's so much to be done here.' The Admissions Room was crowded as usual.

'Ah sure, it's busy. It'll always be busy whether you're working or not.'

'I'd rather be working, Sister. I'm sorry I was late.'

'Could I have some help over here, please?' It was William. 'I'll go.'

Tying her apron behind her back, Jane went over to him. His patient, a woman, lay on an examination couch with her head turned sideways and her hand over her eyes. A lancet lay on an instrument trolley beside a pewter basin. He had drained an abscess in her groin.

'I need a fresh basin of water, please, cotton dressings, and mercurial ointment.'

Normally Jane would have been able to deal with the wound alone, but now she hesitated.

William was studying her, the two vertical lines of his frown deepening. 'I'll help you.' He drew a sheet over the woman's exposed wound and stooped to speak to her. 'Just stay still, my dear. We'll soon have that dressed for you.'

She nodded as he patted her shoulder.

Jane followed him as he wheeled the trolley towards the sluice room.

'I'm sorry for your loss,' he said, as soon as they were alone. 'I feel that ...'

She said nothing and stood watching him as he pumped water to rinse out the basin.

'That time when you came to me in my rooms. I should have done more. I should have taken on your husband's case.'

'Well, it's too late now.' And what of that horrible moment when she had heard him arguing with Wright about Edmond's death? Wright had caught her by the wrist. She had heard Wright accuse him. *You had the means to free her.* 'Dr Wright said you tried to stop Edmond's treatment. That you wanted ...'

'You know me, Jane. I'm the same man that you knew before.' He stopped pumping and turned to her, his gaze intense. 'Do you think I would harm him? Do you think I would do that?'

'I don't know what to think. I'm ...' She faltered and stopped. She remembered him in his consulting room, standing aloof by the window. 'You said you had changed.'

'Changed! Yes, but not in that way. Never! The reason I advised stopping those pills was that I thought they were harmful. Dr Murphy thought the same. And after that I –'

'What's happening with Peggy Reardon?' Sister Aloysius had come to find them. 'She's bleeding under that sheet.'

'I'm just getting a dressing.' Jane hurried off to the dressings press, leaving William to manage the trolley.

She had to make herself focus on the patients.

But that afternoon she met the constant demands of her work with a mind barely present. She sifted through every detail and dwelt on her abduction, blaming herself for going in the carriage, for failing to escape the barn, for being unable to convince Royce of her ignorance of Edmond's gambling. Yet he had no right to snatch her from the street and threaten her with a pistol. She had really believed that he would murder her. He had done it before, she was sure. She thought of the old clothes in the barn: whose bones lay in quicklime on his lands? What were the sources of his wealth? Nellie had spoken of the gangs that controlled

Dublin, and of rack-renting, illegal gambling, extortion.

If there was something she could do to meet Royce's demands, she might be safer to do it. She would recheck Edmond's trunk but, if nothing was there, she might as well resign herself to an inescapable fate. Then her stomach lurched: she had to warn Anna. With her head full of wedding preparations, she would be reluctant to believe that her future father-in-law, so elegant and wealthy, was capable of such an outrage. Yet what would her future be, isolated at Mount Belvedere and married into such a family?

* * *

By the early evening Jane finished work and went directly to Fitzwilliam Square. It did not matter that she was uninvited. She would never forgive herself if she kept silent. There was no point in changing from her work clothes or tidying her hair. Circumstances had rapidly altered her appearance and she could no longer appear as a lady. The sable wrap and all her jewellery, even her wedding ring, were in the pawnbroker's shop, and her clothes had absorbed the musty smell of the tenement.

Yet the housemaid was polite when Jane said she was a friend of Anna's and after a short wait Jane was shown upstairs to the back sitting room. Anna was at a bureau writing letters and rose hastily to greet her.

'My poor Jane … it's been so hard for you … I was beside myself to read of Edmond's illness.' She offered Jane a chair.

'Edmond has died.' Jane remained standing.

'Died?' Anna reached out and embraced her. 'Oh, Jane!'

'Yes.' She shut her eyes and put her forehead on Anna's shoulder. She felt Anna's arms tighten around her and nuzzled her brow against her friend's collarbone. But she did not cry.

'When?' asked Anna after a long pause.

'Yesterday morning, early. He was dead by the time I got to the hospital.'

'I'll come to the funeral. I must pay my respects. I'll do my best to support you.'

'There is no funeral. I could not make the arrangements. The funeral directors are struggling with the cholera epidemic, everything is so expensive, and I had no money, so the hospital buried him somewhere called Broadstone. I don't even know where he lies.'

'Oh Jane, I'm so sorry. I don't know what to say or do. There must be something I can do to help you.'

'I don't think there is. But thank you.' Jane disengaged herself from Anna's embrace. As she did so she suddenly noticed that Lucia Meredith Browne was sitting on a frilled chintz sofa, reading a catalogue.

Lucia stared at Jane's boots, scuffed and muddy from the street. Then she turned her head to her daughter.

'Who, exactly, is this, Anna?'

'You remember, Mama, my friend Jane Verity. You met her. The talented piano player. Her husband is – was – Edmond Verity the actor. He has just died.'

'I don't remember her, I'm afraid.' Lucia's chestnut hair was styled into heavy rolls around her face and neck; it would be a great length when let down. 'Is she applying for the scullery maid's position?'

'*Mama!*'

'I'm working at the Meath Hospital, Mrs Meredith Browne,' Jane interrupted. She was reminded of the painting of the racehorse Lucius, of the glossy red-brown of his coat. Here, surely, was his namesake: the *dear friend*, who had laughed in Theodore Royce's arms as they waltzed, and whom he had bedecked with diamonds. 'They're greatly in need of help, due to the cholera epidemic.'

'Jane has been doing a truly noble thing, in spite of the disaster that's struck her, Mama. You should not judge her by her dress.'

Lucia's eyes returned to the catalogue. 'Don't neglect your correspondence. The invitations must all be sent out by the end of this week.'

'I must speak to you, Anna – about another matter.' Jane wondered how much she could say. Was Lucia promoting her daughter's marriage for the sake of a closer connection with Theodore? She would have liked to have spoken in confidence, but Anna missed the hint.

'Of course. What is it, Jane?'

Jane swallowed. She felt panic rising in her chest. *The pistol shot. The screaming birds.*

'It's about the Royces.' She watched Lucia who was still looking at her catalogue, but no longer reading. 'I was abducted early this morning by ruffians working for Mr Royce.'

'*Jane!*' Anna stared, covered her mouth with her hands, then let them drop. 'What are you saying? Abducted by Alex?'

'No – his father. Theodore Royce. He threatened me with a pistol over some money.'

Anna stared at her, eyes wide, uncomprehending.

'*Unthinkable!*' Lucia slapped the catalogue down beside her on the sofa. 'Mr Royce would never, ever, do such a thing. How dare you come here, in such a disgraceful state, and with your wild stories?'

'I was locked in a barn.' Jane pressed her palms together. Her hands were sweating. 'I saw – I can't say – a chair – old clothes – quicklime –'

'*Outrageous!*' Lucia sat stiff with shock, as though a rat had run across her skirts. 'The Royces are the height of respectability – true gentlemen.'

'You mean they're wealthy.' Jane was convinced now: Lucia must be allied with Theodore Royce. He likely kept her ignorant of his crimes. 'How does Theodore Royce earn his money?'

'He has extensive properties,' Lucia said. 'Commercial, residential – his estate in County Cork ...'

'But I live in one of those properties. It's a tenement. It's in an atrocious state, yet the rent I pay is almost all my salary. I live on bread and black tea.' Jane no longer cared what Lucia thought of her – let her hear the truth. 'If I had not pawned my clothes I'd be unable to buy coal. The tenants are intimidated. If they complain he increases their rent, and if they fall into arrears his ruffians come calling. He threatened me with a pistol because he thought I had some gambling money of his. Are those the actions of a gentleman?'

Lucia stared at Jane. She opened her mouth to protest, but Jane had turned to Anna.

'You should reconsider your marriage, Anna. What does Alex know of his father's business?'

Anna looked bewildered. She shook her head. 'He's never said anything. It's not really my place to ask. But it can't possibly be as bad as you say! Perhaps there's been some misunderstanding? Robert says Alex is respected as an officer, and highly popular. I can't think badly of him!'

'Please, Anna, just don't marry him –'

'Save your melodramas for the stage!' Lucia was recovering her voice. 'Anna, your failed actress friend cannot be permitted to dictate the course of your life. I've always said you're far too impressionable. Now, I suggest you ring for Geraldine to show her out.'

'If you would only reflect, Mrs Meredith Browne?' As Jane spoke, she knew it was hopeless. 'Should you not have more scruples about an alliance with such a family?'

No, Lucia had been seduced – her love of fashion and wealth had turned her head.

'I have nothing to say to you. You will please leave at once.'

Perhaps the wife and daughter of a Dublin Castle official might obtain the Royces some leverage in the administration. As Jane turned to go, Anna jumped up.

'I'll see you out myself, Jane.'

'Make sure she doesn't take anything!' Lucia called after them.

Anna closed the sitting-room door and leant against it. Her face was flushed.

'I'm so sorry about my mother,' she whispered. 'She's awfully snobbish. We'll talk downstairs.'

In the front hall, she stopped.

'What exactly happened to you, Jane?'

'I was lured into a carriage and driven to a mansion. They locked me in a barn. Then Theodore Royce threatened to shoot me. He makes money from bookmaking. He said Edmond owed him some gambling money. A race had been fixed – he'd been cheated. But I don't know anything about it. Edmond lost everything we had and I didn't even know it was happening. I haven't a penny. He said he'd kill me if I didn't find it.'

'Why don't you go to the police?'

'How can I prove anything? In any case, his men would stop me –'

'Anna, what are you doing?' Lucia had come out of the sitting room and stood on the landing.

'The barn. The chair, people's clothes, it was as if they had killed people –'

'*I'm coming up, Mama!*' Anna called out. She opened the front door.

'Be careful of yourself.' Jane embraced her friend.

'I love him, Jane. I can't be without him.'

In Jane's arms Anna seemed insubstantial, as though someone might erase her with a swipe of his hand.

Chapter Thirty-one

OVER OUR HEADS

It had been a hard year so far, a hard time to be a physician in Dublin. The famine had squeezed its victims from the country into the city, and was multiplying the numbers of the dying. It seemed it would never end; week after week there was no escape from the pressure. As summer began, cholera cases continued to rise. He had to harden his heart to the decrepitude of the starving poor who came in at last gasp, and to the keening relatives of the unburied dead. Just as William's body ached with weariness, other problems weighed his mind down like lead.

He attempted a further discussion with Wright after a couple of weeks, hoping that he could do it without provoking him. There was now no way of winning the argument over Verity but, in the unlikely case that Wright didn't know, he wanted to make him aware of how much arsenic was in the pills, for the sake of other patients. He arranged an appointment to see Wright in his office but was kept waiting for half an hour beyond their agreed time, as his work piled up in the wards.

Then Wright disputed William's results.

'It's impossible that my pills should contain a toxic quantity of arsenic. I've prescribed them to many patients with great efficacy.'

'But my analytic methods are well established. I use the Marsh test. All that is required is to digest the sample with pure zinc and vitriol and ignite the gas given off. The smoke creates a deposit of –'

'Of course. Your laboratory – of which you are so proud – I might come and see how the process works.'

Grateful that Wright appeared open to understanding the science, William led him down to his little room in the basement, no bigger than a broom cupboard with a workbench that was merely a shelf along one wall, and explained the process, showing him the black films: control solution in different dilutions, Verity's gastric contents, and the pill he had analysed.

'I thought you should know the strength of your preparation. I'd not want another patient to be harmed.'

'*Hm.*' Wright poked amongst the apparatus, examining the small spirit burner that William used for a flame, the glass vessels, the bottles of reagents. 'You can't keep these materials in the hospital. It's not safe. You could cause an explosion, a fire.' He seemed to occupy all the space, so that William instinctively shrank back until he was bracing himself against the end wall. 'Have you obtained permission from the management committee to dabble with these dangerous chemicals?'

'Well – no – I didn't think it was needed. I got the room – no one else wanted it – from the Clerk of Records. It was too damp for his papers. There's no danger from my equipment.'

'I think it prudent to consult the committee. If these items are safe then you won't object to removing them to your own house.'

'My house? It might mean taking patients' samples home.'

'In any case, I'm a very busy man and I'm sure you have your own work to do. The decision rests with the hospital, not with you or me.'

'But the pills?'

'I certainly will not be changing my well-established and highly respected practice on the basis of your chemistry experiments.'

With that Wright returned to his office.

His jaw set, William locked the room. By late autumn he would be in New York in Professor Charles's laboratory, with no need to fight over a broom cupboard. But what to do about Wright until then? William had hoped for a quiet life before leaving for America, but could see, in all conscience, that this hope was vain. It was impossible to tolerate the man as his superior. In Birmingham he'd despised Wright, who, though salaried as the physician to the workhouse, had rarely attended except to write inaccurate death certificates. Wright had left Birmingham under a cloud. How had he arrived in Dublin with excellent credentials, starting a senior post at the Meath and a lucrative private practice? What if those credentials had been fabricated? Wright's behaviour this year had been highly suspicious, what with Edmond Verity's poisonous pills and the whole business about the wife's insurance claim. Now his response to being shown the science was to do away with the laboratory that had produced it.

But however much he thought about it, it still came to the same question: what possible reason could Wright have had for poisoning his own patient? He wanted to speak to Jane alone, fully explain to her about the arsenic, ask her more about her husband's treatment and whether Wright might have had a motive to harm him. But she kept herself busy and seemed to be avoiding him.

Joseph, on the other hand, was always demanding his time. Once again, he caught William in the corridor for a discussion in confidence. To William's dismay, it was about another of Wright's decisions.

'Can you not speak to Dr Wright about this yourself?' He wasn't yet ready to begin another dispute.

'I don't know how best to approach him – I need the work he gives me.' As they moved to one side to let the orderlies wheel patients past, Joseph lowered his voice. 'I had a young man in with pneumonia. He was doing well, was almost ready to discharge home. Yesterday Dr Wright came in and made me prescribe him a large dose of morphia. When I asked him why he had done that, he said the man was in pain with coughing, and it was to relieve his suffering. But he never woke up again. This morning I certified him for burial.'

'What dose was prescribed?' William was alarmed: Wright was a danger.

'Forty grains!'

'*How much?*' William could not believe what he was

hearing. Ten grains might be hazardous to a man with a lung complaint.

'Forty grains. I said to Dr Wright afterwards that we had as good as killed him. He told me that the man would have died anyway and, when I disagreed, said that had he been sent home to the Liberties he would have brought contagion from the hospital out to his family and neighbours and spread it on the streets when he went begging. The fellow was a singer of ballads, often on Dame Street collecting pennies in a hat – I don't call that begging. At any rate Dr Wright made me certify the man as tuberculous consumption and, when I said that was wrong, he shouted at me. He said my misdiagnosis had led to fatal complications.' Joseph's eyes were red-rimmed: he had taken the reproach to heart. 'I was the one who had to break the news to the wife.'

'Are you sure he'd been improving?' Joseph could be impulsive, thought William, but he also genuinely cared about the patients.

'I'd seen him every day for a week, and the signs of infection were reducing. He would have been well enough in two or three days to go home. Yet Wright didn't even seem to register it. He'd said nothing about consumption when the man was alive. Sister Aloysius wouldn't back me – she said it wasn't my place to dispute a senior's decisions, and that the man had after all been racked by coughing which the morphia had relieved. Will you support me?'

With a sigh, William agreed to accompany Joseph, but their attempt to challenge Wright failed. He was unmoved by Joseph's arguments.

'Dr Murphy, I have already tried to explain to you your

misdiagnosis of this case. And Dr Doughty, I fail to see how this matter concerns you at all, as you had not even seen the case.'

'To be truthful,' said William, 'it's not just my concern. The case ought to be brought before the hospital management committee. That morphia has deprived a young man of his life.'

'I detect, Dr Doughty, a certain malice in your constant attacks on me. I have the right to defend myself and I would remind you both that you occupy a perilous position in your respective careers. As you know, Dr Doughty, I have provided you a reference to Professor Edwin Charles for your proposed move to New York and may write to revoke it. As for you, Dr Murphy, your revolutionary ideas are well known to the medical staff and your latest political outburst at the physicians' meeting has been noted. Know your place as my subordinate, and keep it, or I shall be reporting your seditious tendencies to Dublin Castle. Once that is on your record, you'll find yourself at best unemployable, and at worst sailing in a convict ship to Van Diemen's Land.'

William stared at Wright in horror. He and Joseph had raised a legitimate concern about a patient's treatment and received threats in return. He glanced at Joseph and saw that he was glaring at Wright and had clenched his jaw. He was about to launch an explosive argument which might well lead to Wright carrying out his threats.

'Come, Dr Murphy, there are patients waiting, we can do no good here.' Without acknowledging Wright, William dragged Joseph out of the office and along the corridor.

'What in hell did you say at the physician's meeting?'

Joseph snorted. 'You don't agree with me either. A lot of us though – Irishmen –'

'You're too outspoken. Everyone knows you hold strong views, but –'

'*Strong views!*'

'You must be more careful –'

'The cholera epidemic – we're over our heads in it.'

They were on the half-landing of the stairs and Joseph stopped to draw William into a corner.

'Yet the British government is to deduct half a million pounds from the grants to the Dublin hospitals. Three years' potato crops have failed, the landlords have depopulated the land, so now it must be the turn of the towns to suffer. Our gentry are ruined, our traders bankrupt, taxes sky-high, property worthless – how are we to support our hospitals without the grants? The Fever Hospital at Cork Street will be half-closed down, the fever tents taken away, and what will happen then? People dying comfortless in their hovels for want of care, the Kilmainham Fever Sheds overrun, contagion rampant through overcrowded tenements – in the ruins of houses that were wealthy back in the days when Ireland governed itself.'

'It's going to be difficult.' William shook his head. It was the first he had heard of the grants being curtailed.

'*Difficult!* I'll tell you this now, that out of this cruelty one good thing has come, that all rational Irishmen are united against English misrule, against this indifference to the sick poor, against the burdening of this desperate city.' Joseph's cheeks were red; his blood was up and he gave off a smell of sweat, tobacco smoke and low taverns.

'And the physicians' meeting?' William asked, with a sinking feeling. 'What was said?'

'They concluded we must do more, with less. But I told them: before every person who is able has either died or emigrated, we must drive out our oppressors, by force – why should we be afraid of it? – and proclaim an independent Irish State –'

'You should not have said that! It's sedition!'

'Then can we drive out famine. By driving out famine we drive out disease.' Joseph was in full flow. 'How many lives would be saved if the meat and grain – exported, under armed guard, every single day to England – were forced to remain in Ireland instead? If the people were fed so that they were stronger to resist sickness? What man of honour would not take up arms –'

'Lower your voice, for God's sake!' William put a hand on Joseph's sleeve; he had to try to calm him. 'I share your grief for the dead, and your fear for the living, but much can – and should – be done without bloodshed. An armed uprising? Of doctors?' William had to smile at the idea. 'Everywhere's garrisoned with soldiers – imagine the death toll, and for what? There'd still be famine and disease – no money for the hospitals – and your doctors dead or deported. Save your energy for reform – improved sanitation alone would vastly improve the public health.'

Joseph wrenched his arm away. 'I will not rest,' he snapped, 'until I see justice done in my country.' He turned on his heel and clattered downstairs, his thin shoulders held high.

William sighed. Joseph was right about the situation at Kilmainham – it was bad enough already. For the government to force the Fever Hospital at Cork Street to close their tents and let Kilmainham handle the situation – they were either ignorant of the situation, or so corrupt that they did not care. Recently a local dispensary doctor had come into the hospital to volunteer his help, for which all had been grateful. Dr Enville had said that in one of the fever sheds at the Kilmainham Workhouse he'd seen thirty-five people lying for three days on an area of the floor too small to hold them, so that their bodies blocked the door from closing and let in the weather.

Joseph had strong principles, yet he did himself no favours – always late for work and dabbling in God knows what. After last year's failed uprising in Ballingarry, the military had driven opposition underground, but it seemed that the rebel 'clubs' still operated a network. The newspapers reported trials of men who had sworn faith on the Bible, sworn to **'pursue a traitor seven leagues at sea and bring him back to the committee'**, and sworn to **'visit'** – meaning to intimidate, or even assassinate – any landlord who took a farm from a poor man and gave it to others. Support for the 'Ribbon Clubs' was said to be strong in Liverpool and Belfast, while the authorities in Dublin sought out the men who relayed money and arms to rural areas where clubs existed under other names. Government spies infiltrated their meetings and informed on the conspirators. A list of secret signs and passphrases had seen its bearer sentenced to seven years' hard labour. If Wright were to report Joseph to Dublin Castle the military would arrest and interrogate him. They could be brutal; everyone had seen patients who bore injuries from beatings.

Wright would not care. William ran across him soon afterwards in St Aidan's Ward, striding up and down, shouting at the nurse: 'My patient has to be admitted for an operation by Mr Riley, and you're telling me *no*? Who are you to tell me?'

The nurse said the whole hospital was full of sick people. Anyone could see the ward was overcrowded, with two feverish patients to a bed, and on paliasses improvised on the floor – contagion was everywhere even though they kept the windows open night and day. Dr Wright's patient might get sick if he admitted her.

Jane, with her head down, was washing patients with a rag and bucket. She looked up at William as if pleading for help and he went straight to her. Two lay embraced, a mother and child; she had just brought them up from the Admissions Room. The woman was toothless, shrivelled with starvation, consumed with fever; lice wandered in her hair.

'Will she live?' whispered Jane.

He met Jane's eyes with a brief glance: unlikely.

'She's only thirty-two,' Jane said. She started on the daughter, who was encased in a flannel gown stiff with dirt. There seemed no way of unfastening it.

'They stitch them into their clothes for the winter.' He'd become adept at using the stethoscope through the layers, pressing the ebonite funnel into the fabric as the children squirmed away. The little girl stirred in her sleep and rolled on her back, away from her mother's side. 'The daughter might improve,' he said. 'She looks familiar, somehow.' The child's heart-shaped face was flushed with fever, her chest rose and fell rapidly.

Jane had also recognised her. 'I've met these two, begging by the bank. The mother told me their story once: they were evicted by their landlord. The rest of the family are dead. She'll have to get better, for Orla's sake. Won't you, Margaret?'

Margaret did not open her eyes.

It was hopeless, thought William.

'See if you can get the mother to take some rice-water,' he said, with a sigh. 'Apply cold compresses with vinegar to her head. If you can treat the fever and get some nourishment – however slight – into her, then she might have a chance.'

'Please God,' said Jane, 'let her survive, else what will become of her child?'

Chapter Thirty-two

ORLA

Margaret Keaney, with her last strength, stood up in the middle of the ward with her grey hair flowing, spread her arms and screamed.

'May you die without a priest, Theodore Royce! May you be accursed in the sight of God and hated by your fellow man! May your vile blood burst out of your chest and may you cry for water in vain! May the walls of Mount Belvedere crumble to dust and the Almighty's curse rest upon your children!'

Then she collapsed.

'Theodore Royce must have been her landlord,' Jane muttered to Sister Aloysius, who had crossed herself. 'She had been evicted by him.'

They lifted her back to her bed, but she was unresponsive, her breaths rapid and shallow.

Yet as she declined her daughter revived. Orla sat up in their bed and spoke to her softly, trying to wake her.

Sister Aloysius felt the pulse.

'Not much longer,' she whispered to Jane.

Jane widened her eyes. What would become of the child? She brought her a cup of stirabout.

'Mammy's sleeping,' said Orla. She sipped gratefully at the thin gruel. Children had such powers of recovery, thought Jane: if only it were the same for their parents. 'When will she wake up?'

'Have you anyone else to look after you?' Sister Aloysius asked her. 'You see, child, you're well enough to go home, but your mammy must stay here.'

'I'll go to my grandma,' said the girl.

'Where is your grandmother?' Jane asked. Surely the mother had said that she was dead.

'She's coming from Cashel,' said the girl. 'When we were walking, she had a pain in her leg. She said she'd rest. She went to sleep with my sister, Niamh. Ma and Da made a house of branches over them.'

Jane turned to Sister Aloysius, whose face was furrowed with pity between the white leaves of her veil. She drew the nun aside, lowering her voice.

'I spoke to Margaret once, when they were begging near the Carlisle Bridge. She told me that only she and her child had survived – the rest of the family including her mother and daughter had died on the road from Cashel, the father outside the workhouse gates in Kildare. I think she could not bear to tell Orla that the branches were a grave.'

Sister Aloysius reached out and touched Orla's shoulder. 'Maybe they will not come to Dublin,' she said gently.

'I'll go and look for them.' The sharp little chin jutted out.

'Sure it's over a hundred miles. How will you be doing that?'

'I'll walk.'

'It's too far for a little child like you,' Jane said.

'I walked here, didn't I? So, I can walk back. I'll walk back until I can find my grandma.'

'Child, you must have someone in Dublin you can go to.' Sister Aloysius did not sound hopeful. 'Your mammy-grandma's in Cashel, what about your daddy-grandma?'

'She's in heaven, and so's my daddy now.'

At least she knew the truth about those deaths.

'We went to see Cousin Feargal and Aunty Teresa, but they had gone away. We slept on the bridge. Mammy said that if we had one wall at our back it was a quarter of a house, but I was afraid.'

Later that day Mrs Keaney's face was dappled with the blue-grey shadows of death and her body cooling beside the child who still nestled against her.

'Orla.' Jane nerved herself to explain to the child.

But beneath a tress of dirty hair that tangled across her face, Orla's eyes were already red and puffy. 'Mammy's passed away, hasn't she?' She lay down again, embracing the dead woman, her face to her mother's breast.

Jane went to find Sister Aloysius. 'I don't know what to do.'

'What do you mean? You know you're to get one of the doctors to certify her and then the orderlies will take her for burial.'

'I'm talking about the child – she's well enough to be sent out. We can't send a young child into the street.'

'We're going to need that bed, I'm afraid. I'll send a porter over to the Mendicity Institution to see if they can take her.

She'll get a bit of schooling and be sent into honest work.'

The pain was physical. Jane's arms ached with pity, with memories. 'Maybe I can take her. I'll take her back to my lodging house.'

'Who'll watch her during the day?' Sister Aloysius said in shocked tones. 'You're working here, remember?'

'She can watch herself. I'll leave her some food and water. At least she'll be under shelter.'

'Sure if she doesn't set fire to your room, she'll steal everything and be out the door.'

'Shouldn't we be charitable, Sister?'

'And what will you do with all the thousands of others, all the orphans we see? They'd fill up everywhere, you'll have them sleeping on the mantelpiece and in your presses. Now, you have enough to do, my dear, with your work, and you struggle to keep yourself, I don't doubt. So don't go looking for more trouble. We'll keep her here until we find her a place.'

But after her mammy's body was 'taken to heaven' Orla remained on St Bridget's Ward for days. Jane made her up a paliasse on the floor so that the bed could be used. The Mendicity Institution and all the other orphanages, it seemed, were full. There was the workhouse, but Sister Aloysius, for all her firmness, hesitated. Jane did not need to mention the mother's fear of the 'black bottle'.

For the first week Jane fed the listless, grieving child with mutton broth, fresh bread, and porridge. Orla slowly gathered strength. Jane came in earlier than usual one morning to delouse her and wash her matted hair, which proved to be a glossy dark brown. The blue eyes in the thin face began to sparkle, as Nathan's might have done. On the eighth day Orla began to hum tunes and at fourteen days she pointed her chin upwards and sang like a wren, her strong, clear notes floating from a tiny mouth. She sang lyrics her mother must have taught her: love, heartbreak, green hills, sheltering valleys and flowing water. She even danced, head held high, elaborating patterns with her feet. Then she learned to attach herself to the nurses, spooning medicines and stirabout into the mouths of patients who were too weak to feed themselves.

Sadly, the tide of incoming patients increased: they went from two per bed to three, and then to four; the numbers were too great for the nurses to have any chance of looking after them and the management committee of the hospital ordered that as many patients must be discharged as possible to make way for new admissions; all the physicians were ordered to do more frequent rounds with that aim in mind.

Orla was following Dr Enville when William came round. He raised his eyebrows when he spotted her.

'What's that child doing?'

Dr Enville, who was English, was seeing an Irish-speaking patient, with Orla translating.

'She's been helping out in the ward,' Jane said. 'She's easily earning her keep.'

'If there's no place, she'll just have to go, we can't keep her here,' he said. 'The management committee have issued an order that any patients who can be discharged home must go. For one thing she might fall ill again in this foul atmosphere.'

'She has no home.' Jane bit her lip. She could not face parting from the child. 'She's only seven.'

'We're hoping for a place at the Mendicity Institution,' Sister Aloysius added. 'The best place to take the child but they're crammed full. Maybe the next day?'

'I'll take her,' Jane blurted out. 'Let me take her home.'

'Not appropriate, I'm afraid,' William said. 'Really, not a good idea.' He called Orla over and she scampered up to him and stood contemplating him with her narrow chin held high and her hands clasped behind her back.

'I saw you before,' she said. 'By the bank.'

He frowned at her. 'I don't recollect.' But then something changed in his face and tinged his complexion pink.

'You gave me a whole half-a-crown, to pray for you. I've done it as hard as I could, every night since.'

William shot a glance at Jane. His mouth opened as if to speak, then softened into an awkward grin and he said nothing.

'Did it work?' Orla looked from one to the other. 'No? I'll keep on with it, so?'

William shook his head. 'But, child, the hospital is only for sick people, you see.'

'I'll keep on with it, only, sir – doctor – please don't send me away.'

'But you cannot live in a hospital.'

Orla brought her hands into a position of prayer. 'Don't send me away and I'll pray for you always. To Saint Valentine, like you said, for your heart's desire that can never come true.'

William stared down at the child, his eyebrows drawing together in a frown and his mouth compressed in sadness. Then he retreated. 'I'll go and see who else I can discharge,' he muttered to Jane, avoiding her eyes.

She watched him walk away. What did he still feel?

Sister Aloysius cleared her throat.

'Please continue your duties, Jane,' she said. 'Mrs Houlihan is calling out over there – go and see what the matter is. And Orla, you're not to pester the doctors.'

Jane, as she brought Mrs Houlihan a cup of water, watched William stooping over a patient at the other end of the ward. Saint Valentine had not granted his heart's desire. It seemed she was the source of his sadness and the love that could never come true. Her own longing, she realised, was for the child, but however much she pleaded with Sister Aloysius she was not to be permitted to foster her.

She kept an eye on Orla after that, making sure she got her share of the food that came from the kitchens. It had to go further than in previous weeks, due to the number of admissions, even though many were too ill to eat.

She worked late and one night watched Orla praying beside the paliasse that she now shared with three other children. She wished them all a good night, spreading the thin grey blanket over them, but Orla was the last to lie down.

Jane smoothed the blanket under her chin. 'You must have been praying to your mammy.'

Orla nodded.

'Imagine that her love still covers you like the blanket.'

'And I prayed to St Valentine.' Orla closed her eyes.

* * *

Later, as Jane left the hospital, someone emerged from the

darkness of the portico and called her name. She startled; walking to and from work she was always fearful. She was wary in the streets and kept her head down, hoping to be inconspicuous in her drab dress and bonnet. Yet she had heard nothing more from Theodore Royce and had assumed that he had given up. She had certainly not found the money that he sought; he must have seen that she had not got it. She had searched Edmond's trunk and found only, tucked behind the lining, a calotype of Maud Frith posing as Venus and an unsigned note about racing fixtures. It read: '*Equinox at 15 –1 at Aintree, then a multiplier upon Kilfane at I hope 20 – 1 at the Curragh, and the best I can get at Naas – I'll stake the money as usual.*' A memory had echoed, of Edmond saying: '*This one thing can make me happy, Jane.*' So, she had nothing for Theodore Royce.

In any case, it was William who came down the steps.

'You're late tonight?'

'I wanted to say goodnight to Orla.' She smiled up at him. 'But she was saying her prayers. I didn't want to interrupt her.'

He walked beside her to the hospital gate, where he stopped. Now she must choose, either to stop beside him, or to be unmannerly and walk on alone.

'Were you waiting for me?' she asked. She felt a little tingle in her chest and throat.

'There are a couple of things I ought to discuss with you,' he said. 'Perhaps I could walk with you? It's after nine at night, and the streets can be unpleasant.'

They stood at the corner of Long Lane. Ahead the dark frontages seemed to lean towards each other as if wanting to crush out the sky. The next gaslight was a hundred yards away, through a forest of shadows. As a carriage came along the lane, she flinched instinctively towards him.

'I would be grateful for your company, at least part of the way – I live in Francis Street now.'

'I know it all too well.' He offered her his arm. 'Come.'

She stood still, shocked that he would so quickly cross the distance they had created between them.

'I'd like to speak to you, that's all.'

He kept his elbow lifted; it was hard to refuse him.

She hesitated then linked her arm to his, her lonely fears fading away as she felt the warmth of it under his woollen coat. As they walked on slowly, she relaxed a little into his familiar aroma of cologne, surprised at the rush of longing that followed. They had walked arm in arm like this in the past, but surely now the time for that was gone. Too many betrayed hopes stood in their way.

He was talking about Orla Keaney.

'I know you have a fondness for her, but she's one of thousands.' He heaved a sigh. 'What good can it do? We can't become attached to our patients.'

'Or?'

'Or it destroys us. Think how the families grieve their loved ones. If you were to share in that, and again the next day for another patient, the next evening and the morning after that – within a week you would be so burdened that you could no longer work. We can pity them, we can offer our sympathies –'

'But should that sympathy not be sincere?'

'But what use is it to the bereaved to see their physician

outdoing them in tears? We must remain professional.'

'But the little girl, Orla –'

'Wait until a charity place is found. It will only be a few days. If you adopt her, you'll burden yourself for years.'

'William – honestly – how many children die in those institutions?' She waited for an answer, but he could not reply. 'Orla's mother was terrified of her dying in the workhouse. You know how I lost my son.'

She looked up at him as they passed through the halo of a gaslight. Of course, he knew it well, had even consoled her once, when grief came back to haunt her. But he did not reply. He was an austere figure now, buttoned in on himself, his coat collar up against the cold, the rigid lines of his hat perfectly balanced on his head, his profile in its shadow. She dropped her eyes and saw the mud on his polished boots.

'We're nearly at my lodging. You shouldn't come further with me,' she said. 'It's a bad area ... what will you think of me?'

He snorted. 'Don't you know how long I've worked here? I've been in every laneway, in every tenement, in every cellar. They're poor people, not bad people, that's all. But you're crying ...'

It was true. She sniffed up a tear.

'Are you lonely, Jane?' he said softly. Her arm was still linked with his and he drew her closer as they walked. 'Is that why you want the child? But she's not your own, will never be. She'll never be Nathan.'

So, he still remembered her son's name.

'Nathan ...' her voice was uneven with pain, 'was discarded with the workhouse slops, as if he wasn't human.

I've had to bear that for years. If I can save even one child …'

'You can't. Just – please believe me – she's a vagrant's child, for heaven's sake!'

'Don't walk any further with me.' She broke away from him and marched onwards, dabbing at her tears with her gloved fingers. 'I can walk by myself.'

'I still need to talk to you!'

'No. There's nothing else to be said.'

'About your husband's case.'

She glanced round at him, standing there. What else was there to say about Edmond?

'I don't want to go into all that again,' she said, then hurried on along Francis Street to her lodgings.

She felt her way up the stairs in the lonely dark. Nellie and her family must already have gone to bed. When she lit the candle in her room she saw that someone, the postman perhaps, had pushed a letter under her door. It was from Anna.

Chapter Thirty-three

A TRIP TO MOUNT BELVEDERE

My dear Jane,

First of all, I write to repeat my heartfelt condolences upon your loss. Words cannot fully express my feelings about this irrevocable tragedy. A loss to the entire world of the stage, and you bereft of a handsome and talented husband, as well as your fortune, at a single blow.

I have just returned to Dublin, having been out of town for a fortnight. Alex and I visited the estate at Mount Belvedere which, it turns out, is to be our wedding present from his father. Theodore laid on a banquet attended by over thirty guests from the local gentry. The house (though undergoing some refurbishment) is magnificent, a huge pale-grey edifice with east and west wings. There are over two hundred acres of land, recently converted from smallholdings to pasture, providing ample facility to breed horses. Theodore, finding that the smallholdings were losing him money, had funded – at great cost to himself – passages for the tenants to emigrate to Canada.

Even so, it is a present that I am loath to accept, having no interest in horses. Alex says it is not for me to decide, and that I am not to worry myself, as we will retain an experienced estate manager. Moreover, a housekeeper and a butler supervise the servants: there are twenty-four presently employed and an equivalent number will be found for when we permanently reside there. The word has gone out in the area that extra help is needed by the middle of August. I fear I shall miss Dublin, and my friends, although course I am always enchanted by Alex's company, which ought to be enough in itself. Once we are settled there, I may return to my writing, and in time I suppose I shall be able to occupy myself with our children.

After discussing it with Alex, I did speak to Theodore about your disagreement with him, but he merely laughed and said that he could be a rough diamond at times but meant no harm. He swore that he would never hurt you. I told him that you were a dear friend of mine, and insisted that he must be civil to you in future. I am anxious that nothing – not my marriage, nor your present difficulties – will stand in the way of our friendship.

Please be assured, my dearest Jane, that our mutual love of music and poetry and the way we so freely share our thoughts in conversation will always draw us together. I still have eight weeks before my wedding and am determined to make the most of the remainder of my time in Dublin. I shall be delighted to receive you for as long as you want to see me.

With sincere affection,

Anna

Chapter Thirty-four

THE SOUTH DUBLIN UNION
WORKHOUSE, KILMAINHAM

Jane refolded the letter, then twisted it into a spill. It might be useful for lighting the fire. She looked around her dingy room with a sigh. People from Francis Street did not socialise in Fitzwilliam Square.

Yet she felt sorry for Anna. Her passion for Alex Royce had blinded her and would trap her in the countryside, as a part of his property, in return for his father's wealth that had been invested in their marriage. Anna had been so inspired by Francesca's writing and her political principles, yet now would forsake all that for love.

Margaret Keaney's family and her neighbours might have paid in blood for the two hundred acres *'converted from smallholdings'* for Alex Royce to breed racehorses. Tenants would have been driven out of the cottages that they, or their forbears, had built with their own hands, losing the land they had worked for years to improve, to be turned overnight into vagrants. Jane did not believe the story about

Canada, but even if it were true the tenants might have died of fever in the emigrant ships, or at the quarantine station at Grosse Île in Quebec, a report of which had appeared in the newspapers.

Theodore Royce had more or less murdered Orla's family, and despite Anna's intervention, Jane did not believe that she herself was safe. What agency would Anna have, once the wedding was over?

No. She would not visit Anna, but resolved to write again, perhaps tomorrow, or the next day, or when she had time. She pondered her reply: how to be tactful, in order to maintain the friendship yet lead Anna to question her decisions?

* * *

The next morning Dr Wright made an early start on St Bridget's Ward, doing the rounds with Sister Aloysius. There were fourteen female patients waiting to come up from the Admissions Room, so he was discharging women who could barely stand. They must go home, he insisted – had they not relatives to care for them? They were taking up space that was needed for others. No-one dared gainsay him. Then he noticed Orla. She was fully recovered and required no medical attention. The place at the Mendicity Institution might or might not come up. There was no longer a place for her here, that was the thing, and so she must go to the South Dublin Union workhouse. If she was well enough to be out of bed, she was well enough for the workhouse.

As the child came singing and capering down the ward,

Jane realised she was about to be wrenched away. She could not lose her.

'There's a dear.' Jane rested a hand on Orla's hair, drawing her head close for a moment. 'Now, go and help Mrs McGinty eat her stirabout.'

As Orla went to the old woman's side, Jane pleaded with Wright. 'How can we send her when the workhouse is itself full? I heard of paupers clamouring outside to be admitted.'

Wright smiled as if she had said nothing of any meaning, as if he had forgotten who she was, under her nurse's cap. 'You may return to your duties, my dear, can't you see I'm busy?' He turned his back on her and addressed himself to the next patient.

Sister Aloysius was trying to open the window beside the bed.

Jane went to her side to push up at the heavy sash. 'How can we send her out, alone?' The window unstuck and slid upwards.

'Every day they bring new inmates into the workhouse, as others pass away.' With a sigh, Sister Aloysius wound the sash cord around its cleat. 'If she waits outside, she'll soon be admitted, I'd say.'

'But what to tell her? The workhouse was her mother's greatest fear.'

'Just tell her a new place has been found for her. In fact, why don't you take her over to Kilmainham later? You can make sure that she's admitted.'

* * *

After lunch Jane brushed and tied up Orla's hair. A red woollen shawl, the remnant of a deceased patient, was ample around Orla's shoulders. The child held her hand trustingly as they left the ward.

'Will I come back and give Mrs Murphy her supper? Her tongue is all on one side so she needs me to do it.' Orla had learnt so quickly. It was such a shame to send her away.

'Perhaps one day,' said Jane. 'I'll see to her later, after I've dropped you at your new place. And I'll make sure to put the ointment on Mrs Dillon's bad legs.'

'Has my grandma got to Dublin, do you think? Maybe I'll see her?'

'Maybe.'

The air filled with the steamy scent of malt mash as they passed the Guinness brewery. As they went on it gave way to the workhouse stink. Once they could see the grim buildings of the South Dublin Union and the crowd waiting outside, revulsion gathered in Jane's stomach.

'This is the place.' She could barely say it.

Orla drew closer to her and gripped her hand. The poor child was so small, and stared up at the vast wall with its barred windows. They walked on more slowly, every step reluctant. Ragged paupers sat in a long line with their backs against the wall and their thin legs stretched across the footpath, like skeletons waiting to be entombed.

'Let's walk on the other side,' said Jane, and they crossed the street. She would stand by Orla, was set upon it now. She might ask Nellie to help her.

They stopped where, through the arched gateway, they glimpsed the shadowy buildings that lay behind. From within came the muffled noises of grinding wheels, the thuds of breaking rocks, the high-pitched keening of the insane. Thousands laboured inside a manufactory of suffering. Kilmainham was enormous, even larger than the Birmingham Workhouse, where Nathan's eyes had turned up in his little grey face, and Mrs Burton had snatched his body away, saying it – *it!* – must be disposed of.

Jane put her hand on the small shoulder and received a silent embrace as Orla pressed her head close against her. Sister Aloysius had said she could not care for the child. William had said the same. She knew that she could not take the place of Orla's parents, any more than Orla could replace Nathan, and that life with this child, who had suffered so much that she did not know about, would be hard for her. She was also certain that she was not going to detach those clinging arms, or make Orla go back across the street towards that fearful gate, or wait in line outside that bleak wall.

'Come home with me, Orla.'

They turned away and walked back towards Francis Street.

Chapter Thirty-five

THE LAST DAYS OF JUNE

William had seen Jane leaving the hospital earlier with that child, the youngster bundled in a big red shawl. Sister Aloysius told him that Jane was conducting Orla to the workhouse, that there had unfortunately been no alternative. Jane did not seem to have returned, but now was not the time to look for her.

The morning's chaos in the Admissions Room had been followed by the afternoon's unceasing repetition, walking past the silent gazes of the waiting patients, their faces raised in desperation. Stocks of calomel and morphia were declining. As well as all the patients with cholera and famine fever, the others needed time and attention: the consumptive, the gouty, the paralytic, a man urinating blood, a woman with a purple rash and a heart murmur. Moreover, the nurses were falling sick – five had gone home since the start of the week and there were rumours that one of them was fatally ill with typhus.

Now in the last days of June the cholera epidemic had been going on for six months with no sign of a let-up. No-one knew how it spread. Dr Corrigan of the Board of Health claimed that it was not contagious, but Dr Stokes argued that it was contained in the effluvia of infected patients, and his colleagues were inclined to agree. Whatever the truth, whenever William returned home from the hospital he felt as if contagion had tainted his clothes and skin and couldn't be washed away.

That evening William had out-patients to see at his own rooms. Just as he was starting an orderly came with a message: he was required to attend an urgent meeting at the hospital. He rushed through the consultations in an hour, gulped down tea and a sandwich provided by Mrs Nugent, then returned to the Meath.

The meeting was already in progress in the boardroom when William arrived, but the other physicians made space for him to draw an extra chair up to the long table.

'What's happened?' he asked, apologising for his late arrival.

'Dr Gordon Jackson died today,' replied Dr Wright. 'He was on duty at the Fever Hospital, collapsed and died. It was cholera.'

'He was weakened by overwork,' added Joseph.

The Scot had been a physician at the Cork Street Fever Hospital for the last twelve years and during the epidemic had hurried day and night between there and the Fever Sheds at the Kilmainham Workhouse, as well as doing the rounds of the slums.

'Our army has lost a general.' William felt that Death had wrapped his bony fingers around their hearts, to squeeze away the life. They thought themselves invincible: when you treat a patient, you are healthy, and the patient is sick, else how can you do it? Yet they were all formed of the same flesh and, if unable to avoid infection, might have no more than the space of a day between the home and the grave.

'The Managing Committee at Cork Street have asked for our help.' Wright narrowed his eyes at William. 'They were already short of doctors, have no-one to take Dr Jackson's place, and implore the physicians of the Meath to spare someone, or two doctors if possible, to cover his duties. As you know, these responsibilities will not attract volunteers. The rate of pay ... unfortunately the hospital's grant was reduced by the government, so there's really no choice ...'

William grimaced. What came next was no surprise.

'It has been agreed that you may be released, Dr Doughty,' Wright said. 'I can manage here until Mr Carty will be available to help.'

There would be no refusing.

* * *

The Fever Hospital was the worst place he had ever worked. It was overflowing. Some patients had typhus, some had cholera; it was impossible to separate them so that mostly they ended up with both. He learned to control his breathing, avoiding deep inhalation, to keep miasma from entering his lungs. Every day he saw – or merely glanced at, to his shame – hundreds, prescribing and instructing the few nuns who were themselves exhausted – three would be on duty for over three hundred admissions. Some patients clearly were dying and the only thing for them was morphia, if able to swallow it and keep it down. A few, looking half alive, he examined more closely, diagnosing tonsillitis, pneumonia, scrofula, fistula. Some went home with their prescription; too many remained, awaiting admission.

When the beds had become full the nuns had made up paliasses; now they had run out of those and they just laid the patients down on loose straw; the wards were crammed, the fever sheds were crammed, and the army had erected field tents on the hospital lawn. Pray God the straw would not run out, or the patients would lie in the bare mud.

William's daily routine was reduced to: shave, breakfast, work, supper, wash, bed. After a week he lost the energy to wash and shave and only ate supper because Mrs Nugent had kept it warm for him. At night he was haunted with fear for his patients: how many would be dead by the morning? How many new patients would arrive the next day? He needed whiskey to dissolve his thoughts and submerge him in sleep, even if it left him washed out the next day. He was plagued in the warmth of his bed with an itch in the armpits – the patients were infested with vermin – and rose too early, feeling that if overwork and contagion were to end his life as they had for Dr Jackson, he looked forward to the relief.

A crate was delivered from the Meath to his house: his laboratory equipment.

'There's something broken inside,' said Mr Nugent.

Glass fragments tinkled as the crate was tilted. It was too much to think about, too fatiguing. He would look into it later, he said, but the crate stood in the hall until Mr Nugent, with his wife's help, carried it downstairs to the scullery.

Had Wright willed all this, as a means of getting rid of him? Had he probed too deep into Wright's business, with the analysis of the pills? Perhaps Wright felt he knew too much, and was bent on his destruction. William could not see a way out of the trap and, in despair, prayed for salvation, thinking of the beggar girl Orla, and wishing she had not been condemned to the workhouse. Perhaps she was already dead, and no longer able to pray to Saint Valentine.

Yet his prayer was answered. After a fortnight, Jane was sent to the Fever Hospital, and his heart rose with hope.

They must have allocated her to the fever tents. In the mornings dew dripped from the canvas roof making everything wet; the patients shivered in their sodden clothing. Later in the day, under the June sunshine, the heat and humidity built up, so that they became drenched with sweat. Yet there she was, resolutely picking her way through the stink, slipping on the rotten matter that lay beneath the fresh straw on the floor as she went from one patient to the next.

It gave him courage to have her working beside him. They understood each other with few words, communicating much in a glance or a gesture, from time to time enlivening one another with a smile.

He must speak to her alone, he determined. It was not just about Edmond's pills, but about Mrs Wright's insurance, about Joseph Murphy's patient: it was about Wright. It was something that she might help him think through.

The lawns around the hospital were enclosed by rough stone walls, and in their shade one could get away from the fever tents to cool down in the fresh air. It was here that one day he started to talk to her again.

She said that she'd been made welcome at the Fever Hospital, more so than at the Meath, and however busy it was there was always someone wanting to know where she was from, so that she had become tired of explaining and would simply say 'London'.

'It must seem a long time ago,' he said. 'Another world. To think that only a few months back you were a pianist, so elegant in your black silk, and now – this.'

Her glance incised him, leaving a strange, visceral track of pain.

'Every few years the wheel turns in my life, and I must accept something new,' she said.

'Are you not afraid? Nurses have died as well as doctors, you know. The tents are the most dangerous – full of miasma.'

'I had no choice; they sent me here.' Jane explained that she'd been summoned to see the Matron who had said she had received complaints of impertinence. 'I suspect that Dr Wright wanted me to be transferred. Matron said that a nurse was not an amateur doctor, and that she must learn that obedience to the doctor's orders was the first law of nursing.'

'How did you fall out with Dr Wright?' Even standing an arm's length from her infused William with feeling. He tried hard not to stare at her, focusing instead on a flock of starlings pecking their way across the grass. Above the tents he could see the back wall of the hospital, the top-floor windows, and the chimneys. He reminded himself they would soon have to return to work.

'I had to follow him on his rounds. Often his patients greeted him with reverence, for he'd attended them without charge. Yet I heard him say, quite openly, that the swarms of the indigent were a burden on the city, that they should be extracted from their miserable cellars and returned to the country parishes that deserved to support them. Then he'd ask the patients what work they did. It was necessary knowledge, he said, so many disorders had an occupational basis: mad hatter's disease, chimney sweep's cancer, and so forth. But he prescribed higher doses of morphia for the destitute, and higher for women than for working men.'

'Are you sure of that?' Instinctively they had moved closer together. Now he studied her tenderly: the straight hem of the white cotton cap across her forehead, the fine dark eyebrows beneath, her first wrinkles developing at the corners of her mouth.

'It was a definite pattern. Often two or three times the dose. I may be inexperienced in nursing, but I followed the other medical men – Dr Stokes, Dr Prendiville, Dr Robbins, Dr Stephenson, even Mr Carty the apothecary – their patients did better. I felt bound to question Dr Wright over it. But he rounded on me: how dare I oppose him? Was I so ignorant, that I could not see that the patients under his care were desperately ill? Then he stormed off the ward. Within an hour I was up in front of the Matron. If Sister Aloysius had not intervened, I would have been dismissed. I think Dr Wright was afraid I had caught him out, don't you?' Those eyes of hers probed him.

'I have my own concerns about Dr Wright,' he said. They had not much time, but it could wait no longer. They were out of earshot of the tents, with a thick stone wall at their backs, and no faces showed at the top-floor windows of the hospital. Yet he drew closer, dropping his voice. 'I told you

273

that he was a doctor for the workhouse in Birmingham while you were there – though you say you never saw him – yet somehow he obtained a prestigious appointment here, and a plum practice.'

'I once went to his house on Merrion Square.'

'I've seen it too.' William looked down at his boots. The toes were splitting; he would have to get another pair, yet Wright had his mansion. 'He has land, a racing stables – he's either borrowed heavily or else earned wealth faster than any other doctor. It's suspicious. His late wife was from a well-to-do family, but even so ... There were large sums of life insurance on her and on his mother-in-law.'

'Sister Aloysius told me he benefits from his patients' legacies.'

'Did your – husband – leave him money? Is that why you're forced to work?'

Jane grimaced. 'There's nothing left. Edmond gambled it all away. Supposedly he had a big win, but I've never seen any of it.'

William knew he had to say it now, even though he might release a writhing monster into the space between them. 'I meant to talk to you about him.'

Now it was she who looked away, as if the path that led back to the tents had trapped her attention, showing him the sharp outline of her cheek. How lean she had grown, the poor girl!

Without her searching eyes it was easier. He leant back, against the wall. 'His pills – Wright's pills. I analysed one.'

He saw her shoulders fall as she let out a breath.

'It contained arsenic – a lot of it. I got a sample of his vomit and that was as bad. It would have poisoned him.'

'Edmond was poisoned?' She turned back to face him, slowly, her face registering a new horror. 'That was what killed him? His medicines? Do you think Wright realised it?'

'He didn't want to know.' He kept a level gaze though he shivered. 'I told him, showed him the analysis. Now he's sent me here, closed down my lab, emptied it out. The way he's reacted is suspicious in itself.'

'Edmond took those pills for weeks. Stimulants, he said. I told Wright they weren't making Edmond better, but he insisted.'

'Joseph Murphy thought they were harming him, which was why I did the analysis. When I suggested that he stopped them, Wright was furious with me.'

'I remember Edmond saying his pills were changed and Wright changed them back. Then he accused you, didn't he? The day Edmond died.'

'You should have opted for the post-mortem.'

'I didn't know what to do. I was exhausted, in a state of shock. I find there's something very persuasive about Wright. It's hard to go against him.'

'But why would he have poisoned your husband? Why harm a wealthy client?'

'Maybe it was to do with racing,' Jane said. 'I felt he was encouraging Edmond to gamble. All our money has gone from the bank. Edmond followed the racing results from his bed. I didn't understand how he was still betting. But he left me penniless.'

'Of course, Wright and his horses …'

'Royce said a race had been fixed … he talked about a series of bets.'

'Who's Royce?'

'Theodore Royce. A wealthy landowner – a landlord. He threatened me after Edmond died. I suppose he runs a racing book, amongst other rackets. He claimed his agent had paid out a fortune on Edmond's bet. He said he had been cheated, the race was fixed, and wanted the money returned. He said I was hiding it. Yet I've seen no money.'

But a hullabaloo began in one of the tents. They were needed and without further comment hurried back to work.

The orderlies were restraining a delirious young man so that he could be given a sedative. As he took charge of the situation, William's understanding of Wright crystallised in the back of his mind: he'd murdered for money – the wife's insurance – perhaps Edmond's missing winnings? As to race fixing – who could say? The Turf Club had paid him a visit; Joseph Murphy might know something more.

* * *

After a few days William found that Joseph Murphy had also been sent across from the Meath. When he questioned him about it, Joseph said that he'd been keeping mortality statistics on the physicians' patients. A higher number of Wright's patients had died: one in three, as against Dr Prendiville's one in eight, Dr Robbins' one in eleven, Dr Stokes' one in fourteen. Joseph had insisted on raising it at the monthly committee meeting. He'd proposed that any cases of unexpected death could be presented for discussion at the Dublin Pathological Society on Saturdays.

'Dr Stokes was open to it,' said Joseph, 'but there was

uproar from some of the physicians. They said no individual's practice should be scrutinised in such detail. I argued it was a way that the doctors could study the issue amongst themselves, for their own learning. Without involving anyone else, it might save lives.'

Eventually it had been agreed. Joseph had been given the job of selecting the first case and presenting the details but, before he could begin the task, he found that his duties had been changed without consultation, presumably at Wright's request.

'I've learned that Wright overdoses the destitute with morphia.' William recollected his conversation with Jane. 'Like your singer from Dame Street. Perhaps that's the cause of your statistic?'

'But such a large number of patients? How would that go unobserved?'

'I don't know – he's good at defending himself, at deflecting blame, distraction tactics. The nurses I think are persuaded by him. I wonder, did anything ever come to light about race-fixing?'

'What?' Joseph appeared surprised.

'You know – the Turf Club investigation? The gentlemen who came to see you at the Meath?'

'Oh, that? I don't think anything has ever been proved.' Joseph shrugged.

'But could it have happened?'

'I'd never witnessed it, at any rate.' Joseph puffed out his cheeks, thinking. 'But it's possible, I suppose. He keeps a lot of supplies in his carriage: medicines, dressings – for house calls as well as for the races. It wouldn't be too hard ...'

'I've been wondering, you see,' said William. More of

what Jane had told him replayed in his mind. 'I heard there'd been a large pay-out on a race that was thought to have been fixed. Only the man who should have received it never did – according to his widow. He happened to be one of Wright's patients, and there was arsenic in his little green bottle of pills. You might remember Mr Edmond Verity.'

'Jane Verity's husband?' Joseph seemed to be weighing the information. His eyes widened. 'Are you saying that Wright had put an end to him for the winnings?'

'I'm only surmising,' said William, thinking aloud. 'Like race-fixing, it's a hard thing to prove. But we have to consider the unthinkable: that our colleague may be one who needs money, is motivated by money, perhaps even harbours a disgust for those who lack money. If he's overstepped the limits which honourable doctors won't cross he may have found that there's nothing more to stop him.'

'Except us? Is that why he's after getting rid of us, by sending us to this fever-trap?'

'Very likely. But I don't know that he even needs to do that. It's true we ought to stop him. But it's impossible at the moment. I can't see how to get the law involved – there's not enough hard evidence – unless something else comes to light.'

'Well, I certainly won't be going to the police over it,' said Joseph. 'I'm pretty sure they're watching me as it is. They'll be following me in the hospital carriage, I should think.'

Joseph was to cover the home visiting rounds, with Jane to assist him. William tried not to think of her being out of the hospital for hours at a time, in the company of the handsome and impulsive young doctor.

278

Chapter Thirty-six

OUT ON ROUNDS

Jane did not understand the printed advice she was supposed to distribute on the home visits. As the hospital's carriage set off along Cork Street, she asked Joseph about it. 'What do they mean by: *Sixthly, scrape your floor with a shovel, and wash it clean?*'

He raised a gingery eyebrow. 'You'll see. But it isn't always practical.'

'I can see that if a contagious case comes to the Fever Hospital, their room might benefit from cleaning. But there are many who won't be able to read this advice.' She scrutinised the list: 'There's much to do: keep all windows and doors open for two hours – I suppose that's to change the air – clean the room, wash all the clothes and utensils, steep the bedclothes in cold water then wash in warm water and soap – what about people who don't have bedclothes, or warm water? And how are they to dry everything? It doesn't make sense. Burn straw beds, whitewash your rooms, scrape the floor, wash it clean, and wash the furniture. Am I to help them do this?'

Joseph sighed. 'You're to help me find those whose lives are capable of being saved and persuade them to come to the hospital, which they mostly won't want to do. The very sickest may have to be left, I'm afraid. I've a little medicine in my bag for them, though it's running low.'

The hospital driver followed a list of names and addresses provided by the apothecary. Within a few hundred yards of the hospital the carriage made its first stop. They were between tall tenements in a narrow side road, just off Cork Street. A summer shower had just passed over and should have freshened the streets, but already the stench was appalling. Rats swam in a stream of sewage that ran from puddle to puddle. Rainwater dripped from the empty washing lines that crossed the gap above their heads, joining walls green with slime. Many windows were boarded or bricked up, so opening them would not be feasible.

'Number nine,' said Joseph, replacing the list in his pocket.

He dismounted, heaved down his medical bag and approached the door of one of the most miserable-looking houses. Jane followed him reluctantly.

Crouched on the step was an aged man with a crooked back, smoking a pipe.

'I'm to see Mrs Kitty Keogh,' said Joseph.

'Aye.' The old man ducked his head, as if speaking to the doctor was more effort than he could manage.

Then the door was opened by a little boy of about five or six years, black with filth. Jane stopped short when she saw him, for his eyelids were swollen by infection and his eyelashes stuck together with pus. Joseph asked about his patient and was told 'She's my mam'. They followed the child as he felt his way inside the house and down to the cellar.

Jane put her handkerchief over her face.

What little light filtered down the stairs fell on Mrs Keogh who lay on sacking – there was no furniture – amongst refuse and pools of stagnant liquid. This then, was what was meant by 'scrape your floor with a shovel'. An infant lay screaming beside her and she, half-naked and consumed by fever, stared up unaware with dry and sunken eyes, her skin hanging in folds and her fleshless arms showing every bone and sinew. Her mouth was broken and crusted, and her breathing came in rapid gasps.

Joseph bent to lay a hand on her forehead then looked up at the puffy-eyed boy.

'Your mam's very sick. Will I send her to the hospital?'

'Sure I have three children,' said her husband, who sat beside her on a crate, barefoot. His overgrown toenails were curled like rams' horns. A young girl stood at his shoulder. 'What will become of us without her? What of the babby?'

'She can't look after them anymore,' said Jane. There were others in the cellar, she noticed, other families perhaps, quietly huddled in the gloom on the far side. 'She'll spread the contagion if she stays.'

'Say yeh won't go.' The man reached forward and grasped his inert wife roughly by the shoulder. 'Kitty! Kitty, don't let 'em take yeh!'

'We can care for her,' pleaded Jane, 'at least she'll have a chance.'

Kitty whined. Her husband sat back, grumbling.

281

'The porters' carriage will come for her later,' said Joseph, 'and the whitewashers to clean this place.' He produced a coin from his pocket and handed it to the man. 'Get yourself some oatmeal, make a gruel with salt and sugar and make sure to share it with the children. A pint each, at least. And wash your lad's eyes with salt water.'

The man fell silent, nodding, wondering at the coin.

Surely he had not the means to do it, thought Jane. Where were his stove, his pans, his spoons? There was not even a water jug to be seen – perhaps they drank straight from the pump. And how, in heaven's name, would the whitewashers get this cellar clean, when the wet on the walls was likely the sewage that ran down the street?

'God bless you, doctor, God bless you.' Mr Keogh put the money away in his pocket. The boy had lain down with his head on his mother, as if listening for the beat of her heart, his arm around her and the baby.

'We can do nothing more for ye,' Joseph said. 'The carriage will be here later on.'

They came gasping into the air outside. Joseph made a note on the list, then passed it back to the driver. As the carriage drew away the misery of the scene remained with them; the stench was in their hair and clothes, and both of them knew that she would be dead by the next day.

Joseph lowered his medical bag down from his knees. It landed between his feet with a thud. 'There is a depth of poverty,' he said, 'where everything is lost. People who have nothing cannot save themselves or their families, or avail of help from others. They could not even use your advice sheet to wipe themselves clean.'

Jane was longing already to return to the hospital, but the carriage stopped again only a few yards down the street.

In each tenement the desperate scenes were repeated, with families defeated by disease and unable to prevent its spread. She found ways to be useful, by advising on the care of milder cases of disease, or by consoling the families of the dying.

There was one house, on Marrowbone Lane, that Joseph entered alone. He opened the carriage door and looked up and down the road first. They were a little way from the worst slums, on the way back to the hospital.

'I'll be a few moments,' he said to Jane as he jumped down with his medical bag. The door was opened a few inches to his knock, then she saw him speak into the gap, receive a reply, and speak again before he went inside.

Jane was glad of the brief respite. She kept the carriage door slightly open for air. On the street corner a man in a frieze jacket stood and sang unaccompanied, a crowd gathering to listen. His voice was beautiful. After a few bars Jane recognised the song: it was Anna's rebel ballad, 'Liberty' that she had once set to music – how extraordinary that it could move an audience, even in this desperate place. Then a murmur went through the crowd; it broke up in many directions, the singer at once merging into them. Doorways swallowed some of the people up, others walking steadily away, so that by the time the police came past there was no-one to be seen. Only the fear lingered palpably in the street. She shuddered, feeling strangely exposed, and was glad of her nurse's cap and the hospital vehicle.

Soon Joseph came out again, looking right and left along

the now empty street as he returned. 'Drive on.' He clambered in and dropped his medical bag at their feet. It was lighter; its brass studs tapped the floor.

'This has been the most hopeless of days,' Jane said as they drove back at the end of their rounds. 'How can we prevent contagion when people live like this? Without the means of keeping themselves clean, without proper food, sunken in apathy …'

'It is a slow murder of the population,' Joseph replied. 'All the hospitals in the world couldn't help them. It must be prevented at the source: where houses are ruined, the fields made barren, and tenant farmers forced out to beg along the road. The answer is to allow non-payment of rents, to till the land again, to stop exporting food. Instead the *generous* landlords pay for their tenants to become refugees, to be marched to the coffin ships. Of the many thousands who have emigrated, half are buried – at sea, or on the shores of Quebec. Ireland is ravaged as if by war, yet who is our enemy?'

'Who, then?' They passed the canvas awnings of a row of shops. It was hard to believe in a country at war.

But his voice was hoarse with anger. '*The British government* – with its army, its constabulary – oversees this extermination.'

The carriage had reached the front of the hospital. Joseph dismounted then, reaching a hand up, helped her down.

'In the winter of 1847, we began assassinating the landlords,' he said, dropping his voice. 'At Strokestown the people lit beacons on the hills when Major Mahon was shot. He had cleared thousands off his land.' He put a hand on

284

her elbow, drawing her uncomfortably close, and they went up the steps like that. 'So, twenty-five thousand troops were sent from Britain. It became illegal to possess arms; anyone could be locked up without charge or trial. If there had been an assassination, all adult males in the district were rounded up. They must betray our man or face prison. Yet there were no investigations of murders by the military, when innocents were shot for breaking curfew.'

As they went along the corridor, he spoke of the ensuing rebellion, his voice close to her ear.

'Have you heard of the Young Irelanders? No? Well, last year, the year of revolutions, we were inspired by our brethren in Europe. Yet our men were too weak to fight. With their only power their hatred of oppression, they joined up hoping for food – but we had no supplies. At Ballintray in Tipperary the constabulary defeated a few brave rebels. Then our printing presses were broken up and our leaders captured.'

'What exactly are you involved in, Joseph?'

He looked anguished. 'The British have triumphed by mass starvation of the people that they say are their own subjects. Still this slaughter continues. Can you honestly say that no action can be taken?' His shoulders were tense and shivering with passion for his cause. 'What if a few dozen officials, a regiment of soldiers, had to be exterminated to save a million of the population? What would you choose?'

'Don't speak like that,' Jane pleaded. 'A doctor should respect the sanctity of life, not exterminate it.'

'Even if we better ourselves, through education, employment, wealth, we'll always be inferior to the English, even in our own country. That's what they don't understand,

and what causes the deepest hatred. We must have self-rule – we must be an independent Irish nation. We keep the flame alive and, when the time comes, we will prevail. I hope you understand me?' Even his smile was taut.

'*Good day!*' A familiar voice rang out in the corridor behind them.

Jane stepped back, withdrawing her elbow from Joseph's hand. William strode past before either of them could reply.

Joseph hurried to catch him up. 'How is James Clarence Mangan? Any news from the Meath?'

'Your friend is dead.' William stopped. 'It happened on Wednesday. I heard of it from Dr Stokes: he put him into a private room and supplied him with comforts at his own expense, yet even he could not save him from the cholera, the man was so enfeebled by alcohol and opium.'

Joseph's face crumpled like paper, and he hung his head.

William continued in clipped tones, as if he had no time to spare. 'Stokes sent Frederick Burton to the mortuary to draw his portrait the next day.'

Joseph did not answer and remained stock still in the corridor as William, with an apology, excused himself and stalked away.

His gait betrayed that he had misread them, thought Jane.

She approached Joseph, whose face was creased with pain. 'I'm sorry for that. You have lost your friend.'

'Mangan was an extraordinary writer,' Joseph said at length, choked with emotion. '*O there was lightning in my blood, Red lightning lightened thro' my blood!* The poet of our nation, yet he was destitute. We found him dying in misery in Bride Street and carried him into the Meath. He was forty-six years old. I have lost a friend – yes – but the Irish nation has lost a lover.'

Another poet, a young man whose name was John Keegan, died shortly afterwards. Joseph told her when he heard of it that Ireland was losing her best men: a generation who should have fostered its growth had been crushed. 'There's nothing left but desperation – and revenge.'

Chapter Thirty-seven

THE WEDDING REHEARSAL

My dearest Jane,

I was deeply moved to read your letter about your slum visits with the handsome young Dr Murphy. It must be so distressing to witness the helplessness of the poor people.

I am sorry that my social circle seems so remote to you, when in fact I am in awe of your work and, if I can, I would like to help. I have a friend, Mrs Hester Pearse, who is often involved in charitable projects, and she has agreed that we can distribute clothing and blankets, which might improve the poor people's conditions.

So, they are singing our song, bless them! I had given a fair copy to Francesca who must have passed it to one of her newspaper friends. I hope, though, that we are not identified as its authors. My father tells me that security has been increased in preparation for the royal visit by Queen Victoria and Prince Albert, and nothing remotely suspect can be tolerated. I don't want to miss my own wedding by being locked up!

Alex and I attended a wedding rehearsal at the Chapel Royal. I have six bridesmaids – all cousins on my mother's side, as on my father's side I have only my aunt's family in America. My brother Robert will of course act as best man. The mounted band of the 17th Lancers – twelve musicians, all on grey horses – will play us a fanfare in the Castle courtyard outside.

I am experiencing some anxieties about holding the ceremony in the Castle. We are accustomed to attending balls there in the evenings, but in daylight it is visibly a warren of administrative buildings, including barracks and a prison. Nevertheless we know the chaplain well, a kind and genial man. He told Alex that a marriage was a Christian sacrament and that he must make a habit of attending services in the Chapel regularly. When Alex protested his regimental duties he gave him a knowing smile and said 'regularly is not the same as frequently'.

But Alex is to make a full Confession to him, as it has been some time since his last Communion. I really doubt he will do it. He's so dashing that he could break my heart with a single glance but, honestly, I have never met anyone so lacking in religion. He made excuses, and when the chaplain tried to persuade him, he seemed uncomfortable. There must be something that he doesn't want to confess. I wonder if he has had another sweetheart in the past. If so, I hope she no longer means anything to him.

Hester says that we could follow behind you on your visits, so do get in contact with instructions. I hope I will see you again soon,

With my affectionate regards

Anna

Chapter Thirty-eight

JANE IN LOVE

The government had announced that the cholera epidemic was over, but there had been no sign of this at the Fever Hospital and William worked like a machine. His days were unrelenting, but he also worked until late in the evening because he disliked going home. The Nugents were there, of course, but after a short exchange with either of them about the weather and how busy it was at the hospital, they returned to the basement kitchen leaving him to pick at his supper in a silent house.

It was the nights he hated. He took the whiskey decanter upstairs with him and got befuddled. He had bought a double bed when he had first moved into the house, in those days when he had still had hope. Now he turned from side to side in it, scratching himself, brooding on that sight of Jane in the corridor with Joseph holding her elbow and murmuring into her ear. He'd seen the sweetness and colour returning day by day to her face and it drove him away from her.

But one warm evening as he was in the recovery ward checking through a patient's record, Jane came to sit beside him at the ward sister's desk. She was working on a fair copy of Joseph's report for the Managing Committee. The rich light of July flowed across from the ward windows.

After they had exchanged the usual courtesies he commented that she appeared to have found a new friend in Dr Murphy.

She put her pen down and sat back in her chair, staring at him. 'I wondered when you would ask me about that,' she said. 'I saw you walk off as if we had offended you. What did you mean by it?'

'I ...' he cringed at what he had said – 'I thought ... well ...'

'I know what you thought. It was too bad of you.'

She chided him as openly as if they had been married all this while, and he almost felt grateful for it.

'You should not make assumptions, William. You must know how Joseph talks about politics. He's not my sweetheart.'

'Forgive me. It was base of me to assume. He looked so intently upon you, you see, and you're always together.'

Relief warmed him and he tried to return his attention to the chart: rash, jaundice, fever, always fever ...

But she continued: 'You do realise that I'm required to do the home visits with him? He's taught me a great deal.'

William sighed. 'Be careful of letting him talk. Once he starts he doesn't stop. He's in over his head with the sedition-mongers.'

Joseph was getting more and more outspoken about the political situation. An Orangemen's Protestant march at Dolly's Brae in County Down had led to sectarian violence.

Joseph was angry over the policing of it: shots had been fired on both sides but murderous attacks on Catholic homes had not been prevented or investigated by the authorities.

'He means well. He's stirred up by the suffering he sees, by injustice, and he wants to find a way to stop it.'

William put his elbow on the table and turned towards Jane, resting his jaw on his hand. She resumed her work on the pages in front of her. How much, he wondered, did she realise about what Joseph was involved in?

'You do know that last year there was an uprising? That the leaders were captured?'

She dipped the pen in the inkwell and tapped away excess ink. 'He told me about it.' She put the pen to the paper, and calmly wrote a sentence in her neat script.

'Did he tell you that was when he disappeared for a fortnight? We had to cover his duties. Sooner or later, he'll be in trouble with the authorities.'

'I don't think he'd hesitate to take up arms. He'd gladly sacrifice himself.' She paused in her writing, but only to read aloud. 'Do you think this is safe to write? "*When treating fever, extreme caution has become necessary in bloodletting. The poor are less able to bear it than in the past, due to their degraded condition, the desperate starvation forced upon them having led to exhaustion of the blood from want of food.*"'

'God knows. It's true enough.' He looked down, his lips to his palm, then glanced sideways at her thoughtful expression as she copied out the sentence. 'But you've found someone,' he mused. 'I suppose it's no longer my concern, in any case. In the last couple of weeks, there's something … a new softness in your face. In the mornings I've noticed that you tend to be late … you yawn and smile.'

She replaced the pen in the inkwell and turned her head to him. 'You're watching me then?' Her eyes reflected the sunlight with a metallic lustre, like the silver-grey crystals of antimony.

'No-one could help but notice. It's obvious. You're content.' He sighed. 'You've found a new love.'

'No-one else has commented,' she said with a wry smile, 'but yes, there is someone I care for, only it isn't Dr Joseph Murphy.'

Though he had taken such care to be casual about asking, his heart gave a sudden lurch. So, he had lost her then, even though, after all these lonely years, she had been so close – he regretted his diffidence – and now it was too late. A thousand thoughts roared through his mind.

'I ignored your advice and took in that child.'

His words were slow to come. The heart-shaped face floated into his thoughts. 'Orla Keaney?' He collected himself. 'You're too generous. I warned you not to … but, no, you're very good to shelter a stranger's child. A thankless task, when she could have gone to an institution.' That was what had been agreed on the ward, yet he regretted the callous suggestion as soon as he had made it.

But Jane's smile was a fragment of paradise. 'I couldn't leave her at the workhouse, to face that, on her own. The poor child had lost her entire family. I just couldn't do it. You know enough of me to understand why. She needs someone to care for her, to comfort her. So, I took her back to my lodgings.'

'I don't know how you're managing.'

'Within an hour of getting her home there was a tap on my door. My downstairs neighbour had sent one of her girls up to ask if Orla would like to play. I was so happy to see them together, as if Orla had returned to childhood. Nellie calls her a "little dote" and keeps her with her own children while I'm at work. I pay Nellie something and Orla helps with the chores.'

'Would you send her to school?'

'I'd like to. I tried to teach her her letters. She's a sharp little creature, and sings well. In fact, she's taught her songs to her new friends. Some evenings I play Nellie's piano, and they sing. She'll probably learn musical notation before she learns the alphabet.'

It was a joke, but he still felt he had to frown.

'I'm still trying,' Jane continued, 'but I'm sure that with a better teacher she'd be more able. Perhaps in the autumn I'll find her a place.'

'She's brought you happiness.' William contemplated the new radiance in her face: grief was giving way to hope. 'A kind of motherhood.'

'I'll never be her mother – she calls me Jane. Last Sunday she wanted to see where her mother had been buried, so we went to the paupers' cemetery at Broadstone.' She paused. 'Edmond is buried there.'

William nodded slowly, had seen the place himself: an ugly field with long uneven ridges where clay was heaped upon the burial trenches. There had been a priest stumbling and sliding bravely over the mud with his greatcoat on over his robes, holding his hat on against the bitter wind, and pausing every yard or so to pray.

Jane took a breath that fluttered in her throat like a sob as she inhaled, but her face remained serene, and her voice, when it came, was steady. 'We stood and said a prayer at the edge of the burial ground. There was no point in us going in, for we would not even have known where to stand. All I could tell Orla was that her mother was in there. She said she should have been there at the burial. "Your mother knew you loved her," I told her, "you went through everything together, right up until the end."'

'Did it help her?'

'She cries in the night for her mother,' Jane said. 'I had a makeshift bed for her on my floor at first, but now she sleeps in my bed. It helps her that I'm there. I suppose … I suppose that … it helps me as well.' Her head was bowed.

'It would help her,' he said. He cleared his throat; his voice had sunk to a whisper. Then on an impulse he reached out to where her hand lay on the desk and covered it with his own. He felt a tingling pain, all the way up his arm to his chest. 'God knows it would help.'

She did not pull away, though her face went pink. He had a foolish longing to be in the simple contentment of that poor lodging, to be the one to whom Jane could turn in the night.

'*Ahem!*' The ward sister wanted her desk.

Startled, they separated. Jane put her work away and said it was time she went back out to the tents.

William still could not focus on his patient's chart. His head started to ache. What had he done? He felt ashamed of reaching out for her. He had persuaded himself that everything was in the past. Yet he had been weak enough to display jealousy over Joseph. Now he was jealous over a small child. Holding her hand was a mawkish, stupid thing to do. He must be sure to maintain a distance.

Yet he still needed to speak to her. There were things that needed to be put straight in his thoughts: Edmond's missing winnings, the race fixing, Theodore Royce.

Joseph must know more than he was admitting about Wright's behaviour. After all, he had said he would not report Wright and risk drawing the attention of the police to himself. Perhaps Jane, when out on rounds with Joseph, might get him to confide in her. He would make sure to ask her. There must be a way of proving a case against Wright before he harmed any others.

Chapter Thirty-nine

GOOD WORKS

'I had told her it was an early start.' Jane was explaining to Joseph what Anna had promised.

A barouche drawn by a pair of grey horses had arrived at Cork Street Hospital. The hood was up against a shower of rain and under it was Anna, waving, in a dark-green travelling dress, and accompanied by an older woman, presumably Hester Pearse. They were well in time for the start of the morning rounds and under a tarpaulin had a huge heap of blankets and clothing.

Even in the first street where they stopped, the barouche was surrounded by a crowd of people so that they could not drive away.

'Wait,' said Jane as she returned with Joseph to the hospital carriage, 'or they won't be able to keep up with us.'

'I'll speak to them. There's a long list today. Their intentions may well be noble, but they can't delay us.'

He went over to their barouche and bowed to the two

women, doffing his hat. The rain was easing off and the sun came out. The older woman sat back while Anna, smiling, passed blankets and clothing down to a rapidly gathering crowd.

Jane paused to watch him, thinking of what William had said earlier. He had waited at the hospital entrance to catch her before she went out on rounds. *'Ask Joseph about Wright and what he does at the races. He hasn't told me what he knows. I'm sure of it.'*

Despite the gloom of their surroundings Joseph's russet hair glowed as he stood talking to them. Jane remembered how she had first seen him bareheaded at the Lucan Races, assisting Dr Wright, how the first thing that he had said as he approached them was that the morphia had run out.

The hospital driver shifted in his seat and sighed. Eventually Joseph bowed again, replaced his hat, and returned. He must have impressed on Anna the long route they still had to follow for she covered everything back up with the tarpaulin and the crowd began to disperse.

'The Coombe next,' he told the driver as he handed Jane up into the carriage, 'There are four visits needed there. They'll follow us.'

As they moved off he was full of questions then about Anna and Hester Pearse – how did Jane know them, and who in the Fever Hospital had authorised these women to tag along on his rounds?

'You know perfectly well that giving out those hygiene instructions is useless,' Jane answered. 'How can people wash all their clothing if they have none spare? Anna has out of simple kindness volunteered herself and her friend to offer help. You should be glad of it.'

'It's all very well to have charity from the rich,' Joseph said, 'but if the poor had not been dispossessed of their rights, they would not be living in these conditions in the first place – and perhaps your friends would not be so wealthy.'

'Anna and Hester aren't able to remedy that,' Jane replied, 'and they're helping people who would otherwise have no help. Would you rather they sat idle at home?'

Joseph sighed as if there was no point in arguing. 'She's a lovely young woman,' he said. *'One beamy smile from you would float, like light, between my toils and me, my own, my true, My Dark Rosaleen!* Do you remember my late friend? Mangan, the poet? His words, may God rest him.'

The carriage creaked along and, as it turned off Brabazon Street into the Upper Coombe, Jane mentioned that Anna was engaged to Lieutenant Alex Royce, who had been one of the jockeys at the Lucan Races. Perhaps Joseph might have met him in the course of his Turf Club work?

'An Army wife!' After that, Joseph fell silent and continued the rounds in a sullen frame of mind.

Once all the blankets and clothing had been given away, which took less than an hour, the barouche pulled up beside them.

'We'll come back as soon as we have another load to distribute,' promised Hester. 'The Dublin Compassionate Relief Association is very active, with about fifty members supporting our good works.'

Jane thanked Anna and Hester with genuine gratitude for their kindness, but Joseph said little, though he gazed intently at Anna as if committing her face to memory.

As he and Jane went on in the hospital carriage he stared

out of the window at the tenement houses. The sun had brought ragged children out to play in the street.

'I didn't volunteer for this,' he said. 'I find these visits so difficult, you know. In the hospital we have medicines, equipment. Here we've virtually nothing. To see the conditions that people have to endure ...'

'I suppose Dr Wright sent you here?'

'I was preparing one of his cases for presentation at the Pathological Society when I was sent here. A man who had probably been overdosed with morphia. I think he did not want to see the case presented.'

'So that's three of us now, myself, you, William, that he's put out of the way. It's a pattern. He's doing wrong and he knows it.'

'You think he's doing it intentionally?' Joseph turned his head to study her. 'But why would he do that?'

'I don't know. But what do you think of him, Joseph? You were there when William challenged him about my husband's pills and asked me to agree to a post-mortem. Then he tried to accuse William. He talked me out of the post-mortem. But you didn't say anything. Why didn't you try to persuade me? What were you thinking?'

'Wright had told me that there had always been something ... an attachment ... between the two of you. That there had been a massive scandal in the past, when William's wife had died. So I thought ... it might be unwise to investigate ...'

'But that was nine years ago. We're not even friends any more.' Jane paused. She knew that Wright could damage them by dragging up the past. Harriet had poisoned herself. The affair with William had not yet begun, but Harriet had seen the shift in her husband's affections as he had confronted her with her own dark secrets. Her suicide had been passed off as a natural death, but the rumours had persisted. 'In any case, do you believe William is capable of something like that?'

Gazing at her, Joseph puffed out his cheeks and blew out slowly. 'He's a good doctor, sure enough, but you're a lovely woman.' He raised his eyebrows.

'So did you know that Edmond gambled all his money away without leaving his bed?'

Joseph started. An awkward half-smile twisted his lips as he hesitated to reply. 'No, I didn't know,' he said at length, and looked down at his hands. He had stuffed his gloves in his coat pocket before entering the first house, so his hands were bare and, as he was in the habit of rinsing them at the street pumps, they were red and chapped.

The carriage had entered Marrowbone Lane and was nearing the house that he always visited alone.

She tried again: 'If you know nothing of that, perhaps you might remember something about Dr Wright's behaviour at the races?'

'Why do you say that?'

'You were helping him there. I found out that the Turf Club had been investigating if Dr Wright could have drugged the horses.'

He glanced at the row of houses before telling the driver to stop. 'I couldn't be sure, now.'

'I do remember,' Jane persisted, as Joseph jumped down and pulled down his medical bag, 'that Edmond, before he died, before he went into hospital even, said something about it: *Doctor's orders.'* She tapped the side of her nose.

'I'll be back shortly.' Joseph walked quickly towards the house and was admitted as usual.

Jane could see that he was evading her. Why did he even help Dr Wright so much? He was so on fire for his political cause, so opposed to the government, yet supported races that were for the idle amusement of the gentry and the army officers who jockeyed the horses.

She asked him about that as they were driven back to the Fever Hospital.

'Dr Wright pays well,' he said. 'The hospital pays a pittance and when I help him at the races I earn five times as much.'

'But even so ... with your principles ...'

'The money goes to a good cause. I don't keep it for myself. I live modestly.'

Indeed, Joseph's coat-cuffs were frayed, and he had perhaps gone some days without a clean shirt collar. She did not return his attempt at a smile.

'It goes to help people who are being put off of their farms by the landlords,' he said. 'I can't say more than that.'

There was one more family to visit on the way back to Cork Street. They were all sick, but the eldest son was the only one needing admission to the Fever Hospital. As Jane gave the mother the advice on medications and hygiene, advice that she had given a hundred times before, scraps of what Edmond had said came back to her.

Poor, stupid, gullible Edmond. With her aversion to hearing about his gambling, she had stopped listening properly to him. She had told herself that what he said didn't matter, that she didn't have to believe it, so didn't have to argue with him about money. Now it came to her more clearly. She taxed Joseph with it once they were back in the carriage.

'I think that Edmond said that one of Wright's horses – *Kilfane*? – was going to be on the same stimulant pills as him. But then if Wright's pills contained arsenic – why would he poison his own horse? It doesn't make sense.'

'I couldn't say. I know no more than you.'

She had a brief glimpse of Joseph's blue gaze, every muscle in his face held still. Then the carriage stopped; the driver had been waved down by the constabulary. As an officer tried to peer in at the window Joseph shrank back out of the light.

They heard the driver shout down: 'Cork Street Hospital rounds, sir. No pistols here.'

The constables turned their attention to the vehicle behind. Joseph sat forward again, his shoulders slowly relaxing.

Jane continued: 'Later I found out that the favourite at Naas – Theodore Royce's horse, Lucius – ran badly, broke a leg, and was shot. Do you think he could have been poisoned?'

'I don't see what could be done about it now.'

He wasn't denying it, Jane thought, but neither was he willing to say more. 'I know I'll never be able to prove anything. I don't suppose I can get my money back, or do anything about Dr Wright. But I want to understand what happened to my husband. He had a gambling problem in the past. He gave it up. I helped him – other people helped him – and now … maybe he wouldn't be dead if he had only kept away from it.'

'I'm sorry for your husband, but …' Joseph braced his

arm against the side of the vehicle as it lurched over the potholes on Cork Street. They were nearing the Fever Hospital. 'I have to hold my tongue about Dr Wright. He knows too much about my – affiliations. Otherwise, I wouldn't be assisting him still – you're right in that respect. It is against my principles.'

They stopped at the front of the hospital. Joseph took his bag and jumped down from the carriage; he said he still had to attend the wards and was gone.

But, as William said, he knew more than he would tell, that was clear.

Chapter Forty

AN INAPPROPRIATE ACTIVITY

My dear Jane,

I write this with deep regret, to let you know that my charity visit caused outrage at home. I can see the desperate need in the slums but am obliged to defer to my parents and my future husband. They insist that it is an inappropriate activity for a young lady in my position.

My mother said – in front of Alex! – that I must be sensible that my marriage, which is costing a fortune, will advance me in society. That Theodore, having arranged loans to the administration, is expecting a knighthood. If I am to mix with the highest ranks in society then I must maintain a better class of friends than our neighbour Hester Pearse, whose husband – because he owns a carriage works – is 'Trade' and who even 'has the misfortune to be a Presbyterian'! Being over-familiar with the lower orders is completely out of the question.

Of course, I protested that I was doing good work, and never had I seen such want. That providing clothes to people who were half-naked was of more interest to me than visiting the dressmaker five times a week – which put my mother into such a fury that I was obliged to apologise.

She has a horror of poverty, so I tried to make her understand that even though the poor people have nothing, their kindnesses to one another would break one's heart. When we had run out of blankets, I even saw a man who had nothing to cover his back pass the last coat to a lone mother with children. I argued that these people, the victims of famine, were honourable despite their profound suffering, having been driven off the land by the greed of others.

Alex became indignant and replied, with some passion, that the landlord had to pay a levy to the poor rates for every tenant on his land. He also had to pay interest on the money that he had borrowed, whether that was to improve the land or to provide its produce with a route to market via canals and railways. Rent was not high enough to cover those costs even when the tenants troubled themselves to pay it, so that he was paying to provide them with a home. Did I think it right, that the landlord should pay for the tenants?

My father said nothing to support me, so I had no choice but to agree to forgo our outings. I am very sorry about it.

Alex sounds just like Theodore when he is pompous like that. Yet afterwards when we were alone, I saw his gentler side. He told me that I was far too precious, too beautiful and too clever to be allowed to run the risk of contagion in the slums. As he embraced and kissed me it put my mind in such a whirl that I let the argument go.

Queen Victoria and Prince Albert are, as you doubtless already know, visiting Dublin from the 6th to the 11th of August, so all attention will be on them. Alex's regiment is providing a *ceremonial escort, so he is busy with rehearsals for the next three weeks. Everything must be perfect and the route all the way from Kingstown will be bedecked with flags and flowers, evergreens, and triumphal arches. A detailed plan to present her Majesty with a dove 'en route' is causing my father a headache in itself as he is convinced that what he terms 'the wretched animal' will simply fly away. There is going to be a grand reception at the Viceregal Lodge which I am to attend.*

After that I travel to Mount Belvedere with my mother to view the refurbishments and select fabric swatches. Theodore is to join us on the 14th of August so I expect that the servants will already be in a fever of preparation for his arrival.

Please convey my respects to Dr Murphy. I do hope that I may find a way to rejoin you in the future.

With sincere affection,

Anna

Chapter Forty-one

JOSEPH TAKES THE BAIT

Although Joseph's case could not be discussed at the Dublin Pathological Society, he rose to speak as soon as he had the chance. They were in the lecture theatre of the school of medicine at Trinity. The curved tiers of wooden benches were set at a steep rake so that William could look down at the open abdomen of the cadaver they had just discussed, or at the top of Dr Stokes's learned head.

Unconcerned by his surroundings, Joseph took advantage of the gathering of the top medical men in the city to complain of the working conditions at the Fever Hospital: the interminable hours, the hordes of patients, the abysmal pay, the risk to which the doctors were exposed.

He reminded everyone of the death of Dr Gordon Jackson: 'An irreplaceable loss to our profession. A warning to all of us that we are mortal. Yet Dr Wright has now condemned us – myself and Dr Doughty – to the Fever Hospital as though to our own deaths.'

A shock ran through them. All eyes looked towards William: had he put Dr Murphy up to this?

He was as surprised as they but felt obliged to say something. 'Conditions are bad, it has to be said, although not much worse than at the Meath. I think all of us have dealt with a greater burden of illness in the past few years, since the start of the famine ...'

Dr Wright had got to his feet, his mouth already open to retort.

'Dr Murphy is well known for his extreme views,' he said. 'I myself was forced to endure his diatribe about her Majesty the Queen and the royal visit. Would he care to repeat his views in front of the assembled company? We can then consider whether they befit his position.'

To everyone's dismay, Joseph took the bait. He had a newspaper with him and, as he spoke, he jabbed it with his finger like a crow pecking bones: '*Loyal subjects – an outpouring of affection – a hundred thousand welcomes,* indeed! She is greeted by plague, pestilence and famine!'

Dr Stokes, whom everyone respected, said that he had also read the reports. 'The Queen and her young family are extremely popular. They were met in Cork by large and jubilant crowds, by a festival atmosphere. Likewise in Dublin we are eager for a celebration now that the cholera is coming to an end.'

'*An end!*' Joseph fired off another fusillade. '*There's no end in sight!* The contagion will run rampant through the crowds. All the while the workhouses are bankrupt, the Fever Hospital besieged by the sick poor – all this is being denied, lie after lie, and now the Queen of this ravaged land is coming to Dublin.'

'We shall welcome her courteously,' replied Dr Stokes. 'I shall be leading a deputation from the College of Physicians. We are to go on Tuesday to pay our respects to the royal couple.'

'And to present our city to the Queen as a whited sepulchre, fair and pure, while the evils that lie within are of no concern?' Joseph's vehemence increased. 'How can any physician, working daily with the diseased and the destitute, not realise that is a falsehood? That it makes a mockery of suffering? Does no-one understand how this woman's tyrannical government deliberately murders the Irish, killing the peasantry by deprivation of food and shelter, exposing them on the hillside like the unwanted children of Sparta?'

As Dr Stokes frowned in irritation, Wright got a word in: 'It's untrue that the British intend to murder the Irish. Indeed, the Queen is to visit the Schools of National Education and inspect the children's singing and needlework: is that the action of a tyrant? Of a murderer?'

'*And you – you would know about murder, so?*' roared Joseph.

Without elaborating, he ranted on as Wright sat down: It was all show: beggars and vagrants would be swept from the streets into some charnel house so that they did not offend the regal eye. Sham and lies, that were so constantly accepted as truth that all sense of reality was destroyed.

William watched Wright, who sat with his arms folded and his stocky shoulders hunched, his unwavering stare on Joseph, like a bird of prey. He knew about murder, for sure.

Now Joseph's voice tightened, and he said that one day the royal couple should suffer the same agonies of disease: the fever, the cramps, the bloody flux. Victoria and Albert were not so royal as to be immune to the contagion which destroyed their subjects. He wished them an early death. In his soul he was making a curse which would one day smite them down.

'I think,' cut in Dr Stokes, 'that it's time to conclude the afternoon's business.' There was a general murmur of assent. 'There's no place on the agenda for these harangues. No-one wants to listen to you.'

But Joseph was full of anger and raved on about pishogues …

William interrupted. '*Above all do no harm,* do you not remember the Hippocratic Oath?'

'We'll give the queen a silver comb. We'll roll accursed eggs on the road beneath her carriage and, as they break, they'll release the spell.'

'How can a medical man believe in such superstition?'

With a look so level and hard that it made William wince, Joseph said he believed in history, and had studied a corpus of literature in the Irish language of which English scholars were oblivious.

'But you must be a man of science.' William would not give up. 'You use a system of clinical examination and pathology; you use your stethoscope as a window to the chest; you confirm your observations at the dissection table. There is no magic. That's what we learn here, in this very room.'

The other physicians agreed; Dr Stokes said that the meeting was at an end and that the closing comments would not be minuted.

'There's one more thing,' said Wright, with an apology in Dr Stokes' direction. 'Dr Murphy should tell his colleagues about 18 Marrowbone Lane. I found out from the

Fever Hospital driver that Dr Murphy stops there every time on his rounds. It's never been on the apothecary's list. A house to which Dr Murphy is admitted after reciting a secret passphrase. We're entitled to know the purpose of these visits, made with the hospital vehicle.'

'It's untrue,' Joseph said. 'I know nothing of any passphrases.'

'Why are you so quiet on this point yet so free with your other ideas that everyone avoids you for that reason?' Dr Wright gave Joseph a predatory smile. 'We've all heard enough of the misrule of the country, when in fact the government has spent many millions on famine relief. Yet you deny it and wish to convert your delusions into action. Which is why you visit the house in Marrowbone Lane. Well, the next time you go you may find the house vacant and boarded up.'

At that point Joseph rounded on Wright, leaning forward, his body stiff with anger. William's skin prickled, fearing he would turn violent. What if he carried an armament?

But Joseph was controlled and deliberate, 'At least I'm not a poisoner. Nor am I in the business of drugging racehorses.' He thrust out his forefinger in accusation. 'I've seen the bottles of morphia and nux vomica and strychnine that you carry around in your carriage. *I know now what they're for.*' Then he stalked out of the lecture theatre, ignoring raised eyebrows and exhalations of breath.

* * *

On the Monday they all heard the cannons firing. The Queen and Prince Albert had arrived in the royal yacht, landed in

Kingstown to a great fanfare and cheering crowds, and had been conveyed by the state carriage in procession to the Viceregal Lodge. All the talk for days was of this royal visit: bouquets, blessings, and ceremonial visits to public institutions that had been spruced up for the occasion.

Joseph bore it in silence and as far as William knew he continued his daily rounds with Jane. But on Friday morning he did not come to work. No-one knew where he was. There was simply no-one spare who could cover his visiting rounds and Jane sought William out to ask him what to do. He shrugged.

'The rounds will have to wait until there's a doctor available. In the meantime, there's no point in going out in the district and sending cases in. There aren't enough staff here to treat them.'

'May I speak to you in confidence?' asked Jane. 'Just for a moment.'

If it had been anyone else, William would have said he was too busy. But he still had questions for her. They walked outside, past the fever tents, to beside the boundary wall. He was disappointed when she said she was worried about Joseph. 'One of the orderlies has been to his lodgings to ask if he was sick. The landlady said that he'd gone out and not come back, and that the police had been and searched his rooms.'

'Did you hear he fell out with Wright?' said William. 'In front of the Dublin Pathological Society? He lost his temper and accused him of drugging racehorses.'

Jane gave him a look of alarm. 'That's more than he would admit to me. He told me that Wright knew too much about him and so he couldn't speak out against him.'

'Wright has maybe had his revenge since then? Denounced him to the authorities?'

'It makes sense,' she said. She was gaunt and weary. Yet she had such a lovely face, her dark and serious eyebrows, the symmetry …

'Wright accused Joseph of visiting a safe house in Marrowbone Lane. If he's arrested again and proven to be a member of a rebel club, he'll be transported. For treason the penalty may be heavier.'

'A strange man came to the hospital to find him,' Jane said.

'When?'

'Wednesday morning. I was with Joseph by the hospital entrance, waiting for the carriage to go out on rounds. The man was in such a mess, wild-eyed, with his hat falling off. At first, he seemed drunk. He marched up to Joseph, clapped him on the shoulder and said: "*Are you ready to meet the Queen?*" Joseph said no. "*But she has been in Dublin for two days*" – he must have studied the newspapers. He rattled off the details of her visits and processions. "*I must meet her! We all shall meet her! Even this ravishing young lady*" – he meant me – "*all of Young Ireland!*" He was loud and some doctors who'd been standing talking nearby – Dr Wright was among them – turned round.'

'One of Joseph's political friends, perhaps?'

'I don't think so. Joseph looked uncomfortable. He took the man's arm and said, "*Hush!*" and called out that he had him in charge. Then he tried to calm him by introducing him to me – his name was Daniel Paget. Joseph said that I had done excellent work on our wards and out on the rounds.'

'As indeed you have,' William said.

'Mr Paget bowed graciously. I made a little curtsey. Then he asked if I was for or against Young Ireland and began to raise his voice again. Joseph intervened. He said I was English, but knew nothing of the political situation, only worked to relieve the sufferings of their countrymen. Mr Paget supposed I was loyal to the Crown ...' Jane broke off her account and studied him. 'Are you unwell, William?'

He realised that he was shivering. 'It's cold out here.'

'But we're in the sun.' She widened her eyes at him. 'I hope you're not brewing a fever?'

He shook his head. 'Go on – I'm listening.' But she was right. His head was aching – he shouldn't have shaken it.

'Well, Paget ranted at me. He said: *"I represent our countrymen, I mean to obtain an audience, and if not, they shall reckon with this!"'* Jane's hand went to her breast. 'He looked ready to draw a pistol. I was alarmed but Joseph told him it was best if we took him home. The carriage had arrived, so he steered Paget over to it. We all three got in and Joseph told the driver to go straight to Henrietta Street, where we left Paget outside his house. "He's a harmless eccentric," Joseph told me. "Don't mind what he says." When I asked Joseph how he knew him, he said that Paget was often in the taverns, and that everyone had heard him giving out. Then yesterday, when we were out on rounds, Joseph told me Paget had been arrested. I was relieved that he was no longer at large, but I could see it weighed on Joseph's mind, and he said he should have got Paget entirely out of Dublin.'

A flash of light caught William's eye. Past her shoulder,

in the far distance, sunlight glinted from brass buttons. A constable in a tall black shako, with a musket hung at his side, walked between the fever tents and paused at an opening.

'I wouldn't go in there,' he murmured, then sighed as the officer turned away from the tent and came towards him across the grass.

'We want to talk to Dr Joseph Murphy,' he said. 'A red-haired doctor. I believe he works here?'

William shook his head: that headache again. He frowned. 'He hasn't come in to work – no one knows where he is. Is it something I can help with? I'm his colleague, Dr Doughty.'

'Not unless you were down by the canal last night, doctor?'

'The canal? Why would I be there?'

'Around two hundred men were on the towpath. They were lying in wait for Her Majesty's carriage. She was coming back into Dublin from the Duke of Leinster's estate in Kildare. We got twelve of them and are looking for the rest.'

'I didn't know anything about it,' William said with a shiver. 'I don't know how to help you. Are you saying that Dr Murphy was among them?'

'We took a lunatic into custody a couple of days ago. We were informed that he'd been shouting threats against Her Majesty, had met Dr Murphy here, and was driven away in the company of him and one of the nurses.' The constable's glance shifted to Jane.

'That's appalling,' said William at once. 'I didn't see anything of the sort, and I'm sure you didn't, Nurse Verity?'

As Jane shook her head the constable continued: 'It was fortunate the prisoner told us about the attack, so we broke it up before any harm was done. Her Majesty was not even aware of it. So, if you see Dr Murphy – he's a wanted man – make sure to report him to the Castle.'

'Of course,' said William. 'We'll keep an eye out, won't we?'

Jane nodded. 'We ought to go back to the ward,' she said.

The officer accompanied them across the lawn.

But nothing further was heard of Joseph that day, although one of the orderlies said that he had been spotted very early that morning, at breakfast in the doctors' common room at the Meath.

* * *

One of the patients admitted the next day proved not to have contagion at all, but an injury in his upper arm which had got infected and was the source of his fever. He claimed he had been struck by a runaway cart. William summoned the surgeon, who said there was an abscess there that was turning septic and needed to be lanced.

Despite morphia, the man squeaked with pain as they opened the wound and cleaned out pus. Then something clattered into the enamel dish: spherical and grey.

'That's a Brown Bess musket ball, all right,' said the surgeon. 'I can tell by the dimensions. I've removed these before, from individuals who had a brush with the law. Tell me, how did you come by it?'

'With the greatest of respect to you, doctor, you must be mistaken,' declared the patient, sticking to his story of the accident, which was patently false.

317

The surgeon merely raised his eyebrows. William, who was feeling nauseous, perhaps at the sight of the scalpel blade debriding the purulent wound, did not pursue it.

Re-prescribing his morphia later, William asked him: 'Wherever it might have been that you got your injury, did you meet a man called Joseph Murphy?'

'I never heard the name,' said the man and, turning his head away and closing his eyes.

'A fiery young doctor,' William said softly, 'tall, with red hair? Down at the canal?'

The eyes snapped open. 'Dr Murphy.'

'Yes. I'll shan't tell anyone if you've seen him.'

'God bless him.' He was grey and sweaty; every word was an effort, but now he wanted to talk. 'He bound up my arm. He works here, doesn't he?'

'Is he safe?' William asked. He was sweating himself. It was a warm, enervating afternoon.

'It was after I was shot ... else I'd have bled to death. He got in danger himself by stopping to save me. I'd like to thank him – you must thank him for me when you see him.'

'Was he injured?'

'No, not injured,' said the patient, 'but, if it hadn't been for me, your man would have got clean away.'

'Was he captured?'

'I jumped into the canal to hide,' said the patient. 'I saw nothing more. Your man had told me to come here if the wound got bad. But he's not here, is he?'

'No,' said William.

* * *

That night William shivered, lying still dressed in his bed. Was it just fatigue that contracted his muscles like boiled meat? His head was heavy enough to sink right through the pillow. He covered his head with the blankets, even though it was a warm night, even though sweat crusted his eyes, and his hair was solid with it. He was indifferent to the smell, having got used to the humid filth of the hospital, to ignoring the stink of the patients and even the vapours of the hot turpentine the nurses applied to their bellies.

He lay hunched into a ball, his arms tight around himself, beset by horrors, remembering old cases from the Meath so vividly that he could almost feel their flesh beneath his fingertips, could hear their voices as he strove to understand their complaints. The tobacconist in paroxysms of cardiac asthma, tormented by the apprehension of approaching death – the size of the man's liver! – and the chest full of fluid. The young seamstress with the palpitations, the thyroid gland, and her eyes so protruding that she could not close them – she went blind. Before her the ship's carpenter with a pulsating, bleeding tumour bulging out of his chest. How many children had been hideous with rashes and panting with fever, so that he'd take one look at their sunken faces and know they'd die, however much their mothers pleaded for them? How many tussles had there been with combative patients, the orderlies hurrying to restrain them: the alcoholics with delirium tremens, the rough sailors whose syphilis had infested their brains?

The dawn came and, though his head ached for more rest, he had to get up. He had to work.

Chapter Forty-two

FEVER

In another couple of hours Jane would be finishing up for the day, and leaving the ward to go home, to eat supper with Nellie and her family. She had started to look forward to evenings in that cluttered room, with the windows wide open to the fading sun and swallows darting past along the street. Jane would play Nellie's old piano, sometimes from memory and other times Orla would stand by her, turning the music sheets. Even Michael, Nellie's husband, had stopped complaining about 'that infernal racket' and would lie stretched out on the rug, still covered in plaster dust – he was a decorator by trade – with their youngest asleep on his chest and rubbing his beard as he fathomed Beethoven or Schubert.

But as Jane tidied a pile of clean dressings she looked out of a back window and saw a nurse rushing from the fever tents towards the back of the hospital. The girl was calling out, but Jane could not make out the words. A couple of orderlies came towards her; they conferred for a moment then one hurried back to the tents with her while the other sped across the back yard.

Soon everyone heard him shouting on the stairs: '*Dr Doughty has collapsed in the fever tents!*'

Jane hurtled down the stairs and out to the tents. She could hear the commotion and went to the source.

Three other nurses were there, but no doctor. William lay whimpering in the dirty straw. At the sound of his voice a huge relief flooded Jane – at least he was alive.

'He's the only doctor on duty,' said one of the nurses. 'What shall we do?'

'See if Dr Enville could come over from the Dispensary,' said Jane. It was unlikely as Dispensary was normally besieged at this time of the evening. 'Would someone go and fetch him?'

An orderly hastened away.

William was as pale as paper. Jane crouched down beside him and stroked his hair out of his eyes and away from his hot brow. He stared at her and sighed.

'He has a fever,' said one of the nurses. 'Heaven save the poor man!'

'It's like Gordon Jackson all over again,' said another nurse. 'Barely a month has gone by since Dr Jackson passed.'

It was why William had shivered despite the golden warmth of the sun. When Jane undid his cravat and opened his shirt, they saw a rash like a scatter of red ink amongst the dark hair on his chest and lost hope.

'Oh!' A nurse gasped, and drew back. 'It's the typhus. Be careful, Jane. Try not to touch him!'

'As well to keep him in the fever tent then,' said an orderly, with a nervous laugh.

321

'No. He can't be left here,' said Jane.

'The wards are full.' One of the ward sisters had arrived from the main building. 'The beds filled two or three times over. He mustn't be made to share with the other patients. He might be better kept in here.'

'I'll get him a pillow and a blanket,' a nurse said, and Jane heard her brush through the tent flap on her way out.

'But even if we can't save him,' said Jane, 'he should not be left in this straw, on the ground, like an animal.' She saw now how degraded were the conditions that they all took for granted. It was different when it was someone you knew. Someone you cared about.

'Get me home, for God's sake,' William mumbled.

Jane bent her head to hear him.

'Get me home, Jane. Don't let me die here.'

As she crouched there beside him, she remembered the first time she had ever seen him. She had been nearly dead in the workhouse yard in Birmingham when he had stopped to help her. He had given her the same stare, his eyes wide-open, dark, intent. They had a shared past that could not be discarded.

'I'll take him,' she said.

'Will you not wait for Dr Enville?' The ward sister stooped over William. 'Dr Doughty looks too ill to move.'

'I'll have to take a chance,' said Jane.

'But who will care for him? He lives alone, doesn't he?'

'I'll watch him.'

'You're still needed here,' was the reply. 'Remember we're short of staff.'

'I'll give him into the care of his servants and come

straight back.' She doubted she could keep her promise but would have said anything to give William his wish.

The ward sister relented: the orderlies could help take him to the hospital carriage. As they were preparing to move William, the man who had gone over to the Dispensary came back and said that Dr Enville was very sorry, but he had over forty patients waiting and could not spare the time.

The hospital carriage used to convey patients had a seat for the nurse and a bench upon which William lay. He bumped and jerked about as the carriage rattled along the street, which made Jane flinch, even though he did not complain.

At William's house in Harcourt Street the two servants came out to help bring him from the carriage.

'Mercy!' exclaimed the housekeeper, her face twisting with fear when Jane said it was typhus.

But the hospital driver had left them to it, so there was nothing else to do, and between the three of them they manhandled William upstairs and onto his bed, where he sank down on the coverlet.

'Thank you,' he said hoarsely. He was gripped by rigors.

'What to do now, Waldo?' the housekeeper asked her husband, who, trembling, said he didn't know.

Jane was conscious that in her nurse's cap and apron they expected her to take charge. 'Just help me get him into his nightshirt,' she said, fearing she would be alone in treating him unless she could find him a doctor.

With some effort they got William undressed. 'I'm co–old,' he chattered out through his teeth. The ugly red rash covered his torso.

'Can you sit up, William?' Jane stood in front of him and

gathered his head into her body to keep him upright. Once the nightshirt was on, they pulled the covers back and let him collapse back in the bed, shivering, dull-eyed, and gasping between dry lips.

'Well, Mother Nugent? Well, Miss –' Mr Nugent backed towards the door.

'Jane –'

'Miss Jane, what to do?'

She knew she would have to stay with William. 'Go to 57, Francis Street, Mr Nugent, please, and ask for Nellie, tell her I can't come home and ask her please to mind Orla. Now, do you have any willow bark, Mrs Nugent. Yes? A tea would help the fever. Infuse it and let it cool.' She would have to spoon it in; he could not drink it otherwise.

'We must get him a doctor,' said Mrs Nugent, gathering up the discarded clothing. 'These want steeping in boiling water, I should think. Waldo, you could go for a doctor straight after.'

'Who to ask, Lil?' Mr Nugent started to go downstairs. 'He's never had a doctor to see him.'

'Go to the Meath Hospital,' Jane called after him. 'Say it's for Dr Doughty, they know him there. Ask for any of the physicians – only not Dr Wright. And you could call in at the chemist's shop on the way back. Morphia and calomel is what we give at the hospital. Mrs Nugent, a tablespoon of willow bark in a teacup of hot water, let it steep for ten minutes and strain it.'

She was alone with William. She brought his dressing-table chair to the bedside and sat down.

'Are you in pain, William?'

That dull stare again. His fever must have been at its height, for he had stopped shivering. He closed his eyes and turned his cheek to the pillow. Where his profile rested against the pillowcase the white cotton fabric was worn through. It was an embroidered panel of whitework: fine stitching, tiny pintucks, flower garlands. Jane had seen this pattern, years ago.

Mrs Nugent, bringing the willow bark tea, discovered her leaning over him.

'I was looking at the pillowcase.' Jane got up hastily to take the cup and saucer. 'It's beautifully worked.'

Mrs Nugent, looking at her curiously, said that the fabric was from a lady's chemise. 'Dr Doughty asked me to sew the good parts into a pillowcase. I suppose – he is a widower – perhaps it was his wife's?'

William opened an eye and closed it again.

'Perhaps.' Jane composed her expression, knowing full well it was not. She had packed her belongings in haste and forgotten that chemise on the washing line, in the yard of William's house in Birmingham.

As Mrs Nugent retreated downstairs, Jane propped William up with his pillows and sat beside him spooning in the tea. A drop spilt on his lip, and she stroked it away with her finger. This mouth she had once kissed with such hunger. He had been so formal with her, yet his face, so cold by day, had rested at night on her old chemise. A single ember sparked in the ashes of the past. If these were his last days, she would not leave him.

Mr Nugent came back alone: he had done as asked but no one could be spared from the Meath for a visit. 'I left a message with the Head Porter.' He handed Jane the bottles of morphia and calomel.

'Could you bring me a tablespoon?' She met his doubtful glance. 'I'm familiar with the doses.'

'He don't look very well though, do he, Miss Jane?'

'No,' she said. 'But I must do what I can. Now, please, get me the tablespoon.'

Mrs Nugent brought the tablespoon up shortly afterwards, and with it a sandwich and a pot of tea.

William's fever remained stubbornly high. She stayed beside him through the evening and the fearful hours of the night, napping in the chair. As dawn broke, he woke up shuddering. The rash had spread further, and he groaned in a confused way. She gave him more of the morphia and calomel, trickling it between his chattering teeth.

It was no good: he needed a doctor. She would have to find Joseph. In the early light she hurried over to the Meath Hospital. Making her way through the waiting patients already gathering at the front steps, she went to the porter's desk.

'Dr Doughty is gravely ill and needs help,' she told him. 'I sent a message last night for help.'

'There's no doctor can be spared, my love,' said the porter, looking up from his newspaper.

'I heard that Dr Murphy comes here for breakfast,' she said.

'I haven't seen him.' The porter turned his attention abruptly back to the page. Had Joseph sworn him to secrecy?

Thanking him without meaning it, she went down the narrow corridor to the back stairs. On the top floor was the doctors' common room, where, sure enough, beside a table strewn with medical journals and newspapers, she found Joseph slumped in a tattered armchair with a cup of tea. When she asked him how he was he startled upright, spluttering tea. He looked fit to become a patient himself, hollow-cheeked and weary with his red beard unkempt.

'Don't tell anyone I'm here.' He put his cup and saucer down on *The Lancet*.

'You look awful. Where have you been?'

'They're looking for me. I can't go home. I'm after sleeping in a storeroom in the basement. Thank God for the staff here.'

'I need you to come and see William,' she said. 'He has a high fever, and I can't get it down.'

Closing his eyes, Joseph let out a sigh. 'Is he bad?'

'It's typhus,' she said. 'The rash came on yesterday.'

'Oh, Jesus have mercy!' he said, and sprang up.

He heaved up his medical bag and led the way downstairs.

* * *

'He's sinking, Miss Jane.' Mr Nugent had sat with William.

'Dr Doughty?' Joseph got no answer. 'William?' He drew back the sheet and lifted the nightshirt, exposing the rash. 'Dear God.'

Jane went to the window and adjusted the curtains to let in more light. The trees in the square were alive with fluttering starlings but the city was still quiet. A single dark-red carriage came gradually along the road below. It stopped across the road from the house. A face peered out through the side window.

'He is much enfeebled.' Joseph was examining William. 'The pulse soft and compressible, the tongue brown, the abdomen distended.' He flattened his hand over William's stomach and tapped his knuckle, producing a hollow note. 'I'd give him sulphate of quinine with sulphuric acid, and morphia in the form of the Black Drop, up to sixty drops in twenty-four hours.'

'His fever isn't coming down,' said Jane.

'He's almost at the point of crisis. You may try tepid sponging with acetate of ammonia and ipecac, well diluted. Keep the room well ventilated and change the linen often. Also, rather than giving calomel syrup I would apply mercury, a dram of the unguent each day to each armpit. It's absorbed quickly without irritating the stomach.'

'Should he be bled?' It was sometimes done at the Fever Hospital.

'I would not subject him to it. His pulse might sink. Nor can we apply blisters to the skin, due to the rash.' He stuffed his stethoscope back into his black bag and dumped it with a thud on the floor, the colour suddenly hot in his face. 'He's fought the contagion for so many other people, for so long, that he is utterly exhausted, and can no longer fight it for himself, just when the city is crying out for doctors. And the authorities are after telling us everything's over!'

Opening his writing case on the dressing table, Joseph wrote out a lengthy prescription and was just signing it off when the doorbell rang. Then a series of heavy blows on the front door startled them both. He stood still, not even moving the pen. Jane went back to the window and glanced down at the street. Her breath caught.

'It's the constabulary.'

The officers stood beside the dark-red carriage, training their muskets upon the house. Someone bashed the door again, then she heard Mr Nugent grumbling and his hurrying footstep as he went to answer.

'Hide me.' Joseph shoved his bag and his hat under the bed with his foot and glanced around the room.

'Where?' She could hear boots on the floor below, the banging of doors, the bellowing of an order, Mr Nugent obsequious and afraid. They would be upstairs in a moment.

Joseph dropped to the floor and rolled under the bed. Jane stood at the door, waiting for the knock, hoping that the Nugents had said nothing of Joseph's presence.

Chapter Forty-three

THE MEDICAL BAG

The gleaming muzzle of a musket nudged the door open and pointed at her as she stopped the door with her foot.

'We're looking for Dr Joseph Murphy and his medical bag.' The officer studied her face. 'And the pretty young nurse who's been seen with him, and with a dangerous fanatic, a Mr Daniel Paget. You wouldn't happen to be Jane Verity, would you, *Miss Jane*?'

She denied it without a second thought, giving the first name that came to her head.

'Jane Farthing,' she said. 'I'm a nurse from the Fever Hospital. You're not to come in.' She spoke up to the officer, emphasising her English accent. 'Dr Doughty has a severe case of the typhus contracted from our wards. He's highly contagious.'

'Dr Murphy was seen to enter this house.' His gaze travelled beyond her to the sick bed, where William lay silent and still.

'He has been here to attend Dr Doughty but was in a hurry and left half an hour ago.' Beyond the bed she knew that Joseph's dark-green coat still hung over the back of a chair. The ink was still drying on his signature on the prescription. She kept her tone level and her eyes blank. 'Have you tried the Meath Hospital? He might be there later on.' She gave him elaborate instructions.

A constable came down from upstairs and reported there was nothing up there.

'He has not been seen to leave. My orders are to search each and every room in this house.' The officer pushed the musket against the door again, but she kept her foot in place, resisting his pressure.

'Dr Doughty cannot be disturbed. He's gravely ill – it could kill him. And you'll be entering a highly contagious environment.'

The constable stepped back, and behind the officer's shoulder she saw the fearful face of Mr Nugent.

'You'll put yourselves at risk, and your families too,' she said.

The officer glanced back at his colleague, hesitating.

'Very well. But I may need to ask you some further questions, Miss Farthing, regarding Dr Murphy. May I take your name and address?'

She gave him the address of a miserable cellar in the slums that she had once visited with Joseph, and with a grumble of discontent he went downstairs, ordering the Nugents to inform the police station at Dublin Castle if they saw anything irregular.

She stood completely still until she heard the carriage

move off, then edged towards the curtain and peered down at the street.

'I think they've gone,' she whispered, and Joseph emerged from beneath the bed and got up, putting his back to the wall beside the window.

William was still asleep.

'If they find me they'll hang me,' Joseph said in a low voice.

'What about me?' She was gripped with fear. 'Why are they looking for me? I've done nothing.' An answer came by itself to her mind. 'Wright! It was Wright who saw me with you and Paget. I suppose he wants me out of the way.'

He sucked in his cheeks. 'Likely he's had enough of me as well.'

'But Joseph, what exactly have you done? Why do they want your bag?'

At length he replied, in measured words, that it was no crime to seek justice for the Irish people murdered by deprivation of food and shelter.

She recalled what William had said about the safe house. 'That house in Marrowbone Lane – where I waited outside – you were meeting a rebel club. They want you for treason.'

'You see – the authorities pack the juries with Protestants.' He had a wary look in his eye. 'If I stand trial, then it'll be death or transportation. Sure, Jane, will you not find me some mercy and try to save me?'

She hesitated. He had freely acknowledged that he was outside the law. How could she save him? And yet, she could hardly turn him in.

'I'll be on the Cork train tomorrow morning. It's only until then.'

'Joseph, I can't hide you here – what if they come back? They'll soon find I gave them a false address.'

'Well, I cannot go back to my lodgings. The safe house was raided. I can't go to the Meath now, either, thanks to your directions. If I step outside – they may still be watching this house.'

She stood behind the curtain and moved slightly sideways to check the street with one eye. 'I still can't see anyone.' She raised the sash window and leaned out. 'No-one there.'

He breathed out with relief before peering out into the street himself. 'There's a house on the north side where they might hide me. As long no one spots me on the way.' He put his hand up to his beard. 'Can I shave? And if I can leave my bag here?'

'Why do they want your bag, Joseph?'

'If I can go off without it I'll have a better chance. Can you bring it to Kingsbridge Station tomorrow morning? Meet me at quarter past nine – the Cork train leaves at half past nine.' He felt in his waistcoat pocket and offered her some coins. 'That'll get you a jaunting car.'

She made no move to accept the money. 'But what's in the bag? I've enough to do without running errands all over Dublin. Take it with you, for heaven's sake!'

'It's just for my Turf Club duties. I've to go down to Barronstown. But you heard the officer – they're looking for it. Probably something Dr Wright has told them.'

She digested that. Joseph and Dr Wright – there was still something that Joseph knew. 'When we were in the hospital carriage the other day, Joseph, you said that you could say nothing more about Dr Wright in case he betrayed you to the police.'

'That wasn't what I said. Well, not exactly.'

'It was the sense of it, more or less. You said he knew too much about your affiliations.' She went to retrieve the medical bag from under the bed, hauling it out across the floorboards. 'You've quite a burden here, for the Turf Club. I think you'd better take it with you. It's far too heavy for me.'

'Jane!' exclaimed Joseph.

William shifted and groaned.

Jane put her finger to her lips, then whispered: 'Why should I take it? Why should I trust you when you won't trust me?'

They glanced at William: he had not woken up.

Joseph drew nearer to her. 'What do you mean?' His voice was quiet and clear.

'I think you know what happened between Edmond and Dr Wright, where the money is, and why Wright killed him. You know what happened at the races. Now tell me, or I won't help you.'

Joseph's glance shifted from the bag to her face, then to William, then back to the bag. 'I don't know what else there is to tell.'

'You've nothing more to lose, Joseph. You said yourself that you thought Wright had laid information against you. Why protect him now?'

'If I've played a part in his schemes …' Joseph's mouth twisted as he studied the scuffed toes of his boots.

'I'm not going to do anything against you, Joseph. It's too late. Nothing will bring Edmond back, or recover my money.

I know that. But I want to understand what happened. I want to know how Edmond's bank account was emptied while he was under Dr Wright's care. What happened to his letter of credit? How was he betting on the horses when he was unable to move from his bed?'

'Wright's keen on arranging bets for his patients. He says it's beneficial as it keeps them mentally occupied. Those wealthy widows he sees – they like a flutter.'

'But what stops Royce from knowing it's Wright? I've spoken to him. He doesn't know who has the money that Edmond supposedly won on a multiple bet.'

'Wright's in contact with a large number of brokers over a large number of bets. Your letter of credit could have been changed very quickly for cash.' Joseph put his writing case back into his bag and closed it up.

'Yet he only saw Edmond a couple of times.'

'He gives me notes for the patients; they often send something back via myself. Your husband once gave me six sovereigns in an envelope that I was to take to Dr Wright. I thought it was for settling his medical bills. And – this isn't definite, mind, but a multiple bet might have been arranged a long time in advance. It would be hard to know when it happened.'

'Wright has the money then. Edmond's winnings.'

Joseph humphed. 'He has that many debts,' he said. 'That'll be long gone.'

'And he fixed the races?' The final detail was about to be clear – she felt she already knew the answer.

'Well, there was Naas. The stable lads had got hold of some bottles of stout from somewhere. One of them was almost comatose in Mr Royce's horsebox and Wright went in to deal with him. He said he gave him a stimulant. He might have managed to give the horse something at the same time … he does keep all sorts of supplies in the carriage. The horse ran wild afterwards and had to be shot.'

Jane sighed. Was something she could have done to protect Edmond? Would he still be alive if he had resisted gambling? There was no point in asking Joseph more. 'So, why the Cork train, Joseph? You're not really going for the Turf Club, are you, with the law on your trail?'

'I've some business near Kilmallock, then I'll go on to Cobh and find a passage to France.'

Joseph shaved in William's dressing room, emerging with a handful of red beard. 'You might burn this, if you please.' He dropped it into the fireplace, before putting on his coat and creeping down the stairs.

Jane heard the street door open and close. She put a hand on William's forehead. His fever was still raging, and he could barely respond. She rang the bell and had to wait some time for Mr Nugent to appear, as though he had been keeping out of the way. She sent him out to the chemist with the new prescription.

She supposed she would put the medical bag under the bed. It was the same one that Joseph had brought on their rounds, and taken into the house on Marrowbone Lane. What was it that she had to transport? She opened it up. Beneath a stethoscope and the writing case was a wooden box wrapped in oilcloth, which she lifted out. The lid bore a brass label with the stamp of a Birmingham gunmaker. Inside lay a pair of revolvers, fitted around each other like deadly twins. There were compartments with lead bullets, a powder flask, a tin of caps, and priming instruments. She closed the box, her heart thumping with fear. She hastily shoved the bag under the bed.

Some time after, she heard someone on the stairs. It was Mr Nugent with the new medications and a jug of warm water. She made up the ammonia and ipecac and as she wetted William's face with the pungent solution his eyes opened, he recognised her and moaned.

'It will pass,' she said, hoping she was right, 'the fever will pass.'

He lay helpless on the damp sheet as she stripped him, his limbs heavy in her hands and thumping back on the bed as they came free. She had once loved his body intimately, but it was now that of a patient: stinking, ugly with rash. She rinsed the sponge in the bowl and mopped, wishing she could wash the spots away, coating his skin with cooling damp, then heaved him on his side and peeled away the sheet that had stuck to him, to wash along the bumps of his spine. He was as lean and tough as a reed and she felt sad for him: how hard he had worked, how he had denied himself rest. She remembered something Sister Aloysius had once said: the graveyards of the world are filled with those who thought themselves indispensable.

She applied the mercury ointment then changed his sheets, feeling dull and weary, wishing Sister Aloysius was there to guide her. She rang the bell and Mrs Nugent took away the linen, brought her more tea and toast, and offered to watch Dr Doughty if she wanted to go home. But Jane said no: Nelly would mind Orla as if she were her own. She sat on in the armchair, praying the fever would allow him to awaken so that she could give him the Black Drop.

Around midnight she gave it him, and a dose of quinine. She put the bottles on the side table, then, dizzy with fatigue, stretched out beside him in the bed. If she was going to catch typhus, she would have caught it by now; she was too tired to care.

She lay at William's side, snug against him, inhaling the chemical odour of the sponging solution. In the aura of his feverish heat the ache in her limbs disappeared and she melted, like a pat of butter on hot toast, into a profound sleep.

* * *

She woke to church bells at six in the morning, lying turned away. His arm was around her, and his hand lay on the swell of her breast above her stays. Her clothes were tight and uncomfortable, yet she had not slept so well for years.

She did not turn round, but curled her fingers around his wrist, where the pulse beat steadily, while at her back she sensed his breathing. He was at least alive, his fever down. But to his life, as to hers, was given a finite number of breaths, and of heartbeats – she could not know how many remained. They were precious to her, yet she had wasted them pursuing a hopeless dream, ignoring his loyal waiting. What if it was too late?

His breathing rhythm altered as he woke, but he did not move his hand. 'Something I need to tell you.' His whisper caught in his throat.

At his next words she let go of his wrist.

'About the day your husband died.'

338

'Go on,' she said. Why, at this moment, did the memory of Edmond have to intrude between them? She raised herself up on her elbow and turned to him; his arm fell back.

'It was when I was arguing with Dr Wright. When he held you by the wrist – I could have hit him for it.' He spoke in short gasps. 'Wright said I wanted to free you for myself. I denied it. You know I did not harm your husband. But a lie is more plausible when it's attached to the truth.'

'I'm sorry, William.'

What could she say? His years of loneliness could have been avoided if she had chosen him. But time cannot be reversed. Should she tell him she loved him? It was true, in a way, but she could not bring herself to utter the words.

Instead she said: 'I know it was Wright and not you. I found out from Joseph what he probably did with Edmond's money. And about drugging the horses.'

William nodded slowly. 'Report him to the police. Make sure he's stopped. If I die –'

'Don't die, William.' She lay down again and held him, a pang of regret making her tighten her embrace. 'Nothing else matters, truly …'

'Keep it all clear … in your head …' His voice was fading. 'Stay with me.'

He made no reply, but his hand traced her cheek before coming to rest on her shoulder. She tilted her head back to look up at him. Beneath the stubble she saw how the flesh hung loose on his neck, how hollow his cheeks had become and how furrows had appeared beside his mouth: age and illness might yet steal him away.

She knew she was not in a position to report Wright to

the police – he had already made sure that they were searching for her. She would be lucky to get away with completing Joseph's errand. For a moment the thought entered her head, that she would go to Merrion Square early in the morning, on the way to the station, and shoot Dr Wright. He deserved to be dead. But she had no idea how to use Joseph's pistols. Her hatred soon gave way to nausea.

There was another way of dealing with Wright: she began to form a plan.

Chapter Forty-four

ERRANDS

Jane got up at seven, straightened her clothes, brushed her hair in William's dressing room and rang the bell. Mrs Nugent came up with a cup of tea.

'Could you keep an eye on Dr Doughty this morning?' Jane asked her. 'I think – I hope – he's out of danger. His fever's staying down. I'll give him his medicines first, then I have some errands to run.'

'What will I do if Mr Morrissey calls?'

'Who's he?'

'From the insurance man. He says Dr Doughty owes Mr Lydon money. Twenty pounds monthly premium – fire insurance. He was here last night and I told him Dr Doughty was took sick and to come back the next day.'

'Fire insurance! Tell him Dr Doughty's still sick. It'll have to wait.' Jane sipped the tea; Mrs Nugent had put in too much sugar. 'Twenty pounds is an extortionate premium. Insuring a theatre in London's cheaper than that.' She remembered Davenant complaining about the cost.

'I'd be afraid of yer man, though.'

'Why?' A memory was worming through Jane's mind: *Mr Lydon*.

'He's a rough-looking fellow, you know? He'd break your arm as soon as look at you.'

'What does he look like?' Jane narrowed her eyes.

'A huge ugly divil in a red velvet coat. Neither of his pair of friends is any better.'

'Three of them, then.' Three divils. The men in the black brougham. 'Tell me, is the payment for fire insurance, or is it protection money?'

'I'd say they might set fire to the place if the money wasn't paid,' quavered Mrs Nugent.

Jane took a deep breath. 'If Mr Morrissey comes back, you can tell him I'm going to settle matters with Mr Royce directly. Have you got that? Mr Theodore Royce.'

Mrs Nugent's mouth outlined Royce's name, committing it to memory.

'I hope to be back by lunchtime,' said Jane.

'I'll have a stew ready for you.'

Jane wondered if she would ever eat it. As she thought of the morning ahead, her stomach could barely contain the tea. There was a carpet bag on top of William's wardrobe, which she fetched down and dusted. It was large enough to conceal Joseph's bag on the way to the station.

It was a quarter past eight when she stepped down to the street, her arm through the handles of the carpet bag, wearing Mrs Nugent's oldest bonnet instead of her nurse's cap. An hour to go. She hailed a jarvey to take her to Kingsbridge station and heaved up the carpet bag. It landed in the footwell of the jaunting car with a thud. The jarvey tipped his hat with a grin.

'What have yeh in there, miss, a hape o' stones? Yeh'll be buildin' a wall, so?'

She merely gave him a smile but, as she stepped up, she saw a carriage waiting further down the street. Its driver started the horses into motion.

'Do you see that dark-red carriage?' she said urgently. 'There's a man in it that means me harm.'

'Ah sure, 'tis only the police! We'll throw them off all right.' The jarvey clucked his tongue to his horse and shook the reins. The horse trotted on smartly. They soon crossed Patrick Street and, in the Coombe, gained some distance. But it was market day, and the street ahead was busy. They made little progress and eventually halted behind a brewery dray unloading barrels. The dark-red carriage drew nearer so that she feared that the police would jump out of it and come to detain her.

Joseph had given her three shillings and on the other side of the dray she got up and handed one to the jarvey. 'Let me off here,' she said, 'then drive on.' Heaving up the carpet bag, she descended into the throngs of people heading along a narrow street that led to the New Market. She watched from a shop doorway as the dark-red carriage passed the top of the street, then started to retrace her steps. The carpet bag, with its awful burden, felt ever heavier.

She knew these streets well and some of the people knew her; there were a score of places where she could have briefly hidden, but as she hurried on the cathedral bells struck the three-quarter hour and she quickened her pace. She arrived at the station just after nine. It was bustling but she found Joseph near the ticket office, where he stood perfectly straight and still by the wall, as though facing a firing squad. As he noticed her, he started forward.

'It's inside.' She pushed the carpet bag at him.

He must have seen the fear in her face. 'They're just for shooting horses. At the races.'

'As you like.' She just wanted to be rid of it.

'I have to ask you to do one more thing for me. Only a small thing, now. You'll be in no danger.' He gave her a long, slim envelope. It was crumpled, as though it had been in his coat pocket for days. 'Please, give this to your friend Anna. Tell her I shan't forget her.' Before she could reply, he wheeled around and strode rapidly towards the platform where the Cork train was being prepared for departure.

Relief flooded through her that this part of the morning was done, yet as she left the station by a side entrance, four constables rushed past. She could not help but pause and watch as they boarded Joseph's train. She turned quickly away, before she was seen to be looking.

Without the bag, and in the old bonnet and her plain dress, Jane was an insignificant figure. She slipped unnoticed into the street and soon found a jarvey who knew the way to the house of Mr Theodore Royce, MP. No-one followed them as they headed out of the city. She might have felt grateful when the jaunting car passed unhindered between the black gateposts of Royce Park and rolled slowly up the drive, except that she now had to face the second part of her morning.

The black landau she had once seen at the Lucan races was harnessed to four black horses. Its coachman attended to them while they waited in front of the house to depart. Behind it, luggage was being loaded into a covered carriage.

She paid the jarvey and told him to wait for her. It seemed a long way up the flight of steps to the front door, and the columns of the portico towered above her. She jangled the bell, then waited until a manservant opened the door.

'My name's Jane Verity and I owe Mr Royce a visit,' she said. 'No, he won't be expecting me.'

'Mr Royce is very busy,' the servant said with a scowl, 'and about to travel down to Mount Belvedere.'

'All the more important then, that he sees me before he starts his journey,' she replied.

It was chilly and damp in the hall where she waited for the servant to return. She stared at a pile of trunks on the black and white tiles. She thought of the crack of Royce's pistol, and how the crows would flap their wings and scream. If he did not like what she had to tell him, he could end her life, abruptly cutting her away from the people who cared about her: William – Orla. She imagined herself lying in fizzing quicklime with her clothes thrown in the wheelbarrow to moulder away, while Theodore Royce bowled down to County Cork in his landau with his coachman whipping the perfectly matched horses.

She was shown into the drawing room, where Royce, standing beside the window in a carriage coat, gave her a cold greeting.

'You've found my money, at last, Mrs Verity?' He turned his head to watch the luggage being loaded outside.

'No. But you might ask Dr Wright where it is.' She took a chair, without being asked.

'I've already studied the man and found no proof. Isn't that right?' Royce glanced at someone behind her. Looking round she glimpsed Bernard Morrissey and his two henchmen standing in the shadows.

'We found nothing to link him to the multipliers, sir.' Bernard advanced, heavy-footed.

Jane felt her chair shift as his hand fell on the seat back.

'So what proof is there, Mrs Verity?' Royce stroked his moustache. 'Do you have anything you can show me? Any reason I should delay my journey?'

'I've only what people have told me. Facts you might not know about – facts that form a pattern.'

'A pattern? You've come to waste my time with a pattern?'

'A pattern of poison. And I know what happened to your horse, Lucius.' Jane could see in the way that Royce turned, paused and stared, that she knew something he didn't. 'But if I'm to tell you anything, you must stop extorting money from Dr Doughty. Your men came to menace his housekeeper last night when he lay at death's door.'

Bernard coughed. 'Insurance premiums,' he rumbled. 'One of Mr Lydon's schemes.'

'Insurance premiums?' Jane looked indignantly round at Bernard. 'Protection money! They're afraid of being set afire – a doctor's residence – you should be ashamed of yourselves.'

'How much?' Royce asked.

'Twenty a month, sir.'

Royce shrugged. 'Neither here nor there, is it?'

'No, sir. I'll tell Mr Lydon.'

346

'Do so. You may continue to explain your pattern, Mrs Verity,' said Theodore. He came closer and sat facing her. 'Doubtless all will become clear.'

'I think perhaps you did not know that your two punters, my husband Edmond and Tom Nesbitt, were both patients of Dr Wright?'

As Theodore shook his head, she continued.

'The pills he supplied were poisonous. He gambled their money and poisoned them. He used agents to place the bets – but if you could ever trace the money, you might well find that he has it. Or has spent it – I'm told he is deeply in debt.'

Theodore did not try to contradict her but merely asked: 'What about my horse? Lucius?'

'At Naas, the stable lads were drinking. One of them was comatose in your horsebox. Wright went to help him. That would have provided him the opportunity to drug Lucius. Your horse ran wild afterwards, didn't he?'

'How can you prove it?'

'I can't. But I know enough about how Dr Wright behaves to be almost certain of it. As I said, it's a pattern. It's not just your horse, or my husband, or Tom. Dr Wright's wife, and his mother-in-law – their lives were insured with Mr Lydon. He's a serial poisoner.'

'That's outrageous,' said Royce quietly.

But he was considering what she had said.

'There are other things he has done, things at the hospital, which you don't need to know. If he dislikes someone, he finds a way to get rid of them. So, he's accused me of sedition –'

'You're codding me.' He almost smiled, so that the crows-feet deepened their grasp around his eyes.

'He's done it to silence me. I can't go to the police about him now, Mr Royce, in case I'm arrested myself. They're looking for me.'

'I can't see you as a revolutionary somehow. I can't see it.' Royce shook his head. 'The whole story is … well …'

'Are you saying you don't believe me?' She met his eyes, and held them, willing away his doubt. He was the first to look away.

'What do you think was administered?'

Jane shrugged. 'Wright keeps a whole variety of bottles in his carriage, according to Dr Murphy. Whatever he gave to Edmond, and to Tom, caused them great suffering. Headache, vomiting, painful spasms. Your horse was very likely in pain. Maybe that was the reason he ran badly.'

Royce's moustache wiggled as he sucked his cheeks from side to side, considering her information, as if he had taken a sour fruit into his mouth. Then he looked up. His jaw tightened. 'Lads,' he said, in a cold voice. 'You know what to do.'

'Sir.'

'Go now!'

They filed out.

'There are reasons why I don't go to the police either,' said Royce. 'I make my own laws, and I enforce them.'

Jane rose from her chair. 'I'll take my leave then.'

As she turned to go, he said in a lighter tone: 'But, Mrs Verity, I was about to travel to Mount Belvedere to oversee the preparations for my son's wedding. I believe you're a friend of the bride. Did she invite you?'

'Thank you,' said Jane. 'It's most kind of you, but I have nothing to wear.'

Chapter Forty-five

BLOODLETTING

Where's Jane? Jane?

William called out to her, his groans echoing within his throbbing head, his heart aching for her absence. He was freezing, shuddering, teeth chattering. All his muscles tensed with pain. He burrowed down into his covers, burying his head to keep what warmth he could. Then his fever soared. His heart pounded. He panted for breath. Looking sideways, even at the chest of drawers, gave him vertigo. He begged Mrs Nugent to close the curtains, to shut out the sun. Sweat soaked his pillow and stuck his sheets to his skin.

Through ringing in his ears he heard a fuss downstairs. Someone was coming to help. He heard the gratitude of the servants. But not Jane's voice: a man. Someone creaked along the corridor, then opened the bedroom door.

'Good morning!' It was Oliver Wright, smiling at him with open jaws, with Mrs Nugent whisking the curtains open. Light flooded in, painful light, making William screw up his eyes. He could only peer at Wright.

'I heard you had fallen ill on duty, so I've come to see what I can do.' Wright's voice was melodious, the Nugents harmonising with their respectful thanks. He slid the bottles of medicine around on the tray to read their labels.

'Is this all that's been given?'

Mrs Nugent was apologising.

If only Jane would come.

'He's severely ill.' Wright's fingers pressed at his wrist, then moved up his forearm, pincering around his elbow. 'At a point of *crisis*.'

William's arm throbbed in Wright's grip. He moaned and twisted. The grip tightened, then released.

'Would you fetch me a couple of large bowls, and some towels? Quick as you can. He must be bled at once – to bring the fever down.'

'Yes, doctor, yes.' Mrs Nugent scurried downstairs.

'Bring that chair.'

Mr Nugent obliged and Wright sat beside the bed with his bag at his feet. He took out instrument cases one by one.

'Here's what I want. Large lancets.' He put the case on the bedside table, then replaced the others, waiting for Mrs Nugent to return.

William turned away, curling into a fetal position.

'I think I'll need you to hold him.'

Mr Nugent came around the foot of the bed and placed a hand on William's shoulder to roll him on to his back. 'Like this? Sorry, Dr Doughty, sir.'

William looked into his servant's earnest face. He

summoned up every fragment of voice. '*He's a murderer,*' he croaked out.

'Hush, now, sir,' said Mr Nugent.

'Hah!' Wright snorted. 'He's delirious. It's the fever.'

William struggled to raise his head from the pillow. He was dizzy. *Where was Jane?*

'Keep still, there's a good fellow. Once your fever has been treated you'll be much improved. Ah, very good.' The delphware scraped as Wright arranged Mrs Nugent's bowls on the floor. 'And the towels? Good. Now, madam, if you would hold the hand?'

Mrs Nugent was almost as strong as her husband, whose hands weighed down William's shoulders. William's head sank back into the pillow. Oblongs of sunlight glowed across the ceiling, blurring the cracks in the plaster. He shut his eyes as Wright wrapped the tourniquet around his arm.

It was too loose. What was Wright doing? He felt that pincer grip around his elbow, a little prodding, then a searing pain in his arm that convulsed him. He would have been out of the bed had he not been held.

'Oh, the blood, doctor!' Mrs Nugent cried, though her grasp did not relent.

'The bowl, woman, quickly.'

Now they were silent and William heard his blood going into the bowl. Instead of a leisured drip it was a spurt. *Spurt, spurt, spurt,* the blood splashing out at the speed of his racing heart. His hand went cold, an ache in the forearm muscles becoming an agony.

You've lanced an artery, he tried to say, *it should have been a vein,* but his lips would not form the sounds. He strained and twisted against his servants' hands.

'Damnation! *Ugh!*' The blood must have missed the bowl. Wright's fingers dug viciously into his arm. Then: 'The other bowl, madam.'

William knew he was bleeding out now, that soon his faintness would dissolve into coma, and that he would fade into a pallid nothing. *If only Jane were there. One last sight of her.*

Did Jane come in then? Or was it later?

'What have you done? *Dear God, the blood, all the blood!*' Her voice rose in a crescendo. '*Across the floor, the towels, the bowls! It's an abbatoir. You're killing him. Let go of him!*'

There was such command in her that Mrs Nugent stepped back. But William was too weak to pull his dying arm from Wright's grip.

'No need to be squeamish, my dear.' Wright remained suave. 'His fever needs proper remediation.'

'You're doing that wrong. *You're murdering him!*'

'Nonsense. Bloodletting is essential to relieve fever. I am the physician here. It is not for you to –'

'*Physician?* You're a murderer, Dr Wright. *You murdered my husband.*' Her voice seemed to fade and distort. 'Now you're murdering my –'

'Your ignorance is not needed here.'

Weak and dizzy, William felt he was drowning in a dark vortex. Mr Nugent's hands had left his shoulders. The argument sounded far away. Jane's voice clear and strong over Wright's bluster.

'Ignorance? I know what you did. You slowly poisoned Edmond. You led him back to gambling so that you could smuggle away his money. You poisoned Tom Nesbitt – his money went missing. Heaven knows who else you poisoned, or for what reason. Then, after William analysed your pills you sent him to the Fever Hospital so he would fall ill. You were waiting for this chance to finish him. *Well, you won't.*'

Now someone else was in the room, bringing a smell of stale tobacco. There was a click. A deep voice said: 'Yeh might leave that now, Dr Wright. Mr Royce wishes to speak to yeh.'

'Royce?'

There was a bang, but it was only Wright's chair toppling over as he sprang up. William felt the lancet leave his arm. Someone took his elbow and pressed on the bleeding artery.

'I told him you killed his horse,' said Jane. 'How else could I stop you?'

Through black mist, William saw a huge fellow in a red velvet coat, a pistol in his hand. Then they were gone.

Chapter Forty-six

ABCs

William was improving. Yet he still lay passive on his pillows, heavy and aching, his mind in dull despair. Where was Jane? Perhaps she had no time for him now that he was out of danger.

He sought her in his memories. Her face had been a pale blur as she'd hauled him up on his pillows. That awful tea: he'd only opened his mouth because he had to, and the sponge that reeked of ammonia had made him shiver. He'd been too febrile to be aloof, yet too incoherent to talk to her.

Just once, he'd had a lucid moment, when birdsong had alerted him to the pink light of dawn, a breeze from the open window stirring the half-drawn curtains. His heart had turned a cartwheel, for she had been there asleep, dressed for work, smelling of sweat, and cloves. A treasure in his bed, turned away on her side, unaware that he was awake.

It must have been a dream: leaning up on an elbow and studying her up close for the first time in years, his body stirring into life. Her nurse's cap had come off. Dark wisps of hair had escaped her velvet ribbon. Her cheek had become gaunt, and her mouth had relaxed into sadness. He'd eased himself back down, edging closer, sliding an arm carefully over her waist.

He'd imagined he wasn't sick. He'd protect her, feed her, rest her. If only she'd let him – yet she'd fly into harm if it meant being free.

Then shame had burned through him, stronger than fever. He had seen into the past: he should never, ever, have pursued her, all those years ago. He had been her employer, a married man, a man with a profession. She had been his servant, young and vulnerable, deserted by her lover and grieving for her son, fearing a return to the workhouse if she displeased him. He should not have exploited his advantage. Yet his desire had eroded reason, blinding him to what was decent behaviour.

But he had loved her, he had argued with himself: that must have made it better. He had truly loved her, and loved her still. Had he not paid a heavy price, and been forced to continue through the years alone? Perhaps he had suffered enough. But he could not blame her for having chosen freedom, or for marrying another man. He had no right to exhibit hurt and he should not have refused to help her. He was selfish. Even now she risked contagion by nursing him, and he less than useless in her hands. Painful thoughts had teemed in his mind like tadpoles in a pond.

He'd dozed, but when he'd woken up again, his head had been so heavy and he'd barely caught his breath to speak to her. Had he managed to tell her he that still longed for her? If so, all she had said was, *I'm sorry, William.*

She had gone away. Then she had come back after a while. He remembered Wright and the terrible pain in his arm. Then darkness. Had she been there at all?

Now, Mrs Nugent brought beef tea and biscuits, gave him his medicines, and said nothing of her. William lay in bed, too fatigued to eat or drink, resisting Mrs Nugent's coaxing. He heard the recurring noises of the street below his window: the early morning milk carts, then the costermongers, the newspaper sellers, and always the church bells. At night came the drunks and the soldiers and their women. He heard everything, long after the last echoes of the bells, from gaps in fitful sleep.

After a few days Mr Nugent brought him a copy of *The Dublin Weekly Register*, pointing out an article. The constabulary were investigating Dr Wright's whereabouts. Dr Wright was thought to have fled abroad to escape his creditors. His coachman stated that he had driven him to Eden Quay. A financier and property agent, Mr Vincent Lydon, who had reported the disappearance, also said that Dr Wright's true vocation was not medicine, but his stables and a string of racehorses. This had led to an elaborate series of debts, initially secured on his late mother-in-law's fortune. Each debt paid off a previous one, so that although his losses were heavy, he had maintained the face of prosperity that was crucial for a man of the turf.

'That doctor was here,' said Mr Nugent. 'He had bled you, then three men took him away – that coachman was gone.'

'Did you not report it to the constabulary?'

'Let them find it out for themselves. He was up to no

356

good, so Miss Jane told me. She said he was after letting too much blood off you and she stopped him just in time.'

At least, thought William, he was no longer a danger to patients.

When Jane visited, he heard Mrs Nugent complaining to her outside his door: 'He won't even eat my honey biscuits! Will you not speak to him? Sure I can't manage him when you're not here.'

Jane came in, apologising. 'I should've come before, but I've been busy. I had to work extra at the hospital to make up for my absence, and then there's Orla.'

She had perfected the demeanour of a nurse: kind and polite. He despaired.

'How are you feeling today?'

'Improved.' He raised his nightshirt and showed her his rash, now pale brown, the colour of fading bruises. His abdomen was like an empty bowl.

She glanced quickly. 'You've lost too much weight,' she said, then moved towards the window, waiting for him to cover himself.

'I don't feel like eating.'

'You must try.'

'There's no point. Why did you save me if you didn't want me?'

She stared. 'What do you mean?'

'When I was ill,' he said. 'You embraced me, you lay beside me, we embraced each other, is that not right? I didn't dream it?'

'Yes.' She came back and stood beside the bed. 'I thought I was losing you ... And I was so tired. I had to sleep.'

'Then why so formal now? Now I'm not dying, we're to resume our distance, is that it?'

'We can't go back to the past,' she said. 'You know it yourself.'

'I want you to know that I'm sorry for the past,' he said. He reached and took her hand, looking up pleadingly.

'You do regret our affair then. I thought you would in the end.' She disengaged her hand.

'No. No … I'll never regret it … it's the one perfect memory of my whole life. But I've become ashamed of myself. I chased after you when I shouldn't, and I've rebuffed you when I shouldn't. I'll never get it right.'

'I had to marry Edmond,' she said. 'I should have told you at the time – I should have been honest about it. You were waiting for me and I pretended you weren't.'

'I had no right to expect anything. You had to act according to your situation and what suited you.' He dug into his soul for the right words. 'I shouldn't have put pressure on you. I made it harder for you to tell me.'

Her smile was benevolent and forgiving; he feared that his regrets and apologies were no longer relevant.

'There's no need to go over the past.' Yet her eyes softened – perhaps she felt something after all. 'Is there anything else I can do for you?'

'No.' He sank his head back, staring up at the ceiling. 'Thank you.'

'Please try to eat something,' she said as she left.

He screwed his eyes tight shut, listening to her feet on the stairs. In a moment he would hear the opening and closing of the front door, and she would be gone forever.

But there was a conversation, Mrs Nugent's voice,

pleading. He did not hear her leave. Then after a while he heard music: quiet, then subtly louder. It could only have been Jane at the piano in the drawing room, the same cottage piano from Newhall Street that she'd once played, that time they'd been in love. Music, with its delicate highs and rumbling lows, filtered into his senses like fragrance. He felt hope return. He heaved himself up in the bed, took a honey biscuit from the plate, and let it crumble on his tongue.

* * *

Mrs Nugent must have been overjoyed that he had eaten three biscuits, for it seemed that Jane continued visiting to please her. She was demure and polite when she came to his room: a nurse checking on her patient. He thanked her for her kindness. Her music progressed him from honey biscuits to buttered toast, then to sandwiches.

One day he heard a child's footsteps in the hall downstairs: Jane had brought the orphan. Orla was a lovely little thing, quick and agile, well-mannered with the lilt of County Cork in her voice. He imagined she had been a farmer's child, raised in a quiet rural life until the Great Hunger caught her family in its lethal grasp.

'Why are you in bed in the daytime?' Orla asked straight away when she saw him. 'Are you going to die?'

'Orla!' protested Jane, but the child advanced closer to the bed, her head on one side.

'No – I'm getting better,' he said, feeling embarrassed. What he had suffered was so small compared to this child's loss of her entire family.

'Come away now, my little pet,' said Jane, 'and help me play the piano.'

'I want to see him get better.' There was a mischievous spark in her eyes.

'Do you go to school?' he asked her.

'Not yet. Jane says I have to learn to read and write, so I suppose I ought. I'm scared of school, though.'

'Why?'

'They're run by nuns and I'm afraid of nuns. There were nuns in the hospital, and they used to give me nasty syrup.'

'I expect that was to make you feel better. You got better anyway.'

She nodded. 'My mam didn't.'

'You miss your mam.' He thought to distract her. 'Do you know your alphabet?

She shook her head.

'Sit with me and I'll teach you.' He wanted his desk, and his inkstand, so he put on his dressing gown and made his way downstairs, leaning for support on the banister, to the study.

As Jane went to the piano, Orla perched on a chair by his desk and he pushed a pile of unopened correspondence aside. He had no children's books to show her but drew small pictures with pen and ink: an Apple, a Baby, a Cow. She was a quick learner. He found her a pencil and taught her to trace letters. Her face really was a heart-shape, with its little pointed chin.

Jane was in the drawing room playing a composition of her own. Sometimes gay and sometimes poignant, it floated, weaving soft scarves of beauty in the air. As she played, he imagined the scent of honeysuckle in a summer garden, with Jane in a rose-silk gown, whirling around a ballroom in his arms. The music ended and now she came into the study.

'Look, Jane, Dr William has taught me ABCs. Will I show you?' Orla pointed to the letters in turn. 'A, B, C!'

Jane bent to look at Orla's tracings, and at William's sketches. 'Lovely work. But it's time to go home now, Orla.'

'Can I take the ABCs?' Orla gathered up the drawings.

'Of course.' William smiled at her eagerness as she got down from her chair, but shot Jane a rueful glance, sad that they were leaving.

'She's a clever girl,' said Jane brightly.

'You should have been her mother,' murmured William, thinking it a pity that they were not his family, 'and we should not pretend to be strangers.'

As she left the room, she gave no sign that she had heard.

* * *

At least she continued for now to visit him and, as William became stronger, he'd sit by the piano as of old. Even though she knew most of her repertoire by heart, there were times when he could turn the music sheets for her. Sometimes she would look up from the piano, but he looked away or dropped his eyes to watch her fingers roaming the keys.

He had insisted on paying her for nursing him. If she had been a physician, she would have invoiced him twenty or thirty guineas by now. She had visited regularly for a month and had brought him back from the brink of death. Moreover – according to Mrs Nugent – her influence with a certain Mr Royce had put a stop to the 'fire insurance' demands. It was only fair, he said, that she should receive something.

He was seeing Jane regularly, but he felt they had lost one another again, both of them too distant. And the money increased the distance between them.

It was also enough to secure a passage back to England and several weeks' accommodation, or even to restart her musical career.

When William was well enough to return to his old job at the Meath, Jane said she was leaving for England. There'd been a card pinned up outside the Theatre Royal in Hawkins Street: *Pianist wanted, apply within to the Great Galvini.* The magician, whose real name was Terence Galvin, needed someone to play triumphant chords and crescendos, as he threw knives at his assistant, the dark and careless Coralina, sawed her in half inside a gilded casket, or with his improbably large hands conjured white rabbits out of her scarlet satin cloak. Meanwhile a black-clad youth, Quilty, was employed behind a night sky with a thousand glittering stars and a box of fireworks to make all the illusions work.

So Jane was conjured back to spending three evenings a week in her black silk and black garnets, playing to an audience who gasped and sighed with horror and wonder at the bizarre display. It was not what she wanted to play, still less to compose, but the magic was that it paid well, and when Galvini, Coralina and Quilty planned a move to Liverpool for the Christmas season she said she would go with them. Orla would come with her and might develop into a singer.

When she said it she paused, as if waiting for him to argue, but he merely said it was her decision, and he wished her well. It was not his place to impose his wishes on her.

By mid-September he was strong enough to travel and had finalised his arrangements in New York. Professor Charles had recommended him for a set of rooms on 33rd Street, which he had forwarded a deposit to secure. He would work up until the last possible day at the hospital and refer his outdoor patients on to Dr Stephenson, who had been promoted to Dr Wright's old position. New doctors had been engaged to fill the empty posts. William began to pack up his belongings with the help of the Nugents, who rapidly secured a new post with a surgeon in South King Street.

When Jane next visited, crates were stacked in the hall awaiting the carrier and most of the furniture had been sold. Their footsteps echoed in the rooms.

'You can see that you've entirely cured me – I'm booking my ticket with Cunard tomorrow,' he said. 'There are a few things to sort out at the Meath, some of my books are going to Dun's Library, and after that I'll be ready to travel: from here to Liverpool, then on to New York.'

She let out a little cry, turning her reddening face up to his with her eyes wide.

'New York,' she repeated. 'Three thousand miles away. I can't imagine such a distance. I suppose I might not see you again.'

'You'll be back in the London theatres before long.' He regarded her with a frown, wondering if he saw moisture in her eyes. 'That's your dream, isn't it?'

'I hadn't thought it would be so hard to say goodbye.'

She looked down through squeezed eyelids, fumbling in her skirt pocket for a handkerchief. 'I'm so sorry to see you go … I …'

Then she stumbled forward. Without him consciously willing it, his arms rose up around her, binding her close. Her head ducked into his neck, hot and tense. She was trembling.

'Do you remember how we kissed, when we parted that time, at the station in Birmingham?' He murmured into her hair as his heart pounded against her. 'When you went to London.'

'I've never forgotten. I don't think I can part from you again … I can't.'

In that moment they both knew.

'Come with me, Jane, bring the child. Share my life as you should always have done. There's still time – we still have time.'

'It's not too late?'

'Set your path by mine,' he said. 'We'll face a new country together.'

Her answer was a kiss that, swiftly opening his mouth, made him shudder with delight.

Chapter Forty–seven

THE BEACONS ARE LIT

Thursday August 16th,
Mount Belvedere,
Nr. Kildorrery, County Cork.

My dear Jane,
I write with awful news. Theodore Royce was shot dead yesterday, and I am no longer to be married. I broke off my engagement to Alex last night.

This is what happened: Theodore arrived from Dublin on Tuesday evening. Yesterday morning, as was his custom, he drove himself over to Bowenscourt, along the Mallow road. Alex had offered to go with him, but Theodore laughed and said it was only a short distance, that he had made the journey a thousand times, and he 'enjoyed a spin'. He would not even take his coachman.

There is a stretch of the Mallow road in disrepair, where one must proceed slowly. The murderer must have waited there. A farmer driving a hay-wain found the road blocked by the landau, the horses cropping the grass from the verge, and Theodore slumped in the driver's seat, bleeding out from his wounds.

The area has been locked down by the constabulary, with a curfew imposed, but they fear it is too late to find the murderer and expect to encounter a complete silence in the area. A gun case of English origin was found near the scene, with a brace of pistols, so they think the killer is no longer armed, and that we are not in danger.

Even so, when we saw the fires from the terrace last night, my mother, who until then had behaved with complete reserve, became hysterical. Defying the curfew, beacons had been lit on the mountains for miles around. It seems that Theodore was murdered in revenge for evictions. A similar display took place after conspirators murdered Major Mahon, of Strokestown, a couple of years ago.

The servants laid Theodore's body on a table in the gun room, washed and shrouded with a sheet. Alex did not come to dinner and kept vigil by his father. I went in, as I thought, to comfort him, but found him pacing the floor in a rage and vowing revenge. The remaining townlands would be cleared of tenants and the bailiffs would compel them to demolish their own homes. I went to his side, and tried to reason with him.

'You should not add to the tenants' grievances,' I said. 'It will do nothing to improve the situation.'

He rounded on me. How could the tenants dare to have grievances when his father had done so much to save the estate from bankruptcy?

I thought, Jane, about what you had tried to tell me about Theodore, and wondered how much Alex really knew, despite his denials.

'The tenants your father evicted have died wandering the roads or begging in Dublin,' I said, but he would not listen.

His mind was made up. He could not live here. As Theodore's sole heir he had decided to dispose of Mount Belvedere and its lands, which must be sold unencumbered.

'Alex, if you love me...' I begged him to relent.

'Do you not realise that no-one will buy land occupied by the hovels of the peasantry? They're an obstruction to modern farming.' Then he called me ignorant of the facts!

I was infuriated. How dare he! 'Do you imagine that I will marry into a family who extract their wealth from the suffering of the poor?'

'Nonsense!' he said. 'How can you speak ill of my father, even as he lies dead in front of you?'

The room smelt of blood. Theodore's wounds had oozed into the white sheet. I felt so sick and angry that I could not help myself.

'I've learned that he became rich on illegal bookmaking and rack-rent. That he has the men and the methods to carry out extortion and murder.'

Alex did not ask me for any proof. He must have known, or at least suspected. He merely gave me a vicious glare and said: 'Yet you were enough of a hypocrite to drape his diamonds around your neck.'

'I loved you, Alex,' I said. I felt like weeping. But instead I took off my diamonds and left them beside the corpse. Then I went alone through the corridors of Mount Belvedere to my mother's apartment, where I demanded to be taken home.

At that, my mother broke out into hysterics again. She asked me if I knew how much money had already been spent on our costumes, on the hire of the Shelburne Hotel, on the cake, how many people had received invitations who would now be disappointed with less than ten days' notice, having already bespoken costumes and wedding presents. Did I realise that money would now be wasted?

I replied I would not marry into a family of rack-rent landlords, but she said I was naive, and how did I expect to be supported? 'Money has to come from somewhere.'

When I said that I would rather find a way of supporting myself, she flew into a rage.

Now my mother and I are each keeping to our rooms awaiting my father who is coming to escort us home.

I hope that I shall see you on my return to Dublin.

Ever your friend,

Anna

Chapter Forty-eight

GOD SPEED

15, Place Dauphine, Paris

September 15th, 1849

My dear Dr Doughty,

I hope that you have recovered from your illness and been able to resume your plans for your new appointment in America. I feel I owe you an explanation for my disappearance. You have been aware, I think, that I have been in trouble, and I would like you to understand the reason: no Irishman of conscience can ignore the wholesale slaughter visited upon his country by the misgovernment and corruption of the English.

I was arrested at Kingsbridge Station with pistols in my medical bag and was taken to Dublin Castle. I was locked in a cell and despaired of my freedom, for no-one has ever escaped from those dungeons and the Castle is garrisoned with soldiers as well as being the headquarters of the police.

But within an hour I was escorted to what they called the interview room. I feared I would be beaten to make me betray the Club but resolved to stay silent for as long as I could bear it. Yet at a bare table sat a gentleman in a plain black coat, like a lawyer. As I stood in front of him, he dismissed my two guards, who closed the door behind them. He said he was Colonel Meredith-Browne, and that I might recognise his name, as his daughter Anna had praised my work with the sick poor in the slums.

He then questioned me about the contents of my bag. Owning the weapons was not in itself an offence, but he was anxious to learn where I was taking them. He had been informed that I kept bad company, which was a great shame for a bright young physician like myself. I said the pistols were for shooting injured horses at the racetrack, and that I assisted Dr Wright for the Turf Club. He was silent, in a way that made me feel I had to say more, so I said I was going to a race meeting at Barronstown.

He said he was himself a follower of the turf and was certain there was no race meeting at Barronstown until the thirteenth of September. My destination according to my railway ticket was Kilmallock, further down the line. He wanted to know my plans. If I or my associates intended some mischief with these weapons, his job was to uphold the law and prevent that mischief from being done.

I refused to tell him anything, but he, smiling, said that Dr Wright had given him an address and men had been arrested. He knew that the Club had entrusted me with this burden, and this journey to Kilmallock. He already had enough evidence to hang me if he chose. Perhaps I would inform him as to where the consignment was directed?

I would not.

'Why do you do this?' he demanded. 'An educated young man,

a professional man, yet how you lower yourself by your criminal associations – you have ruined your career!'

I felt as if my own father scolded me and wanted to say that it was none of his business. Instead, I spoke of the evictions around Mount Belvedere. Two hundred acres of land had been emptied of smallholdings. Starving people were dragged in extremis from their pitiful hovels and thrown upon the road, to watch their homes and the last of their possessions consumed by flames. Others had been forced to enter the pestilential ships that bore them to a burial at sea, or to a slow death in the quarantine station of Quebec's Grosse Île. Their landlord, Theodore Royce, was a murderer and must pay the penalty. I said it was only justice: 'If the Government cannot exercise authority, the people will.'

I remember that as I spoke the Colonel brought his hands together and squeezed until the fingertips became dark red. Then he stretched them out and put them on the table edge, as though about to rise. But he did not move. It was as if an internal crisis consumed him. He said he had had a feeling it was Royce. When he met my eyes, his own were full of some unknown grief.

He said he knew well that famine relief monies sent to Mitchelstown, and to Charleville, found their way into Royce's pockets. He knew of the inhumanity of the evictions, the deaths along the roads, the coffin ships. The pity was that Royce had powerful friends. Then with some difficulty he added: 'Theodore Royce has poisoned the wellspring of joy in my life.' He fell silent for a while. I did not venture a reply.

He looked around the room as if to confirm that we were alone, then said that I would continue my journey. His voice was a murmur. I disbelieved that I had heard correctly, and requested him to repeat himself, which he did. He then said he was sparing

371

my life, but it was on condition that I would quit Ireland for ever. My future was in exile.

Then he summoned my guards and told them he was satisfied that the pistols were used by me for purposes to do with horse racing, and that the accusations laid against me and my friends by Dr Wright were false and motivated by professional jealousy.

'God speed, Dr Murphy,' he said.

My identity papers, my medical bag, and the pistols were returned. I was brought to Kingsbridge station by carriage in time to catch the twelve o'clock train. You will probably have learned by now of Theodore Royce's fate. My debt to the Club is now discharged, and I am obligated to them no further.

I sailed from Cork to France and have recently obtained a position as a surgical dresser in the Hôtel-Dieu hospital in Paris. My Latin is better than my French, however, and I have my sights on America once I have earned my passage money. I would be deeply indebted if, once you are established in New York, you could maintain a correspondence with me, and inform me if any opportunities of employment arise.

Sincerely yours,

Joseph Murphy

Chapter Forty-nine

THE JUDGEMENT HOUR

When William showed Jane the letter from Paris, she remembered the crumpled envelope that Joseph had given her at Kingsbridge Station. She ought to deliver it to Anna. It had slipped her mind, in amongst preparations for their transatlantic journey, and arrangements for their wedding, a simple ceremony in the Unitarian church on Eustace Street.

The Unitarian pastor who was to marry them had asked to be remembered to Jane's father, whom he knew from his days as an Abolitionist in London.

'My parents have cut off all contact.' Jane explained her situation.

'But you might try,' he had said. 'They may yet be willing for a reconciliation. I'll enclose your letter with my own, if it will help.'

'You're very kind,' said Jane, 'but after ten years I've given up hope.' She promised to consider it.

Later she even sat down with pen and paper, but the

words would not come to her. Instead, she wrote Anna the letter she owed her. She also owed Anna a visit, for she intended to invite her to the wedding.

A few days later Jane called at the house in Fitzwilliam Square. The fire was unlit in the drawing room, and the house smelt damp. The windows faced east, and in the shadows of a cloudy afternoon the chintz furnishings looked grey.

Anna's footsteps as she came downstairs were the only sound in the house. She forced a smile as she entered the room.

'Congratulations!'

'Oh, Anna.' Jane put Joseph's envelope down on a sofa-table so that she could embrace her. "What a reversal – that I'm to marry while you are not.'

Anna rested her brow on Jane's shoulder. 'It's been horrible. I suppose I oughtn't to have called off the wedding, but I just couldn't go through with it.'

Jane drew back to look at her. 'You've suffered.'

Anna was puffy-faced, her eyes and mouth were sombre, and her girlish freshness had vanished. 'My mother's so low in spirits. She's lost interest in everything. She doesn't even visit the dressmaker anymore.'

'I'm sorry to hear it.' As they sat down together it occurred to Jane that Anna did not realise that her mother was grieving. 'How's your father?'

'Papa's spending long hours at Dublin Castle. He's preoccupied – the famine's never-ending, the potatoes have failed again, the population are facing another winter of starvation and he has not the means to save them. But he did say that it was as well that I'd broken off the engagement. I don't think he ever liked Alex – or Theodore either. My brother Robert shrugged it all off and said that Alex had been cut up about everything but will probably be engaged again by Christmas. He doesn't expect him to be a bachelor for long, at any rate.'

'So, it seems that, of everyone, your mother's been the most upset?' Jane, watching Anna nodding in reply, saw that she was unaware of what lay in her mother's heart. 'Has anything else happened?'

'My parents have had an enormous quarrel. It started over the diamonds that Theodore had given us – I was delighted to return mine to the jeweller, but Mama kept hers. Then Papa said that Theodore's business was dishonest, and much was coming to light about his shady side.'

'I wonder what he meant by that?' Had the Colonel found out, Jane wondered, about the quicklime in Theodore's barn? Did he know what had become of Dr Wright?

'I'm not sure. He said we were to cut all connections, for the sake of his own probity, as an official in the Administration. Mama replied that all he cared about was work. That made him furious – I've never seen him so angry. He started shouting: *"What I care about is honour! I care about self-respect – one's own – the respect of others!"* It was as if he had slapped her. There was absolute silence, then she told me to leave the room at once. I don't know what they said after that, but since then she's kept to her bed, and won't speak to me.'

Jane hesitated, carefully phrasing what she said next: 'As children we see our parents as gods, as infallible; but when we find that their mistakes are not of our making – that is when we enter adulthood.' She met Anna's troubled gaze. 'Do you really believe that you're to blame?'

'I don't know. Sometimes I do regret breaking off with Alex. Maybe Mama was right.'

'Oh, Anna, I'm sorry. I know you adored him.' It would not have been tactful to tell Anna what a relief it had been to read her letter. 'You would have given up everything you cared about for his sake.'

'But how narrowly I escaped a life sentence in the countryside – Mount Belvedere was precisely in the middle of absolutely nowhere.'

'He would have prevented you from becoming anything more than his wife.'

Anna looked at the sofa-table, and her eye fell on Joseph's envelope. 'I was appalled when I learned what was done to the tenants. They were welcome to the whole place as far as I was concerned. Anyway, Alex has it, and I wish him joy of it.'

'You would have been unhappy there.'

'So – as you said – now it is you who are to be married …' Anna, abstracted, picked up Joseph's envelope.

'I would like to ask if you would do me the honour of being my bridesmaid? If you can bear it – you would have been on your honeymoon by now …'

'I'd be delighted,' said Anna. 'And I'm making some new plans …'

'Only don't wear anything too fancy. With all your tulle and taffeta, and Valenciennes lace, and jewels, I won't be able to keep up.'

'But you must have a beautiful outfit for your wedding day.'

'Weddings are frightful things, Anna.' Jane sighed. 'My wedding to Edmond – the whole day was so lavish, so full of anxieties. We had an audience of hundreds: actors, actresses, musicians, scenery painters, wardrobe ladies, stagehands, playwrights. Even the more disreputable members of the aristocracy were there. I remember blankly repeating my vows. I was so nervous that I felt that I shouldn't have been there, and wondered afterwards if I really was. Now I'm keeping all the arrangements simple. Orla will be my flower girl, and the guests will merely consist of a few hospital staff and my downstairs neighbours from Francis Street.'

Jane watched Anna open the envelope and hold a column of newsprint up to the light. 'That's from Joseph,' she said. 'You know, Dr Murphy. You saw him out on rounds.'

Anne read the poem, her lips moving silently. 'Why has he sent me this?' She frowned in bewilderment. '*My Dark Rosaleen? My flower of flowers?*'

Jane frowned, remembering Joseph reciting it. He was a dreamer, although if he had shot Theodore Royce he could hardly dream of winning Anna's heart. 'He asked me to tell you he wouldn't forget you. Obviously, you made a strong impression.'

'I hadn't realised.' A smile warmed Anna's listless face. 'But of course, Mr Mangan writes here that it's an allegory. It's an ode to Ireland, disguised as a love poem. *The Judgment Hour must first be nigh, ere you can fade, ere you can die ...*'

'Joseph's first love is certainly the Irish cause – I wouldn't give him too much thought, Anna. He was accused of sedition, arrested in possession of pistols, and was lucky to be released without charge. He's working in Paris now, and not likely to return to Ireland.'

She would not be telling Anna who had released Joseph, or the reason why.

'Francesca always says that the best men of a generation have been scattered into exile.' Anna slipped the poem back into the envelope. Then she brightened. 'As for me – I'm probably going to America.'

'To America? Oh, Anna!' Jane clapped her hands. 'To New York? I'd be so glad to have a friend there.'

'No – to my Aunt Isobel in Massachusetts. I think it's quite a distance,' said Anna. 'But we may find a way to see one another, or we can always write.'

'Of course,' said Jane, her hopes for Anna rising. 'Tell me more about your aunt?'

'She's Papa's sister. With Mama being unwell, he's sending me to stay with her. She's married to a philosophy professor at a women's academy and enjoys what she terms the 'collegiate life'. She thinks I should study literature for a Bachelor of Arts degree.'

'And will you?'

Anna studied the ink-stained callus on her right middle finger, sliding her thumb back and forth over it. 'I don't know if I'm equal to the task. Mama merely said it would turn me into an old maid – or worse, a bluestocking. But Papa said that was nonsense: I'm not yet even twenty; I'd enjoy it and profit by it. What do you think?'

'It's a perfect opportunity, Anna. Take it.'

'I think studying literature might revive my writing ambitions.' Anna's eyes gleamed. 'Or I could work as a teacher. After all, if I don't go, what's here for me? I might find another husband, I suppose, and be rich, but I'd never be independent.'

'Anna, wherever you go, you'll be besieged by rich husbands. Your task is to evade them for as long as possible and cling to your freedom. There's certainly no danger of you becoming an old maid.'

'But a course of study might take four or five years.' Anna sighed. 'Mama says that gentlemen prefer younger women, and with each year that passes I'll become less desirable.'

'How old is she?' Jane suddenly felt that she had lost patience with Anna's mama.

'I beg your pardon?'

'How old is your mother?'

'I suppose … forty-three or forty-four …'

'You do know that she was having an affair with Theodore Royce?'

'What?' Anna stared, as if at shadows of the past, and was silent, her breath suspended, as if straining to hear distant voices.

'I first suspected it when I saw them waltzing together.' Jane watched Anna's blank face: to think less of one's parent is truly the hardest thing in the world. She went on gently: 'What did you think about all the times she was supposed to be at the dressmaker? You knew that Theodore owned the apartments above the shop. What about the diamonds that she wouldn't give back? Why was that? Was it because they were expensive, or was it because he had fastened them on her himself?'

'Oh, poor Mama …' Anna's hands went to her mouth, then she clasped them together. 'No wonder she's taken to her bed.'

'At any rate,' said Jane, 'you need no more lessons from her on courtship.'

'Papa's view of my prospects was always the exact opposite of hers.' Anna's eyes widened. 'So … Papa knows. He knew of the affair. He must have challenged her with it.'

Jane nodded. 'Hence his assertions about honour and self-respect?'

Anna paused for a moment to reflect. 'Perhaps I'm being sent away so that they can try to mend themselves. I wish there was something I could do to help them.'

'They aren't yet at the age when they need their children to become their parents,' said Jane, with a sigh. 'If there's a reconciliation to be found, they'll find it by themselves. My advice to you is to follow your own path.' Anna was forming her decision, Jane was sure. 'You could accompany us, Anna. We're going on *Cunard* from Liverpool on the 15th of October. William booked an entire two-berth cabin for Orla in First Class, so, as long as you don't mind sharing, it would be lovely to have your company.'

'That was extravagant of him.'

'He said that if he didn't, one of us would end up sleeping on the floor, and he had a horrible feeling it would be him.'

Anna laughed. 'But what will your life be like in America? You disapproved of me giving everything up for Alex. What about you and William? Is he taking you to New York to be his helpmeet? To be a nurse?'

Jane shook her head. 'You may not remember this, but once, when we were talking about Edmond, Francesca asked me if I had someone else.'

'Yes,' said Anna. 'You crumpled up. Then you said, "*My goodness, is that the time?*" and you left.'

'I avoid telling others of my past. Yet I suppose ... I know so much about you now. It's only fair.' Jane glanced at Anna and saw that the lively curiosity had returned to her expression. She paused for a breath, thinking what she was to say. 'Years ago, William and I loved each other, but I had to lead my own life: I had to perform. Now he's someone I can no longer imagine being without. I don't want to chase pointless celebrity. As for performance – I've spent night after night rattling out the same tunes. It's enough.'

'But how can you give up the piano, Jane?' Anna's eyes were wide.

'I won't. I'll continue to compose – it interests me more. Then there's Orla. William wants her to have a good education. But I think she'll follow her own path – all she wants is to sing.'

'And what of your parents, Jane? You know everything about mine, yet have said nothing about your own.'

'They no longer acknowledge me,' said Jane, and explained how they had severed all contact after her elopement with Edmond.

Then, summoning her courage, she admitted to Anna the story of Nathan.

Anna was not, as she had expected, repelled and, after expressing deep sympathy, simply returned to her question:

'Surely you should write and tell your parents of your wedding?'

Jane was not minded to do it: forgiveness was needed on both sides.

But, back in Francis Street that evening, she played the piano while Nellie's husband sang Beethoven's *Irish Songs*. He had proved to have a fine voice, and a love for the old ballads. Orla's voice threaded high and pure through the melody, in an improvisation of her own, as the whole family sat rapt, the children connected to their parents by the sweet linkages of shared music.

Give me the kind spirit
that laughs on its way,
that turns thorns into roses,
and winter to May.

'Beautiful!' Nellie sighed, as it ended.

Yes, Jane thought, *I'll write.*

Author's Note

Has the teaching of Irish history in Britain improved since I was a schoolgirl? In the day, I memorised the dates, spouses and religions of Britain's monarchy and learnt nothing about its colonial past. I got no further than the Tudors before giving up, and I learnt nothing about Ireland, not even the devastations wreaked by Henry VIII and Elizabeth I. So, as a recent immigrant into Ireland, I am self-taught in its history. I hope that readers who are better educated than me will forgive me if I have mangled the truth to suit a work of fiction.

The Great Famine – *an Gorta Mór*, or the 'Great Hunger' – spanned the years 1845–1852. It was not the first famine in Ireland's history but it is the best documented and the most lethal. Out of a population of between 8 and 9 million, the famine death toll was over one million; another million and a quarter emigrated. In Britain, if it is remembered at all, it is spoken of as 'The Potato Famine' – implying that, had it not been for the natural disaster of the potato blight, all would have been well. In Ireland the memory remains and there is an argument that it was a form of genocide, or at least 'genoslaughter'.

The 1800 Act of Union had removed the seat of power from Dublin to London, so that policies were imposed from afar by an indifferent government. Continuing exports of food from a starving land and perverse incentives for landlords to evict their tenant-farmers wreaked devastation. The evicted were forced onto the roads, and if they did not die there of starvation and exposure, they filled urban slums, looking for work or a ticket out. The rural landscape became one of silent villages and neglected fields; the burial sites and ruined cottages are still visible today.

I set my story in 1849, when after years of appalling suffering in Ireland, the British Government lost the political will to provide famine relief. Dublin was overwhelmed in that year by epidemic diseases: cholera and 'famine fever', or typhus. No-one was certain how these infections spread: the germ theory of disease was yet to be developed. Policy-makers ignored the obvious link between poverty and mortality, even though this had already been clearly spelt out to them by the medical profession.

The Great Famine was a pivotal point. The failure of government hardened Irish resolve that British rule must somehow, one day, end. Young Ireland had formed the Irish Confederation in 1847 and, although claiming to be non-violent, the Confederate Clubs were behind the 1848 uprising. But that rebellion was small in scale and easily crushed. Its leaders were prosecuted and nationalism was driven underground.

The British believe to this day in their own freedom. Their faith in the civilising and democratising qualities of their colonial governments has been peculiar to themselves. But in Ireland at the time of my novel, political freedom was heavily repressed; the suspension of *habeas corpus* allowed political prisoners to be detained indefinitely. Young Irelanders whose only 'crimes' had been publishing newspapers were put on trial in front of 'packed' juries before being transported to penal colonies.

The attempt of Jane Francesca Elgee, or *'Speranza'*, to intervene in the treason-felony trial of newspaper editor Charles Gavan Duffy survives in the news articles of the day. In 1849 she had not yet met her future husband, and it has been written that she delighted in her partly Italian heritage and her middle name. She became Lady Jane Wilde, writer, salonnière, and mother of Oscar Wilde.

Although the Ribbon Men, carrying out isolated acts of terror against landlords, were most evident in the north of Ireland, a rural network of sworn-in members also existed in the south and south-west. In September 1849 a small uprising took place in Cappoquin, Co. Waterford. Secret clubs and societies had a variety of different names and for years the newspapers reported prosecutions of members who knew their secret signs and passphrases. There does not seem to have been a unified republican movement for about a decade, probably reflecting the severity of suppression by the authorities and the devastation of the population by famine.

Dr Joseph Murphy is a fictional character but inspired by Dr Kevin Izod O'Doherty, who was moved by the suffering of his patients to join the Young Ireland movement and establish the radical newspaper *The Irish Tribune*, for which he was sentenced to transportation. There were many important Young Irelanders but I omitted them in the interests of economy.

A friend urged me to give James Clarence Mangan a speaking part in my story but I was reluctant to do it – he would have taken over the narrative. Mangan was an inventive writer and poet, an eccentric who frequented Dublin's taverns and strode its streets in a pointed hat with green spectacles and an umbrella under each arm. His prose was Gothic and dramatic; he must have been a spirited, if challenging, conversationalist. His poetry was not anthologised during his lifetime but appeared in newspapers. His miserable death in the Meath Hospital during the 1849 cholera epidemic, despite the ministrations of the leading physician Dr William Stokes, is well documented. His posthumous portait by Frederic Burton is in the National Gallery of Ireland.

At the midpoint of the 19th century, Dublin's hospitals, which had once been merely holding institutions for the sick poor, were evolving into centres of expertise in medicine and surgery. Dublin's hospital doctors, notably Dr William Stokes, were pioneers of clinical bedside teaching and the application of scientific discovery to medicine. Nursing was not yet a regulated profession but the Order of the Sisters of Charity were leaders in working with the sick poor and had set up St Vincent's Hospital on St Stephen's Green. Other Dublin hospitals were also in operation during the period of my story but I focused on the Meath Hospital and Cork

Street Fever Hospital for simplicity and also moved pay wards and fever tents between hospitals to suit my story.

Dr Gordon Jackson was a stalwart of the Cork Street Fever Hospital for many years and his death from cholera in June 1849 was a serious loss to the medical profession.

Dr Oliver Wright's character, though fictional, borrows from that of the 19th century English medical murderer Dr William Palmer, with a few elements of the 20th century scandal that surrounded Dr Bodkin Adams, who was acquitted of wrongdoing.

The extravagant amusements of the wealthy: balls, races, regattas, and hunts continued throughout the Great Famine. Queen Victoria and Prince Albert visited Ireland in August 1849, to be met by cheering crowds and *'Céad Míle Fáilte'* – a hundred thousand welcomes. The attempt by the nationalists to intercept or kidnap the Queen in Dublin failed, Mr Daniel Paget having been the unwitting agent of its betrayal. Prince Albert's health declined during the 1850s and his death in 1861, aged 42, was attributed to typhoid fever.

My other characters are fictional.

Acknowledgements

Thanks are due to:

Paula Campbell my publisher at Poolbeg, and my editor Gaye Shortland for her amazing editing skills.

For beta reading: principally Annette Libeskind Berkovits, Joanna Orwin, Jo Schaffel; also Laina West, Allan Webster, and Julie Bissell.

Wally O'Neill, proprietor of Red Books, St Peter's Square, Wexford, for his labyrinthine bookshop and for nurturing a creative community in Wexford, of which I am lucky to be a member.

Kieran O'Brien, antiquarian extraordinaire, for historical snippets, insights into 19th century Ireland, copies of *The Nation*, and out-of-print books and newspapers.

Professor Colm Quigley for his encouragement and kind gift of *Atlas of the Great Irish Famine* (see below).

Áinnle O'Neill for the UCD Access and Lifelong

Learning course: 'History of Dublin Through Walks & Talks.'

The Irish chapter of the Historical Novel Society especially Katherine Mezzacappa, Susan Lanigan, Patricia O'Reilly, Dianne Ascroft and Catherine Kuhlmann for their camaraderie, encouragement and guidance.

Although I consulted these books, articles and other resources, any errors or distortions of the truth are entirely my own:

William Stokes: A Sketch. Henry W Acland. New Sydenham Society, London, 1882

Observations on the Management of the Poor in Scotland, and its effects on the health of the great towns. William Pulteney Allison. William Blackwood & Sons, Edinburgh, 1840

Ringers & Rascals: A Taste of Skulduggery. David Ashforth. Highdown, Berkshire, 2003

Oscar Wilde and His Mother: A Memoir. Anna, Comtesse de Bremont. Everett & Co Ltd., London 1914

The Cappoquin Rebellion 1849. Anthony M Breen. Drecroft, Suffolk, 1998.

Poison, Detection and the Victorian Imagination. Ian Burney. Manchester University Press, 2006

The Irish Aesthete: Ruins of Ireland. Robert O'Byrne. Cico Books, 2019.

Reminiscences of My Irish Journey in 1849. Thomas Carlyle. Harper, New York, 1882

Selected Prose of James Clarence Mangan. Jacques Chuto, Peter van de Kamp, Ellen Shannon-Mangan. Irish Academic Press, Dublin, 2004

Irish Masters of Medicine. Davis Coakley. Town House, Dublin, 1992

Baggot Street: A Short History of the Royal City of Dublin Hospital. Davis Coakley. Board of Governors, Royal City of Dublin Hospital, 1995

Medicine in Trinity College Dublin: An Illustrated History. Davis Coakley. Trinity College, Dublin, 2014

The History and Heritage of St James's Hospital, Dublin. Davis Coakley and Mary Coakley. Four Courts Press, Dublin, 2018

[These are 21cm x 14cm paper bound booklets of varying length, the 1848 report is only 8 pages] Report of the Managing Committee of the House of Recovery and Fever Hospital in Cork Street Dublin: various years.

Atlas of the Great Irish Famine 1845-52. John Crowley, William J. Smyth, Mike Murphy. Cork University Press, 2012

The Cyclopaedia of Practical Medicine. John Forbes, Alexander Tweedie and John Conolly. Sherwood Gilbert and Piper, London, 1835

'The Meath Hospital, Dublin'. Peter Gatenby. In: Dublin Historical Record, 2005, Vol 58, No 2, pp122-128.

Medical History of the Meath Hospital and County Dublin Infirmary. Lambert Hepental Ormsby. Fannin & Co, Dublin; Bailliere, Tindall & Cox, London, 1888

Dublin Tenement Life: An Oral History. Kevin C. Kearns. Gill & Macmillan, Dublin, 1994

Mad with Much Heart: A Life of Sir William and Lady Wilde. Eric Lambert. Frederick Muller, London, 1967

King Cholera: the Biography of a Disease. Norman Longmate. Hamish Hamilton, London, 1966

'Dark Rosaleen. James Clarence Mangan.' In: *The Nation*, May 30, 1846, page 521.

Henrietta Street: Grandeur and Decline, 1800-1922. Timothy Murtagh. Dublin City Culture Company, 2020

The Secret Societies of Ireland: Their Rise and Progress. Captain H.B.C. Pollard. Irish Historical Press, Kilkenny, 1998

The Miasma: Epidemic and Panic in Nineteenth Century Ireland. Joseph Robins. Institute of Public Administration, Dublin, 1995

Strokestown and the Great Irish Famine. Ciaran Reilly. Four Courts Press, Dublin, 2014

Poems. Speranza (Lady Wilde). James Duffy, Dublin, 1864

Speeches from the Dock, or Protests of Irish Patriotism. T.D., A.M., and D.B. Sullivan, Re-Edited by Seán Ua Cellaigh, M.H. Gill & Son, Dublin, 1953

The Strange Case of Dr Bodkin Adams: the Life and Murder Trial of Eastbourne's Infamous Doctor. John Surtees, SB Publications, Eastbourne, 2000

'Irish Cursing and the Art of Magic, 1750-2018.' Thomas Waters. In: *Past & Present*, Volume 247, Issue 1, May 2020, Pages 113–149.

The Great Hunger: Ireland 1845-9. Cecil Woodham-Smith. Hamish Hamilton, London, 1964

BritishNewspaperArchive.co.uk : various editions of *The Freeman, The Nation* and *The Illustrated London News*.